"If I had to choose one book, just one, to get me through a pandemic—or any other aspect of twenty-first century living—*Four Dead Horses* would be it. KT Sparks writes with a sleight of hand magic that turns sharp humor into compassion and molds lovable characters out of the absurd stuff of everyday life. I'm heartened by the humanity in this novel. Wannabe cowboy poet Martin Oliphant is an unlikely (un) hero who makes me laugh and gives me hope—not the Hallmark card kind— but the gritty, hilarious, intelligent hope we all need to make it through the world today. Definitely one of my favorite books of the year."

— B.K. Loren, author of *Theft*

FOUR DEAD HORSES

K. T. Sparks

Regal House Publishing

Published by
Regal House Publishing, LLC
Raleigh, NC 27612
All rights reserved

ISBN -13 (paperback): 9781646030668
ISBN -13 (hardcover): 9781646031177
ISBN -13 (epub): 9781646030910
Library of Congress Control Number: 2020940213

All efforts were made to determine the copyright holders and obtain their
permissions in any circumstance where copyrighted material was used. The
publisher apologizes if any errors were made during this process, or if any
omissions occurred. If noted, please contact the publisher and all efforts will be
made to incorporate permissions in future editions.

Interior and cover design by Lafayette & Greene
lafayetteandgreene.com
Cover images © by C.B. Royal

Regal House Publishing, LLC
https://regalhousepublishing.com

The following is a work of fiction created by the author. All names, individuals,
characters, places, items, brands, events, etc. were either the product of the
author or were used fictitiously. Any name, place, event, person, brand, or item,
current or past, is entirely coincidental.

Printed in the United States of America

For Mom and Dad

SWEETHEART OF THE RODEO

The devices on my chaps were hearts,
One torn in two, the other red and full.
A romantic take I thought, metaphor,
For rodeo and loves, fits and starts.
Back when I could spur the baddest buckers,
I wrote on the rolls of my Salisbury
Six-O-six roughout kack an inscription,
Something from Ezra Pound, a translation
From the Latin on the Medieval sword:
If your heart fails you, trust not in me.
Oh, words to live by! To say that you're scared,
Ain't nothing wrong in that. But to flee
In the face of chance? C'mon, cowboy,
Roll 'em! Shake your face and let them have you.

SHADD PIEHL

THE FIRST HORSE:

BUSTER

D. 1982

Martin Oliphant had always hated horses. Their staggering stupidity. Their unexplained, unexpected, and ever-explosive snorting. The way they twitched distinct patches of their skin to dislodge flies. The way they shied madly at the most innocuous occurrences: a golf umbrella at fifty feet; a leaf falling from, of all places, a tree; a bale of hay stacked exactly where it was supposed to be stacked and had been stacked for the last month.

Martin Oliphant hated horses, but he didn't, it must be said, wish horses dead. It must be said because horses died around him. Died or almost died. At Martin's hand or almost at Martin's hand. And it was horses, dead ones mostly, that blazed the trail to his life-forging passion. Horses brought Martin to cowboy poetry, and horses, live ones mostly, were cowboy poetry's central theme.

Martin saw his first dying, then dead, horse on May 1, 1982, on the beach at Twin Bluffs, the only resort in his lakeside home of Pierre, Michigan.

He headed to Twin Bluffs that Saturday morning with his mom and dad, Dottie and Carroll Oliphant, and younger brother, Frank, in his dad's week-old Lincoln Continental Mark IV Signature Series sedan. Martin sat in the back seat across from his mom. Between them, encased in plastic film embossed with the Josten's logo, was Martin's special order, plus-size high school graduation gown, a swath of tissue-thin canary polyester bristling with static. The ceremony wasn't until the end of the month, but the XXXL robe had to be delivered early to ensure it fit. Martin poked at the bag, and the garment puckered and creased, like a time-lapse film of a lemon drying out. When he had seen the gown in the catalogue, he had thought that, draped in yards of shimmering gold, he might dazzle as he performed his one duty as the Pierre Public High School's 1982 salutatorian: the introduction of Camilla Lutz, the valedictorian. Though his waistline neared sixty inches, it was, Martin told himself, in harmonious balance with his six-foot-ten frame. Some might call him fat, but he, like the Sears department in charge of labeling outsized children's clothing, preferred "husky." Sitting now with the reality of the robe, its bunchy seams and clinging rayon, he realized the thing would grasp at his buttocks, wedge between his belly and breasts, adhere to his wobbling upper arms. He would dazzle no one. If he could make it to the podium with no rips or visible sweat stains, he would count it as a win.

"It would be so bogus to forfeit to Garth," said Frank. The nominal reason for this rare all-family outing was to cheer on fourteen-year-old Frank in the semifinal match of the Kiwanis Youth Tennis Round Robin. In truth, none of them, including Frank, who had dispatched this particular opponent the month before (6-0, 6-1, 6-0) in the Rotary Classic, had any interest in watching the rout. Frank had been complaining since they'd taken the detour to pick up Martin's gown.

"Why couldn't you have gotten it while you were at school?" Frank asked for the twentieth time.

"I forgot," said Martin, which was a lie. He could have done so yesterday, but he hadn't wanted to cart his enormous saffron cloak of shame through the halls to his locker.

"If I have to forfeit, it will probably be the first and last time Garth ever wins a match. He plays with a wooden racquet," Frank said and tapped his own metal T2000, Jimmy Connors's weapon of choice. Frank's other hand inched his dad's martini toward his lips, as if he thought being slow were equivalent to being invisible. The antiseptic stink of gin overwhelmed the smell of the new leather interior.

"Put it on the dashboard, dear," said Dottie. "And don't be a snob."

Not a trace of irony crossed Dottie's mask of Erno Laszlo cosmetics, applied in the au naturel style favored by the wives who lived out by Pierre Woods Country Club. Led by their high priestess, Bitsy Newport, these women and their husbands—doctors, lawyers, white collar executives, heirs of the founders of The American Glass Co., Pierre's one remaining industry—were what passed for society in Pierre. For years, Dottie had circled and buzzed around them, as if she were an angry fly launching an assault on a sealed jar of honey. Most of the group's communal activity revolved around tennis, so they called themselves the Fuzzy Balls. They played even when lake-effect snow enveloped Pierre in five-foot drifts. They would gather at Twin Bluffs' courts, protected by an overheated and under-oxygenated canvas bubble, for mixed doubles then fondue after at the nearby Swiss Shack.

Several years ago, while waiting for Frank to finish a lesson at the bubble, Dottie had been invited by Bitsy Newport to make a fourth for doubles. Dottie had not brought her racquet and was dressed in what she described as a "poop-brown corduroy jumpsuit from Penney's," her go-to outfit for errands involving her children. Still, she'd been ecstatic about the encounter and, at that evening's celebratory coq au vin family supper, declaimed again and again: "They were so nice to ask."

Since that day, Dottie had sought every opportunity to accompany Frank to the bubble. She always wore full tennis whites and carried two Prince Pros, lest a string break on one. So far, Bitsy Newport's invitation had not been repeated.

Dottie snapped open a compact and scraped with her pinky nail at some microscopic imperfection in her buff lipstick. Martin watched her and wondered why they weren't closer. Who better to understand him? He'd survived a Midwestern public education as an overweight bookworm with neck acne, one who could recite pages of Locke from memory but could name only three of the teams in the Big Ten. Both he and his mom were stuck on the lowest rung of this small town's social hierarchy.

Martin had always wanted to speak to his mom about their common exile. Not even speak. A knowing glance. A wry smile. A shared sigh from the front seat of her Oldsmobile Custom Cruiser station wagon as they watched the Fuzzy Balls families spill onto the Stainbrook-Borden Public Beach for another exclusive bonfire sing-along. They both longed for a bigger life, a yearning neither his dad, with his business, nor Frank, with his tennis, could comprehend. Perhaps the problem was that she thought she could find it in Pierre. Martin knew he had to get out.

And come September, he would. He'd been accepted into the University of Chicago Class of 1986. Come September, his course would carry him across Lake Michigan and into the faux-Gothic sanctuary established in 1890 by John D. Rockefeller and the American Baptist Education Society to meet the new millennium's demand for classically educated Nobel Prize winners, millionaire Adam Smith aficionados, and economic advisers to Latin American kleptocrats. This was Martin's tribe, one that might take him to Wall Street or Michigan Avenue or the LSE graduate program in international relations or Harvard Law, but never back to Pierre. His mom, on the other hand, would die here. And all the way to the graveyard, she'd worry about whether Bitsy Newport had sent flowers.

Carroll, who was now juggling his martini, almost missed the crooked and faded wooden sign indicating "Twin Bluffs, Surf and Tennis and Petting Zoo Family Fun, 1 mile." He banged onto the gravel drive, muttering about "dinging up the undercarriage."

On either side of the one-lane road to the bubble and beyond to the Twin Bluffs cottages and beach, uncut grass fluttered around piles of dune sand and the detritus from failed Twin Bluffs' attractions: A tipped chicken-wire cage that once held a dancing rabbit and a boa constrictor, and then just a boa constrictor; the broken wooden fence through which a probably rabid deer had crashed and led his mangy flock to freedom through a sea of screaming eight-year-olds from the YMCA summer vacation day camp; several tilting Styrofoam monoliths that were to form the heart of the never-finished Chicago Skyline putt-putt course.

These and the other piles of jungle gym parts, ripped badminton nets, and unmatched lawn bowling pins, represented the efforts of the owners of Twin Bluffs, three generations of Pierre's only Italian family, the Dozzis, to keep their resort afloat. They did a decent summer tourist trade for the two, maybe two-and-a-half months of Pierre's annual respite from the subzero winds blasting in off Lake Michigan. But they struggled to bring in any business the rest of the year. The putt-putt, the playgrounds, the animals, and the bubble were all attempts to attract paying merry-makers during the off season.

Of these, only the bubble survived and drew a steady stream of tennis enthusiasts. It couldn't be enough to keep Twin Bluffs solvent, and Martin knew his dad was moving in for the kill. Carroll Oliphant was a small-time corporate raider, a sort of Main Street Michael Milken. He specialized in foreclosing on family businesses. The local Schwinn bike shop or the independent lighting fixture showroom. Places run into the ground by the sons and the grandsons of the original owners. Twin Bluffs had been in his sights for over a year.

Carroll set the emergency brake, threw back the last of his martini, and turned to the backseat.

"I gotta go talk to the Dozzis," he said.

"I think I'll stay in the car," said Martin. The smell inside the bubble, compressed air and aged sweat, nauseated him.

"He should have to watch me," said Frank. He popped open a can of tennis balls and huffed into the cylinder, the kerosene odor his drug of choice this year. "We went with him to pick up his dress."

"Gown," said Martin.

"Nightgown," said Frank.

"Why that's Bitsy's Jeep." Dottie grabbed Martin's hand, squeezed hard, then pulled away quickly, as if she'd picked up the wrong purse off the pew at church. "I'm sorry," she said. "It's just, really. What a coincidence." She shifted her weight left and right and drummed her feet. She patted his hand once, then pushed open the door and trotted up the path to the bubble. Frank followed, yelling over his shoulder, "Make Martin watch me."

Carroll stepped out of the Lincoln and rapped on Martin's window. Martin sighed and joined his dad on the gravel pavement. "I'll go with you then."

Carroll didn't say no right away, and that thrilled Martin, who had always thought he might have an aptitude for the M&A game. He'd even considered talking to his dad about a future joint enterprise. Maybe after an MBA from University of Chicago, a little microeconomics from Milton Friedman, a little finance from Eugene Fama, he could help take Oliphant Investments global. Oliphant and Oliphant. Oliphant and Son.

"I don't think so, Martin. It's hard to close a deal with a fat guy in the room. Not enough air."

Martin shut his eyes a moment and then chose to take that as a compliment. His dad had at least considered it. Weight could be lost.

Martin's mom jogged back from the bubble, swinging her head side to side.

"Have either of you two seen Bitsy? That's definitely her car."

"Maybe she's riding," said Carroll. "The Dozzis brought in trail horses. Not that there are any trails around here. Dozzi Junior saw something like it in Honolulu. Horses on the beach. What he was doing in Hawaii when his old man is about to lose the farm is another..."

The wind died for a moment and a squawk floated over the dunes and down onto their confab, then another.

"What's that?" said Dottie, on the toes of her white Keds, eyes blinking like castanets.

"Seagull," said Martin.

"Bitsy," rasped Dottie.

"Horses on the goddamn beach," continued Carroll. "What next? A luau?"

"Bitsy," said Dottie again. "She needs me. I'm going to the beach." She headed at a speed walk toward a cut-through between two boarded up A-frame cabins.

"Go see what your mother thinks she's doing," said Carroll to Martin. "I'll be hula-hulaing with the Dozzis, if you need me."

It was the alewives that Martin first noticed as he crested the dune that separated the Twin Bluffs' beach from the rest of the resort. The smell of them. It hit him with the same force as the frigid wind off the lake, stippled with splinters of stinging sleet. Since the 1950s, the alewives, a North American shad native to the West Atlantic Ocean, had made their way through the Welland Canal into Lake Michigan, where they expired in massive numbers after a half-hearted attempt at breeding. They died of osmosis, lake water seeping into their every cell and their kidneys too small to process it out, like freshwater fish do. From spring to autumn, on beaches public and private, from Michigan to Wisconsin, rotting alewives served as an unavoidable reminder of the mortal danger of being a fish, if not out of water, then in water of the wrong sort.

So Martin knew what the shoreline would look like before he could spot it through the beach grass: the tiny expired shad would form a boundary between the mud-brown sand and the slate-gray waters that, were there sun, would glitter like heaps of well-polished filigree.

But there was no sun, and when Martin could finally make them out, the alewives resembled only their unromantic essence, a whole lot of dead fish. In any case, he hardly noted them, transfixed by the rest of the scene spread out below him. There was his mom, moving up the beach and toward him with great strides but little speed, her feet sinking to the ankle in snow-melt-wetted sand. With every lunge forward, she would keen, "Bitsy's been thrown, Bitsy's hurt, we must help Bitsy." A riderless roan horse followed her at a stroll, dragging its reins. Beyond her, just above the line of dead shad, stood Bitsy New-port, in hip-boots, water-soaked jodhpurs, and a tight azure blazer, her left foot lifted just an inch or two off the ground. She didn't look hurt. More like a great blue heron deciding if it were worth it to bend down and eat an alewife. And beyond her, in the roiling Lake Michigan wa-ters, a slight teenager, Bitsy's youngest, Julie, danced dangerously close to the flailing hooves of a second horse, this one tar black. As she waved her arms and screeched commands to the beast to rise, it rolled in the shallow surf, throwing up sand and fish bodies and banging its head into the waves.

Martin lurched down the dune toward his mom, who reached out to him and panted, "It's so terrible. An awful accident."

"What happened?" Martin asked, putting his hands on his mom's heaving shoulders. She seemed near hysteria, and he considered shak-ing her to stop her compulsive gulping.

"She was thrown. The horse is wild. It should never have been rented out by those stupid, stupid Dozzis."

Martin looked at the roan horse, now trying to snap at the razor-sharp beach grass along the bottom of the dune, drawing its black lips back to reveal teeth like cracked hunks of yellow quartz. It didn't look wild. It looked hungry. And a little bored.

"It fell, and she wrenched her leg dismounting. She just avoided being crushed. Crushed! You can see in its eyes, it's evil," said Dottie.

The roan sighed into a prolonged fart, then stretched its neck back and pointed its snout to the sky, as if it expected oats to rain down like manna from horse heaven.

"What about Julie?" said Martin. "Looks like her horse is pretty crazy too." He gestured toward the water, and the roan startled, pivot-ed, and trotted back toward Bitsy.

"That's Bitsy's horse in the water," Dottie sobbed. "That's the beast that threw her. And Julie won't stop fussing with it. Bitsy might have broken something. Come, please, Martin." Dottie wrapped both hands around his arm and tugged at him. Martin felt a thump at his chest, as if he'd swallowed a slug of Diet Rite too quickly. His mom needed him. Bitsy Newport needed him. Perhaps there was a chance to exit Pierre on a note of, if not heroism, then at least competency.

He followed Dottie down to the shoreline, watching Julie all the while. She was a powerful swimmer. Already, in her sophomore year at PPHS, she'd shattered the girls' record for the 100-yard butterfly. She was on her knees at the horse's thrashing head. Waves regularly doused her, and once the horse's muzzle caught her in the jaw, she went under.

When Martin and Dottie reached Bitsy, she looked up and said, "I'm fine, but aren't you nice? Maybe just a stick to lean on?"

"You are so brave." Dottie looked as though she were about to fall to her knees and bawl, a cripple at the feet of a bemused Jesus Christ. Instead, she slung her shoulders back and said, "I will get that stick. Martin, find your dad and tell him to bring the Lincoln as close as he can." Dottie turned and ran to a driftwood pile, dove toward a branch, then tilted further forward, windmilling both arms. Her feet flew back, kicking up silver slivers of shad.

"That is exactly how my horse fell," said Bitsy, in the quiet tone of someone talking to herself about the weather.

Martin jogged after his mom, who jumped to her feet. Her legs, from the pink border of her footies to the edge of her Fila tennis skirt, were covered in sand and fish guts. Her Lacoste polo had ripped at the front, and blood seeped through the fabric under her right breast.

"Mom, you're hurt," he said.

She ignored him, bent down, and grabbed a piece of driftwood from the ground, carefully wiping the fish scales from it.

"I've got to get back to Bitsy. Go get your dad. Go," she said.

Dottie scuttled sideways, right arm pressed to her side, left fist raised, brandishing the walking stick, Lady Liberty with her tricolor. Martin considered staying with her until it was clear how bad her injuries were. But she wouldn't want that, or anything that might interfere with her opportunity to be of service to Bitsy Newport.

Julie yelled from the water, "Goddamn it, Martin, help me. This horse is drowning."

Martin looked to see if his mom had noticed. She should be pleased. Julie Newport knew his name. And sought his counsel. Unfortunately, he wasn't much of a swimmer. Given his size, people expected buoyancy of him, but he had never floated. Even at the YWCA beginner's class, where every minnow was allowed to cling to a kickboard, he would still sink. He remembered there had been a kind of peace there underwater, listening to the gargled bellows of the instructor, Mrs. Thurk. Peace, but not aquatic competence. He thought of relaying that history to Julie, but held back, sensing the time was not right. Anyway, it didn't look like more than a couple of feet deep, when the waves weren't crashing over the horse and the girl. And he did truly want to be the sort of man who would bound to the rescue in this sort of situation, without overthinking exactly what this sort of situation was. He made his ways through the alewives and into the lake. He hadn't worn the right shoes.

"Hurry! I can't hold his head anymore."

The horse rolled onto its back and churned its legs, one hoof dangling at an odd angle from the fetlock. Its massive jaw gaped, and its nose spewed green foam. An eye spun around, then fixed on Martin, and the upended animal froze. Martin used the moment to strategize his approach.

Before his plan gelled though, the horse groaned and smashed onto its side, its back hooves kicking into the space into which Martin had been about to step. Damn it all, he needed a hero's playbook here. Who was he supposed to save? Julie? The horse? Himself? Went with himself. He bicycled back to dry land.

"Don't go," Julie sobbed. "We've got to keep his head up."

"Don't be ridiculous," said Bitsy, walking to where Martin stood. Dottie hobbled behind, still clutching the driftwood branch. "They'll have to shoot the nasty thing anyway. Martin, I believe your mother is injured. Perhaps time to go for your father?"

"Buster, his name is Buster," screamed Julie, hugging the horse's stilling head. "Martin, please. He's dying."

He so wanted to dive in, prop the horse with one arm and Julie with the other, take in the yelps of surprise and admiration from his mom and Bitsy Newport. And Julie. But not this time. Not yet. Martin turned and trudged up the dune toward Twin Bluffs' offices.

When Martin returned with his father and two Dozzis, Buster's corpse was beached. A bedraggled and weeping Julie sat legs splayed in the alewives, cradling the horse's head.

"I'm afraid we've had a little accident here," said Bitsy, as if she were the queen apologizing for her corgi lifting a leg on a potted plant.

Dottie, propped on the driftwood stick, croaked, "Bitsy needs to see a doctor."

Carroll's eyes swept over the tableau, and he smiled at the quaking Dozzis. "Don't suppose you've got liability coverage," he said.

Bitsy Newport sustained only a minor sprain and was able to host her annual Kentucky Derby party that afternoon, a sprig of mint tucked rakishly in the folds of the Ace bandage around her left ankle. Dottie Oliphant watched 21-1 long shot, Gato del Sol, win the 108th Run for the Roses from her bed at Swinehurst Hospital. The gash at her sternum took eleven stitches to close, and she broke a rib on her right side.

There were two fatalities on the beach that day: Buster, of course, and the Dozzis' dreams for their resort. By the next Friday, Carroll Oliphant had purchased Twin Bluffs at a bargain basement price, agreeing to assume legal responsibility for the riding accident. He bet that the aggressively genteel Newports wouldn't think of suing over something as trivial as a sprained ankle, and he was right.

By August, Carroll had stripped the place of every rental Sailfish and nautical-themed decorative item and sold it all to a couple starting an inn on Florida's Longboat Key. The only asset he couldn't monetize was the bubble. No one seemed to know how to take the thing down. So he gave it to his wife, who spun it into social gold. Soon she was hosting the Fuzzy Balls' Mixed Doubles tourneys, carpooling with Bitsy and her husband to the Swiss Shack on Thursday evenings, and partnering with Bitsy in the bubble's regular Tuesday morning ladies league. For a brief time, Dottie soared, riding the social updraft she had always known she was meant to catch. Even after her crash, Martin in equal part envied and took comfort in the fact that she, at least for a couple years, had been able to inhabit her own version of the American dream.

Frank won his semifinal match 6-2, 6-0, 6-1.

THE SECOND HORSE:

CHOPO

D. 1986

Seventy-Sixth Annual Conventional of Rotary International

Emergency Plenary Session

"WOMEN IN ROTARY IN THE ERA OF E.R.A."

May 28, 1985

Kansas City Convention Center
Kansas City, MO

All ROTARIANS are invited to an EMERGENCY PLENEARY SESSION to take place during the SEVENTY-SIXTH ANNUAL CONVENTION OF ROTARY INTERNATIONAL to discuss a UNIFIED and INTERNATIONAL response to the continued attempts of women to infiltrate the ranks of SOME (former) ROTARY CLUBS and the impending decision of the SUPREME COURT OF THE UNITED STATES on the validity of ROTARY INTERNATIONAL's expulsion of the Rotary Club of Duarte, California, for the admittance of THREE females in 1976.

10:00 a.m. Welcome and Benediction
The Very Reverend Bill Beaverton, Chevrolet Mission Baptist
Church of the Redeemer in Faith
Rotary Club of Milledgeville, Tennessee

11:30 a.m. "Stop in the Name of Love: What to Do When the
Ladies Come a-Callin':
Handling Applications from Women: A Discussion"
Mitch Ragsdale, Rotary Club of Fort Worth, Texas

12:30 p.m. Luncheon and Keynote: "No Girls Allowed: Keeping
the Gals Out of the Clubhouse, for Their Own Good,
and Ours, and the Nation's"
Carroll Oliphant, Rotary Club of Pierre, Michigan

1

1985 was a fine time to be at the University of Chicago. On any given day, Saul Bellow and Alan Bloom might be discussing Kierkegaardian relativism in front of twenty-year-olds who read their first chapter books the year Bellow won the Nobel Prize, while Eugene Fama, still a quarter decade from his Nobel, drew supply and demand curves for an Econ 101 class. Muddy Waters regularly headlined at Buddy Guy's Checkerboard Lounge, ten blocks north of campus; Jimmy Cliff and Run DMC appeared at Mandell Hall; and the Lascivious Costume Ball, an annual mélange of porn flicks, professional strippers, Ancient Greek erotic poetry, and naked nerds, raged at Ida Noyes.

From the day of his matriculation, Martin took to U of C like bacteria to an agar plate. He read *Plato's Republic* until three a.m., played Space Invaders in the basement of the Woodward Court dorms with his laundry quarters, and cheered on the hapless varsity Maroons as they took to storied Stagg Field to be decimated by various junior colleges.

C—H! Chicago!
C—H! Chicago!
What is C—H for?
Methane!

He spent summers at the front desk of the Regenstein Library, shivering in the overextended air conditioning, getting a jump on his reading for the next quarter, and making the pocket money that would keep him in Eduardo's stuffed pizzas and Morry's subs the rest of the year. Summer before his junior year, he moved to one of the student slums on Blackstone Avenue with two roommates he rarely saw. Like him, they used the apartment for sleeping and changing underwear and the library or the classroom for the rest of life. He was alone much of the time, but no more alone than the majority of his classmates, who drowned themselves in books the way most college students of that decade drowned themselves in grain alcohol mixed with Hawaiian Punch and cocaine.

So it was not unusual that he stood alone outside his apartment that day in March of 1985. He picked at the hem of his Levi's cutoffs and watched his dad help his mom out of a Checker Taxi and halfway into a curbside snowbank. He'd last seen his family two months ago at Christmas break. They'd all be together again in less than a month for spring break with a coterie of Fuzzy Balls families at Jimmy Sneedle's Tennis and Dude Ranch in Arizona. The unprecedented level of togetherness made his stomach buzz with unease.

Dottie waggled a slush-sheathed red pump, and Carroll took her arm, then both arms as her clean foot shot under the idling taxi. Frank came around the back, cracking his neck. Martin walked down the path from his apartment building to the sidewalk.

"Hey, welcome to Chicago. Sorry about that."

"Never mind," she said, pulling her mink tight around her. "Where are your pants, Martin? It's freezing."

Martin was sure his mom had lost weight. Even under her fur coat, which puffed with static like a cattle-prodded cat, she looked like Nancy Reagan, a starving and tense starling. That was the style, he supposed.

"Show us some leg," Frank cackled, and Martin wished he'd worn the full-length jeans he had initially pulled out of his closet. But the temperature reached fifty-two this morning, and that meant spring at U of C. Shorts, Frisbees, and legs as white as the scrap paper upon which students noodled through the millionth or so decimal place of Pi.

"We should probably get going," Dottie said, took one step forward, then sank to her knees on the sidewalk, talking the entire time. "Or maybe a quick sit, to get one's breath, just a moment, or a glass of water, that might be the thing."

Carroll tugged at her arm with one hand, while the other brushed dirt from her coat. "She's all right. Just overheated. A thousand dollars' worth of fur, she better be overheated."

"Mom?" Martin said and walked to her, went in for a hug. Damn, she was thin.

"I'm fine. Just tired." She started to sag down again. Carroll put an arm tight around her waist and bounced her once. Her mouth gaped open and snapped shut, but she stayed upright.

"I think I'll probably just sit out the tour," she said.

A college tour for Frank was the ostensible reason they had gathered today. Martin had his doubts. Frank was an average student with an above average backhand and, last Martin had heard, was interested only in Stanford. Certainly not the U of C, whose teams did participate in the NCAA, but in division III, and with a great sense of irony.

"There's a café on Fifty-Fifth," Martin said.

Martin looked back from the exit of the Café Medici to where they had left his mom. She sat across a rough and scarred table from a frizzy redheaded boy in a poncho translating *Die protestantische Ethik und der Geist des Kapitalismus*. She held a mug of chamomile tea in front of her mouth but did not drink. Instead, she stared at the laboring student, as if he were a gorilla inventing the wheel and she were Jane Goodall, catching it all from behind a mufungu tree. Martin followed his dad and Frank out.

"Let's get a drink," said Carroll.

"Great idea," said Frank.

Martin considered pointing out that it was only eleven in the morning. Martin considered pointing out that it had been five years since Illinois had raised the drinking age to twenty-one, and, in any case, Frank was only seventeen. Martin considered pointing out that even the most basic tour of the U of C campus, one that skipped the interior of Frank Lloyd Wright's Robie House and the Oriental Institute's special exhibit on the excavations of Persepolis, would still take at least two hours. But he did not. To do so would have been to assume his father could get through more than an hour of interaction with his family without a drink, preferably stiff. To do so was to assume a college tour for Frank had ever been anything but a fiction. To do so would have been to delay finding out what really rocketed his family out of their well-loved world and into Martin's, a distant moon in which they had shown little interest in the past.

They walked in silence down Fifty-Fifth Street to Woodlawn Avenue and pushed inside Sammy's Tap. Smoke hung low, though none of the daytime regulars were smoking. Martin inhaled and shut his eyes, savored the smell of ancient cigars, stale beer, and yesterday's sauerkraut. Frank hacked and put a hand over his nose.

Carroll turned to the bar. He elbowed between an old woman in a plastic rain hat and a burly man in a black White Sox T-shirt. "Martini, dry, rocks, twist, and…" Carroll raised an eyebrow at Martin and Frank.

"Coffee, black," said Martin.

"Miller, Genuine Draft," said Frank.

The bartender cocked his head, shrugged, and turned away. Martin trailed Frank and Carroll to a Formica table on the opposite wall. As soon as Frank sat, he launched into a monologue about some tennis match during which he felt he had been cheated or treated with less than adequate respect. Carroll clasped both hands in front of him and stared at Frank, nodded, grunted. It was like watching *Meet the Press*. Except dumber. And Martin couldn't change the channel.

"We're not three blocks from where Enrico Fermi first split the atom," said Martin, which silenced the other two until the bartender slouched over with their drinks.

As Carroll lifted his glass, he said, "So, you see how it is with your mother? How she was back there?"

"What's wrong with her?" Martin took a sip of coffee. It seared down to his gut. His mom hardly ever got sick. Everybody in Pierre went around for half the winter with chapped lips, feverish eyes, and crumpled tissues poking out of the pockets of their parkas, but never his mom. She didn't even buy Kleenex. The rest of the family had to spend the flu season blowing their scabbing noses on toilet paper.

"She's got cancer," said Carroll, poking the lemon peel into what was left of his drink.

"What?" Martin pushed back in his chair. The legs screeched against the floor like skewered peafowl.

"Cancer of the…women's parts," Carroll answered.

"Ovarian cancer?" Martin squeaked. A girl in his European Literary Realism class sophomore year had ovarian cancer and didn't even make it to the end of the section on Balzac.

"Breast," said Carroll.

Martin shook his head. Bile crept up his esophagus, bypassed his mouth, headed for his eyes.

"I'll get us another round." Carroll returned to the bar, and Frank followed, empty mug dangling from his hand. They both talked for a while to the bartender. Carroll slung an arm over the shoulder of the old woman. Frank hooted something at the Sox fan.

Martin thought, perhaps, they were giving him a moment to take in this terrible news. He tried to envision his mother laid out in a casket, white, lined in burgundy silk, he in a new suit taking the hands of the mourners. Looking into the eyes of their neighbors, the Burrows and that older son who never recovered from Vietnam. Accepting an awkward hug from Bitsy Newport, who would be in black Dior.

He felt sorry for his mom. Why hadn't he been kinder to her? Why hadn't he listened, or reacted at all, during her weekly calls, shown a little enthusiasm for the shake-up in the cotillion decoration committee or concern for the progression of Gra Gra Newport's gout. Granted, their communications had followed a set pattern that didn't allow Martin much more of a return than "that's great" and "neat" to Dottie's volley of bullets on the Fuzzy Balls. But Martin hadn't even tried. He'd been so caught up in his newfound life of the mind. And now she was dying, and for all his reading in the constructive and cultural studies of religion (two quarters, Eastern and Western), he could find no meaning in her impending demise, just regret. And a little resentment. Maybe. After all, she could have made even the teensiest effort to understand him, appreciate, even celebrate, his accomplishments, which were not insignificant. But it was always Frank she fawned over, his backhand down the line, the wave in his golden hair, his popularity with the PPHS cheerleading and lifeguarding set. Who cared that Frank read at a sixth-grade level? Who cared that he dented her Oldsmobile on a beer run to that place in Baroda that doesn't card?

Carroll and Frank returned to the table, and Frank returned to narrating the disputed tennis match. Martin interrupted.

"How long does she have?"

"She's not going to die, you moron," said Frank.

Martin looked at his dad.

"She doesn't have to die," Carroll said, as if this were his wife's choice, like deciding whether to get Ho Hos or Chips Ahoy at the Hilltop Grocery. "Betty Ford didn't die."

"Right," said Frank, "but tell him about the operation."

Carroll drained his glass. Dottie was scheduled for a full mastectomy the last week of May. She'd be in the hospital at least ten days, depending on how it went, then home with another few weeks of bed rest. The timing of this, which depended on the schedule of "the best breast man money can buy," was terrible. Frank was due at Dick Gould's Junior Summer Tennis Camp in Palo Alto the weekend before the operation.

"And I gotta go to this." Carroll pushed a flyer toward Martin. "For Rotary. In Kansas City."

Martin looked at the single mimeographed sheet. "Isn't the ERA dead?"

"Still in the courts. This is an emergency meeting. A club in California let in women, two women," said Carroll.

"And you're putting together a posse to ride from Kansas City to oust them?" said Martin.

Carroll poked at the flyer. "I'm a keynote speaker, look at that. I'm representing all of the upper Midwest."

"At least all the males," said Martin.

"Don't kid yourself, smartass. There are a lot of women who don't think they should be in Rotary either."

Martin sympathized. He'd attended a Rotary meeting five years ago in the company of the PPHS assistant principal, Mr. Jimkowski, as a reward for a high PSAT score. They were served partially rehydrated mashed potatoes, canned peas, and breaded perch for lunch; a speaker from Plasti-Fab Inc., a four-man tool and dye shop specializing in safety and warehouse signage, droned for forty-five minutes on the dangers—economic and environmental—of recycling; and the meeting closed with a song about the benefits—economic, environmental, and spiritual—of manhood. Those who didn't join in the chorus with enough verve had to throw a quarter into the tin can provided by the Pierre Rotary Committee for Crippled Children.

"I'm speaking on the day Dottie goes to the hospital. And she can't drive herself," said Carroll.

"That's exam week," said Martin. "Let Frank be late to summer camp."

"Are you listening?" said Frank. "He said Dick Gould's Junior Summer Tennis Camp. Twelve weeks. Invitation only. Dick Gould's Junior Summer Tennis Camp, as in Dick Gould, as in McEnroe's coach. McEnroe, as in John McEnroe, as in the best player of all time."

"It's what your mom wants," Carroll said. "She knows you're good at school. You can make up your work."

"I am good at school. But final exams," Martin said, with less resistance. Had his family discussed this, decided that he was the one best suited to take on the awesome responsibility of caring for his mom on her deathbed? That he was the one smart enough and compassionate enough and strong enough? Had someone, his dad even, sat at the dinner table, the same table where Martin had endured countless, endless, incoherent tales of Frank's tennis victories and his dad's business conquests, and said, "Martin's the man for the job"? His face warmed, and he blotted his forehead with a scrap of tissue from a metal napkin dispenser.

Frank muttered into his empty plastic mug. His cheeks blinked orange in the neon light of the malfunctioning Schlitz sign over the bar. He lifted his head and said, "You know, I'm having to miss my exams, too."

Of course. Nothing new here. Martin swiveled to see if he could snag a witness. He expected Frank to point out next that there was "no *I* in *team*." The bartender held up a stubby finger.

"Set 'em up," Carroll said, and Frank giggled like a tipsy schoolboy, which, Martin supposed, was the case.

"What about Mrs. Newport, couldn't she take care of Mom for a few days?"

"Well, here's the thing," Carroll said. "Dottie doesn't want anyone to know. We're telling people she's going in for surgery, but on her elbow. Tennis elbow."

"So you see," Frank said, "Mrs. Newport can't take her to the hospital, because she'll see that mom is going into the breast wing and not the elbow wing."

"Tennis elbow," said Martin. "Jesus." He stood up. "I won't do it."

"Think about it," said Carroll. "I need you. Frank needs you."

"And Mom," mumbled Frank and looked into his lap. His face hollowed out, became the face of the five-year-old their dad had shoved, shivering, out to the end of the high dive. Martin had liked Frank back then.

"We can talk about it more in Arizona," Carroll said. "But it's not like you've been pulling your weight in the family lately."

"Your considerable weight," said Frank and snickered.

Martin dug in his pocket to find some money. He wanted to throw it down, say something dismissive, like, *This is for the coffee, see you in hell.* His shorts were a little tight, though, and it took a while to pry out what he thought was a dollar bill but turned out to be a receipt from the Korean wash-and-fold. His dad and Frank had already returned to talking tennis anyway. Martin exited, distressed and relieved that neither called out to him to wait.

Martin took the seat across from his mom and ran his finger through the milky coffee blob left by the Weber acolyte. The mug, half full—or Martin supposed, in this circumstance, half empty—sat in front of her. Her palms pressed flat on the table.

"How was the tour?" she said, head down. "I need a manicure."

"We didn't do a tour," said Martin. "Dad and Frank are at Sammy's getting drunk."

Dottie nodded, as if she he had known that. "I suppose I should join them." She didn't move.

"They told me about the operation."

"Oh," she said. "It's nothing. Tennis elbow. I don't even think they put you out for it. I tell you what needs a serious operation. These cuticles, that's what."

She looked up at him with empty eyes.

"They told me it was cancer," Martin said. "Breast cancer."

"Tennis elbow," she said.

Martin put his hands on top of hers. Her bones shifted under thin skin. She pulled her hands into her lap.

"When Bitsy had her operation on her tennis elbow, she was back on the courts in no time," she said.

And then she started to cry.

April 7, 1985

Dear: Oliphant Family, Cabin #14

Yee-haw! Welcome to Jimmy Sneedle's Tennis and Dude Ranch. We hope you are settling in fine, and if you have any questions or concerns, please contact Mary Anne in housekeeping (x-4359), Tricia at the front desk (x-4350), or Bibby Jean in the dining room (x-4952). If all else fails, head over to the Sunshine-on-my-Shoulder Saloon in the main lodge. As bartender Tommy Tonic says, "Ain't no squeaky wheel a Long Island Iced Tea can't grease."

Dinner tonight is at 7:00 p.m. in the Chow Wagon Dining Room, and we'll be offering our traditional Sunday supper of Oysters Rockefeller, Celery Rémoulade, Beet Salad with Dijon Crème Fraîche, and brandied pears for dessert! The cocktail special of the day is Sex on the Beach!!

At 8:30, we'll hold an orientation session around the grand fireplace, and you can get more information on all the fun activities we've got planned this week. Sign up there for midnight poker (adults only), a tasting of 1980 Bordeaux led by Jimso himself (with an opportunity to bid on a case from Jimso's personal cellar), the round robin tennis challenge (junior, ladies, and adult brackets), Marketing Director Mark Buffington's slide presentation on upcoming real estate opportunities at the ranch, child care (full day and overnight options available), and so much more. We'll also give you the out-west-low-down on Jimso's Jamboree and Talent Show, our end-of-the-week entertainment extravaganza.

After orientation, the bar will be open until 2 a.m.

with rumba dancing to the Latin beat of the ever-popular Jimmy Sneedle house band—Músicos con Queso!!

For those interested in horseback riding, barn manager Beaufort Giles will offer a mandatory safety briefing at 9:00 p.m. in the billiards room.

Welcome again to a week of WILD WEST FUN, so hold onto your ten-gallon hats and make sure the cat gut's tight on your racquet, because HERE WE GO!!

Happy Trails!

Jimso and the entire Jimmy Sneedle's Tennis and Dude Ranch Staff

2

Martin spent the first half of his spring break week at Jimmy Sneedle's Tennis and Dude Ranch in Wickenberg, Arizona, trying to get Carroll or Dottie to explain the extent of her deterioration and Martin's role in her recovery. But should the *C* of cancer even form in his frontal lobe, his mom would dart away to take a fly-fishing lesson, and his dad would lasso the nearest employee to discuss the capitalization challenges of a dude ranch. Dottie seemed healthier than she had in March, perhaps rallying in the presence of the Newport family and the rest of the Fuzzy Balls royal court. But the operation was still on. Martin had received a Xerox of her hospital appointment reminder in the mail a couple of weeks ago. In the top left-hand corner of the sheet, Carroll's secretary, Janet Priebe, had typed: "FYI, from your father. Bless you." Mrs. Priebe was long serving, loyal, and didn't range anywhere near the borders of Fuzzy Balls society. Martin supposed she would keep his mom's secret.

He attempted again Wednesday at lunch. Dottie and Frank had left early to sit for a mother-son caricature by the ranch's cowboy cartoonist. And again, Carroll cut Martin short, waving over Jimmy Sneedle himself, "Jimso" to paying guests. It took little prodding for him to hold forth on his purchase of the thousand-acre ranch from the Giles family, who had run it as a cattle operation for over a century.

"I got big plans, Mac," Jimso said, waving a pudgy hand at Carroll, who didn't challenge the nickname. He often complained that his given name ran counter to the essential virility of his character, and he never protested when he was assigned a more masculine moniker, no matter how random.

Jimso flapped his paw toward the dining room's picture window. Palo verde trees and saguaro cacti glinted in the noon sun. He described a Robert Trent Jones golf course covering the riding trails; a Michael Graves-inspired clubhouse taking the place of the eighty-five-year-old barn; low-fat cooking classes instead of square dancing, California wine tastings instead of end-of-week gymkhanas. He would get rid of the horses and their sky-high liability insurance premiums. And he would fire barn manager Beaufort Giles, who "never goes a goddamn day without shooting me the stink eye." Jimso and Carroll then fluted off into a martini-fueled duet on the ingratitude of underlings. Martin headed for the barn to read Shakespeare.

It was there that cowboy poetry first found him: April 10, 1985, not six weeks before the First Annual Elko Cowboy Poetry Confluence in Elko, Nevada. Martin lay on a pile of rough blankets, his head on a saddle, his feet propped on a pile of *Western Life* magazines and thumbed a ratty paperback copy of *Hamlet*. Sequestered behind a wall of hay bales stacked two high, he read to the clump of horse hoof on old wood and the mumbles of the ranch hands.

Hamlet's grousing and Gertrude's nagging drifted past him, like the sweet tang of horse manure floating in the barn's stratosphere. He didn't know why he was bothering. His professors for Macroeconomics II and Ancient Law had refused to let him reschedule final exams. Only the Shakespeare scholar on loan from Cornell was willing to accept a paper in lieu of the last test. He'd probably have to repeat the entire trimester.

He focused on the page, but Claudius's elucidation on the nature of grief tangled with another soliloquy beaming in from somewhere beyond the hay bales.

> *I'll tell you, boys, in those days*
> *Old-timers stood a show,*
> *our pockets full of money,*
> *not a sorrow did we know.*

So simple, the metaphor and rhyme. Martin's cohorts in his English literature discussion group would have gone after the doggerel like picadors to the bull, poking it full of holes with exquisite irony and obscure references to Chaucer. As would have Martin had he been back in Hyde Park. But in this barn, the lines, more than any of Hamlet's self-indulgent bellyaching, struck in him a minor chord to which he had not previously resonated.

It had to be in the delivery. Martin peeked past the hay to confirm the baritone twang was Beaufort Giles's, a lean man with crackling brown skin, as if he had been cured next to the tobacco in the Marlboro always affixed to his bottom lip.

But, how times have changed since then,
we're poorly clothed and fed,
our wagons are all broken down
and horses most all dead.

Beaufort stood, right leg a little forward of the left, knees soft, right hand extended and cupped, as if cradling an invisible Yorick cranium. Three wranglers faced Beaufort, backs to Martin, their leather-clad legs a row of null sets.

Soon we'll leave this country,
then you'll hear the angels shout:
"Oh, here they come to Heaven,
their campfire has gone out."

Beaufort shut his hand and gave it a little shake. The wranglers broke out in loping applause. One whistled through his fingers and two horses whinnied in reply.

"That's really good," Martin said, before he remembered he was terrified of Beaufort, whom he had seen coldcock a foaming mustang two days earlier. "Did you write it?"

"Christ no, son," said Beaufort. "That's Ben Arnold. He died in '22. He was one of the greats."

"Greats?" said Martin.

"Great cowboy poets," said Beaufort.

"What's a cowboy poet?" Martin asked, unaware he had just posed the question the answer to which would give the rest of his life purpose.

Beaufort dug a boot toe into the barn's dirt floor, spun a silver spur with a rust-brown finger, and hacked a nicotine-scented chortle. "Showin's better than teachin'. Why don't you practice with us, for the show?"

Martin had heard all about Jimso's Jamboree and Talent Show from his mom, who was working up something with Bitsy involving kazoos. Beaufort explained that the performance always concluded with a cowboy poetry recital by the barn staff and any guests who might want to join. If Martin started practicing now, he could earn himself a solo spot.

Martin pursed his lips, a prelude to demurring, but before he could, one of the wranglers, the one with a handlebar mustache that drooped the length of his neck, said, "Get that in a knife fight?" He flicked a rough hand at a small scar on Martin's top lip, where he had sliced it on a chipped espresso cup.

"Sure," Martin answered and found he meant both the scar and the poetry practice.

Over the next three days, between leading trail rides, Beaufort schooled Martin on cowboy poetry. Classics like Henry Herbert Knibbs's "Where the Ponies Come to Drink," and modern works like Bob Barnhardt's ode to bull busting, "Born to Buck."

Often, Beaufort's daughter Ginger would stop by to listen. She was seventeen, a champion roper who threw her saddle on her silver cutter with the authority, fluidity, and grace of the kind of man Martin hoped to be someday. Yet she was not a man. Martin was aware of that.

She'd put her hands on her narrow hips, cock her head, drawl a backhanded comment like, "Not bad for an Eastern fella," or "You won't learn that at your university." She'd wink or smile, and Martin would choke or blush. Beaufort would have to snap his fingers and jangle his spurs to get Martin to focus again.

On the afternoon before the Saturday show, Martin and the hands ran through their performance for the last time before Beaufort and the others left to lead the sunset rides. Martin remained in the tack room, eyes closed, whispering the words to "The Campfire Has Gone Out" to himself and running his fingers along the swirls tooled in the leather fender of the saddle on the stand before him.

"Do you study stagecraft in Chicago?" said Ginger.

"Jesus," Martin squeaked and coughed to lower his voice back down to his practiced baritone. "I didn't see you. Where did you come from?"

"Born here on the ranch, like my daddy and his daddy before. And you?"

"Michigan," he said.

"The big lake they call 'Gitchee Gumee'?"

"No, I think that's Superior. We're near Lake Michigan, you know, the one that steams like a young man's dreams. Gordon Lightfoot's great."

Ginger nodded. "Could have been a cowboy poet. So you study theater or poetry?"

"Political science," Martin said and watched Ginger squint. He wished he had a better answer, like "welding" or "animal husbandry."

"Well, that's a waste, a man who can recite like you."

Martin straightened his shoulders, sucked his belly in. He couldn't remember anyone calling him a man before.

"So I'll come see you tonight." Ginger patted dust off her boy-cut Levi's. "And maybe after, we can take a walk."

Martin stopped breathing for long enough that black flecks cartwheeled in front of his eyes. She was talking about sex, right? Or at least the prelude thereto? Sex with him. Sex between him and Ginger. Ginger, who smelled like leather and horse and desert rose. Ginger, whose denim-draped thighs could hold onto a bucking mustang while she twirled a lasso over a charging bull's horns. She was saying it in her old-timey Little-House-on-the-Prairie idiom, but she meant sex. Martin knew it as sure as he knew his lines for Jimso's Jamboree and Talent Show.

"It'd be an honor, ma'am," Martin answered and cursed himself silently. This was not the time to channel Curly from *Oklahoma*. "I mean, sure, that would be neat," but Ginger had already slipped out the door.

Martin sagged against the saddle stand, anemia washing over him as his body's store of blood rushed to his cock. It wasn't that Martin was new to sex. True, in high school, his heft, his lack of athletic prowess, and his aptitude at the cerebral arts meant he didn't get a chance to partake in the freely given gifts of the cheerleaders or the swimmer girls. He had, of course, self-pleasured to the exploits of the forever-fortunate correspondents in his dad's *Penthouse*s, hardly hidden under a two-year-old copy of *Life Magazine* in the drawer of a bedside table. And he and Camilla Lutz had spilt fluids in the backseat of his 1972 Dodge Dart in an apple schnapps-induced haze after the PPHS Senior Prom.

At U of C, his was a more sexually active demographic. In his freshman year, he had enjoyed regular and robust encounters with a budding Austrian geneticist almost as big as he. And just last month, he had been dumped by a bony seminary student, who had declared a major in asceticism with a minor in abstinence. As she had often smelled of garlic and cabbage and would usually cry throughout their otherwise silent lovemaking, Martin supported her decision and the split was amicable.

But sex with Ginger, that would be explosive. He would breathe hot into her sunset-hued tresses and, like a bull bucking at the brand, mount her strapping thighs, naked, he hoped to God, but for her supple leather chaps, and take her amidst the sage and sand of the Arizona desert floor. This would be sex between a man and a woman. A Western woman and the sort of man Martin had been reading about and riding with, at least in his mind, in the four days since Beaufort introduced him to cowboy poetry.

Martin took a deep breath and tried to replace the image of Ginger's dimpled smile with the visage of his ancient law professor, a puckered woman with coffee-stained teeth. His rigidity yielded enough for him to make his way up to the lodge for his pre-theater meal.

After dinner, salmon aspic and a green salad, Martin hid out in the ranch library, not allowing himself to look around the main lodge to see if Ginger had been good to her word. He spent two hours thumbing through back issues of *Western* magazine before he was called to the stage by a slurring and sniggering Jimso through a mic screeching with reverb. Martin centered himself, his back to the massive stone fireplace, and looked out. The ambitious wattage provided by the lighting team—Beaufort and the hands armed with Black and Decker spot flashlights—rendered Martin as blind as an elk about to be flattened by a semi, so there was no hope of spotting Ginger. Probably a good thing. It would no doubt distract the audience from his paean to cowboys of the past if he intoned it while sporting a throbbing erection.

He did not remember starting the poem, or whether he had tilted his head at the end of the second stanza, as he had practiced. He remembered nothing of the performance at all until he reached the final lines:

Oh, here they come to Heaven,
their campfire has gone out.

Applause shook the pine-paneled room. Martin lifted a crooked right index finger to his temple in salute, as he had seen Beaufort do. Martin could hear Beaufort whistling now, a sharp and painful shriek, as if he were garroting a prairie dog rather than blowing nicotine-scented air through gnarled fingers. He had to set down his flashlight in order to whistle effectively. The respite from the glare allowed Martin to see out into the crowd.

There weren't as many guests sitting in the semicircles of wooden chairs spooning the stage area as there had been when the show started. Most of the Fuzzy Balls, Martin's parents included, had slipped into the bar in back of the big hall. A few of the others appeared to have snuck out or joined the Fuzzy Balls. Here and there, ranch employees filled in for the defectors: a couple of the busboys; most all of the groundskeepers; the youngish waitress whom Martin's dad had taken to patting on the ass; the shaggy-headed tennis pro who sold Frank pot.

Julie Newport, now in her first year at the University of Michigan, was also there, in the front row, clapping with great, broad bangs of her mannish hands. In the three years since they had witnessed Buster's death on the beach at Twin Bluffs, she had grown, both as a swimmer and as a physical presence. She had set records at PPHS in every girls' event except the 100-yard backstroke, and U of M put her on the varsity squad as a freshman. Tonight, she had the fierce look that Martin imagined she must wear while blazing down the lane during the butterfly. Her massive shoulders swiveled in and out as she applauded, and her head bobbed with each strike. Next to her, leaning away from Julie's pumping appendages and also clapping, but with lither movement, was Ginger.

The barn staff joined Martin up front to acknowledge the ovation. For the bow, wranglers on either side of him grabbed his soft hands in their calloused ones, like Dunkin Donuts Boston cremes wrapped in sandpaper. He hoped they didn't notice. After the third curtain call, Martin hustled to where Ginger stood, smiling and applauding.

"Really nice, cowboy," she said and placed a hand on his chest.

"Martin, who knew?" Julie pushed Ginger's arm out of the way and pressed her ample breasts to Martin's ample stomach. He was a head taller. He could smell whiskey on her breath, and bubble gum. She cupped his groin with both hands.

"I'm happy to see you too," Julie continued. "I've got some hash back in my room. Want to go see if we can take care of this?" She gave Martin's swelling balls a squeeze through his jeans.

Martin looked over Julie's chlorine-green-tinged blonde shag to Ginger's retreating back. He moved to go after her, forgetting for a moment Julie was there, bumping into her. She responded with another clutch at his balls.

Martin realized right then that the genes driving blood to his cock, like cowmen behind a stampeding herd, were half contributed by Dottie Oliphant. Those genes could not help but lust after a Newport, no matter how improbable or crass Julie's advance might be, no matter how enticing or life-changing his alternate adventure with Ginger might have been.

"Let's go," he choked to Julie and looked down her gaping checkered shirt to her freckled and unencumbered breasts.

They didn't make it back to her room. They ducked into the darkened billiards den. Martin leaned back on the table, hands clutching at the green felt. Julie unzipped his jeans and ran a scratchy tongue up his rigid shaft—as impressive as any on the cover of the bull semen catalogues Martin had seen on Beaufort's desk. Martin's hormone-addled brain only lit for a second on the question of why Julie, who had said more words to him tonight than in the previous decade of their acquaintance, was ministering so expertly to his manhood. Only much later did he recognize that Ginger's interest must have fueled the ever-competitive Julie's desires. Only much later did he learn that, prior to coming to the ranch, Julie had been cut from her college swim team and from her sister's bridal party because of weight gain, the freshman forty slowing her in the water and straining the seams of her Neiman Marcus custom-tailored full-length bridesmaid's gown with bustle. Only much later did he hear that, since arriving at the ranch, Julie had offered blowjobs to, and been refused by, Frank, the tennis pro, three wranglers, the pastry chef, and Jimso.

No, that night, as Martin sprayed and convulsed like the Colorado River charging through the Grand Canyon itself, he credited it all to cowboy poetry. Every spasm of pleasure offered up by Julie's virtuoso lapping, every frisson of titillation excited by her roaming hands, every pang of sweet regret brought on by his missed coupling with Ginger, every swell of his breast puffed up by the remembered evening's ovations, every moment blessedly free of thoughts of his family, and college, and cancer. All of it was cowboy poetry. And even much later, when he had accepted the less lyrical facts of that fine night, he still attached the feel of it—the sounds, the smells, the sex—to cowboy poetry, and only that.

The Campfire has Gone Out
Traditional

Through progress of the railroads,
our occupation's gone;
we'll get our ideas into words,
our words into a song,
first comes the cowboy—
he's the spirit of the West;
of all the pioneers I claim
the cowboys are the best.
We'll miss him in the round-up,
it's gone, his merry shout,
the cowboy has left the country,
his campfire has gone out.

You freighters, our companions,
you've got to leave this land;
can't drag your loads for nothing
through the gumbo and the sand;
the railroads are bound to beat you—
so do your level best,
give it up to the granger
and strike out farther west.
Bid them all adieu
and give the merry shout,
"The cowboy has left the country
and his campfire has gone out."

When I think of those good old days
my eyes with tears will fill;
when I think of the tin can by the fire
and the coyote on the hill.
I'll tell you, boys, in those days
Old-timers stood a show,
our pockets full of money,

not a sorrow did we know;
But, how times have changed since then,
we're poorly clothed and fed,
our wagons are all broken down
and horses most all dead.
Soon we'll leave this country,
then you'll hear the angels shout:
"Oh, here they come to Heaven,
their campfire has gone out."

3

Frank arrived in Dottie's brown-fake-wood-on-lighter-brown-exterior station wagon at noon on the Saturday of Memorial Day weekend 1985 to take Martin and his worldly possessions back to Pierre. Martin had transferred his lease to his roommate's girlfriend, figuring he could always come back to campus before the next trimester and find another place. Legions of pre-meds would spend their summers retaking organic chemistry, and most would fail. That would leave plenty of overpriced and underfumigated dwelling spaces from which to choose.

Frank exited the car, and Martin trundled down the path from the apartment foyer, extending the hand not clutching a black trash bag full of dirty laundry. "Thanks for coming."

"Not my choice," said Frank. "You know, today is opening day of the beach season."

"Pierre's beaches are public," said Martin. "They're open all the time. And not my choice either. I'm not the one going to California tomorrow, Mr. McEnroe."

"Well, I'm not the one who got cancer. And we're not supposed to say 'cancer' at home, by the way. Mom and Dad don't like it." Frank looked at Martin's still-outstretched hand and grasped it.

Frank's grip was firm, no surprise there, and Martin firmed his own in response. They bobbed hands a moment, then Martin stepped back, looking toward the street, the side elms, the traffic, the berm's patchy grass. Anywhere but Frank.

"These all going?" asked Frank, kicking at a pile of ten or so cardboard boxes piled at the curb.

Martin nodded. He didn't speak, worried that the words might come out cracked and loving, and that would make for a long ride home.

"Goddamn, this is heavy," said Frank, hoisting the top box. "What's in here, beer?"

"Books," said Martin.

"*Pffft,*" hissed Frank. "To each his own. How much more of this shit is there?"

Martin thought of the fifteen boxes stacked in his room, each labeled in green magic marker: "common core physical science texts, deutsche Sprache, Grammatik Bücher, Wörterbuch, Kafka, Brecht, Western and Non-Western Civ." Then there was his Brother Cassette Correct-O-Riter I in its hard shell case; his posters (Wham!, National Geographic World Map, 1979 Tutankhamen Artifacts Tour) secured in a tube; a mesh-bagged collection of half-melted, scented votive candles, and two bottles of Prell Shampoo left by his ex-girlfriend; his own toiletries—toothbrush, Crest, plastic combs, nail clippers, Vaseline Angel Skin lotion, one unwrapped bar of Life Buoy, Head and Shoulders, Gold Bond Medicated Powder—all fit neatly in a Converse shoe box. It was a point of pride for Martin that, despite his body's great size, he could care for it with minimal amendments.

They rode the elevator to the second floor. The door opened, and Martin held its rubber edge.

"You want to keep it here, and I'll get the rest of the stuff?" he said.

"Nah," said Frank. "I want to see your place."

But what Martin wanted was for Frank not to see his place. Frank couldn't help but find it, at best, grim. No decoration, save the books stacked on and around two-by-four board-and-cinderblock shelves. Windows without curtains painted shut and smeared with black grease of unknown origin. That smell endemic to Hyde Park student apartments: leaking gas, rotting food, unwashed sheets. Martin was already finding it uncomfortably easy to abandon his Chicago home. Frank's disapprobation would only fuel the disquiet that threatened to develop into a full-fledged existential crisis.

But once in the apartment, Frank's only comment was about the lack of alcohol in the kitchen's battered and moldy refrigerator. They got the car loaded in just under two hours, and Martin made one last trip up the elevator to leave his keys. There was no one to say goodbye to, there or anywhere outside the building. Saturday before exam week, and everyone was at the Reg.

Martin offered to drive the three hours around the bottom of Lake Michigan back to Pierre, and Frank accepted, explaining he wanted to nap. The Cubs were in Philly, and Martin switched the radio on low to listen to Vince and Lou narrate the inevitable defeat. Martin didn't follow sports as a rule, but he made an exception for the Cubs. That a team so hapless could remain so beloved always filled him with the sort of hope he felt he needed to stockpile if he was going to make it in this wide world. He preferred listening to losses, which this one was shaping up to be by the time he pulled off Stony Island and onto I-94E and the Chicago Skyway.

From the late 1950s through the 1980s, to get to points east and south of the University of Chicago by car, you had to scale the Skyway then descend toward the Indiana border. The road swooped away from Hyde Park, with its promises of cerebral employment, stimulating conversation, and clean nails to skim over the circle of hell that was the flats of Gary, Indiana—sidewalks empty of people, streets empty of cars, tree boxes empty of trees; soot-stained bungalows sharing side walls, and concrete yards fenced with chain link; bent TV antennas sending thick black wires to the tops of tar black poles and then into a messy grid of overhead electrical lines. All this sat against the backdrop of the steel mills and their smokestacks, eternally flaming and spewing the gray smog that turned every Gary day to constant dusk. Go to a good college and finish well or pick up your lunch bucket, report to the line, and hope you don't die of emphysema before your union-negotiated pension kicks in.

Frank didn't wake up until Martin had taken the Indiana Toll Road ticket from the graying and probably diabetic attendant, who might well have been born in that booth.

"Jesus. Gary," said Frank and put his hand over his nose and mouth. The odor was sharp and unique and almost as strong with the windows up as with the windows down. It was as if someone had decided to boil urine down to a thick paste and had burnt a good deal of it onto the bottom of the metal pot.

"Do you have a beer in one of those boxes?" Frank said and sat up.

"Just books," said Martin.

"Ron and I went to the bonfire last night. Fuck, we got wasted. Do you think mom has aspirin in here?" Frank popped open the glove compartment. In it was the owner's manual, still sealed in its plastic wrap, and the faux leather-covered book that Lou Cheely, Pierre's

Oldsmobile franchise owner, provided gratis to all customers to re-cord their service visits.

"Just books," said Martin.

Frank slammed the compartment door. "I saw your girlfriend Julie Newport last night."

"Not my girlfriend," said Martin and shifted in his seat to ease the electric tingle that moved into his groin with the mention of Julie's name.

"That's not what I hear. I hear you fucked her at Jimmy Sneedle's."

"I did not." Martin was fairly certain that that was technically true, though sex act taxonomy had not been a topic covered in the PPHS health class syllabus. For the males, that curriculum had consisted entirely of a short film about how teen fatherhood could really screw up a promising high school long-jump career.

"Did she say something?"

"She said you were after that Ginger chick, you know, the barn guy's daughter," said Frank. "Did you fuck her?"

"No," said Martin. Ginger. He squeezed his legs together and took a deep breath. Ginger.

"Ginger's hot. My type, an athlete," said Frank.

Martin felt the incoming tide of blood washing over his genitals and face reverse course behind a wave of fear. "Did you?"

"What?" said Frank.

"You know, do it. With Ginger," said Martin.

"I totally would fuck her, but no. She wouldn't even talk to me. Except once, and that was to ask about you. You missed your chance, man. She totally would have fucked you. I could tell."

The bubbled back of the two-toned Pacer in front of the station wagon swam in Martin's tearing eyes. Oh Jesus, he was going to cry. And from what? Relief that Frank hadn't fucked Ginger? Joy that Ginger might have fucked Martin? Regret that Martin hadn't fucked Ginger?

"What'd Ginger ask about me? And can you please stop saying fuck?" said Martin.

"Christ, I can't say 'cancer,' and I can't say 'fuck,'" said Frank, "What am I supposed to say?"

"Just tell me what she asked about me."

"She asked how big your dick was, and I said, 'Ever seen a roll of Certs?'" Frank bayed. Martin didn't join in. He jerked the station wagon around the Pacer.

Frank tried another laugh, this one less authentic and less harsh. Martin remained silent.

"I'm sorry, man. I don't remember what she said, but I remember thinking she would have f—, had intimate relations with you, if you wanted."

Martin eased up on the gas, took a deep breath. "Thanks," he said.

"No fucking problem." Frank shut his eyes again. "'Fucking' isn't the same as 'fuck,' right?" His head drooped, and he hacked out a snore.

Frank slept as I-90 gave way to I-94, and the factories gave way to scrub trees and furrowed fields, greening here and there with early corn. Martin's thoughts about Ginger gave way to more thoughts about Ginger. In the six weeks since he had returned to Hyde Park from Arizona, he'd managed to convince himself that the carnal adventures he had had, without complaint or regret, with Julie Newport had come at no cost, except maybe the premature extinction of a sweaty fantasy about a sweet ranch hand's daughter. Ginger and he could never have coupled, he knew that. The mighty Mississippi was the least of that which separated them. There were their families, their lifetime income expectations, their social classes, their equestrian abilities, or lack thereof, their familiarity with the pre-Socratics, or lack thereof. He had convinced himself that their meeting was a fluke, a brief and meaningless flirtation of two unlike souls over the words of the cowboy poet Ben Arnold.

But they had met. And they had flirted. And he had read "The Campfire Has Gone Out" with the vim of a seasoned hand reciting around the chuck wagon after a hard day on the Chisholm Trail. And she had stood and cheered. And he could have made love to her that night. He could have fucked her, Frank said, so it must be true, because Frank was a savant when it came to the sexual proclivities of teen girls. Maybe, then, it was not a fluke. Maybe, then, Martin and Ginger could meet again. And they could flirt again. And they could this time let the bonds of cowboy poetry lash them together in sublime physical union, saddle to stallion, calf to teat, bacon to beans—dare he imagine it?—husband to wife. It could happen, he knew, just as sure as he knew it could never happen in Hyde Park, Illinois. Not in a place where poetry is examined as an artifact rather than recited as a creed. Not in a place where hands are for typing dissertations and ropes are for designating academic honors. Not in a place that smelled of burnt coffee and molding books instead of sunburnt dust and gunfire.

Martin noodled on like this all the way to the Michigan border, there adding remembered snippets of verse learned from Beaufort and pornographic daydreams featuring Ginger's body and Julie's tongue. By the time Martin pulled into the Oliphant's garage, he had come to believe his early departure from U of C might not be the disaster he had assumed, might even be an opportunity to be of honorable service, to live a life, at least for a few weeks, of action and meaning. A life he'd be proud to tell Ginger about, when they met again. In Ben Arnold's words, "to strike out further West." Technically Pierre was due east of Chicago, but spiritually, with the issues of life and death and family duty Martin was taking on, it seemed to be a few degrees further west than even Jimmy Sneedle's. And for this reason, he waited a minute after the automatic garage door thumped closed, breathing the air that smelled of exhaust fumes and, maybe, freedom, then gently shook, rather than slugged, his sleeping brother awake.

Where a family fell in the caste system in place in Pierre in the 1980s was best predicted by what time they sat down to their evening meal: 5:30, 6:00, or 7:00. The half-fivers were the factory workers (the ones that were left), the shopkeepers, widows, fruit farmers, hairdressers, plumbers, secretaries, small-engine repairmen, and residents of the Oaks Home for the Aged. If it was eaten during the five-o-clock hour, it was called supper. Those who ate at six, ate dinner: middle managers, junior professionals, golf and tennis pros, unmarried teachers, the younger car and insurance salesmen, people who had grown up dining at 5:30 but added a cocktail half-hour to the evening routine and felt modern as a result. Seven p.m. was for the elite, those with trusts funds and continental airs, families who went to Austria for Christmas or to Aspen for spring skiing, people who had been to

Rio or might one day go. Seven p.m., of course, was when the Fuzzy Balls ate.

And thus it was when the Oliphants ate. Before Carroll's acquisition of the bubble, though, they'd been solid six-o-clockers. At exactly that hour, Dottie would snap off her Liberty London print apron, switch on the kitchen black-and-white, and sit down. They raised their first forkfuls to the local CBS anchor wishing them "good evening" backed by a fanfare of recorded trumpets.

Now that dinner was at seven, it was a less orderly affair. Carroll watched the news in his den, usually with a second pitcher of martinis or a bottle of wine from his new cellar, just like the one Bitsy's husband had. Dottie would struggle with a recipe from *Julia Child and Company*, cursing the scorched puff pastry around the ham pithivier. Frank often ate at McDonald's after practice with his best friend and doubles partner, Ron Seeds. And Martin, for most of that period, was in Chicago.

The evening Martin returned to Pierre, he and Frank arrived at 6:45 p.m., so they had missed neither dinner nor the surrounding chaos. Martin hadn't fully extracted himself from the front seat when his dad threw open the door from the house to the garage.

"Come in, come in," he slurred, one arm waving them forward, one swinging an open bottle of wine. "It's the commercial, but Dan Rather's about to do a bit on a new drug, the LSD of the eighties. Ecstasy! What do you think?"

"I think I'll go say hi to Mom," said Martin and squeezed around his dad, who swayed in the open door.

"Put this on the table for dinner then," said Carroll and handed the empty bottle to Martin.

"I'll be with Dad," said Frank.

"That's my boy," barked Carroll. "Ecstasy!"

Martin continued to the kitchen, a rectangular space, running along the backside of the house and bifurcated by a half island separating the cooking area from the dining nook. He passed the dinner table, noting that it had been set with cloth rather than paper napkins and that the usual centerpiece, a fruit bowl except at Halloween when it was a pumpkin, had been replaced by a columnar candle with Day-Glo orange, lime, purple, hot pink, and yellow stripes. Wisps of smoke formed a cirrus cloud over the stove, and the room smelled of fireworks and bait minnows, as if there had been an explosion in a fish cannery.

Martin rounded the island. His mother sat on the tile floor, legs splayed, staring at her reflection in the oven door.

"Welcome home, dear. I think I've burned the cod," she said.

"Are you okay?" Martin said. He felt he should give her a hug, but there was no way to accomplish that without getting on the ground too. He feared that would leave them both stuck until his dad and Frank finished educating themselves on the latest recreational narcotics. Martin settled for patting her on the head.

"I'm great," said Dottie and leaned forward at the waist until her forehead rested on the oven door. "How are you? Easy drive?" She turned to him, one temple still on the oven. "Why don't you put that on the table and call your dad and Frank for dinner?"

"Empty," Martin said and waggled the bottle.

"Then open another. Your dad brought up three. Open them both." Dottie pulled her legs underneath her and reached a hand toward the sky. Martin bent toward her.

"Let me help you." He wondered whether this was a preview of his summer's employment.

"No," said Dottie. "I want the bottle. Bitsy and I make goblets out of them."

Martin put the empty bottle in the sink, then placed his hands under Dottie's arms and boosted her to standing. It was too easy, like hoisting a grocery bag of packing peanuts. She gasped and all above her neck palsied.

"I'll get the wine," she said. "You get the others. It's seven."

The new centerpiece was what Dottie called a "Conversation Candle," a staple, she explained, at Fuzzy Balls' dinner tables. Everyone was to stay seated for the forty-five minutes it took to burn through one band of florescent wax, enough time to move beyond the petty disputes about who got more rice and why they never had sloppy Joes anymore and onto more serious subjects. Such as his mom's cancer, Martin thought, and wondered how that would go, given the ban on talking about it. He was also curious how his dad would fare through forty-five minutes of sedentary small talk. He couldn't remember Carroll sitting still for longer than fifteen minutes, save for car or airplane trips, those punctuated with, on land, finger drumming, radio switching, and lane changing or, in flight, restroom visiting, tiny-bottled-gin drinking, and stewardess-ass patting. But he seemed calm tonight. He was also smashed, more so than usual. He'd probably gotten wind earlier of the impending confinement period and liquored up appropriately.

Frank, on the other hand, was clearly caught by surprise and spent the first fifteen minutes of the candle's flaming appealing the sentence. He had to pack. He had to say good-bye to Ron. He had to shower. He had to say good-bye to the PPHS JV cheerleaders, especially those he had not gotten around to deflowering yet.

Frank went on until Dottie pulled the Midwestern Methodist version of breaking into hysterical sobs: She folded her hands on the table, pursed her lips, blinked several times, and started her sentence with "I just wanted…"

"I just wanted to talk about what we're all going to do this summer, since we won't see each other again…" She paused, and Martin feared she might be at a full stop, which was far more information about her illness than he was prepared to take in over charred fish.

"…for quite a while," she finished.

"At least you and Martin will get to spend some time together," said Carroll and poured a healthy measure of Cabernet down the side of his glass.

"And you too, Dad, right?" Martin said, deploying his napkin to dam the river of red wine headed toward his placemat. "Isn't your speech Tuesday?"

"The conference goes until Thursday," Carroll said. "And after that there's a business I want to look at in Kansas City. A pet cemetery deal."

"Like the Stephen King book, which I read all of," said Frank, throwing Martin a look that invited him to challenge.

"I heard you could read now, congratulations," said Martin.

"Boys," said Dottie. More lip pursing, more blinking. "I just wanted…"

"Not like Steven King at all," said Carroll sharply. Martin always marveled at how, no matter how much his dad drank, when discussing business, he rivaled Carrie Nation in his sobriety. "The idiot running it has no idea what he's got. Pet morticians located next to funeral homes. Be buried with your beloved Fido. Franchise possibilities out the wazoo. I want to open one in Pierre."

"Okay," said Martin. "But you'll be back for when mom comes home from the hos—"

"The procedure," barked Dottie. Frank raised an eyebrow and shook his head. The linguistic obstacles to navigating this summer were mounting, Martin thought.

"Then there're these sports stores in California," continued Carroll. "One is right near Frank's camp. People out west, they exercise."

"Like Jane Fonda," Dottie said.

"Right. Just like her. And men too. I gotta think about the next generation." Carroll inclined his head toward Frank. "Once this guy here's done tearing up the pro circuit, he'd be great at the sports equipment racket." He guffawed at his pun.

"Don't you have to be able to do long division to run a business?" asked Martin and took a mouthful of haricots verts. He didn't like the way this was going. Seemed like he was expected to abandon the U of C so his dad could spend three months making sure Frank would have gainful employment someday.

"And Martin would be great at putting animal carcasses in the ground," said Frank.

"Right," said Carroll and reached over his shoulder to pluck the final bottle of wine from the island. "Exactly," he mumbled and poured a full glass.

"Of course, you won't be gone the entire summer," said Dottie with a weak laugh. "It would get kind of lonely, just Martin and me, and you'll need clean clothes." Her voice became quiet. "Won't you?" Martin almost couldn't bear to look at her.

Carroll didn't seem to notice. "Oh no, hotel laundries are the best. They've got these machines that do the pressing, and they bring it back on hangers."

"I just thought, I guess I thought..." Dottie's voice trailed off, a handful of pebbles plinking into a deep well.

Carroll's head jerked up. "Dottie, Jesus, we talked about it. I'd be in the way. You'll be busy, busy." He looked around the table.

"Recovering," offered Martin, which won him a grimace from Frank.

"Of course," said Dottie, her face smoothing back into the cold and gracious smile she'd worn pretty much continuously since Carroll bought the bubble. "Summer is all about the ladies leagues, isn't it? Bitsy and I will hardly have a moment to spare, organizing for the July Fourth round robin and the Dog Days Challenge Ladder at the club."

"So what about you, Martin? What are your plans for the summer?" said Carroll, in the hearty tone of a sitcom dad, obviously relieved that the emotional interlude had passed and without any crying. "Probably a little late to get a lifeguard job, eh?" Frank snorted at that. "But you heard your mom, she's gonna be swamped, so you stay out of her hair."

Martin looked hard at his dad then harder at Frank. With popping eyes and contorting lips, they both telegraphed the same message: Go with it.

Martin bowed his head. Was silent sacrifice nobler than heralded deeds? Not according to Homer or Virgil. But maybe according to Ben Arnold. Or Beaufort. Or Ginger. Who remembered the names of the countless cowboys who tamed the frontier and fed the nation? No one asked them to ride the cow trails, to brave the summer storms, to turn the deadly stampede. They did it because that's what needed to be done. They did it without much in the way of recompense or acknowledgement. It was enough for them to know that, at the end of the day, the angels would greet them: "Oh, here they come to Heaven, their campfire has gone out." It was enough for Martin too.

"This summer, I think I'll…"

"Times up," shouted Frank and pushed back his chair.

"Martin, would you clear please," said Dottie, also rising.

Martin stayed seated. "This summer," he said, pausing for dramatic effect, though he was certain no one was listening, and Frank was already out of the room. "This summer, I'm going to make a study of cowboy poetry."

Jimmy Sneedle's Tennis and Dude Ranch Chronicles: Summer Edition, May 15, 1985, p.4

The View from My Corner of the Barn, by Beaufort Giles

Well, another dude ranchin' season's come and gone, and Ginger and I are packing our gear and getting ready to head out to our summer's employment. We said goodbye to the barn hands and a heap of the wranglers on Sunday: Travis, Beau, Wylie, Jesse, Tray, Jeb, Herbert, Quentin—we'll miss each and every one of you. On Monday, the last two went: Zane and Lucky Robert loaded the ponies up in the trailers and made for the cooler pastures of the K Bar T Ranch in Little Springs, Montana. Of course, Ginger kept her cutter Minnow with her, and she'll be traveling the rodeo circuit, running the barrels and adding to her pile of silver buckles. I head out tomorrow to Elko, Nevada, to meet up with a few other old-timers and recite some rhymes. It's the First Annual Elko Cowboy Poetry Confluence, a pretty high-falutin' name for a bunch of worn-out hands tossing around the prairie coal, if you ask me, but as usual, no one has.

From the bottom of our hearts, Ginger and I want to thank the guests at the ranch here for allowing us to spend one more season on the Giles family homestead. I pray to the good Lord that he sees fit to have our trails cross again someday and to bless you and yours with starry nights, placid dogies, and a soft saddle. I leave you with a couple of verses from the great Badger Clark. May they bring you the comfort they have always brought me.

A Cowboy's Prayer

(Written for Mother)

I thank You, Lord, that I am placed so well,
that You have made my freedom so complete;
that I'm no slave of whistle, clock or bell,
nor weak-eyed prisoner of wall and street.
Just let me live my life as I've begun
and give me work that's open to the sky;
make me a pardner of the wind and sun,
and I won't ask a life that's soft or high.

Let me be easy on the man that's down;
let me be square and generous with all.
I'm careless sometimes, Lord, when I'm in town,
but never let 'em say I'm mean or small!
Make me as big and open as the plains,
as honest as the hawse between my knees,
clean as the wind that blows behind the rains,
free as the hawk that circles down the breeze!

4

The leitmotif of denial that had marked the Oliphant's Conversation Candlelight dinner dogged the rest of Martin's summer. When he dropped his mom at Swinehurst Hospital for her mastectomy, he didn't even go to help her check in. They shook hands on the curb outside the in-patient entrance, as if he were a long-time chauffer depositing the lady of the manor for a fortnight in the country. While she was recovering, he visited every morning. They would sit in her antiseptic room, watching reruns of old black-and-white sitcoms on the wall-mounted TV, never discussing her sunken chest, the drainage tubes sprouting from the short sleeves of her gown, or her prognosis. When *The Andy Griffith Show* came on, Martin would make his exit, return home, and continue to watch daytime TV. In the evenings, his anesthetic of choice was a bottle of wine from his dad's cellar and a Dick Francis paperback from the stash in the den.

After two weeks, Dottie moved back home with the help of Nurse Hawkins, a rounded woman who smelled of starch. Martin's routine hardly changed, except that he watched both his morning and afternoon TV in the basement rec room, while his mom and Nurse Hawkins used the set in the master bedroom. Another two weeks and Nurse Hawkins decamped, professing herself satisfied that her patient was on the mend and that Martin could handle the caretaking duties on his own. After all, how hard was it to warm up a can of Campbell's Chicken & Stars or scramble an egg?

Not that hard, fortunately, because by mid-July, Martin accepted he was on his own. His dad had announced he was proceeding straight from closing on the Final Paws Pet Mortuary 'n Cemetery of Kansas City to Palo Alto, where a failing sports equipment store chain was headquartered. From there, he'd also be able to keep an eye on Frank, who'd almost been kicked out of Dick Gould's Junior Summer Tennis Camp for an incident involving a missed curfew, a bottle of Boone's Farm Strawberry Wine, and a bikinied Stanford grad student, who was old enough to know better. Martin appreciated that he should be angry with his dad, but Martin also appreciated that his dad was reacting to Dottie's frailty the only way he knew how—from afar and with lots of cash. He instructed Mrs. Priebe to collect and pay the bills and dispense whatever spending money Martin deemed necessary, no questions asked. Martin recognized that addendum for what it was: the only attaboy he was likely to receive for taking on solo the terrifying task of waiting for his mom to get well, or not.

He knew it was bad. The mastectomy had gone as planned, but as the summer weeks ticked by, Dottie didn't get better. She remained skeletal. She limped. She needed help getting out of bed. Martin was sure the cancer had spread. When he expressed that concern to their family physician, Dr. Elliot Broad, he answered, "the body is an amazing thing" but offered no other comments, diagnoses, or timelines. Martin's mom complained but only of tennis elbow.

Once, at the beginning of August, Martin battled back his ennui enough to make a trip to the Pierre Public Library to start his planned study of cowboy poetry. The outing was a failure. The scratched oak file drawers held no card for Ben Arnold, nor for any of the poets Beaufort and the hands had performed: Bruce Kiskaddon, Henry Herbert Knibbs, Badger Clark, S. Omar Barker. Martin found no anthologies of the classic cowboy poets' works, no listings for cowboy poetry in *The Readers' Guide to Periodic Literature,* no librarian familiar with the canon of that particular folk art. When he left the central-air chilled sanctum, with its perfume of carpet glue and mimeograph ink, he left convinced that, in Pierre, he was alone in his passion for cowboy poetry, alone and without resources.

And he was half right. It would be a few more years before NPR's Saturday night staple, "The Cowboy Poetry Hour," would introduce Western verse to Midwestern sensibilities. In Pierre in 1985, Martin was indeed cowboy poetry's sole devotee. But he would have been wrong to think he could not have found a solid grounding in the art on the shelves of the Pierre library. Cowboy poetry—recited, sung, and translated (for many of the earliest campfire performers were vaqueros from south of the border)—was first chronicled among the stockmen working the cattle drives after the Civil War. These were men who had, in school, memorized Longfellow, Shakespeare, and the Bible and, in parlors, listened to Robert Service, Rudyard Kipling, and

Edgar Allen Poe, such orations being one of the most popular American entertainments of that era. Thus primed, and with six months to kill while trotting up the Chisholm, Shawnee, or Goodnight-Loving trail, cowboys would create their own ballads and odes. To the beat of horse hooves on packed dirt, they would rework "Gunga Din" or a Shakespeare sonnet to feature a few more skittish calves, a just-broke stallion, and a honky-tonk whore with a heart of gold. If Martin had bothered to look, he could have found the forefathers of cowboy poetry all over, and rarely checked out from, the Pierre Public Library stacks.

He did not connect again with his passion for cowboy poetry until the late August night before he was to pick up his dad and Frank from O'Hare Airport. He wandered into Carroll's home office in search of the index card on which Mrs. Priebe had typed the number and time of the flight from San Francisco. He sat in the desk chair, leaned back, sniffed at the Vitalis that had soaked into the pleather headrest, and struggled to work out how he felt about the return of the other half of his family. He had become accustomed to floating alone in the timeless stream of nescience that had become his summer. Mrs. Priebe had sent in his tuition for the fall trimester at U of C, but Hyde Park seemed a million miles from his and Dottie's days of Stouffer's Macaroni and Cheese, three o'clock naps, and *The Dick Van Dyke Show.* Dottie, on the other hand, was elated and had claimed she was already feeling better knowing that "my boys" would soon be home. Martin saw no evidence of improved health on her part, just the opposite in fact, but he chose to believe it because she did.

He pushed around the mail on top of his dad's blotter: J.C. Penney's catalogue promising an "acid-washed summer of denim fun"; the First Methodist of Pierre's newsletter, *A Pew Words;* a March of Dimes appeal; a flyer for twenty percent off on an oil change at Dougie's Engine Shoppe. And, at the bottom of the pile, *Jimmy Sneedle's Tennis and Dude Ranch Chronicles: Summer Edition.*

Reading the masthead quickened Martin's breath and hardened his cock. He scanned the front—an announcement of a name change, come October, to "Jimmy Sneedle's Tennis and Golf Ranch;" a boxed invitation to purchase, at a "friends of Jimso" rate, one of the "clubhouse view timeshares"; a photo of a barren patch of desert, a

bulldozer, and a sign that read FUTURE HOME OF THE JS EN-
TERPRISES CHAMPIONSHIP GOLF COURSE. Martin thought
the bulldozer was parked where the barn used to be, but he couldn't
be sure, as he recognized nothing familiar in the picture. No horses,
no cacti, no sagebrush, no cowboys, no Ginger.

He flipped the newsletter over and gasped. There it was, covering
the back page: A column by Beaufort, a couple of verses of poetry,
and a large black-and-white photo of Martin performing "The Campfire Has Gone Out." Martin thought he could make out the back of
Julie's head in the front row and next to her, Ginger, leaning forward.
He had not imagined it. His life had changed that night.

He read Beaufort's article with care, noting that the Elko Cowboy
Poetry Confluence he spoke of attending had long passed but also
that he had called it the "first annual" of such events. Martin vowed
then to be at the second. He turned his attention to the Badger Clark
poem, "A Cowboy's Prayer," subtitled "A Prayer for Mother."

How could he not believe this, and the note above it, was a missive
for Martin and Martin alone? He gently tore off the back page, vow-
ing, starting immediately, to practice reciting the poem until he knew
it as well as "The Campfire Has Gone Out." But that night, he only
got as far as the first lines—*I thank You, Lord, that I am placed so well,
that You have made my freedom so complete*—before the phone rang. He
picked it up.

"Hello?" It was Frank, via clicky long distance, Pierre to Palo Alto.
"You're coming to the airport, right? I think there's something wrong
with dad."

Martin scanned the passengers disembarking from the TWA SFO-
LAX-ORD red-eye. Though only ten a.m., the heat of Chicago in
late August made the planes outside the terminal windows wave and
bend, as if they were tuned in on the kitchen RCA. He had promised
to meet Frank at the end of the jetway to help with Carroll who was,
in Frank's words, "acting strange, even for him." But that was last
night and the flight took five hours, enough time for the chronically
distracted Frank to forget he even had a brother. If Martin missed
them, there would be panicked calls to his mom, who was not well
enough to pick up the phone. There would be frantic white courtesy

phone announcements. There would be an impossibly expensive cab ride home and recriminations all around and somehow, inevitably, it would all be down to Martin. So he noted each deplaning passenger with the intensity of General Custer astride his horse, scrutinizing the horizon, waiting for that first Lakota or Oglala or Miniconjou to come and shoot him dead.

Martin spotted his dad first. He walked with a starboard tack and his right jowl slouched a good three inches lower than his left. He passed by Martin; less a snub, Martin thought, than a lack of vision out of a sagging eye socket, so loose the eyelid had completely covered the pupil and most of the iris and was working its way through the bottom half of the sclera.

"Dad," Martin said and reached a hand to the shoulder of the listing man's checkered travel blazer. "Are you all right?"

"I know," said Frank, a step behind Carroll. "He won't stop doing that." He wore a shiny tracksuit in Stanford red and black and carried a matching bag sprouting three tennis racquet handles.

"What'd you say? What'd you say?" Carroll's good eye ping-ponged between Martin and Frank.

"He does that too," said Frank. "Maybe his ears are clogged."

"How long has he been like this?" said Martin.

"I dunno," said Frank. "A couple of days. Since he came to see me play on Wednesday. But sometimes he's okay. Like he can drive fine. He keeps both hands on the wheel now. His face, though, it's messed up. Anyway, we should get our bags before some asshole takes them. I have valuable stuff in there." By "valuable stuff," Martin assumed Frank meant drugs.

"Where'd you park?" Carroll angled his head so the left side addressed Martin in a sharp voice infused with familiar and oddly comforting vibrations of contempt. He sucked in a breath. Maybe it wasn't so bad. Then the right side of Carroll's lip let loose a cord of spittle, which shimmered and twisted in the light from the floor-to-ceiling plastic windows.

"Did you go to a doctor?" Martin asked.

"Flu," spat Carroll.

"You think I should?" said Frank. "You think it's catching?"

"No. For Dad," said Martin.

Frank shrugged. "He says he's fine, just needs some sleep. He's probably fine. It's probably not catching. Let's get home. How's Mom?"

At the baggage carousel, Martin pressed for more details on the contour of his dad's evident infirmity, but Frank didn't respond, too busy elbowing his way to the front of the scrum at the conveyer belt, brandishing his baggage claim, and cross-checking it against the tag on every black hard-shelled Samsonite that looked like his, which was all of them. Carroll continued to talk out of the dextral side of his jaw, telling Martin about the great impression Frank had made at the tennis camp. Martin tried to quell a rising bile of terror, one he could taste as regurgitated airport hotdog and Crown Cola. He was meant to return to the U of C in less than two weeks. But to do so, he needed to relinquish his nursing duties vis-à-vis his mom. And now this with his dad, who looked like he was going to require more therapeutic intervention than what was available in their medicine cabinet in Pierre: Vicks VapoRub and a half bottle of Anacin.

Suitcases, golf clubs, and yet another racquet collected, Martin, Frank, and Carroll navigated the parking garage, trudging in single file, Carroll listing to the right and banging his shins on the bumpers of Chevy Caprices, Honda Civics, and the occasional Pontiac Fiero.

"Watch where you're going, asshole," he yelled and slapped an open palm on the trunk of each vehicle as he passed.

Once Martin got the baggage loaded in his mother's station wagon, and once he had safely merged onto I-90, he asked his dad again what had happened.

"Flu," he answered and fell asleep, expectorating right cheek pressed to the passenger-side window.

Martin left his brother and the functioning half of his dad wrestling their bags out of the back of the wagon and headed to the house. He needed to decide what to do first: warn his mom about the fractional state of her husband, or help her to her feet so she could appear, if not well, then better than she usually did. He opened the door from the garage, and Dottie stood in front of him, eyes shut, upright, clutching in one hand the end of the faux antique chinoiserie screen that separated the entryway from the family room and in the other, a neon yellow tennis ball.

"Welcome home, boys." She exhaled and opened her eyes. She dropped her hands, and her shoulders sagged. "Where's your father?"

"They're coming," said Martin.

"You caught me doing my grip strengthening exercises," she whispered, head drooping, looking not at Martin but down at the rug on which he stood. This sounded to him as if it were a practiced line and practiced not for him.

"I may need to sit," she said.

She slumped forward, and Martin leaned to catch her under her puny arms. He realized her hail-fellow-well-met routine must have exhausted her. How long had she been there, pressing that ball and grimacing like the teaching skeleton in Dr. Broad's waiting room?

The tennis ball dribbled from her hand and rolled next to the bar refrigerator. Martin two-stepped Dottie backwards and around the screen. He maneuvered her to the far end of the room and onto a tweed couch covered in a nubby gold-and-orange fabric that looked like a weave an ophthalmologist might choose for his second-best suit. Martin gathered a few needlepointed throw pillows and arranged them around her, sandbags to keep her from eroding into a pile of bone fragments and dust.

Frank followed a minute later, dropped his Samsonite in the middle of the living room, and pushed next to Martin.

"Hi, Mom. You look great." He kissed her cheek then whispered in Martin's ear. "I gotta get out of here. Please, man, just for a little bit."

Martin looked into Frank's shell-shocked eyes and gave a tight nod. He was just a kid. And Martin was a man, he realized, hatched out sometime over the long summer. A kid ran. A man stayed.

Frank grinned and leaned back down to Dottie. "I'm going to Ron's. Dad said okay. You really do look wonderful."

"Thank you, dear," said Dottie and descended sideways until her head stopped on the armrest.

Carroll, dragging his golf bag on his good side, where it was well positioned to clip and collapse the screen as he came into the den, shouted at Frank, already back out the garage door, "Don't forget, work on your serve, five hundred tosses a day, that's what Gould said.

Five hundred a day." Carroll shook his head at the answering rumble of the Custom Cruiser turning over.

"Welcome home," said Dottie, still propped on her ear at about a thirty-degree angle to the couch, eyes shut. "How was California?"

"What'd you say? What'd you say?" Carroll yelled. "Who's dat? Who's dat?"

Martin would come to recognize those two particular questions as rhetorical, primitive communications from the stroke-ruined regions of his dad's brain, the parts where neurons continued to fire but only blanks. But now he took Carroll at his word and chose to answer the second inquiry.

"That's Mom. She not feeling well."

Dottie tackled the first. "Can you hear me, Carroll? Are your ears plugged from the plane?"

"Who's dat? Who's dat?" Carroll repeated. His good eye darted nervously. "What'd you say? What'd you say?" He crouched and raised his hands, like a child mimicking an attacking lion.

Martin stepped closer. "It's Mom. She's not well." He punched out each word, as he would for a non-English speaker, even though he sensed it would not help.

Dottie moaned. "My poor Carroll. You've gone deaf."

Good an explanation as any, Martin thought. He could work with that. A hearing aid, everyone speaks up, maybe his dad learns to read lips. As for the disintegration of half of his dad's face, well, if his mom could ignore it, so could Martin. A disability denied is a disability discharged, their new family creed. Martin reached for the bag Carroll had dropped on the carpet.

"I'll take that," the ravaged man yelled and ran out of the room empty handed.

Excerpt from the file of Carroll Oliphant, male 51
Dr. Elliot Broad, GP

Office visit, 8.22.85

Carroll Oliphant, male 51, patient since 6.15.58, presented with hemiparesis in dextral side of frontal cranium, dysarthria evident in approximately 50% of patient's speech, signs of dementia (patient claims to have "banged the shit out of" Barbra Streisand, played trombone for F. Sinatra orchestra, no evidence of either event) and disassociate amnesia (no memory of wife, see file Dorothy (Dottie) Oliphant, female 48). In-office tests, patient self-reporting, and declarations from son Martin (see file Martin C. Oliphant, male 21) and employee of Oliphant Holdings, Inc. (see file Janet E. Priebe, female 57) indicate that patient exhibits normal if not hyper-competence at mechanical (e.g., driving) and employment-related (e.g., mergers and acquisitions) tasks. No indication of external head or brain trauma or pre-conditional oxygen deprivation.

Diagnosis: Possible transient ischemic stroke or strokes.

NOTE: Add to file, article from July New England Journal of Medicine, Armengard P.W., Situational Dementia: Coronary Causes, Pathological Presentation **(Done!!— Nurse Treble)**

Recommendations:
*Referral to Mayo for CT scan, possible endarterectomy. Explained limitations of imaging technology, carotid artery surgery for past cardiac events. PATIENT REFUSED REFERRAL.

*Referral to University of Illinois Bartolucci Brain Injury Center for speech and physical therapy. PATIENT REFUSED REFERRAL.

*Referral to Pierre Nurses-on-the-Go for in-home therapy and assistance with D. Oliphant (ductal carcinoma, radical mastectomy, 6.28.85, Swinehurst Hospital, Dr. Sumner Fensterwald attending). PATIENT REFUSED REFERRAL.

*Discussed care options with son Martin, who will coordinate henceforth. Weekly home visits for patients C. and D. Oliphant scheduled. No further medical intervention required at this time.

Transcribed by Nurse Treble, 8.26.85

5

"Situational dementia brought on by a small stroke, maybe several small strokes." Dr. Broad closed the file marked "Carroll Oliphant" on its outer cover in red Magic Marker. Martin shifted, and the white paper pressed between his rear end and the exam table crackled. Sunlight from the window behind his shoulder bounced off the bell of the stethoscope clipped to the pocket of Dr. Broad's white coat and shot into Martin's left eye.

"Can we talk someplace else?" Martin said. He didn't like the way his legs dangled. He felt seven years old. He'd come here for his annual physical ever since he could remember. He would strip down to his skivvies and sit cold in this exact place, waiting for Nurse Treble, a bulldog who smelled of sweat and peanuts, to burst in and jab him with a horse needle. Dr. Broad would show up after the initial scream and proffer a clear bowl full of plastic rings and toys. They were cheap trinkets, inferior to what he could have procured for a nickel in the machine at Zitta's Five and Dime. But back then, Martin, and every kid he knew, would rather have one of those crappy rings than a bag of real gold. They signified an escape from pain and terror for one more year, FDR's promised freedom from fear.

Dr. Broad held that bowl now. It was only about a quarter full, and it occurred to Martin that it might not have been topped up since he was in elementary school. It looked to be almost all rings, none of the tiny red sedans that had once been there.

"How about I sit up there with you?" said Dr. Broad. He hopped on a metal footstool, swiveled himself next to Martin, and bounced the bowl on his leg.

"Should Mom hear this?" said Martin.

"She said she'll wait for you out front. She also said she knows perfectly well what's wrong with her husband, exhaustion. I don't think she is willing to take in any more, and I don't recommend telling her more in her current condition. Your father said he was going back to work. That hasn't been a problem? Driving, working?"

"No. He hasn't been home a week and he's already closed on a stockyard in Stevensville and a Far-Out Jeans Emporium in South Bend," said Martin.

"Increased proficiency is often a symptom of situational dementia," said Dr. Broad.

Martin felt his back sweat. "Situational dementia," he said. "I've never heard of it."

"The brain is an amazing thing," said Dr. Broad. He hooked a purple ring on his right pinky and twirled it. "We ran several tests. In some areas—Frank's tennis career, your father's own work with struggling small businesses, the rankings in the Pro-Am Western Challenge for the last thirteen years—your father's mental function is not only sufficient, it's first rate. And in other areas..." The doctor paused, shook off the purple ring, dug for something near the bottom of the bowl.

"Like my mom," said Martin.

"Like your mother," said Dr. Broad. "In such areas, he's almost one hundred percent demented."

"What does that mean?" said Martin.

Dr. Broad abandoned his search and looked at Martin. "I read about a case in which a stroke patient couldn't recognize, or comprehend in any way, any of the cruciferous vegetables. Not cabbages or radishes or even Brussels sprouts."

"But this is my mom, his wife."

"Kohlrabi, arugula, turnip, rutabaga, tatsoi." Dr. Broad looked over at Martin, seemed surprised to see him there.

"What do we do?" said Martin. "I'm supposed to go back to school next week."

"This is a difficult situation," said Dr. Broad and offered the ring bowl to Martin. He picked out a yellow taxi he had spotted while the doctor was doing the roll call of the crucifers.

"You know," the doctor said, "your mother doesn't have tennis elbow. Or she might, but it's the least of her worries right now."

"How bad?" said Martin.

"Bad," said Dr. Broad. "We're talking weeks." He sighed and snagged a mood ring, cupped it in his hand, huffed on it. "I've talked to your mother about getting a nurse. She flat out refuses, says it's a waste of money. And I talked to your father, just now. He flat out refuses. Won't pay medical bills for a stranger."

"I'm supposed to go back to school," Martin said again. And his mom was dying. This he could not say out loud.

Dr. Broad nodded. Dug a small grave in the plastic toys, lowered the mood ring in, mumbled something, perhaps a little prayer? Martin thought of the poem on the page tucked in his wallet. "A Prayer for Mother."

I thank You, Lord, that I am placed so well,
That You have made my freedom so complete;
That I'm no slave of whistle, clock or bell,
Nor weak-eyed prisoner of wall and street.
Just let me live my life as I've begun
And give me work that's open to the sky,
Make me a pardner of the wind and sun,
And I won't ask a life that's soft or high.

Martin mouthed the words. He knew them by heart, spoke them every night before bed, every morning when he rose. But today, this minute, was the first time he really understood why Beaufort had put them in his column for Jimmy Sneedle's newsletter, a message surely meant for Martin. He thought back to his hours in the barn, how Beaufort had insisted that Martin practice pronouncing "pardner." Martin, in his denim Dockers and checked yoke shirt with the mother-of-pearl snaps. Martin who came no closer than ten feet to a horse all that week. Martin who was, when it came down to it, afraid of horses. He had been since Buster's death, before that, too. He claimed allergies—dangerous, throat-swelling, eye-bloodying, anaphylactic-shock-inducing allergies. But it was fear, just fear. Beaufort must have realized, and yet he had gone all Henry Higgins on Martin—"Paaah-dner, Paaah-dner, one more time, boy"—even though the old rancher had to have known, Martin was not a *pardner*, not a *pardner* at all.

But maybe there was still time. The poem was a life rope, wasn't it? Beaufort had tossed the lasso, locked it around Martin's bull head, was pulling him out of the rapids and into the salt cedars at the river's edge. Because Martin was in danger. In danger of sweeping unconscious through the University of Chicago's common core and (very fine) political science research curriculum until he washed up in some grey fabric-covered cubicle at a think tank with a name like The Center for Applied Thought Metrics. Beaufort had been trying to save Martin from *a life that's soft or high*. But Martin hadn't seen it. Forgot all that hard-won wisdom shared through coffee-brown teeth and whiskey-scented whispers. Forgot the words of the cowboy poets passed down voice to voice, hand to hand, and for one half of one fine week, to Martin. He had forgotten it the minute he got back to school, the minute he marched back through Cobb Gate with its gables and gargoyles. Ridiculous! Gothic garnish on Chicago's South Side—land of Johnny Lee Hooker, Muddy Waters, and bad, bad Leroy Brown, not Louis the Sixth. But he marched in without hesitation, glazed eyes and willing heart, an eager *slave of whistle, clock, or bell*. He marched through the last six weeks of the trimester, high on Aristotle's *Metaphysics* and Marx's manifestos; high on Sammy's watered-down Stroh's and joints from the used-bookstore guy who was in year twelve of his Ph.D. in Eastern Religions; high on the fog of all that classics-fueled, academically charged, self-indulgent, abstract certainty. Certainty that he, and those like him, knew the most, thought the deepest, comprehended the world at its center, and would, like Plato's philosopher kings, one day rule with undeserved benevolence over the fit and fatuous masses who made up everyone else.

But they didn't make up everyone else, did they? There were the cowboy poets too. Men like Beaufort and the barn hands and Jack Thorpe and Ben Arnold and Henry Herbert Knibbs and Badger Clark. And Ginger. Women like Ginger. Men and women who had embraced him for the best four days of his life.

> Let me be square and generous with all.
> I'm careless sometimes, Lord, when I'm in town,
> But never let 'em say I'm mean or small!
> Make me as big and open as the plains,
> As honest as the hawse between my knees,
> Clean as the wind that blows behind the rains,
> Free as the hawk that circles down the breeze!

Christ, how careless he had been. How consumed with returning to his libraries and his books and his endless thinking without doing. He was needed here. Here, where the woman who had given him life lay dying. And he, Martin, was the one, the only one, to shepherd her to a peaceful grave. So thank you to Badger Clark and your western God and Beaufort. And Ginger, always Ginger. Thank you to his mom, his poor, simpering, status-addled, fading mom. Thank you even to Dr. Broad and his bottomless trove of cheap plastic rings. Martin had again, here, thigh to thigh with the doctor, realized the gift of cowboy poetry, of the hope of a life in which the only lexicon was action, the only emotion, earned. *Free as the hawk that circles down the breeze*. He had received the gift before, at Jimmy Sneedle's, received it and walked away. And now, on this narrow bench, the sanitary table paper starting to tear under Martin's chinos, he received it again.

Martin hopped from the bench, snatched the bowl of toys from Dr. Broad's lap, and headed for the door.

Martin settled Dottie in the front seat of the Oldsmobile, maneuvered to the driver's side, and got in. He passed her the ring bowl. She mumbled something, the fish-gray tip of her tongue escaping out the right side of her lips every second syllable or so.

"How was your appointment?" said Martin.

She slumped and shook her head, picked through the bowl, slipped artichoke bands on every finger, fluttered them in front of her face, and hummed "Copacabana." She didn't give the bowl back until after they had pulled into the garage. Martin got out, squeezed to her side, and offered his arm. She spread her bedecked hands, two green plastic starbursts, and hissed, "At the Copa, don't fall in love."

Inside, the house had smelled as it had all summer: burnt ramen noodles, Pledge, and that sickbed stink—artificially sweetened urine and iodine—that clung to his mom's belongings no matter how often Martin laundered them. But underneath all that, he could sense a shift in the prevailing winds. Horse manure, desert night, pine. He yelled to Frank that they were home and to make sure Mom got some dinner. He ignored the yelps of "wait" and "cold" from Frank's bedroom and headed back to the garage. His mom would be fine for a few hours. But right now, Martin needed to be with men who worked with their hands.

The early '80s had been kind to neither farm nor factory, and Pierre, Michigan, sat on the border between the rust and fruit belts. In such a town, men drank at four o'clock, an hour after the three o'clock whistle, not that there had been a three o'clock whistle for years. At three, they would rise up from the plastic–covered couches and Formica kitchen tables where they'd been having a coffee, reading that morning's *Leader Telegram,* resisting the urge to turn on the boob tube. They would rise to the unblown whistle like dogs to a silent call, pull on their tan car coats, leave notes for their wives to find when they returned from shifts at the Holiday Inn. *At the Buck,* they would scribble. *Back for supper.*

The men were already hunched over the scarred pine bar at half-past four when Martin, still clutching the ring bowl to his chest, entered the smoky haze of the Silver Dollar Saloon. He extracted a stool from between two of them, both in pale yellow polo shirts and bent over half-full mugs of boilermakers. Martin signaled the bartender, Hank, a pink bowling ball of a man with perfectly round eyes and a perpetually surprised oval of a mouth. Hank puckered his lips and flared his cheeks.

"What'll it be, son?"

"A beer, I guess," said Martin, wishing he had the guts to order one with the depth charge of whiskey, a boilermaker, like the regulars did. He wondered if that were a universal working man drink, one that a cowboy poet might slug down after a day walking the fence line and chasing reluctant dogies out of aspen stands. Or was it just a Midwestern drink, a drink for guys who trafficked in steel, carburetor parts, assembly lines, and tires?

"What's that, son?" said Hank. "I'm a little hard of hearing."

"Um," said Martin.

"Over here." A voice floated from the far bend of the bar.

Martin looked in its direction and made out a gnarled branch of an arm swiping at the smoke clouds. "Martin Oliphant, join us."

Martin did, leaving Hank muttering to the two regulars.

"Mr. Lattner," Martin said. "Hi."

Bob Lattner was the doggedly alcoholic and violently bitter editor of the *Leader Telegram,* which, every morning, brought the 8,000 or so residents of Pierre "local news of national import through a global lens." Or so claimed the paper's motto, featured in the boxed ear to the left of the masthead. The slogan was mostly aspirational. Editorials on the bravery of the Lake Michigan Polar Bear Club or in-depth interviews with that year's acne-scarred Cotillion Grand March leaders were typical of the paper's fare. Only occasionally did the editorial staff, which consisted of Lattner and a revolving roster of recent college English grads, venture into issues such as AIDS or Ronald Reagan's second term. Martin had never spoken to Lattner before but knew who he was. Pierre was a small town, and Lattner's presence was a given at any event of even the slightest significance. If not beloved by his many readers, he was tolerated as a necessary piece of public infrastructure.

"Master Oliphant," said Lattner, "what's your pleasure?"

Martin wondered how long the newspaperman had been at the tavern. "A beer?" Martin said, then added, "A Stroh's?" inspired by the aqua neon sign behind the bar. It bathed Flip, the donut shop proprietor sitting next to Lattner, in an undulating blue light.

"A fine choice for the young prince. A Michigan beer for a Michigan man," said Lattner and yelled to Hank, "One Stroh's with a Jim Beam chaser. On me."

"Stroh's is piss water," said Flip. "Coors is what you want. But you can't get it here. My brother's gonna bring me a case when he comes out. It's the water out West. It's pure. Don't catch on fire and shit, like Lake Erie do."

"You are a victim of advertising and corporate manipulation, my friend," said Lattner, "a shill in the three-card monte game known as manufactured scarcity."

Flip nodded, as if he had known that all along. "How's your mother doing?" he asked, lifting his drink with both hands and taking a sip. "Piss water," he mumbled.

"Okay," Martin said, horrified to hear his voice crack.

"Good to hear," said Flip, burying his face in his stein and shutting his eyes.

"Excellent news," said Lattner. He patted Martin's hand, now flat on the bar, moved to do so again, seemed to think better of it, waved off a nonexistent fly.

The editor made a show of studying the Stroh's sign while sneaking glances at Martin. In sympathy, perhaps. More likely concern. Concern that Martin might start blubbering. Martin understood. He shared that concern.

Hank arrived with Martin's mug of Stroh's and the shot of Jim

Beam. He kept his hands in his lap on the bowl of rings and stared at the two glasses, the mug filled with bubbling liquid that was, Flip was right, urine yellow, the shot glass almost overflowing. Before Martin could stop himself, he leaned over and sniffed at it.

"Like this," said Flip, snatching the shot glass from under Martin's nose and dropping it into the beer. Bubbles followed the pony as it floated to the bottom of the mug. A thin layer of foam slid over the side and puddled around the base.

"Pretty," said Flip.

Martin, as nonchalantly as he could manage, set the bowl of rings next to a crusty ketchup dispenser. He picked up his boilermaker by the handle and sipped, he hoped not too delicately.

The first taste was all beer. He took another sip, one he thought might even be described as a slug. This time a flicker of whiskey licked at his sinuses, cigar in its undertones, a bit of gunpowder on the tongue. He downed three quarters of the drink in one go. And hardly choked at all. Lattner laughed and pounded him on the back.

"Another here," he called to Hank. "And one more for me as well. You're okay, Martin Oliphant."

Martin nodded, coughed once more. He was okay. That's why he was here right now and not at home warming up Banquet Salisbury Steak Dinners for his mom and Frank. He was okay here, away from Hyde Park, among the men who worked with their hands. Or pens. Or fried dough.

"So," said Lattner, "headed back to school soon? Chicago, right? Fine school. Saul Bellow's there, if I'm not mistaken. Bit over the top in their economics, but I don't suppose you're studying economics."

"Political science," said Martin, "but not anymore. I quit." And Martin realized that, in fact, he would quit.

"Shame," said Lattner. "What's next for you?"

Martin finished his drink, caught one-handed the fresh mug Hank slid to him, drained half the glass, banged it down as he had noticed an old man at the other end of the bar had done, shot the whiskey, and slugged back the rest of the beer.

"Another," he rasped. "And what's next for me is poetry."

"Capital," said Lattner. "Next round's on you. Not too many poets here in Pierre. An open market."

"I'm a limerick man myself," said Flip.

Martin wiped a tearing eye with the back of his hand. An eye tearing not with grief for his infirm mom or his newly aborted academic
career. An eye tearing from the alcohol-infused stomach acid that had
somehow lodged itself in his nasal cavity. Martin wasn't much of a
drinker. And he hadn't had anything to eat since a bowl of Lucky
Charms that morning. But he found he liked this drink, this boilermaker. It could well be the perfect drink. Had it been made with
Coors beer followed by a shot of rotgut brewed in some Montana
outlaw hidey hole, it would have even more fit his mood, his hunger,
at the moment. But this was close to what he needed, damn close.

His third boilermaker arrived, and this time he dropped the shot
glass in the mug with a splash that raised a cheer of "huzzah!" from
Lattner and a "that's the way" from Flip. Martin wiped the foam from
his upper lip and grinned.

Two men, closer to Martin's age than Lattner or Flip, pulled out
stools on the long side of the bar around the corner from Martin.
They both wore tight bell-bottoms and matching denim vests over
button-down poly-blend monochromatic shirts, one mustard, one
burgundy. Both had wet hair slicked back into tails that licked at their
collars. One had a well-trimmed mustache; the other, a scar that ran
across his right cheek. Their aftershave reminded Martin of the smell
of cabs he had taken from the South Side to downtown Chicago:
pine, cardamom, coffee, Lysol.

Hank brought the two men beers without either ordering. Martin
noticed they didn't get the whiskey shots and wondered if boilermakers were an old man's drink. Martin motioned Hank for another
round in what he thought was an understated flick of his finger but
might have been a bit more because Flip snorted, and Lattner chirped,
"Ride 'em, cowboy."

"Cowboys," Martin said to no one in particular as his fourth boilermaker arrived. "Cowboy poetry, to be precise."

"Arthur Chapman," said Lattner.

"Excuse me?" Martin said.

"You said, 'cowboy poetry' and then I said, 'Arthur Chapman,' who,
if you know anything about cowboy poetry, is a cowboy poet. Perhaps
the best known of the cowboy poets." Lattner stood up, tapped the
bar with one bony finger, and recited:

Out where the handclasp's a little stronger,
Out where the smile dwells a little longer,
That's where the West begins...

Hank deposited the next round in front of Lattner, Flip, and Martin, and Lattner bowed, arm stiff across his stomach, toward his latest beer. "These are on Martin," he said. "The cowboy poet."

Martin didn't protest, just stared at Lattner, who bowed again, this time immersing his thin nose and rectangular mustache into the beer, like a perpetual-motion dipping bird sans red top hat.

"I don't know that one. Arthur Chapman?"

"You don't know Arthur Chapman? You don't know the classic 'Out Where the West Begins'? What"—he hopped back on his stool, mustache dripping—"do they teach in the Pierre public schools these days?" He cleared his throat, closed his eyes, poked Flip, who had put his head on his arms, and trumpeted:

Out where the sun is a little brighter,
Where the snows that fall are a trifle whiter,
Where the bonds of home are a wee bit tighter,
That's where the West begins.
Out where the skies are a trifle bluer,
Out where the friendship's a little truer,
That's where the West begins.

"Out where the dongs are a trifle longer, out where they pull a little stronger. Trifle, trifle, trifle, West," said Flip, sitting back up. The two men to Martin's left sniggered.

"Is that it?" said Martin.

"No," said Lattner. "It goes on forever. Do you need a job, by the way? Maybe the *Leader Telegram* should start a regular poetry column. Cowboy poetry. Or maybe, for the local audience, angler poetry, or sailor's poetry. Or small-town blowhard poetry."

"Really? Of course," said Martin. Lattner was probably kidding, but Martin was drunk, and Lattner's nonsense was making more sense, at the moment, than anything he had studied at U of C.

"Bowling poetry," said Flip and put his head back down.

"Ah, but can I trust an inexperienced college dropout who doesn't even know 'Out Where the West Begins'? How are you with limericks?

Flip is always saying we ought to do a limerick column." With one finger, Lattner fished for Flip's latest shot and pushed his own empty glass back to Flip's side. Without lifting his head, Flip said, "There once was a woman from NAN-tuckett."

This was another sign, of course. That Martin had found someone who knew of cowboy poetry—who knew more than Martin did about cowboy poetry—in Pierre. He was in the right place. He was being called.

"What we ought to do," said Lattner into the thinning hair on the back of Flip's head, "is a multipart series on the life of Arthur Chapman, concluding on Sunday with an entire edition devoted to his poetry. 'Out Where the West Begins,' of course, but also, you know, the rest of them."

"That's a great idea," said Martin, more loudly than he had intended. Flip snorted.

"And Martin will write it," said Lattner and threw back Flip's shot. "Martin will be my assistant, my muse, my journalistic journeyman, my literary...lug nut."

"I will," said Martin. "I will."

"What about that other guy?" said Flip. "Greg, Greg? Greg Lugnut?"

"Greg Lange," said Lattner, "is a muscle-bound moron. I'm firing him tomorrow."

"He can sure write about basketball." This from one of the denim-clad men, the one with a mustache not unlike Lattner's, though more carefully trimmed.

"And you can't," said Flip to Lattner.

"Point taken," said Lattner. "We'll no longer cover basketball, though that will mean the end of the paper, as most of our readers only open the broadsheet for the PPHS scores. But no price too high for art. No price too high for cowboy poetry, right?" He gestured at Martin without looking at him.

"Another round?" said Hank.

"No," said Martin.

"Of course," said Lattner and Flip at the same time.

"No drink too many for cowboy poetry," said Martin as Hank went to fetch their order.

One of the younger men looked toward Martin with bright eyes. For a moment, Martin thought maybe he had found an ally, the ally he knew he was to find in this bar, this bar of men who worked with their hands, the reason he knew he needed to come here this night, this night he had committed himself to cowboy poetry and a life of action.

"Is that Dr. Broad's ring bowl?" the man asked. "Goddamn, you know I think my brother got the only good thing he ever put in that. A Swiss Army knife." He looked at Martin. "My name is Todd, by the way."

"I'm Eric." The other man reached a hand across to Martin, which he took and shook without knocking over either of their drinks, perhaps his last graceful move of the evening. "And there's no way there was ever a Swiss Army knife in there. I would have found it. I practically emptied that thing out every year looking for something that wasn't a goddamn ring. Let me see."

Flip grabbed a green ring from the bowl and pushed it toward Eric. "They didn't have this kind of shit when I was a kid."

"They didn't even have shots, did they? Didn't you all just get polio?" said Todd.

"Ignorant youth," muttered Lattner, waving at Hank, though his mug was still half full. He swayed on his stool, or maybe Martin's vision doubled.

"Some jewels, my good man," said Lattner, though it came out "mush god-man."

Eric laughed and tossed a handful of plastic at Lattner. A couple of the rings slid to a stop in the beer river winding its way between the bunched-up paper napkins scattered around Lattner's drink. The rest of the jewelry bounced over the bar's polished brass rim and skittered on the floor. Lattner jerked sideways off his stool and fell to his knees with a thud. He brushed at the peanut shells with outstretched fingers, mumbling about "sweeping once in a while."

Eric took more rings and other toys out of the bowl and lined them up according to color. "Why so many green?" he said.

Lattner rose back up, almost whacking his head on the underside of the bar. "Photosynthesis," he said.

The evening loped on unsteadily. Another boilermaker that Martin didn't remember ordering showed up, and Hank removed the last one that Martin didn't remember drinking. A woman with short black hair and a low-cut orange T-shirt advertising the Star Bright Brushless Carwash walked behind Todd, grabbed a bunch of his hair in a fist, and kissed him hard.

"Marry me," the girl said.

Flip stumbled backwards toward the men's room. Lattner pulled Flip's abandoned stool close and lay a shoulder on it, his head held rigid, his eyes unblinking and aimed at Martin's mid-torso. More people pushed into the bar. The two old men who had been there when Martin came in were long gone. Martin recognized some of the newcomers, high school classmates, his year and the one or two after. The mostly men, mostly former members of the PPHS swim team, gathered around one of the booths, their noses still capped white with zinc, still wearing their "Horn of Plenty Beach Lifeguard" shirts from the afternoon shift. They were at the end of their summer breaks from University of Michigan, Michigan State, or the other regional state schools that everyone said were just as good. Each new entrant to the booth was greeted with yelps and gargles, as if the greeters were still underwater. A harried Hank carried pitchers of beer, two at a time, to their table.

The other guys—the ones who didn't finish high school, or who finished but just barely and started immediately at the gas station or road construction jobs they would hold for the next fifty years, if they were lucky—gathered around Todd and Eric. And Martin, for Dr. Broad's rings had made him a valued member of the young working man set. Women too. Girls Martin remembered from high school, smirking through sex-ed in tenth grade because, as was well known, they had already done it. Pompon squad girls who worked now as cosmeticians-in-training or waitresses at The Seashore, Pierre's other bar, the one with ferns, a kids' menu, a Christopher Cross-dominated soundtrack, and no one drinking boilermakers. Girls with big breasts and full lips and hard red nails. Girls who smelled of french fry grease and gasoline and saltwater taffy. Martin leaned into one's side now, snuffled at her cleavage, and offered her a green ring.

The swimmers' table had girls too, but they were younger, or younger looking, mannish shoulders propping up Izod collared shirts, straight-legged blue jeans or faded gym shorts, green-tinged hair brushed back straight. Some had lifeguard shirts of their own. They sat on the boys' laps and checked their watches and eyed each other with the air of people who had someplace else to be.

A microphone squawked somewhere up near the front of the bar, Hank rumbled something, and a guitar started twanging at what might have been "Cat's in the Cradle." At some point, Hank switched from the plastic mugs to red plastic cups. Martin lifted his drink and hummed along with the guitar, now plinking doggedly at "Let's Hear it for the Boy."

"So you sing too." The breath in his ear smelled of ash and bourbon.

Julie.

His last memory of her, that night at Jimmy Sneedle's just four months ago, was of the top of her head, her straw-blonde hair parted almost down to the scalp, and the smell of bleach, of pinion smoke from the scented candles in the dining room, of mold from the leak in the back of the billiards room. He felt his dick harden. Again, cowboy poetry had brought him this.

"He is a singer, and a dancer, and a poet," said Lattner.

"Oh, I know," said Julie. "I've seen him perform."

He hadn't remembered she had green eyes. Or that her face was as round as the moon.

"Poetry? You've heard him perform cowboy poetry?" said Lattner.

"That too," said Julie.

Martin grabbed the last handful of rings from Dr. Broad's bowl, which had ended up in front of him on the bar, though it must have traveled some distance before, since everyone he could see was festooned with cheap jewelry. "Marry me," he said to Julie. "Or blow me." And he rained the flashing green down on her.

"You must recite for us," said Lattner, grabbing Martin's hand and tugging him away from Julie, who was picking plastic off the front of her shirt. Yes, Martin thought. Yes, he must perform. Recite cowboy poetry and have sex with Julie Newport because that's how it went. He was back in the arms of the range, the wide-open range, and he would shed this Martin skin, this Martin death-tainted skin of failure and unearned superiority and loneliness, and he would recite cowboy poetry. He would recite cowboy poetry in this bar, in The Silver Dollar, and he would recite poetry in Elko and in Wickenburg. He'd recite on the Chisholm Trail while sitting with Beaufort and the hands from the barn. And Ginger. He would recite cowboy poetry and drink whiskey and have sex and marry Ginger and father ten round babies, who in this drunken fantasy, were Mexican.

As honest as the hawse between my knees,
Clean as the wind that blows behind the rains,
Free as the hawk that circles down the breeze!

"How's your mom?" shouted Julie as Lattner led Martin past her and toward the microphone and the shriveled man with a long white ponytail in a Grateful Dead shirt cowering and crooning behind it.

"Dying," Martin roared back. "Dying, almost dead, thanks for asking. Dying, as we all are, buzzard fodder and bleached bones in the desert sun."

Martin started taking off his shirt before he got halfway to the microphone. He yanked at it so hard the last two buttons popped off, one pinging onto the bar in front of his eighth-grade biology teacher. He felt his breasts rolling independently, like the pistons on a locomotive, spattering bystanders with droplets of sweat. He kept moving while unbuttoning his Wrangler's, paused to step out of them, and bellowed:

Through progress of the railroads,
our occupation's gone;
we'll get our ideas into words,
our words into a song,

The diminutive guitarist held his hands up, as if being mugged, and called to Martin, "Whoa there, guy, slow down! It's cool, it's cool."

Martin squinted at the tie-dyed little man. All those colors on him. All that pointless music in his fingers. He needed cowboy poetry. Like Martin, like Lattner, like Flip and Todd and Eric and Julie. Especially Julie. Like everyone in this bar, in this pathetic town, in the world. They all needed cowboy poetry. And Martin had it. Martin had it to give.

He felt such a need to be naked, a need like he had never known before. To be naked before God and the good people of Pierre and

The Silver Dollar and Julie Newport and cowboy poetry. No scrap of foul cloth would stand between him and the words that would save him, save them all. They would see, they would know. They would witness the life-giving verses writ large across his naked loins.

> *First comes the cowboy,*
> *he's the spirit of the West;*
> *hf all the pioneers I claim,*
> *the cowboys are the best.*
> *We'll miss him in the round-up,*
> *it's gone, his merry shout,*
> *the cowboy has left the country,*
> *his campfire has gone out.*

He dropped his Fruit of the Looms and turned to the crowd.

Letter to the Editor, Pierre Leader Telegram
August 26, 1985

Maybe Mayor Vernon should have waited a few days before "spouting off" about how great a place Pierre is for families (*Mayor Tells Chamber Downtown is 'Super-Duper-Kid-Friendly', August 20, 1985*). If he had, like me, been walking his miniature schnauzer on Main Street in the vicinity of The Silver Dollar Saloon at 11:30 p.m. on Thursday, August 22, he would "right this minute" be issuing an apology to every parent who happened to hear his misleading address.

At that very time, with that very dog, I witnessed a "drunken mob" pouring out of the said tavern, singing, screaming, and vomiting. The most shocking part of the spectacle—even to me at the "ripe old age" of seventy-four (think of the scars it would leave on "our youth!")—was the leader of this parade: an obese man, entirely and utterly "buck naked!"

When President Reagan was elected, he promised us "morning in America." To most of us "family men," that meant the end of "free love," "women's lib," and "the counterculture." "Good riddance" to it, I say. It will be a "sad day," if night in downtown Pierre becomes known for debauchery, and worse.

Gordon Ziemke

[ed. note: I was a member of what Mr. Ziemke has termed a "drunken mob" outside The Silver Dollar Saloon on the night of August 22. He has many of the salient facts of that fine evening incorrect. The gathering was less of a bacchanal than a symposium in the style of the ancient Greeks, complete with epic poetry recitation and other elevating entertainment. And, yes, one of the key participants— "Obese" is inaccurate. I would have said "tremendous"—was nude, exactly as heroes were depicted throughout the Hellenistic Period. Also, Gordo, I printed your letter as you typed it, but next time, be warned, I'm charging by the quotation mark. "Sincerely," BL]

6

Martin recalled nothing of what happened after he left The Silver Dollar, but when he woke the next morning, lying bare-assed on splattered porcelain tiles among strewn toiletries, he deduced he had spent the early morning hours retching and rolling between the shower and his bathroom floor.

His attention for the rest of the day was focused on not vomiting. That left Martin without a neuron to spare to contemplate the fallout from his introduction of cowboy poetry to the drinking folk of Pierre. He was sure that, once the tides of physical suffering wrought by alcohol poisoning receded, the waves of humiliation and regret would pound down. And so he hunkered, sipping broth, gulping aspirin, the old man who refuses to leave his shanty ahead of the hurricane.

By evening, he could bear to picture himself at The Silver Dollar, his sweating lips forming each word of "The Campfire Has Gone Out." Picture, but no audio, the silent image of his naked self, waving his arms over his head, underarm flab rippling, black hair and droplets of sweat shooting from his armpits like flames out of a cartoon rocket ship.

It wasn't until the following Tuesday that Martin felt prepared to meet the world again, or at least his family. He dressed in pressed jeans and a faded U of C T-shirt and padded into the kitchen. Dottie and Frank sat at the breakfast table, a PPHS gym bag at his feet, scrambled eggs and bacon half-eaten on a plate in front of him, two new spiral notebooks to his left. School must have started up again while Martin was in boilermaker purgatory.

"Good morning," Martin said, waited, added, "Mom. Frank." Waited some more.

Martin stared hard at Frank. This was his moment. This was when Frank would let Martin know exactly what the entire town of Pierre thought of him. The Silver Dollar had been packed, plenty of people who knew the Oliphants, or Frank, or who knew people who knew the Oliphants or Frank. Martin was surprised his performance, complete with photos and a review from the *Leader Telegram,* hadn't already appeared on the front page. He was sure the story had been told one hundred, one thousand times, at every beauty shop, service counter, and parking lot. Every time Eric filled up someone's car, or Flip custom-frosted a cruller for a pudgy housewife, or a newly vaccinated kid complained to Dr. Broad about the missing plastic rings. The story had to have been told and reenacted and embellished, though it was difficult to think how it might be embellished. So Martin waited for Frank to inform him just how bad this all was.

"Want my toast?" said Frank. "I haven't touched it."

Martin started. What was this?

"Honestly," said Frank. "Not even a bite."

Martin examined Frank's blank and smiling face.

This was a miracle, that's what this was.

Martin accepted the toast.

As that day, then that week, unfurled, Martin marveled as the miracle swelled. Todd's mother, a checkout lady at the Hilltop, let Martin sign for his groceries and even wished him a good day, both firsts. Flip delivered a dozen apple-glazed donuts to the house. Julie waved to him from across the drug store parking lot, and with one hand mimed, *I'll call you,* which she did not, but still. Not one word about The Silver Dollar. But they knew. He could see it in their eyes. They knew, and they were not going to speak of it. They knew, and they thought more of him for it.

A miracle.

And here was the biggest part of it: Martin realized that he didn't look back on the evening at The Silver Dollar as a humiliation. Oh, he tried. He knew he should. But they had seen him, seen him as he had thought he might be and now was sure he was. As a cowboy poet, though he didn't expect they knew the moniker. But he did, by God. As of that night, he knew what he was. He knew his name.

The day after Labor Day, Martin received the job offer Lattner had promised. Greg Lange, the *Leader Telegram's* incumbent reporter and assistant editor, had not been fired but left for a position at a used bookstore in San Francisco. Lattner needed someone of Martin's poetic attitude to "keep cranking out the shit for the local peons,"

or so Lattner had said on a message left in a slurred voice almost completely obscured by the clankings and cursings of The Silver Dollar weeknight regulars. Martin had intended to call the next morning and accept, but before he could and before he had had his first cup of coffee, Mrs. Irene Trinkle, Lattner's longtime secretary, appeared at the Oliphant doorstep in a burnt-orange knitted two-piece suit, matching umbrella, and felt hat. She refused to come in, inquired after Dottie, and presented a warm mason jar of homemade chicken soup.

"He is a good man, Mr. Lattner," she said, just as Martin was running out of small talk. "Maybe a great man. But drink has him in her siren grip and will not loose him enough to let him ascend to the level where he should and could dwell." Mrs. Trinkle spoke in a skewed and formal tone that Martin would later learn was co-opted from Scholastic Books' Sunfire historical romance novel series, Mrs. Trinkle's own secret dependency.

"Mr. Lattner could use an intellectual like you, a man who can challenge him, make him rise above his demons and do the work God meant him to do," said Mrs. Trinkle. "Also, one who can spell. You can spell, can't you, dear?"

Martin said he could.

He went into the *Leader Telegram* offices the next day for a few hours after Frank went to school and while Dottie napped. Lattner had him edit an opinion piece on the scheduling of the Lion's Annual Broom Ball and the PPHS homecoming dance on the same night. Martin struck the words *megalomaniacal* and *imbecilic* (twice) from the text, but otherwise deemed it a reasoned analysis of the conflict. Mrs. Trinkle agreed.

From then on, Martin showed up when he could, which, as Dottie slept more and more, was oftener and oftener. The time Martin spent in the *Leader Telegram* offices or covering Pierre events, like the Congregationalist's Faith is Fun Fall Fest or a PPHS cross country meet, was time during which he was happily distracted from Dottie's disintegration.

And disintegrating she was. Martin watched through the Michigan autumn—one week of glorious arboreal color, followed by bitter subfreezing winds and snow by Halloween—as she shriveled into a shivering clump of patchy hair, musty chenille robe, and bruised skin.

Sometimes it sickened him. Other times, it hit like a Molotov cocktail to the chest. He felt closer to her than ever before.

Carroll, on the other hand, seemed to be getting better. By November, his face drooped a fraction of the amount it had two months earlier, though he still showed no signs of recognizing his wife. He slept in the guest room and rarely addressed her directly, but what relations there were, were civil and, perhaps, when viewed through her morphine haze, appropriate and enough. She didn't complain, nor did he. Domestic life, at least as far as interactions with his dad went, started to resemble one of the blander 1960s sitcoms Martin had followed all summer, not particularly funny, but predictable and safe. Plus they were getting rich. Oliphant Holdings, Inc. thrived in its founder and CEO's post-stroke months. With the shutting down of the part of Carroll's brain that governed the always messy emotional stew of marital relations, he had been able to zero in on what he did best, preying on failing small businesses, circling like a buzzard whenever he caught a whiff of road kill on the highway of commerce.

So with Dottie drugged most of the time, Carroll at the office or traveling to some desolate small town Main Street to feed, and his brother virtually adopted by his friend Ron's family, Martin had time that autumn to embark on the career in journalism he had never imagined or intended. In the process, he reminded himself daily of his clarion call—that which had dragged him from the limestone towers of U of C—cowboy poetry.

In late September, Martin finally wrote Beaufort, apologized for the delay in corresponding, explained the senior Oliphants' unique declines, asked after Beaufort's health and that of the hands and that of his lovely daughter, Ginger. Martin explained how sorry he was to have missed the First Annual Elko Cowboy Poetry Confluence, how sincerely he wished for a list of the poems featured, how welcome some lines from a few of the newer works would be. He added as a P.S. that he had recited "The Campfire Has Gone Out" for a largish local crowd and thought it had made an impression. He addressed the whole thing to Beaufort Giles, care of the Jimmy Sneedle's Tennis and Golf (Dude) Ranch reservations desk at an address he found on some stationery in his dad's office. At the last minute, Martin added "and Ginger" to the end of Beaufort's name on the envelope. And then a small smiley face. And then he scratched out the smiley face, stamped the letter, walked it three blocks to the post box, and shoved the missive through the clanking door. His letter came back three weeks later, marked in purple ink: NO LONGER AT THIS ADDRESS and more ominously NO SUCH ADDRESS. Someone had scribbled on the back, next to a line of handwritten numbers, *Try Montana*. Martin waited a week, then called the number for Jimmy Sneedle's on the stationery, but the line was disconnected. He sent his letter to "the sponsors of the Elko Cowboy Poetry Confluence" c/o Elko, Nevada General Delivery in hopes they would forward it to Beaufort. In the same package, he included a note to the sponsors inquiring about the possibility of attending the second event, scheduled, he assumed, for May 1986. He imagined heading to Nevada, packing one rough burlap duffel with a couple pairs of jeans, his Roget's Thesaurus, a copy of Plato's *Republic*, his IBM Selectric, and a small brass-framed picture of his mom, smiling in tennis whites, before she got sick. The reverie concluded with him—fully clothed, thank God—intoning the last verse of a poem to a room shaking with the claps of rope-burned hands and the stomp of desert-bleached boots.

Dear Martin Oliphant,

I hope this will find you before the New Year, and I hope the New Year will find you well. I find myself riding the range again on land not my own, but there is a freedom in owning naught but a good horse and a saddle and a rope and the wits to use them and the pen and paper to write it all down. Word has come that your mother is ailing, and so I enclose Jack Thorp's little book in hopes that it might bring her and you some comfort. It was my father's, and I'd appreciate it if you would see fit to return it when we meet again some day.

Yours truly,

Beaufort Giles

P.S. Ginger sends her best and wants me to let you know she has entered a university, inspired as she was by your love of book learning. She continues to ride better than a bull nurse twice her years and has been crowned rodeo queen in four counties in Wyoming and two in Arizona.

7

The package from Beaufort came the same day that O'Brien's Pharmacy and Medical Supply delivered the hospital bed. The O'Brien twins, home from CMU for winter break, stripped the plastic wrapping off the gurney and shoved it next to the Christmas tree at the far end of the living room. Martin fussed as they maneuvered, making sure the branches of the balsam didn't scratch the bed's real oak laminate retractable table. It would eventually sit at the front end of the living room, where the Oliphant's baby grand was now, but the Lemons Piano Tuners and Movers, who had to come in from Watertown, weren't due for another hour. Martin had hoped that the O'Brien boys, both heavyweight-class wrestlers at school, might have been able to remove the Steinway, but he had learned that piano transport was an art requiring trained specialists and unique truck configurations.

That was just one of the many tidbits Martin had picked up over the last couple of weeks of phone calls and faxes procuring the bed and moving out the piano. He also learned: that hospital beds could be left or right handed; that the Oliphant family health insurance covered wheel chairs but not adjustable beds but maybe beds with wheels or wheelchairs that flattened to beds; that hospital bed mattresses take specialized sheets; that it's hard to find those specialized sheets in anything but stiff waterproof material; and that for patients in the latter days of stage IV breast cancer, it's best to go with the waterproof design in any case.

Martin flicked a balsam needle off the mattress top and went into the kitchen to get himself a spiced cider. The cliched clove and cinnamon perfume drifting from the stove reminded him of an argument he had had with Lattner and Mrs. Trinkle over the best-smelling holiday. Martin had led with Christmas. Lattner countered that Christmas didn't smell good, it just smelled as expected, and that, at any other time of the year, all that nutmeg and pine and wood fire would be dismissed as toothpaste and toilet cleaner and cigars. He had posited Fourth of July.

"It smells American," Lattner said. "Gunpowder, barbecued meat, sweat. It smells like war. It smells like freedom."

"Thanksgiving, then," Martin said. "You've got your burned flesh as well as pumpkin pie and Brussels sprouts. That smells like America to me."

"Smells like genocide to Indians," said Lattner.

A door banged and a pocket of cold air brushed by Martin's neck, interrupting his sniffing and musing.

"Deck the halls with boughs of holly," sang Carroll.

Martin followed the sound into the living room. "Why aren't you at work?" he asked.

"Who am I? Scrooge McDuck? I told everyone to go home," Carroll said.

"Christmas isn't for another two weeks," Martin said.

Carroll continued to sing as he draped tinsel around the hospital bed. "Where's my elf's hat?" Martin pointed toward the front hall.

Carroll had been like this for about a month—baking pfeffernüsse cookies, festooning the windows with holly and fir roping, dragging in a seven-foot Christmas tree, setting it up by himself, and covering it with lights and ornaments. Dr. Broad posited that it was the latest manifestation of the strokes Carroll had suffered last summer. The doctor had offered again to set up some rehabilitation therapy, and again Carroll had refused. Martin didn't press the point. Carroll seemed happy enough. And besides, he was assuming the burden of planning what otherwise promised to be a grim holiday celebration.

"Mail call." Carroll reappeared in the elf hat, arms full of letters and a couple of packages. "Look at the Christmas cards." He dumped the delivery on a mustard club chair, one of two situated at the side of the living room, both already holding several days of unopened correspondence and bills. The bustling Olde Christmas Village squatting on the front hall table left no place for incoming mail.

Martin poked through the thick red and green envelopes. Nothing from Elko, as usual, but one package addressed to Martin, return address: "Post Office, Medicine Bow, Wyoming." He ripped into the brown paper and almost tore through the tattered cover of an old manuscript stained with coffee and two greasy thumbprints. Martin read the title out loud: "*Songs of the Cowboys*. Jack Thorpe. 1908." He opened it and a piece of notebook paper fluttered down to the golden shag of the living room carpet.

"Let it snow, let it snow, let it snow," sang Carroll.

Martin picked up the paper, scanned it, mouthed first, "Beaufort," then, "Ginger." Someone banged on the front door. He read the letter again. More banging and a shout: "Mr. Oliphant?" Martin put the letter back in the book and the book into the pile of mail, walked to the foyer, and let in four Lemons Piano Tuners and Movers, trailing them back into the living room to watch them transmute the familiar space into a sickroom.

Over the next two days, each step in the living room's metamorphosis opened further the wound that the arrival of the hospital bed had cut: Frank's return from school and refusal to help Martin move the hospital bed from under the tree to the empty space left by the absent Steinway; Carroll's agreement to help move the hospital bed from under the tree but only if Martin would join in singing "Over the River and Through the Woods" as they did it; Dottie's slow and unsteady trip downstairs; her hysterical sobs at first sight of the bed; her escalation to hyperventilation as Martin demonstrated how easy it was to fold her table up and down and adjust the bed into its fifteen customizable comfort configurations; Frank's anger at Martin for buying the bed because "it's already making Mom sicker"; Martin's horror as his mom did get noticeably sicker.

After dinner on that second day, the doorbell rang out the first bar of "Winchester Cathedral," and Martin's dad, who had been rearranging the Christmas tree ornaments to get a better red-green symmetry, bolted for the front door. Martin stayed at his mother's bedside, holding a mirror under her nose. She had been sleeping since breakfast, and he was debating calling Dr. Broad.

He heard the rubbery pop of the door sucked back into its insulated frame.

"Not carolers," Carroll said, returning to the tree.

"But who was it?" Martin said.

"Some fat girl," Carroll said.

Martin noted a faint murking of the mirror, exhaled his own puff of relief, and went to see for himself.

He opened the front door to a giant white snowman, squinting in the light thrown off from the flashing display covering most of the colonial's front façade.

"Julie?" Martin said.

"Can I come in?" said Julie Newport and did so without waiting for a reply. Her down-stuffed jacket rustled as it knocked miniature candy canes off the festooned entryway. She pulled back her hood by its rabbit fur trim and tugged off her white ski cap. "I brought something for your mom. From my mom." She nodded toward a tinfoil-covered paper plate in her right hand.

"Great," said Martin. "We moved her downstairs."

Julie handed the plate to Martin, unzipped her coat, shook it off, and tossed it over the staircase landing, where it settled like a well-felled polar bear. Though she no longer appeared as if she were encased in bubble wrap, Martin still found himself staring at her bulk. He was positive she had not been this heavy when he saw her at The Silver Dollar last September.

Frank skidded down from the second floor, flinging himself over Julie's coat.

"Who's your fa——?" He reared back, stared open-mouthed at Julie. "Julie? Shit." He laughed, stopped. "Shit."

"Sixty pounds since school started in September, almost one hundred since I graduated PPHS, okay?" she said, catching and holding Martin's eye.

"No, that's fine. That's great. Good to see you." Frank slithered to the doorway to the den. "I'm going to Ron's," he said and vanished.

Martin stared at Julie for a minute more.

"Mom's asleep, but she'll want to see you," he said finally. "Do you want a cup of coffee, or…?" The grandfather clock in the den struck eight, as if correcting Martin. He waited until it was done. "…or a drink, a beer, or some brandy?"

"Brandy would be good," said Julie and followed Martin to the kitchen. She sat down at the dinner table and took the foil off the plate to reveal a pile of lumpy cookies in the shapes of holly leaves and Santa hats. She picked up one and pushed the rest away. Martin retrieved two brandy snifters from the bar in the den as well as a three-quarters full bottle of Christian Brothers. He set the glasses down and splashed some in each. Julie gestured for more. He poured her a second measure and took a cookie too. Julie picked up her brandy snifter with both hands and stared into it.

"I left school," said Julie, picking out another cookie and licking the green frosting from its top. "In October."

Martin put down his cinnamon-ball-encrusted reindeer and took a small sip of the brandy. It burned the back of his throat, evaporated before he could swallow.

"How's your mom?" Martin said.

"Good," said Julie. "No. I don't know. She's a bitch. We don't talk. I made these fucking cookies, you know. Her best friend in there," Julie waved toward the living room, "dying in the room with the Christmas tree, which is weird by the way, and Mom doesn't even bother to sign her Christmas card."

The Newports' card had come a couple of days before, a cardinal on a snow-covered pine branch, "Season's Greetings" scrolling on the top, inside, stamped in gold, "Best Wishes For a Happy Holidays and a Healthy New Year, the Newport Family." Martin remembered thinking it was kind of classy, the custom printing. He had not understood that the name stamp was sending a message, not of Christmas cheer, but of social distancing.

They chewed and sipped for several more minutes, until Martin could bear the teeth clicks and throat gurgles no longer. "What have you been up to since you've been back?" he asked. He knew he sounded like an out-of-town aunt making conversation with a niece she had met only twice before, but he couldn't seem to control the platitudes spilling from his sugar-frosted lips.

"Therapy," said Julie. "Can I have another shot?"

He poured the drink and topped off his own.

"Therapy," he said. "Physical?"

"Mental," she answered. "My mom thinks I have an eating disorder."

It had begun over Columbus Day, when Bitsy Newport and her husband, Winnie, surprised Julie at U of M's parents' weekend. They had found her on the lawn of the Phi Kappa Alpha house, representing her newly pledged sorority, Delta Sigma Theta, in the pizza-eating contest, which she won handily, two pies in seven minutes thirty-two seconds, a campus record. She downed two cans of Budweiser while the other contestants chewed it out for second place, an act of poor sportsmanship, but not so bad that it warranted Bitsy's tremolo scream as Julie, tomato sauce smeared on her chin, crushed the second empty on her head.

"They drove me straight to the psych ward at Swinehurst," Julie explained. "They've got a floor for eating disorders now. It's quite the rage. I think Mom thought I could catch one, like the flu. She told the shrink that the problem wasn't that I binge, which I do, but that I don't purge. The problem is, that I am fat, and Bitsy Newport does not have fat children. She wants me to be bulimic, or even better, anorexic, because it's less messy. The first doc, the one that admitted me, yelled at her. Said she was the one who should be in the loony bin. Said don't you know how serious eating disorders are? People die. Look at Karen Carpenter. Mom told him that Karen Carpenter was love-ly—by which she means skeletal—and she would have been fine had she had someone to help her manage her situation. Anyway, she got me this other shrink, not even a doctor, like a guru nutritionist scam artist who wants me to meditate with him and eat only vegetables. I go three times a week and he plays bells and I nap and he draws up a menu, which I take home, and my mom serves me lettuce rolls and rice cakes, and I smile and eat them and then I go to Dunkin Donuts and get two boxes of donut holes for my ride to Beamers Liquors to buy peppermint schnapps, Jack Daniels, and *People Magazine* to keep me company in my room until I pass out."

"Martin, who's there?" Dottie's voice floated into the kitchen, as strong and clear as he had heard it in months. "Is it Bitsy? Bring her to me."

"Let's go," Julie said and picked up her glass. "It's me, Mrs. Oliph-ant. Julie." She took a step, hesitated, turned back, grabbed the bottle. "Do you think your mom will want some?"

"God, no," Martin said, also rising from the table. "She's barely had a sip of water in the last week."

Dottie leaned in the doorway between the living room and the kitchen and said, "Don't be silly." She clutched both sides of the raised doorframe, and the veins on her hands popped like blue twigs tossed on white tissue paper. Her pale peach nightgown drifted to her feet, as if it were suspended from the ceiling by fishing line, no substructure of body holding it up from underneath. But she was standing, somehow having extracted herself from Mount St. Hospital Bed, and she was smiling.

"Get me a glass, Martin," Dottie said, "and let Bitsy come with me to the living room."

Martin fetched the glass. Julie disappeared with the bottle and her own snifter. By the time Martin joined them, his mom was back in the bed and showing Julie, who had pulled up one of the club chairs, how the morphine pump worked.

"Bitsy was telling me how she was thinking about applying to the nursing program at Lake Michigan University," said Dottie. "Isn't that exciting?"

Martin raised an eyebrow at Julie. She shrugged. "Pour your mom a drink."

"Yes, Martin, do," said Dottie, "and then leave us to catch up."

Martin poured the drink but held onto it. "You think? With the drugs?" he said. Julie smirked and waved a hand.

Dottie said, "She is a nurse, you know."

Martin handed the glass to Julie, who set it on the retractable table. "This is Julie, Mom. Julie Newport, Bitsy's daughter. She's not a nurse. Or a future nurse." He poked Julie's back. She turned, frowned, and waved him off again.

Dottie halted her brandy snifter in mid-heft, set it back down. She leaned over the table toward Julie, who leaned in. Dottie placed a hand on Julie's cheek and blinked.

"Well, so it is. Little Julie. I'm sorry, my dear, but you are so like your mother. So beautiful. So very, very beautiful."

With that, Julie started to sob and didn't stop until they all consumed two more brandies and decided that Julie would stay at the Oliphants' at least through the holidays.

"Good night, Bitsy," Dottie whispered, right before her eyes, dulled and heavy with booze and opiates, shut. "We'll talk more in the morning."

Author's Preface, *Songs of the Cowboys* by Jack Thorpe, 1908

To the Ranchmen of the West this little volume is dedicated as a reminder of the trail days and round-ups of the past. To the younger generation, who know not of the trip from Texas to Dodge and the north, it will tend to keep alive the memories of an industry now past.

I have gathered these songs from the cow camps of different states and territories. They embrace most of the songs as sung by the old-time cow punchers. I plead ignorant of the authorship of them but presume that most of the composers have, 'ere now, "Gone up the dim narrow trail."

I mount this little book on one of the best cow horses that ever lived and start it on its journey; together may they meet all the old-time cowboys and receive a welcome at their hands, is the earnest wish of

THE AUTHOR.

8

Julie slept on the living room couch that first night and the next morning returned to the Newports' beach mansion to retrieve her things. The rest of the Newports had already left for their Christmas trip to Aspen to ski the peaks of Snowmass, so Julie's run home was unmarked by any family fracas. She picked up her clothes, a couple of Harlequin romances, and a battered stuffed pink elephant she had had since she was two. From the idling Oldsmobile in the driveway, Martin watched her shut the door on the childhood home she would not enter again until six years later, when she would be married on its wooden deck overlooking Lake Michigan.

Carroll, accustomed as he was to having strangers appear in the house and take residence, seemed not to note Julie's occupation of the master bedroom recently abandoned by Dottie. Frank grumbled about "fatties taking over the world" when he was home, which was hardly at all. Dottie reacted most positively, sitting up, eating, chatting as she hadn't for weeks. About half the time, she confused Julie with Bitsy and demanded details about a long-forgotten or never-happened tennis round robin at the club or the menu for this year's cotillion. But Julie rolled with it, sitting by Dottie's bedside for hours at a time, calming the dazed and dying woman as she slipped seamlessly between ego and alter ego.

On her third day in residence, Julie found the *Songs of the Cowboys* in a hamper she had taken from Martin's room. She had started doing their laundry. Martin imagined that described well the depth of her desire not to return to the Newport house. She presented the book to him at the dinner table that night.

"This is that stuff, you know. From The Silver Dollar and the ranch. The poetry. It was in your dirty underwear."

Martin flushed. "Cowboy poetry. It's cowboy poetry. Beaufort Giles, from Jimmy Sneedle's, sent it."

"You had a thing for his daughter, what was her name? Clover? Sugar? Something culinary like that?"

Martin couldn't believe he'd forgotten about the book. Julie put it down beside her plate.

"It's pretty good. I read some to your mom this afternoon. She liked it. Especially the poems about horses. There's one called "Chopo," I think, that she made me read about ten times."

You've good judgment, sure footed, wherever you go,
You're a safety conveyance, my little Chopo.

"Safety conveyance, that cracks me up. I practically have the thing memorized."

"Hmm," Martin answered. He hadn't heard the poem before. And he hadn't read the book yet, which wasn't really his fault. Not with all the upheaval lately. But he found he didn't like Julie reciting cowboy poetry. And maybe he didn't even like his mom enjoying cowboy poetry. He considered for a moment that Beaufort had said he was sending the book to provide comfort to his mom, but she hadn't been the one who'd performed at the ranch. And Julie wasn't the one who'd stripped bare and proclaimed cowboy poetry from the stage at The Silver Dollar. What had they risked for it?

He thought it, but he didn't say it. He couldn't think how to and not sound small, selfish, a tad insane. And that was the opposite of what the art form promised.

That night, he refused the snifter of brandy Julie poured for him. She shrugged, pushed the book across the counter, picked up her drink, and retired to the basement to watch *A Chipmunk Christmas*. From the easy chair in the den, where he withdrew to read, he could hear Alvin and the other weasels piping out "Silver Bells."

There are only twenty-three poems and fifty pages in the 1908 version of *Songs of the Cowboys*. Martin read them all in less than an hour. Devoured them like he was a starving coyote, and they were a slow-moving pack of disoriented shih tzus. In that short time, they sang to him of the loss and hope and sadness and joy of his twenty-one-and-three-quarters years: He sobbed for his mother as "our little Texas stray—poor wrangler Joe" was crushed to death by a herd of stampeding cattle. He jigged with the Dutchman, the Cornishman, and the "Johnny Bull from Leeds" at "The Cowboys New Year's Dance." He struggled through that fetid summer with the hunters on

"Buffalo Range" and raged with them against the perfidy of a boss who would not pay, at a world that did not recognize hard work, at a land that defeated the best efforts of "all able-bodied men." He glowed with admiration for "my chico Chopo" and felt closer to his mom because she had discovered the pony. He forgave Julie and his mother for reading the little book first, for loving it too. How could he not?

He rose from the chair and, with the book, walked into the living room, where Dottie slept, bathed in lights from the Christmas tree, the same red, green, and gold that colored the falling snow outside. He kissed her cheek then retreated to the kitchen and picked up the glass of brandy Julie had poured for him earlier. He hesitated, then picked up the bottle too and descended into the dark of the basement to join Julie on the couch, just in time to hear Perry Como sing "I Saw Three Ships" with the concussed-looking chipmunk. She scooted over, and he spread out into the warm she left.

On Christmas night, Martin stood at the end of his mom's bed, its retractable table open and positioned before him. He looked down at the book, propped against a cup of eggnog, and read:

> *Way out in Western Texas, where the Clear Forks waters flow,*
> *Where the cattle are a brewin' and the Spanish ponies grew,*

"That doesn't rhyme," said Frank. He sat cross-legged under the Christmas tree, fiddling with a warty, canary-yellow Sony Walkman.

"No doubt the result of the evolution of the Western idiom and pronunciation patterns," said Lattner from one of the club chairs. A bottle of 1979 La Mission Haut-Brion sat on the occasional table next to him, one of four he had brought to the celebration. Another hung loosely in Carroll's hand, and he slugged from it occasionally as he leaned in the doorway between hall and living room. The emerald pulse from Dottie's drug pump infused Lattner's balloon glass, and stars of flashing green danced across the ruby liquor. Julie, eyes half shut, leaned back in a chair pulled up next to the hospital bed and mouth-breathed regularly, a comforting background soundtrack. Bits and pieces of the remains of dinner perfumed the air: roasted turkey, yeast rolls, a tang of cranberry, a frizzle of burnt chocolate.

"You go on, Martin. You're doing a good job," said Mrs. Trinkle from her seat opposite Lattner.

Martin looked down at the page. He should have memorized it. But "The Cowboys' Christmas Ball" was one of the longest poems in *Songs of the Cowboys*, and there had been so much to do. Getting several days' worth of the *Leader Telegram* written, edited, and printed, so they wouldn't have to work over the holidays; settling his mom in the living room; adjusting to Julie whistling Captain and Tennille in the mornings, showering through the hot water in the evenings; corralling and managing his dad's epic Christmas celebration plans: returning the live goose, canceling the Victorian Chorale, extinguishing several practice figgy pudding flame outs.

"Is it over?" Frank said.

Martin decided to skip a few lines.

Where the antelope is grazin' and the lonely plovers call
It was there that I attended the Cowboys' Christmas Ball.

"You missed the mockingbirds singin' and the monstrous stars winkin'," said Dottie as she revved her mattress into its most upright position. Julie reached over the gasping woman, punched the button on the morphine pump, and eased her back into her pillows. "I'll read you the whole thing later," she said.

"And the double mountains slumbering in heavenly kinds of dreams." Martin watched the tension melt off Dottie like high sierra snow in the spring. She took Julie's hand and muttered, "Antelope grazin'...lonely plover...call."

Dottie was still dying as much as she had been two weeks earlier, when they moved her to the hospital bed. You could smell it on her, see it in her. But she seemed so much better now, listening to the poetry as Martin read. He continued to the end, not lifting his head until the last stanza, then gazed a moment at the tilting star atop the Christmas tree and shut the little book softly. Dottie, revived, sat up, hands clasped in front of her chest, cheeks flushed.

"Oh, Martin," she said, eyes sharp and clear, for a rare moment, of the haze of drugs and death. "That was just wonderful." She leaned toward him, clapped twice, then fell back. "I'm a little dizzy."

Lattner and Mrs. Trinkle picked up the applause. "Bravo!" Lattner called and Mrs. Trinkle added, "Well done."

"Done?" said Frank, propping his head up on one hand. Three verses into the recitation, he had collapsed face down into a pile of balled-up gold tinfoil, knotted curly ribbons, and gift tags bearing sled-riding snowmen. "Really and truly and finally done?"

"Will you read 'Chopo' now, Martin? I think we all want to hear it," said Dottie, shutting her eyes. "It reminds me of when I was a girl."

"A little of this first," said Julie, punching at the morphine pump's button again. "That was great, Martin." She gave a couple of claps, her long nails, painted red and green, flicked festively.

Not the thunderous applause Martin remembered from the audience at Jimmy Sneedle's. Or the cheers and shouts from the patrons of The Silver Dollar. Not the tidal wave of sexual release, the touch of a woman's tongue, the slap of a man's palm. Not the smell of sweet sweat or spilled beer or horse manure or soft leather. Not this time. This time, his mom's smile, weak, through medicine-stained teeth. His dad's quiet attention, the stilling of his crazed and addled brain. Lattner's thumbs up. Mrs. Trinkle's twittering laugh. Julie's fluttering nails. Even Frank's reluctant presence. For Martin. For cowboy poetry. Not what Martin had planned. Not what he'd ever wanted. But a merry Christmas, a happy new year. And cowboy poetry. This time, it was enough.

Page torn from *My Scarsdale Diet Log*, found inserted in a used paperback copy of *The Thornbirds* donated to the Pierre Salvation Army Thrift Shoppe by Julie Newport on May 18, 1988

DAY: 3   DATE: 3/6/86

<u>Breakfast:</u>

1/2 grapefruit
One slice of protein bread toasted
Coffee or tea (no sugar, cream or milk, no honey)

Notes: *No protein bread, Brown Sugar Cinnamon Pop-Tart instead, scraped off frosting.*

<u>Lunch:</u>

Tuna fish or salmon salad (oil drained off) with lemon and vinegar dressing
Grapefruit, or melon, or fruit in season
Coffee/tea/diet soda/water

Notes: *Tuna Fish with packet of French dressing, 1/2 banana, Diet Rite.*

<u>Dinner:</u>

Sliced roast lamb*, all visible fat removed
Salad of lettuce, tomatoes, cucumbers, celery
Coffee/tea/diet soda/water
* Can be substituted with fish, seafood, chicken or turkey

Notes: *No lamb (yuck), bbq chicken breast instead, 1 only, Skim milk with dinner, 3 brandies after (no ice cream!!), but no salad, some rice.*

<u>Exercise:</u>
Jane Fonda's workout VCR tape, 30 minutes beginners level.

<u>Quote of the Day:</u>

When you lose weight, your heart gets closer to the surface, and everyone can see you, beautiful you, for who you really are!!

—Maria Tosi, third Mafia girl, Season 2, *Miami Vice*

9

By nine a.m. on the morning of Boxing Day, Carroll had abandoned his obsession with Christmas and locked himself in his den. Martin could hear him yelling on the phone at various Oliphant Holdings, Inc. employees, ordering them home from the extended vacations he had ordered them on two weeks before. At one point, he slammed the phone down so hard, the handset cracked. They had to wait until after New Year's for AT&T to replace it.

Martin spent most of those final December days at the *Leader Telegram* offices, helping Lattner and Mrs. Trinkle put together several year-in-review pieces. Julie continued to read to Dottie from *Songs of the Cowboys*, and she ghostwrote some last-minute college applications for Frank. Many, Martin included, who would one day struggle to fathom the bond between Julie and Frank, would have done well to pay attention to that collaboration. Though it would be years before either could acknowledge it, they fell in a sort of love hunched together over a manual typewriter, Julie tapping out an apologia for Frank's academic record to date and a declaration that it would improve were he to be welcomed into the storied ivory towers of (in order of preference): Stanford, University of Michigan, Michigan State, Western Michigan State, South Bend College, and Olivet City College.

And Colorado State. Julie insisted on this. Several of her more water-logged former teammates from PPHS had matriculated at this school, known for its wild parties and applicant-friendly admissions process: a one-page form that asked only that the future collegian be able to type his name and address on, or close to, the printed line indicated. That and the twenty-five-dollar application fee.

Shoulder to shoulder at the kitchen table, Julie forgoing her first evening brandy for a Diet Rite, Frank's eyes scrunched in concentration, they fell into conversations far deeper than Julie had had thus far with Martin and far deeper than Martin would ever have with Frank. Julie later explained that, in pushing Frank to use Dottie's cancer in his "greatest challenge" essays, she came to understand, underneath

Frank's teen angst, he, like she, was mourning a lost parent. And Frank later explained that, in discussing the feats to include in his "greatest accomplishments" essays, he came to understand, underneath Julie's excess adipocyte cells, she, like he, was a passionate athlete.

Julie and Martin spent New Year's Eve taking down the Christmas tree and packing up the boxes upon boxes of trimmings that Martin's dad had nailed, taped, and hot glued to most of the house's surfaces. Julie picked some tinsel off an inflatable gingerbread man and said, "I can't go back, you know. And I can't stay here."

Martin had wondered how long it would take her to bring up her family, due soon to repatriate to Pierre. He nodded.

"Because?" asked Martin.

"I'll get a job," Julie said.

"Okay," said Martin. And that was it for a while.

Julie didn't get a job, or even try, but it didn't matter. They didn't need the money. Carroll continued to focus what was left of his diminishing mental resources on the pure pursuit of cash. He no longer even took interest in what happened to the Oliphant Holdings, Inc. profits, simply amassed them and deposited them into a household account. Dr. Broad again attributed the behavior to the stroke, but Martin wasn't so sure. The lust for pure plunder seemed to be closer to his dad's existential rule than it was to an exception. Not like his newest tic, blurting out crude demands when in the presence of any female. "Show me your pussy," he'd bark at Julie as she passed him the salad bowl. "You're welcome," she would answer, perhaps unwilling to upset the founder of her substantial daily feast.

Besides, Julie had a job of sorts, caring for Dottie as she approached death. "Any day now," Dr. Broad would say on his weekly visits. "Any day."

It could have been the opiates or the cancer, perhaps having crawled to her brain by then, but in her lucid moments that late winter, Dottie hardly ever presented as herself anymore. Sometimes she was Bitsy Newport's imaginary twin sister and would chat to an invisible Gra Gra Newport, who had taken to haunting the left corner of the bed. Other times, Dottie became present-day Bitsy herself, fussing about the quality of the chocolate at the club's Valentine's Day dinner-dance or the scheduling of the bubble's mixed doubles league. Martin suspected that Julie herded his mom's delusions onto this particular trail. More than once, he had come in on the two of them holding hands, and Julie explaining earnestly her side of what sounded like long ago mother-daughter disputes. "Of course, you should get to decide what to wear," Dottie would mumble. Or, "I always thought you were the smart one." But most often, what Martin heard Dottie say was, "Oh no, dear, oh no. You are so beautiful."

Martin couldn't understand why all of a sudden his mom had chosen to become the mom she had never showed any interest in being in the past. A mom who saw the internal beauty of her fat offspring. Martin had been fat, and with ample internal beauty, long before Julie started packing on the pounds. Who knew what he could have become if some of that support and charity and love had been focused on him, back when he needed it, before he learned to live without it. Not that he cared anymore, now that he had the promise of cowboy poetry, again simmering like a tin coffee pot on the back of the campfire, waiting for him to heed its final rattle and blast of bitter steam, waiting for him to fulfill his destiny, somewhere out West, somehow with Beaufort and his like, with Ginger and her, well, with Ginger. He would not settle for less. Cowboy poetry, as soon as he could shake off this last, but weakening, stranglehold of Pierre and its close horizons and gray skies and watery sunsets and steel instead of sand and inland seas instead of trout streams and old boys instead of men.

Given all this, he should have been more understanding of the fervor with which Dottie took to the *Songs of the Cowboys*. Sometimes, he would read her "Top Hand" or his favorite, "Educated Feller," and would see how she leaned into the words, her eyes grabbing at his lips, as if the verses were the rope tethering her to this earth. He knew how cowboy poetry could cinch you in like a well-thrown lariat, hogtie you to purpose and life again. But he could not help but feel that the gift had been given to him, and now his mom, who would not live to see another year, was using it up.

March is the most dismal of the months in Pierre. Elementary school teachers paste up construction paper tulips on classroom windows, but even the youngest know this is a lie; adults nurse the colds they've had since before Christmas, and their skin scales from radiator heat;

old women break their hips on slick walks; family dogs lose their feet to frostbite; and emphysemic World War II vets down fifths of rye and shoot themselves with their service weapons in the dim of their paneled basement bars.

As that March came in like a depressed and bilious lion, Frank began to receive rejections from college admissions offices. First Stanford, a mimeographed paragraph askew on the page without salutation and without mention of Frank's tennis prowess and performance at camp the summer before. Then University of Michigan, more carefully typed but equally cold, then Michigan State, and the lesser regional colleges, just Olivet City College taking any time to sound even the slightest bit sorry. By mid-month, only the application to Colorado State remained extant. Frank reacted with typical bad grace, criticizing Dottie's refusal to heal, mimicking Carroll's obscene outbursts, ignoring Julie's concern, retreating to Ron's.

Julie's mood also turned sour. Dottie was physically no worse than she had been three months earlier, which was days from death, but mentally she was all gone. It had been weeks since she had made an appearance as Dottie Oliphant. Even the preferred alter ego, as far as Julie was concerned, the remade and motherly Bitsy Newport, showed up only for rare cameos. Her new character—one that, from the grumbling Martin heard over dinner or brandy, he assumed was not much to Julie's liking—was the *Song of the Cowboys'* "young Patty Moorehead, the Pecos River Queen."

> *She can rope and tie and brand it as quick as any man,*
> *She's voted by all cowboys an A 1 top cow hand.*

Dottie slept through early March's dusky days, waking about the time Martin got home. Though it was Julie who had so faithfully read *Songs of the Cowboys*—the source, it seemed, for almost all Dottie's knowledge of the West—it was Martin with whom his mom wanted to reminisce about her fictional life on the range as Patty Moorehead. She lamented never taking a husband, lamented testing her lover's heart one day by riding "across the Comstock Railroad bridge, the highest in the West."

> *For he told her would gladly risk all dangers for her sake,*
> *But the puncher wouldn't follow so she's still without a mate.*

But in the end, the conversation always came back to "my little Chopo." She would grab Martin's hand and say, "What I would give to see my little Chopo one more time."

"Chopo," Julie would snort. "The poem isn't even any good."

It's unclear whether it was because Julie had no interest in Patty Moorehead or because Patty Moorehead had no interest in Julie, but she again started talking about moving back home. Martin thought it unlikely. Her family had returned from Aspen in early January but had done so without a word to her, not phoned in or in person, not to ask how she was faring, not to wish her a happy New Year, not to see whether she still wanted her Elton John albums. The only communications were from her mother and through the mail, the occasional article clipped from the *Leader Telegram* or *Tennis Magazine* on weight loss or exercise regimes. Julie clearly wasn't wanted there, and besides, Martin needed her to hang in here, with him, until his mother died, until he could get himself packed up and head west to find Beaufort and Ginger. He didn't think that he could do it alone. And it wasn't like Julie was getting nothing out of the deal. Free room, free board, a lot of board, free remodeled mother figure to burnish up the badly bruised self-esteem.

On the ides of March, a week before Martin's twenty-second birthday, he spent a Saturday afternoon trying to calm his mom by reading from *Songs of the Cowboys*. She had been restless all day, cranking through her mattress's comfort positions and moaning for more morphine. He recited "Speckles" that night, another of the horses featured in Jack Thorpe's little book. He'd been cuing it up on the play list for a while now, hoping he might divert his mom's affections from her little Chopo. Julie was right. It was a crappy poem. And having read it perhaps two million times, he would do almost anything to escape from its limping rhythms and stilted syntax. Chopo my pony Chopo my pride Chopo my amigo, Chopo I will ride. Chopo Chopo Chopo.

"Oh, Chopo," mumbled Dottie, and Martin upped the volume on "Speckles."

But for single and double cussedness 'en double fired sin,
The horse never come out 'o Texas that was halfway knee high to him.

K. T. Sparks

The doorbell rang and Julie and Frank yelled, "Got it" from up-stairs at the same time, but it was Frank's size ten Adidas Martin heard jumping down and into the hall.

"I want Chopo," groaned Dottie.

"Julie," Frank yelled. "Your mom's here."

Martin reared back. The ladderback he had pulled in from the kitchen tilted and teetered. He tangled his legs in its legs. The chair clattered down. He caught his tailbone on the edge of the upended seat and boomeranged the back of his head off the living room car-pet. Black, then stars, then a bathtub-shaped series of cracks in the ceiling he had not noticed before. He had to get up, shake off the almost certain concussion and spleen rupture, and somehow get to Julie before Bitsy did. And then do what? KO her? With one giant fist, send her bony cranium tumbling down the front walk? Say something, anything, to sum up all that Julie was that Bitsy didn't see? And that would be? That would be?

"Chopo?" Dottie whined. Then, "Julie? Julie dear?"

Martin raised his head, dropped it back when his abdomen muscles would not engage sufficiently to bring him upright. He rolled to one side, winced as he cracked through the chair arm with his right hip-bone, made it to his hands and knees.

"Oh my God, you are fatter than ever. Have you read even one word I sent you? Your father said not to bother, but I thought, I thought..."

Too late. Martin crawled over to his mom's bed and hefted himself up, hand over hand, on the metal leg.

"I thought maybe you had a shred of self-respect. A shred of, I don't know, class."

"Mom," Julie wailed.

"Chopo," Dottie cried, mimicking Julie's cadence.

Martin made it to the doorway of the hall. Julie stood two stairs up, rooted, one hand gripping the metal bannister. Bitsy shook off her black-and-white boucle wool jacket and untied the scarf covering her thin, sand-brown hair. She dumped her outerwear into Frank's arms. He stared down at it as if she had just deposited a clubbed and bloody seal there.

Bitsy addressed Julie: "Well, I didn't come to see you, in any case. I came see my friend. My best friend. I ran into Dr. Broad at the Spring Fling, and he said poor Dottie's taken a turn for the worse."

That was enough to jolt Julie out of her catatonia.

"You fucking bitch," she screamed and leapt at her mother, arms spread, fingers splayed, as if the scrawny woman were a grenade and Julie was about to earn a posthumous Gold Star for jumping on it.

Martin got as far as a bleated "Julie" and one step into the front hall.

"Can it, Martin," Julie screeched. "I'm going to kill her."

Frank dropped Bitsy's coat and ran into the den. "I'm going to Ron's," he yelled, and the door to the garage slammed.

Julie stood panting, not an inch away from her mother, who was staring into the intricate pattern knit around the neck of Julie's Shetland sweater. Martin hadn't remembered Bitsy being so short, and perhaps she hadn't been last time he saw her. Perhaps, having run out of girth to reduce, she had started taking pounds off the top.

"She's been dying for ten months, your best friend," Julie snarled. Spittle landed on Bitsy's puffed-out do and winked in the light from the overhead brass chandelier.

"I didn't know," she said and sidestepped her daughter. "I assumed she was healthy, healthy enough to take on the burden of caring for you and your mental illness, it seems. I wish I had realized what a burden..." she paused and looked Julie up and down as she repeated "burden." "I would have stopped in earlier. Hello, Martin. How are you?"

"Um, fine," said Martin.

"Martin," Julie yelped.

"Right," said Martin, putting his hands on Bitsy's shoulders. He knew what he needed to do. "I think you better go."

"Don't be ridiculous." She looked up at Martin. "I've come to see Dottie, and I will see Dottie. Then I'm taking Julie home. I apologize for the inconvenience her emotional disarray and physical ruin has caused you and your family at this difficult time. I am sure Mr. Newport would be glad to discuss some sort of monetary compensation with your father."

Julie sputtered and pawed the ground. "Get out of the way. I swear to God, Martin, I will kill you too. Prison is as good a career plan as

any. Orange is the color of my parachute, bitch." Julie feinted left, and
Martin deflected her with his hip. They polkaed in place at each other
for a few steps. Sweat trickled down the small of Martin's back to the
waistband of his Fruit of the Looms. He smelled the fried eggs he had
had for breakfast; that, and the hall's winter perfume of wet rubber
and moldering wool turned his stomach, and his vision tilted twenty
degrees to the left. He was almost sure he had suffered a concussion.

The door to the garage slammed again.

"Bitsy, it's been too long. Great to see you." Carroll two-stepped
around Martin and Julie and enveloped the tiny woman in a hug, then
pushed her back with both hands and smiled: "Bitsy."

"Lolly." This was Bitsy's take on the hated "Carroll." "I am so sorry
about Dottie."

"Yeah," he said, still grinning, "I hear it's bad." He leaned in, as if
for a hug, seemed to reconsider, then reached for her left breast and
gave it a full-handed squeeze.

"You always had great tits, Bitsy. Great fucking tits. Make sure Julie
gets you a drink. You'll have to excuse me."

Martin silently thanked his dad for exhibiting this particular manifestation of cranial rewiring at this particular moment. It sucked some
of the venom out of the hall. Or at least smothered it with a blanket
of embarrassment and confusion.

"Julie dear, is that you? Come in and sit with me for a minute,
darling." Dottie's voice floated in.

Julie stopped shifting. Bitsy was patting her breast, as if checking
to make sure Martin's dad hadn't walked off with a chunk of it and
didn't seem to have heard. Julie's eyes unfocused and she smiled.
Martin knew what she was thinking. What fate to Bitsy Newport
was worse than death? Getting one-upped, that's what. And here
was Dottie, reprising her role as Julie's good mother, just in time
to one-up Bitsy Newport into oblivion. Christ, Martin thought, his
chest expanding with pride, his parents were deluding on all cylinders
tonight.

"Let's go in together, Mom," said Julie in the saccharine tone favored by matricidal maniacs from Lizzy Borden to Norman Bates.

She took Bitsy's hand away from her breast and led her into the
living room. Martin followed, but at a distance that would allow him

to brake and reverse when the crash came and bumpers and gasoline started flying all over the place.

"I smell urine," said Bitsy, standing at the side of the hospital bed but not touching it, as if she thought the undeniable stink of death might wipe off on her Ralph Lauren chinos. "Who's your housekeeper? You shouldn't stand for that, Dottie." She addressed the back of Dottie's head, which was all of her that was visible in the heap of sheets and pillows. "Is she alive?"

Julie moved the pieces of the crushed chair aside with her foot and leaned over the bed. "Mrs. Oliphant, are you awake?" Then, with a look at her own mother, "Mom, Mommy, it's Julie, your daughter. Remember the bully I told you about? She's here to see you."

Dottie turned her head, her pellucid eyelids still clamped tight. She moaned through grey lips, then said, "Chopo?"

"It's Bitsy, dear. I've come to visit." Bitsy shot Julie a look and pushed in front of her.

"The woman I told you about," said Julie, shoving her mom back with a quaking arm. "The one who called me fat. She's the one who said I was hideous."

"I never said hideous," said Bitsy.

"Tell her." Julie looked ready to crawl into the bed with Dottie, who had opened wide her terrified eyes. "Tell her I'm beautiful."

"Oh, Julie," said Bitsy. "This is not fair."

"Tell her," Julie grabbed the sick woman's arm, just skin badly stapled to bone.

Dottie sat up and looked at Martin. Her arm was still in Julie's hand. "Who is it? Where's Chopo?"

Martin stepped toward the bed. This had to end.

"Chopo's right here." He placed a hand on Julie's shoulder, which was shaking hard. "And this is Bitsy Newport, you remember Bitsy. She used to be your friend."

Julie started to sob. Bitsy said, "Hello, Dottie. How are you?"

"She used to be your friend," Martin said, not dropping his eyes from his mom's. "But now she works for the glue factory. She's come to take your Chopo away."

Dottie turned to her old friend, her best friend, and screamed.

March 23, 1986

TO: Bob Lattner, editor

FROM: Martin Oliphant, reporter and assistant editor

RE: Feature article on the 50th anniversary of the death of Arthur Chapman, cowboy poet

---

Miss Stanley, reference technician (her nomenclature, not mine) at the Pierre Public Library, pursuant to my request submitted in September of 1985, has turned up two volumes of Arthur Chapman's cowboy poetry: *Out Where the West Begins* and *Cactus Center*, both published in 1921. She has also, to her and my great delight, procured from the New York Public Library a microfiche copy of Arthur Chapman's *New York Times* obituary, which shows he died in December of 1935.

I propose to write a feature Sunday article introducing cowboy poetry to Pierre based on these books, the brief bio of Chapman included in the obituary, and an interview with Miss Stanley about her adventures obtaining the microfiche (which she claims are legion, and she'll tell you more if you ever buy her that Singapore Sling you've been promising, "you sly dog," her nomenclature, not mine) **[TYPIST NOTE: Mr. Lattner: It is unfair to string that poor girl along just so you don't have to look up things on your own. Plus she is too young for you. IJT]**. I also can draw from *Songs of the Cowboys* for other and earlier examples of the art form, a scoop of sorts, as I have reason to believe (stains, wear, and tear) that my copy is quite rare.

You should be particularly interested in Chapman (as I am) because, according to the NYT, he both started, middled, and ended his cowboy poetry career as a journalist: *Chicago Daily News* (1895-1898), *Denver*

Republican (1898-1913), *Denver Times* (managing editor, 1913-1919), and the *New York Tribune* and *New York Herald Tribune* until his death.

I have finished the research you asked for (notes on your desk) on the new Chi Chi's and hepatitis, so I am available to start this piece posthaste.

MCO/ijt

10

The day before Martin's birthday, Mrs. Trinkle organized what she called "the intervention." The previous week's brawl between Julie, Bitsy Newport, Dottie-Oliphant-cum-Bitsy-Newport, Dottie-Oliphant-cum-the-Pecos-River-Queen, Chopo, and Martin had left few physical scars, all on Martin, who saw double for three days and still sported a bruise the shape of Alaska on the right side of his chest. But emotional wreckage was rampant: Bitsy had keened and skittered her way down the Oliphant front walk and into her Mercedes Benz 190E and had not been heard from since. Julie stopped bathing, stopped speaking to anyone, and started consuming her, Martin's, and a small Cossack regiment's share of Christian Brothers alone in her room each night.

Mrs. Trinkle made a reservation for them at Emilio's under the pretense of celebrating Martin's birthday. Carroll was in Denver for business, so it was Mrs. Trinkle, Lattner, Martin, Frank, and Julie. Frank was a last-minute addition. He usually avoided any public appearances with his family, but he was in an expansive mood, having received an acceptance from Colorado State in that afternoon's mail.

"Like a fucking reprieve from the governor," he explained to Lattner, who met them at the restaurant.

"Cheers, young man," said Lattner, setting down the martini glass he had dragged with him from the bar. He took a place at the head of the table, snapped open a red cloth napkin, and tucked it into his collar over an already sauce-splattered tie. "So, Martin," he said, tipping his chair back, losing his balance for a moment, then clunking back down, "share with us the wisdom of your twenty-two years on this great planet."

"In a moment," said Mrs. Trinkle, with one finger edging Lattner's martini glass away from him. "First, let's drink a little toast to Julie."

Mrs. Trinkle had read a *Redbook* article on interventions—heroin addictions, albeit, but she was certain the principles were the same for any sort of what she called "mental hobgoblins." She had explained this to Lattner and Martin that afternoon. Lattner obviously had not heeded.

"Okay, to Julie. And to Martin's birthday. But mostly to Martin's birthday or why did I spend twenty-five dollars I could have used on Jameson's on a cake from Bit o' Swiss?" said Lattner.

Excellent, thought Martin. He hoped it was Black Forest. The evening was looking up.

Mrs. Trinkle ignored Lattner, pressed on as if reading from the *Redbook* playbook. "Julie dear, we are all here for you to help you cope with your fraught domestic situation."

Julie smiled, practically the first Martin had seen in a week. "Great," she said. "Let me tell you what I'm thinking."

Martin listened to Julie spill out her plans and recognized, for the first time, the Bitsy Newport in the girl. She knew her mind, twisted as it might be, and expressed it clearly, not as opinion but as fact, not as a hope but as a finished blueprint. Lattner and Mrs. Trinkle nodded at her, mumbled agreement when she stopped to take a breath. She had hijacked the intervention.

The gist of Julie's self-help plan was this: She would get a job at the *Leader Telegram*, filling in for Lattner when he was too drunk to finish his copy, helping Mrs. Trinkle with the editing. She would get Martin's job, he realized as she continued to talk. He would give up his job so Julie could feel better about herself. Happy birthday, fat boy.

"What do you think, Martin?" Lattner took a sip of a new martini. "She'd be pretty good at the newspaper game, I reckon."

Mrs. Trinkle put a hand on Lattner's arm. "Well, you know, Martin has been doing quite a lot lately."

Lattner tilted his head, took another sip, and, after way too long, said, "He has, he has. Julie, I have a reporter already." Another too long pause. "Martin!"

"But Martin is going to go out West after his mom dies," said Julie, "which is any day now. It's all he talks about. And it's not like I expect to get paid until he leaves."

This set all the heads, except Martin's, bobbing happily. Over plates of paglia e fieno and spinach manicotti and pasta puttanesca, the table, except Martin, discussed where Julie would sit, investigations she might conduct, copy editing she might undertake. All, except Martin, agreed the situation was win-win: a better *Leader Telegram* and a happier, healthier Julie. After what seemed like several hours of this, the waitress brought Martin's cake.

"Then it's settled," said Mrs. Trinkle, smiling and clearly pleased with herself. "Martin, why don't you cut it?"

Martin picked up the knife the waitress handed him, briefly contemplated shoving it into Julie's fleshy throat, then sliced into the creamy topping. No candles, no "Happy Birthday, dear Martin" mumbled out in embarrassed disharmony, no "make a wish, Martin."

No need. No problem. He could see the Rockies now, peeking out from the far horizon. He could smell the hay, feel the tickle of barn dust on his nose. No matter, all this. He'd be with Ginger soon.

One week into Julie's employment at the *Leader Telegram,* and Martin began to think it wasn't such a bad idea after all. For one thing, there was his mom. Amoya Higgins, the Jamaican nurse Martin had hired while Julie was in her post-matricidal funk, stayed on. She was competent and kind and Dottie, though she slept just as much and improved not at all, seemed to sleep easier. For another, Julie's presence in the *Leader Telegram* offices forced Martin to up his game. He had been simply ignoring Lattner's incessant and bellowed requests for "someone to make some goddamn sense out of this presser from the Art League" or "an interview with the Stevenstown Blossom Queen—no photos, this one is preggers and showing." But Julie jumped at such commands, like a Jack Russell to the rat. And Martin began to too.

And that was perhaps for the best. Because, since the night at Emilio's, Martin had come to understand that he needed to put meat on the bleached bones of his, as Julie pointed out, oft-asserted plans to relocate. Did he really think he could just show up somewhere west of the Mississippi, and Beaufort and Ginger would come galloping in to sweep him up? Did he really think Beaufort would jump at the chance to hire him on as a hand? That Ginger would insist on a seat for him in her Rodeo Queen court? That he would get a job reading cowboy poetry aloud? He, who had performed in front of a crowd only twice, both times to loud acclaim, though never paid and once naked?

No, cowboy poetry might be the train that would take him to his western destiny, but his job at the *Leader Telegram* was his ticket. He'd do it the way Arthur Chapman did, according to the *New York Times* obituary, which Martin had quoted extensively in his article on the 50th anniversary of Chapman's death. Lattner had finally let it run, albeit on a Tuesday and under a recipe for Potato Chip Fried Chicken Cutlets. It had only inspired one reader response, which was both negative and misinformed: the owner of Zick's Bowling Lanes complained that the article had displaced the cartoon strip, "Mark Trail," which had in fact moved to the sports section the week before. But Martin was proud of the byline and inspired by Chapman's history, a Midwesterner who never rode the range but became the most famous cowboy poet of his time. Martin could do the same: hone his journalism acumen here, in the heart of the heartland, just as Chapman had in Chicago, and then move it west. Carry his clips and his thesaurus like a saddle and a lariat, and take the stockman literary world by dust storm.

Martin pulled the Custom Cruiser out of the driveway and heard the first clinks of April sleet hit the back window. He regretted volunteering to cover the Orchard Mall opening. Six-thirty in the morning. It was still dark. The ribbon-cutting ceremony wasn't until ten, but Lattner had wanted a few pictures of the eager shoppers lining up to get the first J.C. Penney rose velveteen blazer or takeout chop suey from the food court's gleaming new China House.

No one was lined up when Martin pulled into the expanse of black-topped parking spaces, frosted with a crunching layer of ice. Workers in blaze orange vests were setting up a stage at one end of the lot. To the left, in a roped-off area, carnies milled around a collapsed Tilt-a-Whirl and haphazardly painted trailers promising TERROR TERROR TERROR. A fun fair. Of course. What Midwestern cultural event was complete without rickety thrill rides, E. coli-laden corn dogs, and rigged games of chance? Martin snapped a few pictures of the "Welcome to Orchards Mall" banner going up over the stage, then wandered to the carnival to see if he could find a churro.

Which he could not. He took some more pictures: tattooed carnies smoking hand-rolled cigarettes; a stilled Scrambler, one bent metal arm reaching for the gray sky; a midget in a diaper and a down jacket applying white clown paint. Diane Arbus reincarnate, that was Martin.

He thought he smelled coffee and headed in that direction. He passed a dented white trailer and was hit with the scent of horses. It deluged him. Beaufort, the hands, the straw, the leather, Ginger, the dry heat, the poetry, Ginger, the sweet horse sweat, Ginger, Ginger. He swung around, almost sure he would see her behind him, leading her silver mare into the stall, laughing at his posturing as a photographer.

But, of course, behind him, no Ginger. No churro and no coffee either. Just an old pony being led by an even older man. Martin knew him. Earl Dewitty of Dewitty's Delightful Pony Rides. There was not a county fair, church homecoming festival, or community ice cream social to which Dewitty didn't bring his string of stunted nags. Every kid in Pierre had ridden one of them at least once. And what status, what joy, to be the beloved child whose parents sprung to have Earl haul his herd to a birthday party. Martin did not have such parents. Martin had never even been invited to a birthday party of a child who had such parents.

Martin watched Dewitty hook the pony into a complicated chain metal harness, which was, in turn, attached to a rusty disk. The gray pony's back was so swayed, there'd be no need for a saddle. Dewitty could just wedge a kid in there. Martin almost felt sorry for the beast, though he was pretty sure this was the same animal that had tried to take a chunk out of his thigh about fifteen years ago at the Blossomtown Fest. He snapped a picture, got closer, noticed a line of sores where the saddle had rubbed the nag raw, snapped another.

"Get the fuck out, you sorry nag, or I'll ship you on the next boat to France, where they'll eat you for lunch." Dewitty's voice echoed out of the trailer, followed by several loud clomps and what sounded like a woman screaming but could have been a pony's wail. A minute later, Dewitty emerged, this time tugging on a sorrel pony that was tugging just as hard the other way. Martin could see the same pattern of sores on this one. He snapped several pictures, and several more after Dewitty got the sorry steed hooked up to the wheel, picked up a board, and began beating the animal with what looked like well-practiced strokes, not stopping until the pony fell to its knees. Martin leaned in and shot a close-up.

"No pictures," Dewitty snarled. "Pictures are two dollars, rides are two dollars. Pay separately. No discounts. Use your own camera."

"That's okay," said Martin. "I'm out of film anyway."

He took two weeks to write the story. He showed the pictures of the saddle sores to Dr. Hall, the local vet, who gave him great quotes like "worst I've ever seen." Martin discovered that Dewitty's Delightful Pony Rides had had several complaints filed against it with the Better Business Bureau and interviewed all of the complainants, most of whom had hired Dewitty and his foaming beasties for birthday parties. But the final of these interviews, with Treena Wentworth, the director of the Pierre Humane Society, provided all he needed to finish his piece.

He had suggested that they rendezvous at the Baroda McDonald's, twenty minutes east of Pierre. He relished the deep throat aspects of the interview, even after the dressing down he got from his source, a committed vegetarian, on his choice of meeting place. They settled into a molded plastic booth.

"Thank God someone is finally paying attention," she said and stared down into her coffee, as if examining its murk for stray cow entrails.

"Did you go to the police?" Martin asked. He tried to bite into his Big Mac discreetly.

Treena laughed. "You know who owns it, don't you?" Her breath smelled of cloves. Martin shook his head no, did not open his mouth, wished he had told them to hold the onions.

"Arnie Stem."

Martin sat back. Ah, Arnie Stem. No idea who that was.

"Arnie Stem," she repeated. "Arnie Stem. Sheriff Arnie Stem. The sheriff of Pierre County."

"Of course," said Martin, with feigned surety. They didn't go much for politics at the *Leader Telegram*. They were more of a high school musical and bake sale operation. But once she said the name, he did recall the posters around town; it had to have been from several years back. A beefy man, as all Midwestern sheriffs seem required to be, pictured on a campaign sign waving a bulbous cherry-red thumbs up.

Treena looked at her watch. Her face said what a waste of time she was finding this. "Look, are you going to run something? Because let me tell you, you're going to get blowback. Arnie makes a fortune from that business, keeps him and his mistresses in Michelob and Cheetos. The week I filed with the BBB, my mailbox got shot up, and my car was towed for parking violations."

"Well," said Martin, "the Pierre constabulary is known for its rigorous enforcement of the traffic laws."

"It was in my driveway," Treena said. "But look, on the half chance you have the cojones to go after those bastards, I'll give you my notes. I've been watching them for a year. I've got pictures, even one of Earl dumping a dead horse in the back of that swamp he calls a farm. Maggots in the food, saddle sores, no water for days. He gets the ponies out west, pets of kids who have grown up or lost interest. He hauls them back here and works or beats them to death. Most only last a couple months." She shoved a bulging file folder toward Martin and stood up. "Good luck."

Martin choked down the bite of his burger he had been chewing and yelled at her back, "So Arnie Stem gets the money. What does Earl get out of the deal?"

She turned, one hand on the door.

"Earl? He just likes hitting horses."

Martin presented the story to Lattner to run in the Sunday edition the first weekend in May. This was also the kickoff weekend for the annual Blossomtown festivities, the closest thing Pierre had to a Haj. Lattner had complained every day for the last month about having to cover the weeks of parades, Boy Scout pancake breakfasts, and disturbing toddler beauty pageants, so Martin assumed the editor would welcome the serious exposé.

Instead, Lattner told Martin that he was thinking of dedicating the entire Sunday spread to the blessing of the blossoms, the gathering of Pierre's priests and pastors, and a rabbi—if one could be enticed to make the drive from Chicago—to bless the peach buds in a local orchard, the traditional first Blossomtown event.

"Last week you said it should be called 'the last rites of the blossoms,'" Martin pointed out. Lattner had argued that almost every year, the peach crop was wiped out by a late frost, which often coincided with the Blossomtown closing ceremonies. He had said it gave the area's German Lutheran farmers a socially acceptable excuse for their genetically predisposed depression.

"What about the Blossomtown Tiny Parade of Beauty?" countered Lattner. "The sheriff's grandkid, Becky, is in it. She's a frontrunner."

"It has not escaped my notice," Mrs. Trinkle said, "that Sheriff Arnie Stem's highly average spawn have received extensive coverage in this paper."

"I swam on the team with, what's that scrawny one's name?" said Julie.

"Hank Stem," said Lattner. "So much potential."

"Whatever," said Julie. "You put his sorry ass on the front page. 'PPHS Olympic Hope.' The kid backstroked into the wall his first meet."

Mrs. Trinkle looked up from her typing. "Maybe you're right, Robert. Perhaps Sheriff Stem is as innocent a victim as those poor ponies. He's shown such compassion in other matters, like his leniency in the, how many? Eight? Nine times he has pulled you over for drunk driving?"

Lattner slumped into the chair in front of her desk. "He'll throw me in jail for fifty years."

"Maybe you should stop drinking for a while," Mrs. Trinkle said.

"Or driving," Julie said.

"Just keep my name off the fucking thing," Lattner said.

Martin and Julie climbed the stairs to the *Leader Telegram* offices the Monday after Martin's story ran. They could hear phones ringing before they were halfway to the top. And a bellow, like a bison gut-shot from a west-bound train.

"You tell him to call me when he gets in."

The door above them slammed, glass rattled, and Sheriff Stem barreled down the stairs. Martin reared back at the slap of Old Spice, old cigar, and old cheese that accompanied the sweating uniformed man. Greasy hair, bulging neck, protruding eyes, the sheriff looked as if he were on his way to audition for the part of the law enforcement rube in the next installment of *Smokey and the Bandit*.

At the bottom of the steps, he turned back. "You better watch out, Oliphant. It wouldn't take much to push that mother of yours over the edge."

"Be my guest," Martin said. "I'll just warn you, she's got a mean left hook for an eighty-six pound, semi-comatose invalid."

He and Julie entered the office and greeted a wild-eyed Mrs. Trinkle, standing at her desk, telephone receiver in one hand.

"The answering machine is full," she said. "Your phone has been ringing since I got in. The mayor wants to talk to Lattner. And the sheriff's department is having a press conference about it all at ten. A TV station is coming in from South Bend and maybe one from Detroit. Martin, this is big TV."

Martin accepted a pile of pink slips from Mrs. Trinkle and wandered back to his office, a converted storeroom where he shared desk space with stacks of Xerox paper, but at least it had a door. He shut that now and ignored the clanging of the phone. He closed his eyes. He would let the story play out, cover the press conference, follow up with Treena, maybe a photo of her hugging him in gratitude. He'd package it all up and send it to the *Denver Post,* and they would beg him to come out, join the staff, maybe even the editorial board. They would be surprised when he brought up the idea that, along with his Pulitzer-prize-worthy reporting on travesties of justice and unfathomable wrongs done to the noble oppressed, he would like to start running a column of cowboy poetry. Why not, they would say. Give him a chance, they would say. Genius is as genius does, they would say. Beaufort would see it, call Ginger. Remember Martin Oliphant? How could I forget? I'm going to Denver. She would saddle up her mare, and in the pounding rain, which would make it difficult for Martin to tell if she was crying, but of course she would be, she would ride into the gates of his...

"Martin, phone," Mrs. Trinkle stood in the office doorway.

"Can you take a message?" Martin grabbed a pen and scribbled his own name on a pad.

"It's your mom."

He picked up the phone.

Of course, it wasn't his mom. She hadn't spoken an intelligible word since Bitsy Newport's visit a month before. And she hadn't used the phone for several months prior to that. It was Amoya, the nurse. Martin was needed at home.

"Chopo"
By Jack Thorpe

Through rocky arroyos so dark and so deep,
Down the sides of the mountains so slippery and steep,
You've good judgment, sure footed, wherever you go,
You're a safety conveyance my little Chopo.

Whether single or double or in the lead of a team,
over highways or byways or crossing a stream,
You're always in fix and willing to go,
Whenever you're called on, my chico Chopo.

You're a good roping horse, you were never jerked down;
When tied to a steer, you will circle him round,
Let him once cross the string, and over he'll go,
You sabe the business, my cow horse Chopo.

One day on the Llano, a hail storm began,
The herds were stampeded, the horses all ran,
The lightning it glittered, a cyclone did blow,
But you faced the sweet music, my little Chopo.

Chopo my pony, Chopo, my pride,
Chopo my amigo, Chopo I will ride,
From Mexico's border 'cross Texas Llanos,
To the salt Pecos River, I ride you Chopo.

11

Martin had to pour three cups of highly sugared green tea into Amoya before he could get her to explain the crisis. Through sobs and slurps, she blabbered about the demon Keshi, a mythical horse that Krishna killed. Martin didn't know, nor did he particularly care, how that Hindu archfiend became enmeshed in Amoya's version of Obeah theology. But he did need to understand why she was convinced that Keshi had possessed Dottie's fragile soul.

Amoya told Martin she had run through her morning routine as usual. A sip or two of Geritol for the semi-conscious patient, a warm bath, new diapers and a fresh nightgown, back to bed, where Amoya read aloud, usually the Bible. Today, however, she had decided on the Sunday *Leader Telegram* and Martin's blockbuster story on Dewitty's Delightful Pony Rides.

"She's so proud. She loves you like a son," said Amoya.

"Good to know," said Martin.

Dottie had listened to the story, according to Amoya, with her usual lack of consciousness. But she woke up when the nurse held the front page up to display the byline: by Martin Oliphant.

"She rose in the air like a *Moka Jumbie* and did the zombie dance, yelling, 'Keshi, Keshi, Keshi!'"

"Any chance she was yelling, 'Chopo, Chopo, Chopo'?" Martin said.

Amoya looked at him with wide eyes, held up one broad hand, and guillotined the air three times.

"Like this?" she asked, shook her head no, then said, "Maybe."

Martin knew what his mother had seen. It was not his name in Times New Roman font. No, it was the two pictures below that, before and after shots, in color. One was a corn-husk-hued pony with a light-tan mane rigged out in a purple-and-red woven halter. A tiny girl with blonde braids sat astride the little beast, smiling out from under a red straw cowboy hat. The pony's head angled toward the camera, and it flashed its teeth in what looked like a smile.

The reader was asked to believe that the photo next to that happy scene was of the same horse, which even Martin would have questioned had he not seen the brand himself and talked to its former child owner, now a realtor in Dallas. Nothing suggested the healthy pet in picture one was the broken animal in picture two. Martin had caught Earl in the act of bringing down a board on the pony's swayed back. It was already on its front knees, its head drooped. Earl's mug was tilted toward the camera, and his teeth were bared.

Of course. Dottie saw the pictures, not the byline. She saw, not the granddaughter of a successful Texas oilman atop her birthday present circa 1972, but her young and entirely fictional self atop her beloved Chopo. Martin could only hope she hadn't made the connection between the first and the second pictures, but he feared she had. His mom had been many things in her life—neglectful, jealous, petty, delusional—but she had never, never been stupid.

"Martin?" Dottie's voice floated in from the living room. Martin and Amoya followed it to her bed. She spoke so infrequently, every word was treated by them both as possibly her last. Amoya scrambled for a notebook.

Dottie was up on one elbow, eyes open and sharp. "Not you, Amoya, just Martin." She dropped her head back down but kept her eyes wide. She breathed irregularly. Martin sat beside the bed. There was almost nothing left of the woman he had known, all the chill melted from her cheeks, all the avarice washed from her eyes. Just fever and fear now, and he hated himself for liking her better like this. He turned to the window and the front yard beyond, where three robins pecked at the weeds in the perennial border.

"Martin," Dottie said again, and he felt her hand on his, cold, as if drained of blood. "Earl's got Chopo. You've got to get him back."

Martin returned to the office at the same time as a sweating and grumbling Lattner arrived. "Christ, it must be ten miles from my house," he said. His button-down shirt clung to the concave of his chest. Martin could not stop looking at the silver-dollar-sized nipples poking through the wet and transparent fabric. The man smelled like a feverish bottle of Jack Daniels.

"You walked?" asked Mrs. Trinkle.

"We discussed this," said Lattner.

"You can drive if you don't drink," said Mrs. Trinkle.

"Noted," said Lattner. "Should there come a morning I choose not to drink, I'll keep that in mind."

Julie came around the fabric partition separating her desk from the reception area. "I got you the stuff from the press conference. It was ridiculous. First Mayor Vernon went on about how they take animal abuse very seriously, and these allegations will be investigated, and that birthday party planners should rest assured blah blah blah. All the while, that little turd Earl Dewitty is sitting in the front row in a suit that looks like it came off a Skid Row weatherman. Then Sheriff Stem got up and said that, of course, the laws against animal cruelty would be enforced, but innocent until proven guilty was still the controlling legal principle around here, and that he was not about to start harassing innocent small businessmen on the word of a couple of besotted yellow journalists…"

"He said 'besotted'?" Lattner stood in the doorway to his office. He had removed the sodden shirt. His tie still hung knotted around his bare neck.

"Or something like that," Julie went on. "And he talked about property rights and prayer in schools and putting the 'Christ' back in 'Christmas.'"

"That was it?" said Martin.

"No," said Julie. "That lady from the council spoke, the one whose kid was the glue sniffer."

"Paul Marietta," said Martin. "He was in my class. I think his mom's name is June, or Judy. She taught nursery school at the Y, remember? Paul used to eat paste."

"Elmer's and Magic Markers, gateway drugs," said Lattner. "So what did Councilwoman Judy Marietta say?"

"She said that the council would take up the question of whether to honor their contract with Dewitty's Delightful Pony Rides for the Blossomtown Parade this year at their next meeting," said Julie. "Then two freaks from PPHS shouted something about getting the U.S. out of Nicaragua, and Earl yelled, 'Git out of here you fucking commies,' and the sheriff took the microphone back and said, 'If you want to live in a place without due process where honest businessmen get railroaded out of their honest businesses, then Nicaragua would be a good place to move, and also that if you don't sit down and shut up, I'm going to due process your sorry asses into the county lock up.'" Julie looked at her notes. "I think that's it."

"Mrs. Trinkle," said Lattner. "Can you go to Butlers and get me another shirt? Also stop at the courthouse and find out when the council meeting is. I'll have two editorials for tomorrow, one on Dewitty and one on Nicaragua, again. Not that it will get through the Swiss cheesy craniums of the David Stockman cultists that run this town, but if there is a windmill, I must tilt." He backed into his office with a sweeping bow.

"You going to write up the press conference?" Martin asked Julie. Of course, she would, or should, say no. This was his story. She should hand over her notes, let him make a few calls. He could already picture the look on the *Denver Post* editor's face when he opened Martin's package, a series of clips, Martin's work all, exposing not just a ring of animal abusers, but a city government and constabulary rife with corruption, incompetence, and unprofessional press operations. "What's this?" the editor would mouth and pull on his tortoise-shelled reading glasses. "Why have I not heard of this reporter before?"

"Yeah," Julie said, "I already did it."

Martin blinked out of his reverie, and before the good part when the editor figures out Martin is only twenty-two and willing to relocate to Denver sometime around yesterday. Martin tried to keep the hurt out of his eyes.

"It was just because you weren't here," said Julie, looking concerned, but not concerned enough to turn over the story. "How's your mom?"

"Bad," said Martin. "And Chopo's back."

Martin had to admit Julie's story was decent. It got nowhere near the reaction his story had, though, and was pushed to page three by an outbreak of fires in several peach orchards where farmers had placed smudge pots to stave off another killing frost. The air in town was still tinted gray and smelled of tar two days later when Martin went to cover the council meeting on Dewitty's Delightful Ponies and the Blossomtown Parade. The issue was the only thing on the agenda after the "Official Honoring of the Blossomtown Princesses and

Their Families." The meeting started at six p.m. and Martin hoped the abbreviated agenda would mean he could pick up dinner at Wright's before they shut.

His hopes dimmed as the Alex Baily Council Hall and Community Room filled with Blossomtown princesses—coiffed, polyester wrapped, and sashed—accompanied by family members stuffed into their Easter Sunday best. For a moment, he wished he had eaten dinner at 5:30 as all these people no doubt had. But he need not have worried. The fug of Clearasil and pink bubble gum lip gloss that accompanied the princesses soon smothered any desire he had for Wright's olive-and-mayo burger.

Martin settled in to wait for the council to act on the Dewitty matter. He sat, less and less placidly, through thirty-two votes on thirty-two separate proclamations on the wit and beauty of the thirty-two Pierre County city, township, and village Blossomtown princesses. Martin wondered if this is what it would be like to cover the Politburo.

It was past two a.m. when the final princess, who had been snoring into her green tulle neck ruffle for the last hour, stumbled up to the front for the vote on her resolution and picture with the mayor and the council. As the members returned to their seats, shuffled their papers, and retrieved their coats from their chair backs, Councilwoman Judy Marietta caught Martin's eye.

"Dewitty?" he said.

"Aw, shit," she answered. "One more thing, folks." A few of the council members groaned; one looked wildly about, as if a gaggle of unfeted princesses might be hiding behind the Michigan and U.S. flags.

"I move that we put off the decision on Earl and the parade until the official council visit to his farm on…whenever that is," said a councilman with a stringy black comb-over. He was already in his car coat and halfway out the door.

"May 22nd," said Judy. "And I second. All in favor?" A bunch of raspy ayes. "Then so moved, meeting adjourned."

"Wait," Martin shouted. "What visit?"

The councilwoman slipped on her pink raincoat and belted it. "Arnie asked us to put it off until we could go see the place for ourselves. Seems fair enough."

Martin just stared at her.

"You should have asked me before the meeting, honey. You could have avoided all that princess rigamarole."

"Shit," Martin whispered.

"Unadulterated Blossomtown shit, dear. Give my best to your mother."

Over the next two weeks, Lattner editorialized a few more times on the scandal, the last piece to remind readers there was a scandal. The Blossomtown festivities kicked into full gear with the usual craft fairs and the usual drunken teen formal dances and the usual-yet-still-shocking teen deaths in car accidents after the drunken teen formal dances.

At home, Dottie continued to keen, sometimes for hours at a time, for her Chopo. "I saw him; he's alive. Bring him to me," she wailed, grabbing at her sheets and scratching at her arms until they bled.

Amoya begged Martin to call in a Hoodoo root worker for an exorcism. Martin consulted Dr. Broad instead and asked whether his mom might be better off in a hospital.

"They'll tie her down, Martin. She's more on the dead side of the ledger than on the alive. But I've seen this before. They wait for one last thing, their brother to make it to the bedside or a baby to be born or a spinster daughter to be married off. Is there any way you can get a visit from this Chopo? It's a horse, right? Her horse? I think she might go then."

"Chopo is a literary fiction circa 1908," said Martin. "But she saw a picture of a horse she thought was Chopo. One of Dewitty's."

"Ah," said Dr. Broad. "Well, could you hire him to bring it over? He did my daughter's birthday party, it's got to be twenty years ago. He was very reasonable."

"I don't think that's a possibility." The doctor clearly hadn't read Martin's story.

"Well, that's too bad, because a few minutes with this Chopo, whether it is the real one or not, might be all she needs to pop her over to the other side," Dr. Broad said. "Pop her peacefully," he added.

"Please, Martin," Dottie moaned from her bed. He had thought she was asleep. "Please bring Chopo."

Lattner twisted the wheel of Mr. Trinkle's extended cab F-250, on loan for what they were calling "Operation Chopo," and dodged a deep scar in the dirt road leading to Dewitty's stables. A metal piece of the undercarriage scraped on a rock, and Julie's temple smacked audibly into the passenger side window. Martin could smell horse manure and something else, smoke, maybe a neighbor barbecuing. He experienced a moment of longing for the comfort and certainty of Beaufort's well-ordered tack room, the leather and horse dung tang of the corral, the hardy back slaps of the hands, the sight of Ginger, one long leg swinging over her mare. *What you got going today, city boy?*

But as they got closer, the tableau dissolved, like in a movie when the lover's face melts off to reveal a Russian spy or, in this case, a junk-filled barnyard reeking of sulfur and tar. The shadows blurred the jagged lines of the piles of trash dotted throughout the yard: naked bed springs, a rusted freezer door, a broken black plastic bag spilling open cans, rye bottles, McDonald's wrappers, and rotting lettuce. Martin's nose tingled with the scent of seared meat. It could be the smoldering remnants of trash burned a day or so earlier, though it didn't look like Dewitty had been engaged in much trash disposal recently, or ever. The place was devoid of poetry and hope. Also devoid of people, which was fine as far as their mission went, and devoid of ponies, which was not.

"Do you think he ran for it?" Martin asked. "Cut and run before they found out how bad it really was?" The council's inspection tour was scheduled for the next afternoon.

Lattner shook his head. "The rumor at The Silver Dollar is that he's gone out West to pick up some healthier horse flesh."

"What did he do with the ones he had?" Martin asked. Julie opened her window, sniffed at the smoky air, looked at Martin, drew a finger across her throat.

The smell. Against his better judgment, Martin said, "Smudge pots?"

"Okay," Julie answered. "If that's what you want."

Martin slumped back in his seat. Of course, it would be a relief if Earl Dewitty was out of town. What would not be was if Dewitty had offed the Chopo lookalike on his way. Hard to rustle a dead horse.

And they needed to rustle Chopo, or a reasonable facsimile, if Dottie was to go in peace. Martin would carry her into the sunset on his own back if he could, but he couldn't. He had tried for ten months. Ten months of walking her to death's door, holding her hand, urging her along, assuring her it would all be fine, wiping the snot from under her nose, and making sure she didn't wet herself along the way. He had done it as well as he knew how, he had tried and sacrificed and not been thanked nearly enough, and yet she would not go, not without Chopo. He needed Chopo. He hated Chopo.

Unbidden, a verse from "The Cowboy's Lament" popped into his head, and he mouthed the words as Lattner navigated around the potholes and fallen branches and pulled onto a patch of bare dirt next to Dewitty's barnyard.

My curse let it rest, let it rest on the fair one,
Who drove me from friends that I loved and from home,
Who told me she loved me, just to deceive me.
My curse rests upon her, wherever she roam.

Julie jumped out of the truck and strode toward the barn for a few steps, stopped, turned.

"Are you coming?" she said.

"I think breaking and entering violates my parole," said Lattner.

"And horse theft doesn't?" said Julie. "What parole? Oh, forget it. God."

She stood, hands on hips that were significantly narrower than they had been last March. She'd been drinking less, eating better, playing tennis with Frank several times a week after work. She'd even spoken to Bitsy, quickly and by chance, but without fisticuffs. Martin had witnessed the encounter from across Main Street where he had just picked up tuna sandwiches for their lunch from Dino's Deli. He couldn't hear what words were spoken but saw Julie bend her head to her mother's hand, and Bitsy raise her hand to her daughter's cheek. He didn't ask, and Julie didn't give him details, just berated him for forgetting to request extra garlic dills. The scene had made him feel the impending loss of his own mom more keenly than he ever had before.

"You don't have to do this," said Martin.

"I want to," said Julie. "Your mom is kind of my hero. I've never met anyone like her before, who knows who she's supposed to be and goes for it."

"She's delusional, you know," said Martin.

"I guess," said Julie. "Anyway, it is an honor to do something for her."

Julie was braver than he was, Martin thought, part in admiration, part in irritation. Was she the one to whom the poem referred, the fair one who had deceived him? She had abandoned his mom, despite her revived interest now, and tried to steal his job. She was losing weight, which felt like an unspoken reproach. She was enjoying Frank's company, finding the good in him, another reproach. Martin couldn't deny she had helped him, was helping him. But he had never loved her. Lusted, yes. Liked, yes. Loved, no.

She resumed her march to the stables. Lattner and Martin got out of the truck. Lattner leaned on the back bumper and hooked his thumbs in his belt. Martin watched Julie enter the dark barn. Her blonde hair disappeared into the gloom of a half-opened wooden door, like a candle snuffed at fifty yards.

"Hope she took a flashlight," said Lattner.

The deceiver couldn't be Ginger either, thought Martin. They had never talked of love, or really of much at all but cowboy poetry and his University of Chicago elitist and, he now realized, ridiculous views on philosophy and utopic world order. If anything, he had deceived her, eschewed her company, and maybe the start of love, for the immediate gratification served up by Julie. He had no reason to curse Ginger, and maybe she had some reason to curse him, though he suspected he had not made that much of an impression.

"Found him." Julie's muffled voice carried from inside the dark stables.

Oh, why fight it? Martin knew who the fair one was, had known it for a while now. Cowboy poetry. Sweet, singing, always promising more, more for Martin, more sky, more air, more love. Always promising, always singing in his ear of a place where wit and honesty and a strong handshake and a way with rhyme was enough to get you the girl and a plot of land where you could husband your own destiny. Cowboy poetry and its lies and its false, false promises trapping his poor, shallow, grasping mom in its soft leather riding gloves, choking the old woman to death, making him an accessory to the crime. Cow-boy poetry was the whore. The callous whore. *Her heart was as cold as the snow on the mountains.*

"I suppose we ought to go help," said Lattner and moved not an inch.

Once they figured out the horse was starving, they had no problem moving ersatz Chopo. Julie held a Red Delicious from the bag she had brought along in front of the snorting animal's nose. She did a slow, and to Martin's eye, dangerous dance, waving the fruit, then jumping back as the pony bared its yellow teeth and lunged at her outstretched fingers. He flashed back for a moment to the beach at Twin Bluffs, when Julie risked her life to save Buster and Martin did naught. This time, he'd be an equal partner in the equine rescue and maybe even the hero he could not be four years ago.

As Julie inched her way across the dark and open paddock toward the truck, Martin joined Lattner and prepared to load the beast. They pulled out the two-by-fours that Mrs. Trinkle had thought to add to the pick-up bed to serve as a makeshift ramp.

"Shit," Lattner barked. "Splinter."

Martin hushed him, and Lattner answered, "No need, James Bond, we're the only ones here. Us and that probably rabid nag waltzing with Julie."

Julie worked her way to the end of the plank leading into the truck bed. The pony dove at her, and she jumped behind the wooden boards.

"How are we supposed to get it up there?" Julie asked, crouching lower as the pony snarled. "It would help, Mr. Cowboy Poetry, if you had some idea how to get the harness on."

Martin sighed. "The body of work with which I am familiar is heavier on lyricism than on practical advice. It's got a lead rope on." He nodded toward the noose around the animal's neck. Lattner, a finger to his lips, tiptoed to the side of the horse and made a grab for the loose end of the rope. The pony kicked laterally and viciously at Lattner's hand, missing it, but just barely.

"Wow, he must be double-jointed," Lattner said.

Julie tossed the apple to Martin. "Throw it in the cab. Maybe he'll go after it."

Chopo's rectangle of a head swung toward Martin and a rope of spittle from its foaming mouth slapped his shoulder. The pony's eyes were bleeding red, and it gurgled and growled. Amoya had been right: the demon Keshi. Martin relayed the apple into the back of the truck, and the pony leapt up the ramp in two hops. Lattner kicked the boards away and slammed the tailgate.

"He's so hungry," said Julie. They watched the pony finish the apple in one bite then submerge its snout into a bucket of water.

The pony's back glistened. Someone had put some sort of salve on his saddle sores, the ones that had made a front-page appearance over Martin's story, and they looked a little better. But the animal had had no food for days, it seemed.

"Why do you think Dewitty left just him?" Julie asked, tossing another apple into the truck bed.

"He was on the front page and not looking too good," Martin said. "It's going to be kind of suspicious if he's not around for the big inspection."

Martin watched the pony drain the bucket and wondered how long he had been without water. Dewitty was a cruel man and a stupid man. If whatever he had cooked up to fool the council was this half-assed, Martin could count on penning a nice dénouement to the first expose within the week. That is, of course, unless he was busy planning a funeral. That was the point of this, after all, sending his mom off to the "Grand Roundup, where the cowboys with others must stand." Maybe after, he would adopt Chopo, find a nice stable near town to house him, let him eat apples and rest out his days, which, given that he looked about three-hundred-years old and not well, had to be numbered.

Julie dumped the rest of the bag of apples in the back of the truck and Faux Chopo rooted around for them, snarling and sneezing.

"Not too grateful," she said. "Let's get out of here while he's occupied."

Lattner bumped the truck down Dewitty's long driveway and back onto paved roads, though not the main ones, lest some night owl catch sight of the captive in the rear, who was not going along with the caper quietly. Having finished off the last of the apples, the pony had taken to kicking at the tailgate with his back hooves.

Julie maneuvered on the back seat's cracked plastic bench and peered out the rear window into the cab. "He's putting some nice dents in there. Won't Mrs. Trinkle be angry?"

"She hasn't driven this since Mr. Trinkle went," said Lattner.

"When did he die?" asked Martin, as always, amazed at his own self-involvement. He had never thought to ask.

"He didn't die. He moved to Cabo," said Lattner, "with his lover, Maurice McJunkin."

"The Harley guy?" said Martin.

"Yeah," said Lattner. "She goes down there for vacations, stays with them. Nice condo. I've seen pictures."

Martin nodded, struck speechless by one of those glimpses of the great chasm of complications and connections that are other people's lives. The rest of the ride passed in silence, save for the clang of hoof on metal and the putter of the F-250's engine.

When they reached Martin's, Lattner backed into the driveway. The plan was to bring Dottie out through the garage, open the door, give her a quick look at Chopo in the back of the truck, settle her back into her deathbed, return the horse, and get back in time for *Saturday Night Live*. Martin went around to the front door and was surprised to find it locked and the house lights off. Carroll was away on business, as he was most of the time these days, and Martin had not wanted Amoya to stay for this. He was pretty sure that witnessing Keshi in the flesh might push the kind woman over the edge. That left Frank to babysit while they were gone, not much to ask, Martin had thought.

He found his key and was jiggling the lock when Julie came around the corner. "Hurry up, the beast is getting restless," she said. Martin heard a loud whinny.

"Frank, the asshole, isn't here." He pushed open the door and picked up the note on the hall rug.

mom a
    sleep at
rons

Julie looked over his arm at the scrawl. "A regular ee cummings, our Frank," she said.

"He couldn't spare a couple hours from his busy life of skipping class and smoking pot? Mom could have died," said Martin.

"Well, that's the point, right?" said Julie.

Martin winced. So maybe it was. He didn't want his mom to die. He didn't want her to live. He felt a molten sphere of anger form underneath his rib cage. It was unspeakable, all this. Unspeakable and unfair. Even the cowboy poets had nothing to say. How was he supposed to know what to do? Where was the trail map that showed him how to live, or her how to die, on this forsaken mountain route, so cruel and so hopeless?

"Is that you?" Dottie's voice floated from the dark living room.

"Yeah," Martin and Julie answered in unison. She probably hadn't meant either of them.

"Time to meet your Chopo," said Julie, pulling the wheelchair out of the front hall closet, unfolding it, and pushing it to the hospital bed.

"C'mon, Mom, let's go see Chopo." He lifted her from the bed and set her in the wheelchair.

She started to cry. "Thank you, thank you."

She kept up a sort of sobbing, laughing, and chanting as they pushed through the hall, the den, and out the door into the garage. Martin wanted to slap her. He wanted to hold her. He wanted to be held by her. He punched the garage door opener.

The door let out a last groan and settled into its overhead berth. Faux Chopo's head hung over the tailgate, and a gray tongue lolled out between black lips. A little in front of that stood Lattner, looking quite pleased with himself, holding the end of the rope around Faux Chopo's neck.

"Impressive," said Martin.

"Your pony," said Lattner, with a bow to Dottie. The rope tightened and the horse tossed his head and coughed.

"Don't kill him, Christ," said Julie.

"Oh, Chopo," said Martin's mom.

Martin wheeled her toward the tailgate. She reached for the pony's flailing head, leaned forward in the chair. Julie placed her hand on the frail woman's shoulder.

Martin hesitated. He wasn't sure he ought to push her within reach of the animal's clattering teeth.

"Forward, Martin. I want to touch him," Dottie said. Martin

snapped to and pushed. His mom's voice had not rung so clear in over a year.

Faux Chopo, perhaps sensing this moment might provide his salvation, perhaps even recognizing the once-girl in blonde pig tails who had sat so softly on his back so many Texas summers ago; that girl who was not now Dottie Oliphant, but no matter. This whole charade depended on everyone playing a role not really theirs, a role dictated by that muse of muses, that temptress of temptresses, that promiser of open ranges and deliverer of, in the end, just words. Cowboy poetry.

"Put me on Chopo. I want to ride him." Dottie again. And she was on her feet and out of the wheelchair, striding—striding!—toward the truck. "Give me the rope, Robert, and open the back."

"Don't give her the rope," Martin yelled.

Dottie had made it to the back of the truck, reached up, and patted the pony firmly on the nose. It took this without budging, perhaps as stunned as the rest of them at the sight of what had been, seconds ago, mostly corpse, now transformed into the Pecos River Queen, ready to unload her trusty cutter and get started on the cow work.

Lattner did not hand her the rope, something he raised in his defense later, but he did drop it when he figured out what Dottie intended to do. He dropped it and lunged toward the woman but too late. She flicked open the latch with a practiced hand and let the gate fall.

"Out you come, dear Chopo," said Dottie, and, clearly annoyed that the pony wasn't heeding, reminded him:

You're always in fix and willing to go
Whenever you're called on, my chico Chopo.

As Dottie Oliphant's last earthly words echoed among the lawn mowers and rusted bikes in the garage, the pony sunk back on his haunches and jumped.

It would be many years before Lattner would talk to Martin about the specifics of what happened that night, and Julie never would. For Martin, forever, it would flip through his head like a washed-out slideshow, each flash of scene marked with a scream, a wail, a crack of hoof on skull, a crack of bat on bone.

There: his mom upright, open arms to the airborne animal, then a pile of flesh, horse and human, on the concrete, the pony's front hoof in a spray of blood. The striations on the horse's hoof, the chink before the horseshoe, remembered in detail, no memory at all of its crash into his mother's skull.

There: Chopo crumbled in front of him, Dottie's arm stretched on the driveway, one hand opened and lightly cupped on top of the kitty litter spread to soak up spilled car oil.

There: his childhood Louisville Slugger leaning against the garage wall.

There: his fist on the handle. Not his fist. A fist.

There: the arc the bat defines. Again. Again.

There: the blood and mane and blood and one red eye dangling down.

There: two deaths, not one. Martin's fury draining, mingling with horse blood, Dottie's blood. Julie's screams fading.

There and there and there, always there, putting it all to music. Cowboy poetry.

Beat your drums lightly, play your fifes merrily,
Sing your death march as you bear me along,
Take me to the graveyard, lay the sod o'er me.
I'm a young cowboy and know I've done wrong.

INTERLUDE

In May of 1986, the Second Annual Elko Cowboy Poetry Conflu-ence concluded on the same day Dottie's funeral was held in Pierre. Martin recited Herbert Henry Knibb's "Where the Ponies Come to Drink" over her casket, which was closed. Even the eldest and most skilled Stark brother of the Stark Family Funeral Home could not reconstruct the crushed skull Dottie was said to have sustained when tumbling from her bed on her last day in this mortal realm.

On that Saturday, Martin listened to a cowboy poet named Vess Guffry host an NPR special featuring clips from several of the con-fluence's performances. This was the first *Cowboy Poetry Hour*, the weekly two-hour Saturday night live variety show that, for the next thirty years, would popularize the Western arts among public radio lis-teners. In each of those years, the *Cowboy Poetry Hour* would broadcast live from the Annual Elko Cowboy Poetry Confluence, Vess Guffry would never miss an Elko show, and Martin would tune into all but the last.

In May of 1987, Martin again didn't go to Elko, as he had intended. He stayed in Pierre to cover Earl Dewitty's trial on charges of ani-mal cruelty, fraud, bribery, breach of contract, and criminal battery. The year before, Councilwoman Judy Marietta had stumbled over the mangled body of a dead pony on her way down the back path to Earl's porta potty before the council's inspection of the Dewitty's Delightful Ponies' stables. Dewitty had tried to stem her hysteria by slapping her repeatedly. He got twenty years.

In May of 1988, Martin went as far as to inquire via post after tickets to the Fourth Annual Elko Cowboy Poetry Confluence, but before he received an answer, Julie decided to move to Denver to study to be a vet tech at Colorado State, and Martin stayed in Pierre to help her pack.

In May of 1989, Martin planned to drive cross-country to Elko, but two days before he set out, his right foot was crushed by a runaway Shriner's minibike at the Blossomtown parade, and he was unable to make the trip.

In May of 1990, Martin went west, but not to Elko. He and his father attended Frank's college graduation. They stayed two weeks, during which Martin discovered Julie was living with Frank in his one-bedroom apartment.

In May of 1991, Martin again went to Denver rather than Elko. This time, it was to explore taking on, with Frank, a chain of sports equipment stores Carroll had pillaged from two elderly brothers. It took Martin exactly four days to figure out he neither cared about nor comprehended the capillary action of various wicking athletic bras. Frank, on the other hand, was a natural. Carroll turned the stores over to Frank, Frank renamed them "Frank's," and Martin returned to his job at the *Leader Telegram*.

In May of 1992, the Eighth Annual Elko Cowboy Poetry Confluence was not an option for Martin. Its final days coincided with Julie's wedding to Frank on the deck of the Newport's home on the shores of Lake Michigan. Martin served as best man.

From May of 1993 through May of 1996, Martin hardly thought of the Ninth through the Twelfth Annual Elko Cowboy Poetry Confluences. He had latched onto the Serenity Prayer from a scrap of the AA literature Mrs. Trinkle often provided Lattner, and Lattner always threw out. Martin decided to accept his absence from Elko as a thing he could not change. He dated a former Blossomtown queen and current orthodontic hygienist, practiced TM, listened regularly but with only half an ear to the *Cowboy Poetry Hour* (though he always caught the live Elko broadcast), and considered taking up jogging. The hygienist ran off with her boss in December of 1996, and Martin began ordering cowboy poetry books off Amazon.com.

In May of 1997, Martin scotched his plans to attend the Thirteenth Annual Elko Cowboy Poetry Confluence after Carroll suffered a heart attack that kept him in the ICU for twenty-three days.

In May of 1998, Martin listened to the Cowboy Poet's live show from the Fourteenth Annual Elko Cowboy Poetry Confluence from Carroll's room at the Baroda Better Acres, a very nice home for the demented. Carroll had moved there only the day before, at Frank's insistence.

In May of 1999, Martin did not attend the Fifteenth Annual Elko Cowboy Poetry Confluence in a fit of pique. He had decided the previous January, he would apply to perform and was rejected by the Fifteenth Annual Elko Cowboy Poetry Confluence Selection Committee the following March.

By May of 2000, Martin had begun to soften and even eyed with some enthusiasm last-minute airfare deals to Salt Lake City, a short drive, by high desert standards, to Elko. But in the second to last week of that month, Lattner, who had diagnosed the *Leader Telegram* with terminal intellectual and financial degradation a decade before, put the paper out of its misery with one last issue published on Sunday, May 23, 2000. In it, he memorialized in ink each rumor, slander, morsel of gossip, and indelicate confession that each bastion, official, and blow-hard in the greater Pierre metropolitan area had whispered, disclosed, or bragged of to Lattner in his thirty-plus years of drinking at The Silver Dollar. The morning the final edition came out, Lattner disappeared, leaving only a collection of Jägermeister bottles dating back to the 1930s, a burgundy leather couch in remarkably good condition, and a 1984 edition of *Roget's Thesaurus*. Martin spent the week of the Sixteenth Annual Elko Cowboy Poetry Confluence consoling Mrs. Trinkle, fending off defamation lawsuits, and filing for bankruptcy.

In May of 2001, Martin passed the week of the Seventeenth Annual Elko Cowboy Poetry Confluence helping Carroll to fulfill his dying wish: to see his son Frank at the helm of his own thriving business. Martin and Carroll, who should not have been allowed to travel, travelled to the Denver suburb of Greenwood City to spend six days in Frank and Julie's over-air-conditioned family and guest rooms.

In May of 2002, during the week of the Eighteenth Annual Elko Cowboy Poetry Confluence, Martin read Sharlot Hall's "Beyond the Range" at Carroll's funeral. Martin chose the work less for the poet's final words of religious redemption than for its third stanza paean to the art of rapine:

> *Now, stake for me a last, last claim*
> *And lay them there to rest,*
> *The trailworn feet, the weary hands,*
> *The still heart in my breast.*
> *Earth's last prospecting trip is done,*
> *But somewhere, strong and sure,*
> *My spirit seeks the motherlode*
> *Whose treasure shall endure.*

In May of 2003, Martin hardly had time to tune into the *Cowboy Poetry Hour*'s coverage of the Nineteenth Annual Elko Cowboy Poetry

Confluence. He had, early in that month, finally rented out his child-hood home and moved to a second-floor apartment above Murphy's Cameras in downtown Pierre. Further, the Confluence coincided with several meetings with the local bank and Frank, via Skype, over the level of investments necessary to render Final Paws Pet Mortuary 'n Cemetery, Martin's bequest from his father, a functioning financial concern.

In May of 2004, Martin spent the week of the Twentieth Annual Elko Cowboy Poetry Confluence in Pierre rather than Elko, comfort-ing Julie, who had returned to her childhood home to recover from a double mastectomy, chemotherapy, and divorce.

In May of 2005, Martin again traveled west as far as Denver, but not as far as Elko, for Frank's marriage to CeeCi Seaborne, former head of athletic footwear sales at Frank's Sporting Goods and present motivational speaker.

From May of 2006 to May of 2013, Martin, sometimes adamantly, sometimes resignedly, put traveling to the Twenty-Second through the Twenty-Ninth Annual Elko Cowboy Poetry Confluences out of his mind, though he stayed devoted to the art form itself. He continued to apply to perform each year, and his applications continued to be rejected.

In May of 2014, Martin spent the week of the Thirtieth Annual Elko Cowboy Poetry Confluence in Cabo, visiting Mrs. Trinkle, her ex-husband, Paul, and his lover Maurice.

In May of 2015, Martin was again in Cabo instead of Elko, this time for Mrs. Trinkle's burial at sea. He recited Arthur Chapman's "Men in the Rough" over her batik-shrouded body.

Men in the rough—on the trails all new-broken—
Those are the friends we remember with tears;
Few are the words that such comrades have spoken—
Deeds are their tributes that last through the years.

Men in the rough, prairie and mountain—
Children of nature, warm-hearted, clear-eyed;
Friendship with them is a never-sealed fountain;
Strangers are they to the altars of pride.

Men in the rough—curt of speech to their fellows—
Ready in everything, save to deceive;
Theirs are the friendships that time only mellows,
And death cannot sever the bonds that they weave.

THE THIRD HORSE:

ZACH

D. 2015

Martin stood at the entrance to his childhood home and watched Bev Pitzke of Pierre Premier Households wrestle a For Sale sign out of the back seat of her Jetta. It was only mid-September, but already someone was burning leaves, and the smoke registered in the cold tip of his nose, like all those dry winter smells do.

"Need some help?" Martin called, hoping he'd waited long enough for the answer to be no.

"I got it," she said. She leaned into the car and tugged left then right, her helmet of slate hair bobbing in time with her shoulders, like a metronome clicking out the cadence of her continued patter: "Just...need...to...get...it...over...the hump and, whoopsie-daisy, here it goes." She staggered backwards onto the front walk and hoisted the sign, almost as tall she, which was not very. "Nils put the post hole in yesterday, so we don't have to worry about that," she said, lugged the sign onto the lawn, and propped it up with another robust "whoopsie-daisy," stepped back, and added one more "whoopsie-daisy," this one quiet and thoughtful, in the tone of visitors to St. Peter's coming on Michelangelo's *Pieta* for the first time.

Or maybe Martin just heard it that way. Because everything about this moment felt epochal. Because, more than he had wanted but exactly as he had expected, the evening's task, finally putting the Oliphant home on the market, hollowed him out. His heart pounded in his throat and his breath came in whistling gasps. He put a hand on one of the front portico's faux pillars to stop himself from charging the tiny realtor, chasing her back to the VW, and chucking her sign through the rearview window.

Renting out the place after his dad died had been so much easier. Mrs. Priebe arranged it all: lined up Dr. Sharma and his family, just arrived from India, to occupy the house; got rid of all the furniture, via Goodwill and a yard sale, except the kitchen table and chairs, which the Sharmas kept because they fit the space so nicely; handed over the rent collection and maintenance scheduling to a young local lawyer, who had just opened his own practice and needed the work. Martin had only visited once in the last thirteen years, a reception for the Sharmas' eldest son newly graduated from Columbia Medical School. In a haze of curry fumes and tandoori smoke and through the crowd of what had to be three-quarters of the Swinehurst Hospital staff and all of the Sharmas' home state of Goa, Martin recognized little. It was like one of those dreams where the familiar was still familiar and also decidedly not.

"This is where our piano used to be," he had found himself telling a pre-teen girl in a red silk half-sari over a sequined blue blouse.

"That's Vishnu," she said, inclining her head toward the statue that was the current occupant of the plot. Martin half-bowed to the god, and the girl smiled him a mouthful of braces and darted off. He left the party five minutes later.

It wasn't that he wanted to keep the house for himself. As far back as the summer he left Chicago and moved back in, he felt his presence here in this red brick colonial, in Pierre at all, was temporary, a way-point on the long and one-way expedition west. He still felt it. And because of that, guilt—guilt that he had never been able to do more than squat in this, his ancestral home.

"We're going to lose our light soon." Bev materialized next to Martin's elbow, toting an armful of shiny blue folders. "Maybe we should start looking around without Judy."

"Julie," said Martin. "And I want to wait for her." He didn't care that he sounded brusque. He hadn't wanted to use Bev. She wasn't from Pierre, had moved here only a few years ago after marrying the State Farm Insurance rep, Stephen Pitzke. He'd been on the PPHS swim team with Julie, and she argued to Martin that Bev's ignorance of the house's history would make it easier for her to sell it. Perhaps, he thought, but it would also make it impossible for her to value it. Julie was the one who had wanted to put it on the market, though, so he acceded to her.

"That's got to be her," said Bev. A white Chevy Cruze, pulsing with rental car vibe, rounded the corner into the cul-de-sac and skidded to a stop a millimeter behind the Jetta's bumper. Julie emerged from the driver's seat clutching a paper bag. Even at twenty yards, Martin could spot the familiar black neck of a Christian Brothers brandy bottle poking out of the top.

"Great, let's start here," Bev said. "Meticulous landscaping, mature trees with well-tended auxiliary plantings. I'm just going to put these inside." She pointed her chin at her folders and stepped in the front door.

"Nice to meet you too," Julie said to Bev's back and pulled Martin into a hug. She had to stretch past his sixty-inch waist, maintained since high school, and her 36D chest, acquired after her 2003 bilateral mastectomy, and could just reach around his neck. She still managed to clock him with the liquor bottle at the base of his skull, and he saw stars. "I hope you still have our tumblers in there," she said into his ear.

"Julie." Bev rematerialized on the porch, hand extended, whitened front teeth beaming like tractor headlamps. "Stephen talks about you all the time."

"Really," said Julie. "Because I've been clear with him, phone sex is as far as I'll go with a married man." She locked eyes with Bev for a moment, then matched her frozen smile, Julie's teeth smaller but just as iridescent. "Let's do this," she said.

Martin had never bought or sold real estate before, so he was happy to leave to Bev and Julie the negotiations over what would get fixed, repainted, or discounted. They feinted and dodged like Siamese fighting fish in adjacent tanks, ready to go all in should somehow the glass walls come down. Julie seemed to be winning on points and only stumbled once in her absolute certainty about the maintenance requirements and outstanding features of a house she hadn't been in for over twenty years. It happened in the driveway.

"Have you thought about resurfacing this?" Bev gestured at a constellation of blotches on the concrete, most of which were motor oil but one or two of which might have been blood.

"No," said Martin.

"Never," said Julie.

"We tried kitty litter a long time ago," said Martin.

"That's an urban legend," said Bev. "I think redoing it will get you your investment back and then some. The oil stains interrupt an otherwise yummy street-to-ingress eye feel."

"That's not happening," Julie said. "It's not oil, not all of it. It's blood, and it needs to stay there. Like a memorial." She looked past Bev with wide eyes, and Martin knew she was seeing the truck, the horse, Dottie, him. And blood.

Bev's smile reversed to a frown, and Martin thought he could hear her cheeks creak with the unaccustomed unfurling. "Someone died here?" she said.

Martin and Julie spoke at once: "No." Then Julie: "A pet did, a cat. The family cat. Martin's brother, Frank, he ran it over. Tragic." She blinked, as if trying to wake up from a nap she hadn't meant to take.

"Our beloved cat," said Martin, shaking his head.

Bev put a hand on his arm. "I understand. Stephen and I have four kitty-babies, and we love them like they were real live babies. What was your kitty's name?"

"Chopo," said Martin.

"Dottie," said Julie. "I loved her like a mother."

"Dottie," said Martin.

"Say no more," said Bev. "Let's go inside and talk about the diminishing role of mullioned windows in the twenty-first century."

After two hours of searching for fuse box labels, counting rings on ceiling water spots, and scouting a location for a future basement bar, Bev left Julie and Martin at the kitchen table to mull over the listing agreement and a pamphlet titled "Motivated Seller, Monetized Asset." As soon as Martin heard the front door click shut, he shoved the paperwork away and cracked open the Christian Brothers. He took a slug from the bottle and leaned back, head swimming in nostalgia and the burped-up almond aroma of heavily fermented grapes. Julie lifted the bottle from Martin's hands and poured a good five inches into a Starbucks to-go cup she had retrieved from the Chevy.

"So you can drop the papers off?" Julie said. "And mail me my copy. I'm going back tomorrow, early."

Martin frowned. "I was going to take you to Tommy's for brunch. It's new downtown, with a chef from Chicago who was on some reality show about circus freaks and pâtissiers, though I don't think he's either. But bottomless mimosas and the crab cakes are good."

"I got a job, starts Monday," said Julie. "A vet in Conifer. Also, the Inn at the Lake is almost $300 a night. Gluten-free muffins for breakfast and five o'clock wine-and-nibbles. In Pierre, who would have thought?"

"Money's bad?" Martin said.

"The settlement's mostly gone, except for my half of your house," said Julie, then buried her nose in her cup and slurped. For the last decade, she had lived off the lump-sum payment Frank had offered

to avoid a family court fight. She rented a converted loft in Denver's
LoDo neighborhood, blogged about breast reconstruction, founded
a feminist beer tasting group, volunteered with the ASPCA, and occasionally made noises about upgrading her vet tech BA from Colorado
State into a VMD. Martin assumed she was content. He probably
should have checked on that assumption once in a while, but they
didn't have that sort of friendship.

"I could give you a loan," said Martin. In truth he couldn't, so he
pursed his lips hard and tried to signal to her subconscious that she
should refuse. He had recently put Final Paws into substantial debt to
purchase a top-of-the-line pet incineration system.

"It's okay," said Julie, her cup in front of her face, her voice echo-
ing mournfully in the paper chamber. "Like Bev says, the house will
sell. And the job at the vet's isn't bad. Housing's cheaper in Conifer,
and I get health insurance." She put the cup down and poured another
measure. The bottle was a quarter gone, and Martin had only had one
sip.

"Fuck, I need this," she said and gulped at the brandy. "And I'm
sorry about that freak out in the driveway. I'm not sure why it got to
me. I've been looking forward to coming here again, which wouldn't
have been true not that long ago." She stared into her brandy. "I used
to have nightmares about being in this house, worse after I got cancer.
But they stopped in the last few months."

"Maybe you've moved on?" said Martin, who still had those nightmares.

"No. It's because I've been trying to figure out what the hell I'm
going to do with the rest of my life. I realize that living here, well, that
was a good few months for me. It was a happy time, right?"

Martin folded his hands and stared down at his knuckles a full
minute before answering: "I'm not sure *happy* is the word I would
pick." He thought about Julie back then, what a disaster she'd been. A
motherless anti-waif, drinking, eating, and keening her way around the
sick-smelling psych ward that had been this house.

"We were doing something," said Julie. "I knew who I was, even
if I was a mess. We got that Dewitty story. We pulled off the Chopo
heist. That might not have gone as planned, but it was grand, like
the end of a Shakespeare play, or an X-Men movie, or one of your

poems. For a while, I was really good at being me. I was good at taking care of your mom. I was good at being a reporter. I was good at veterinary science. I was even a good wife for Frank. And then the fucking cancer."

"Just like my mom," said Martin, remembering Dottie's brief heyday with the Fuzzy Balls. He put the bottle to his lips, thought better of it, set it back on the table and kept his hand around its neck.

"Not just like. She got to die. I got to become a survivor." Julie said it as if she were Gregor Samsa complaining of becoming a cockroach.

"Isn't being a survivor the point?" Martin said.

Julie shook her head, then made a sound in her throat like she was winding up to spit. She reached across the table, wrenched the bottle away from Martin, filled her cup almost to the top, and began to rail against the "breast cancer industrial complex," the barbarism of current medical treatment protocols, and all things pink. Martin would have many chances over the next eight months to rehear her rant, and it would always contain the same premise: that breast cancer survivors were the lepers of the twenty-first century, isolated on rose-tinted islands of infirmity by the cruel compassion of those who walked for the cure, ran for the cure, sang for the cure, stood up for the cure, but never actually cured anything.

"The cancer's gone, though, right?" said Martin. "You look great." She did look good, if not great, even in her borderline hysteria. Certainly better. Her hair was a little thinner, but still blond and long again. She had none of the pinched demeanor that Bitsy Newport had had, with less excuse, at the same age.

"They'll never tell you it's gone," said Julie. "The few nice docs will give you a thumbs-up and a NED, no evidence of disease. Most of the others don't say anything, just check over your file to make sure your advanced medical directive is in order. They want you to thank them for your *survival*, wear your goddamn pink ribbon like it's a purple heart, and they were the ones who provided the covering fire while you crawled into the machine gunners' nest. But surviving is worse than dying. It's spending your days doing full body mole checks and reading WebMD. It turns you into a narcissist at the cellular level, on constant guard against that one allele that will betray you. I'm done with it. I want to reset to the Christmas I showed up here. I want to be of use again, feel what it's like to take care of someone else, to accomplish something. I want to have a plan for my life, like you do, Martin. I want to help you like I helped your mom."

"But I'm not dying," said Martin. In fact, he had recently had an annual physical during which Dr. Broad's replacement, Dr. Bonnie Sun, informed Martin that he might be the only man in the U.S. of his age and weight class not required to be on HMG-CoA reductase inhibitors.

"Of course not, you ghoul," said Julie. "I didn't help your mom die. The cancer did that all on its own, with that little last nudge from Chopo. I'm talking about helping you reach your dream, get to your poetry thing. The cowboy poet compadres."

"The Elko Cowboy Poetry Confluence," said Martin.

"Right," said Julie. "Anyway, when we were in Cabo, you said you thought this was your year. I want to help you get there."

Martin didn't remember saying that to Julie, but he probably had. Since Mrs. Trinkle's funeral, he'd felt optimistic about his chance of capturing a spot at Elko next May. In Cabo, he had recited "Men in the Rough" with such verve that it left tears in the eyes of even the waiters passing the light apps to the mourners on the beach in front of the Hacienda Cocina y Cantina. He sensed that, finally, his voice was strong enough to impress the Elko Cowboy Poetry Confluence Selection Committee—strong enough to ring among real cowboy poets and to be heard by the champions of his youth and his still youthful heart: Beaufort and Ginger.

But that had nothing to do with Julie, not anymore, not for a long time. Cowboy poetry was his quest, his obsession, and now it would be his victory. He was sorry she had had cancer. He was sorry Frank had ditched her. He was sorry she was lost. She was a good friend, probably his best friend. But why was it always he who had to step aside, alter his course, to clear the trail for another? Why did he always have to share?

He picked up the bottle, took a sip, and pushed it back to her. He wanted to say no but in a way that honored their past, preserved their future, and kept her from screaming at him. He didn't have those words yet, and he hoped his silence would speak for him. After a few minutes of Julie drinking and chattering, he realized she was taking his stony negative for a humble positive. She had come prepared with a list of ideas on how he could improve his application to the selection committee: a professionally shot test video; an article or two on cowboy poetry in Western-themed literary magazines; some cowboy resume-building activities like lessons in rope braiding or horseback riding.

Though he answered her only with grunts and nods, her enthusiasm didn't flag, even as her voice slowed and slurred. With about an inch left in the bottle, it occurred to Martin that, since Jimmy Sneedle's, he had not had a discussion about cowboy poetry of this length with another human, certainly not a discussion in which he listened more than he spoke. And he liked it. And her ideas were pretty good. Maybe this was one of those situations so rare in Martin's life that he had thought the breed extinct: a win-win.

About the time Martin was ready to agree outright to Julie's proposed alliance, she put her head on the table and began to snore. He gathered up Bev's paperwork, placed the empty bottle in the sink, and shut out the lights. He dug Julie's keys out of the chaos of lipstick and paper wads at the bottom of her purse, half-carried her to her car, and drove her back to the Inn, wrangling her up the wide plank stairs and depositing her in the foyer. He was halfway to the sidewalk when she cried out his name:

"Martin. Martin, wait. I need this. I really need this."

He didn't turn, just gave one finger a wave above his head, a head wrangler's salute to the greenhorn bringing up the rear.

Three weeks later, at his desk at Final Paws, Martin clicked off Skype and waited for Julie to blink to black. Since she had declared herself Tonto to his Lone Ranger, she had taken to calling every day during her lunch hour to check on his application video, which was not due for another three months, and his attitude, which was uncharacteristically upbeat. Along with her practical suggestions on how he should prepare his package for the selection committee, she'd been offering advice on how to apply mindfulness and positive thinking to the task. Plus she sent gifts. Just the week before, a package from Sheplers. com: Lucchese cowboy boots; a size 4XL Scully rose and horseshoe Western shirt in turquoise with black cuffs and yoke; two pairs of relaxed fit, prewashed denim Wrangler jeans in indigo; and a Nocca belt with multi-tone calf hair set on genuine leather. The note on the bill of lading said: "You gotta look the part, but I thought a hat was too much. Love, Julie." The final bill was $683.79.

Today, over the squawks of the recovering budgies in the Conifer Veterinary Associates' break room, he and Julie had discussed NPR's announcement that, in seven months, the *Cowboy Poetry Hour* would end its thirty-year run with a live broadcast from the Thirty-Second Annual Elko Cowboy Poetry Confluence. Devastating news, of course, but softened by Martin's firm conviction that he would be there for it and as a performer. Even without the aid of one of Julie's affirmative visualization exercises, he could see it so clearly that he believed for a moment he'd already gone and felt around his desk for a memento: a performer's name badge, a backstage pass, a swizzle stick from Stockman's Casino. He found instead a receipt for *Anyone Can Ride!*, beginners' horseback riding instruction at the municipal park stables for which Julie had signed him up. As she had reminded him ten times during their twenty-minute chat, the first lesson was that afternoon.

The intercom crowed, and the voice of his assistant, Annie Tree-horn, inquired whether there were any more copies of his eulogy for the last of the lingering mourners from the funeral luncheon for Mrs. Pinehurst's tabby. He told her to run off twenty extras and that he was leaving soon for the day. He gathered his riding togs from a plastic Walgreens bag under his desk and left a note on top about the only other appointment of the afternoon: a client discussion of the funeral arrangements for the McDows' whifferpoo puppy-mill puppy, gone too soon, as the stone in the Final Paws Memorial Garden would soon read.

Martin ducked into the Grieving Guardians restroom, changed into his Shepplers.com outfit minus the Scully creation, which he had swapped out for a plain black T-shirt, and admired the result in the mirror over the sink. With the little lift the boot heels provided, he looked okay. If he squinted, he could even say badass.

He exited the mortuary through the back door so as not to disturb any mourners left in the chapel area with his inadequately somber getup. He headed to the Pierre Historic Trolley whistle stop directly outside Final Paws and waved down the free conveyance run by the city. He was pretty sure that at no time in Pierre's past had trollies like these traveled the roads. The vehicles were bright blue, open, outfitted with train whistles, and operated by grumpy retirees in striped conductors' outfits. But his transportation options were limited. The 2000 Lincoln Mark VIII that Carroll had bequeathed Martin had been in the Bitner brothers' back lot for the last two years with a blown head gasket. The trolley and proximity of Martin's downtown apartment to Final Paws had weakened his resolve to save up the $1,500 it would take to get the car rolling again.

He boarded and greeted the driver, Sam Earhardt, a retired tractor and chainsaw salesman who had told Martin, more than once, what he thought about a grown man who did not have his own working vehicle. Martin had refrained from replying, more than once, what he thought of a grown man who dressed up as a train conductor to supplement his Social Security.

The trolley travelled past the Wal-Mart, the Jiffy Lube, the Five Guys Hamburgers, the All You Can Eat Chinese Good Luck Buffet, and the mini mall with the women's golf wear shoppe. As they turned into the historic downtown and bumped along the cobblestone streets, Martin shut his eyes. A church bell rang twice, paused, and rang again, as if the hunchback needed to check his watch. The breeze carried the scent of autumn in Pierre: grass clippings rotting in green municipal trash bags at the curbs, which city workers were supposed to have picked up last July; coffee roasting at the café where out-of-towners had taken over the space from recently bankrupted feng shui consultants; naan burning in the tandoori oven at Taste of India, where Martin ate dinner every Sunday night.

Sam blew the whistle again and announced: "*Bozho*—'hello' in the language of the Potawatomi, for whom Potawatomi Municipal Park, and this stop on the Pierre Historic—"

"Save it," Martin said, exited the trolley, and headed for the stables.

Martin looked over the crowd of chattering schoolgirls in ponytails and English riding pants. He had figured he might be one of the oldest in the class, which began right after school let out. But he had hoped for one or two other adults. Having Julie back in his life made him realize how sorely he had missed having a trail partner.

The instructor entered the corral from the barn, clapping her hands and leading a knock-kneed, mustard-brown pony. "Okay, girls, gather round," she said. "My name is Kim, and I'm going to go through some basic safety information with you."

Cooing and squeaking, the little riders-to-be swarmed Kim and reached for the pony's nose. Martin held back. When he had imagined the class, he had imagined horses like the ones in Jimmy Sneedle's barn. Twitching, snuffling, stomping at the dust. Terrifying to be sure, but Martin had prepared himself for that. What he wasn't prepared for was a pony that could have been a healthy version of one of Dewitty's nags. What he wasn't prepared for was Chopo.

"Gentle," Kim said. She batted what looked like a toddler away from the pony's leg just before it shot a hoof back. The animal craned its head around, then drew back its lips and bared yellowing teeth. Martin thought it looked disappointed that there were no brain bits or lifeless child bodies in the dirt for its efforts.

"This is Poppy, and Poppy is a pony," said Kim, gathering her long hair in one hand, twisting it into a scrunchie with the other. She bounced on the toes of her hip-high riding boots and tugged at her tight purple and white T-shirt. It read "PPHS Girls Volleyball 2012." She couldn't have been over twenty years old. "Poppy's going to help me teach you today."

As the girls cried, "He's a baby!" and Kim explained the difference between ponies and horses, Martin circled the little beast. He couldn't figure out how anyone might find it cute or think it young. He certainly hoped he would not be expected to ride Poppy or any of its brethren. He had not considered there might only be a string of bitter Poppies from which to choose.

Of course, Martin had not expected that any municipal animal could measure up to Hero, the Cowboy Poet's mount, the horse against which Martin judged all other horses. He didn't know what Hero looked like in the flesh. He'd only seen the promo pictures, most taken through a wide-angle lens on Vess Guffry's Colorado ranch. The poet rarely brought the mustang with him to the weekly tapings of the *Cowboy Poetry Hour,* which was actually two hours, recorded on Friday nights and aired live on public radio stations across the nation. Sometimes, when the show was performed in larger venues, Hero joined Guffry on stage, Pyrois to his Helios.

Of course, the radio couldn't capture Hero's radiance, and most of what Martin knew of Hero's looks came from the verses of the Cowboy Poet himself:

He's as blond as the sun.
He's as broad as the skies.
As mighty as a gun,
Like a bullet he flies.

That particular ballad went on for multiple stanzas and added ample physical detail—for instance, Hero's forehead was emblazoned with *heaven's own star*. Martin had many times imagined himself on the mustang, staring off into a fiery Western sunset, both man and horse alert to the coyote's call, his evening song of loneliness, one that only a cowboy poet could fully capture and repeat in rhyming iambic pentameter.

Kim had moved on to assigning horses to the class, all of whom but Martin squealed and bounced each time a horse name was announced, as if they were going to be mounted atop the front men from a hot new boy band.

"Maribeth on Streamers. Vanessa on Beaucoup. Ellen Catherine on Tigerlily. Maguire on Sunshine, Vivian on Whiskey, and Martin on…" Had she really paused or was it just Martin's nerves slowing time? That often happened to him before minor traffic accidents or great humiliations.

"…Zach."

A gasp went up from the crowd, both the mothers along the fence and the daughters already straddling their ponies. Another instructor, almost identical to Kim down to the hip boots and the high school athletics T-shirt, led out a colossal black draft horse, a Percheron. Martin gasped too. Even he recognized Zach. The horse was famous in Pierre: hauling the float for the queen's court every Blossomtown parade; pulling the cart with the pretend dead Union cavalry generals every Memorial Day; serving as pace horse for the Pierre Penny-Farthing Bike Festival every July; hauling Santa's sleigh down Main Street every Christmas. Zach was not Hero, but he was a storied, even legendary, steed, and Martin stood a little taller knowing they had been paired.

"He's the only horse we have that can carry your weight," said the second instructor as she dragged a stepstool over to where Zach was accepting pats and apples from the mothers. Martin recognized most of them. He'd written their grandparents' obituaries for the *Leader Telegram,* covered their graduations from PPHS, and interred their parents' last Irish setters. A six-foot-plus freckled dirty blonde, Susie Coyne, gave him a small wave. He had buried her ferret just a couple of weeks ago.

He didn't think he needed the stool to mount Zach, having imagined many times swinging into the saddle with the grace and ease granted by the extra room in the thighs and seat of his Wranglers. But then again, Zach was taller than any of the horses on which he had mentally practiced.

Martin put his left foot in the stirrup and reached for Zach's mane with his right hand, as he had watched the girls do. A single, festive bell tied on the horn with green ribbon jingled softly, and Zach snorted, reared his head back, and sidestepped away from the fence. The horse's momentum caught Martin mid-leg-swing, and he ended up, his stomach on the saddle, flopped crosswise to Zach's body. Zach continued to wriggle and throw his head.

"Quit kidding around," Kim said over her shoulder as she strode after the line of ponies and their riders walking placidly into the arena. The mothers followed outside the fence, each tossing a piece of advice to Martin as she went:

"He likes his ears rubbed," said Clarissa Bottom, Flip's granddaughter.

"Sing to him in Spanish," said Flower Parrott, the second wife of Pierre's municipal attorney.

"Don't touch his rump," said Jeanne Belski, the Lincoln Elementary school secretary.

Zach had probably, at some time or another, at some civic event or another, carried each and every one of these women and their daughters and the instructors at the stables today. Carried them without incident. Martin feared he was about to become the first resident of Pierre ever carried with incident by the great and gentle Zach.

By inching on his stomach forward and left, forward and left, forward and left, Martin managed to smash his right testicle onto the back of the saddle and his left ear into the horse's coarse mane.

Balanced on those pinpoints, he leveraged himself up and into his seat. He grabbed the thick leather reins, but before he could set his feet in the stirrups, Zach took off at a full and lopsided gallop after the line of girls.

Zach's front and back legs churned as if controlled by two different nerve centers. The front pair would skitter left while the back pair stumbled right. His back buckled and swayed, he reared and bucked. Martin gave up trying to fit his feet into the stirrups and concentrated on hanging onto the saddle horn. His rear end swung with Zach's gyrations, and Martin worried his shifting mass was further unbalancing the canting equine.

"Remember what I said to do if a horse starts rolling," yelled the instructor, both hands now tugging on her ponytail.

"Calm DOWN, pull UP, get ready to get OFF," chanted the girls. Martin did not recall that chapter of the prelaunch briefing.

"He's not rolling," Martin yelled back, "he's convulsing."

And then, Zach was rolling.

At first, this appeared a welcome development. Zach stopped yawing and fell to his front knees. Martin pulled up on the reins, which moved the titanic horse's head not one whit. Zach's belly heaved with irregular gasps. He threw his head up and rolled his eyes. He collapsed onto his right shoulder and, like a glacier beginning to calf, crumbled onto his side. Martin pushed away from the dropping animal and rolled clear. He lay panting in the dirt, eye-to-eye with Zach.

"Zach, Zach, Zach." Martin could hear the girls wailing somewhere deep in the arena.

"Off your horses for safety," the instructor wailed back. "Zach is just trying to cool off."

Martin stared into Zach's white, blank eye. He didn't have the look of one indulging in a refreshing dust bath. He had the look of one dying, if not already dead. Martin knew companion animal remains when he saw them.

Or maybe not. Zach pulled back his lips, exposed a row of chipped and bloodstained teeth, and blew a raspberry at Martin. Perhaps there was a chance to exit this day with some grace, even honor. CPR. Did not Martin have a card, somewhere between his AAA membership and his Kroger's valued customer credentials, that certified him to perform CPR on adults and children? Sure, this was neither a human adult nor a human baby, but the card was expired anyway. The principle was the same. Martin had seen it done on *Animal Planet*.

Martin would save Zach's life. He would become a hero in the town, a legend as great as Zach himself. Ballads would be written, were Pierre the sort of place where ballads were written, which it was not, so keys to the city would be handed out. Martin would ride Zach in town parades. Business would pick up at Final Paws. He would give Annie a raise. He would save up for his move west. He'd pay Julie back for all she had invested in his bid to recite at Elko.

He would have a true and personal story of redemption and resurrection to versify in his cowboy poetry.

Zach rotated onto his back, slowly bicycled his hooves in the air, as if shooing flies. Martin crawled toward the beast's massive left breast, scrambled onto his knees and pounded on the horseflesh, one, two, three, was it five or ten pumps? Three or five puffs? Horse sweat sprayed from under his fists and burned into his eyes. He skittered up to Zach's mouth and puffed into an opening in his black lips that Martin widened with his fingers. One, two, three, had to be enough. Martin tasted hay and something sour, like regurgitated aspirin. Skittered back to the chest. Pounded five times.

"Stop hitting him, stop hitting him, stop hitting him," the Greek chorus of girls moaned in the distance.

Zach lifted his great head and neck, whinnied, rolled one eye back toward Martin. He grabbed at the front of the horse's mouth, a last kiss of life to seal the deal, to make Martin the hero of Pierre. He pressed his lips to the horse's lips.

The Percheron heaved an oaty breath and life departed with a shudder, a roll, and a spray of blood-specked spume.

THE FOURTH HORSE:

HERO

D. 2016

March 21, 2016

Dear Mr. Oliphant,

Thank you for again for sharing your cowboy poetry and your recitation videotape with the 32nd Annual Elko Cowboy Poetry Confluence Selection Committee. Your work and your reading impressed us all. We particularly admired "When My Midwestern Heart Does the Western Two-Step."

But as you know, the key criteria the committee considers are quality of performance, quality of writing, appropriateness of genre to the event, and the connection or deep understanding of modern-day ranching and cowboy culture. As in years past, your work has fired mightily on the first three cylinders but petered out on the last. We do understand that you are employed in a profession that requires harmony with animals, some of which might be found on ranches (though it is a stretch to compare burying cats to driving cattle, poetic license notwithstanding); that you attended and enjoyed a dude ranch in Arizona as a young man; and that you have heard almost every show recorded by this year's keynote speaker, Vess Guffry, the Cowboy Poet. You surely have the heart of a cowboy poet, Mr. Oliphant. But I have an old three-legged dog with the heart of a stallion, and I won't be breeding him to my mares anytime soon.

So I am afraid we again cannot invite you to perform at the Annual Elko Cowboy Poetry Confluence. As a longstanding member of our sponsor, the Western Folklife Center, you will, we hope, take advantage of early tickets sales and join us in the audience at the end of May. And feel free to submit again for the 33rd Annual Elko Cowboy Poetry Confluence should you manage to pick up some hands-on cowboy and ranching experience by then.

See you in Elko!

Sincerely,
The 32nd Annual Elko Cowboy Poetry Confluence Selection Committee

12

Martin tried to tell Julie about the letter the day he received it, a chilly March Wednesday. He punched her cell number as soon as he saw the FedEx envelope in the pile of crematory urn catalogues and utility bills on top of his inbox. Perhaps it had been foolish to pay the extra $12.95 for the selection committee to send their decision overnight, but he was so sure it would be good news.

For the last six months, nothing could shake his certitude that he had turned the herd toward Elko and was finally headed home. Not even Zach's death. He had not been blamed. In fact, he was chosen to preside over the Percheron's funeral, held at the Pierre Bandshell-by-the-Lake and attended by half of Pierre. *USA Today* had printed a small article on the service, mostly favorable and scarcely tongue-in-cheek, which was picked up by the *Niles Township Tattler,* a weekly and the closest thing these days to a local paper.

The call went to voice mail, and Martin clicked off the phone without leaving a message. He wanted to take his time, rolling this moment over his taste buds like a pretentious sommelier with a 2008 Spottswoode Cabernet. He pulled the golden package out of the orange, white, and blue mailer. A firm hand had addressed the internal envelope with a fountain pen. He could see three or four infinitesimal ink splatters that gave it away. This must be what letters that travelled by pony express looked like, the letters bringing news of deaths or marriage proposals or new lands ranched or new ranges rode. He held the envelope to his nose and inhaled: dust and desert and horse manure and nervous cattle and saddle leather. Also Old Spice. Old Spice was the FedEx guy's aftershave.

Martin slit the envelope with a silver-plated opener. The black brand of the Thirty-Second Annual Elko Cowboy Poetry Confluence marked the upper corner, and the text of the missive paced across the page in elaborate cursive. By the time he got to the final decisive no, tears fogged his vision and he put the paper down. He felt the floor beneath him turn to sand, then quicksand, then straight-up abyss. He would not go to Elko. The application, thanks to Julie, was stronger than anything he had submitted in the past and was stronger than anything he could imagine compiling in the future. What had gone wrong? Had he misheard the dots and dashes coming in over the telegraph? Misread the smoke signals floating on the horizon? Had he led his entire adult life faithful to a code he didn't really understand? This was his truest shot. And he missed.

His cell trilled out "Streets of Laredo." Julie. He picked up and croaked a "hello," not in the voice of a cowboy poet. The western song within him was already on the retreat. He greeted her as a fifty-two-year-old Midwestern pet mortician.

"Howdy, cowboy," said Julie. "So? What'd they say? Do you know which group you're in? Is it like college, where you find out who your suitemates are so you can decide who brings the chaps and who's in charge of the barbequed pork rinds?" She giggled, and what sounded like a basset hound kept up a steady bay in the background. "Can you hear me? Shut up, Winston. I wish I was there with you, we could celebrate proper. Shut up, Winston! Christ, you would think I was pulling out his toenails. I bought my tickets for the confluence yesterday, all four days. I need to get a hotel reservation. Where do they put up the performers?"

"I don't know," said Martin.

"We ought to coordinate travel. Don't book anything without me."

"I won't," said Martin.

"Goddamn it, Winston. I gotta go. He's bleeding on my smock. But I'll call. I love you. Thank you for this. We did it! You don't know how much that means." His screen flashed back to Julie's contact page, and he considered it for a second, thinking how many problems he could solve by blocking her number.

Because he did know how much it meant to her. Because he didn't know how he could tell her. As she had nurtured his confidence, hers had flourished alongside, a symbiotic relationship, like the basil that thrives under a tomato plant, enjoying the shade and repelling the hornworms. She credited all that was positive in her new Colorado life to her collaboration with Martin. And though he couldn't see the connection, she believed in it mightily, and he hadn't argued. A win-win. She was happy. She'd found free housing with her boss, who traveled often with Critter Clinicians without Borders and needed a housesitter. She made a new set of outdoorsy girlfriends in Conifer and started hiking fourteeners. And Martin thought she might be dating again. She rarely spoke to him of her day-to-day realities, and he rarely asked. She just thanked him, every call. He had shown her what was possible; he had taught her to breathe the air of lyricism and hope again; he had let her be a part of a beautiful dream.

So of course, he couldn't just blurt out the news of his rejection. He would need to be careful, sensitive. But. He looked down at the letter and felt the rising burn of resentment creep through his chest and up his esophagus. But here he was again, pushing aside his own considerable injury to minister to the wounds of another. Julie had barely been grazed, while he had taken a Winchester .44 round to the chest. And yet it was he who was supposed to drag himself, bleeding in the dust, to help her open up a Band-Aid packet.

He couldn't do it, maybe not for a while. He needed a proper period of solitary bereavement. He wouldn't answer the phone or look at email. He'd write her when he was ready. He'd mourn what he had lost—Elko, Beaufort, Ginger, even his mom, his dad, the *Leader Telegram*, his move West, Ginger, cowboy poetry.

> *You think of things he did and said, and of the ways he had.*
> *And now to think that he is dead. It makes you feel plum sad.*
> *It brings the old days back again, you live them one by one.*
> *You think of things that happened then, and what you should have done.*

Bruce Kiskaddon understood. Grieve alone, take as long as it takes.

> *You do it when you've time enough to make a quiet ride.*
> *To see the fleecy clouds above and watch the shadows glide.*

The phone twanged again. Julie again. Martin muted it, slipped the letter from the committee into his top desk drawer, put his head in his hands, and cried.

Two months later, three weeks before the kickoff of the Thirty-Second Annual Cowboy Poetry Confluence and on the day Vess Guffry brought his Cowboy Poetry Hour Farewell Tour to Pierre's Theater-on-the-Lake, Martin arrived at Emilio's to meet Julie. He still hadn't told her about his rejection, despite his every intention. But whenever he'd tried to bring it up, she hijacked the conversation with her own announcement of plans for their trip to Elko.

First, she informed Martin that she'd procured them tickets for the Pierre stop on the Cowboy Poetry Hour Farewell Tour, the show's only Upper Midwest engagement. She got them through one of her mountain-climbing friends, who hosted a syndicated preschool counting program on Denver Public Television. WBEZ, the Chicago public radio station of which Martin was a sustaining member at the booster level, had sold out their allotment to those in giving circles several grades above his.

Next, she proclaimed that her boss had granted her a month of leave so she could road trip with Martin to Elko. "Like the Chisholm Trail, but sideways," she had enthused over Skype, while Martin slipped the selection committee's letter back in his desk drawer. Soon after that, she called with the news that her boss, who Martin was beginning to think was going for some sort of Conifer Chamber of Commerce employer-of-the-year award, was lending her a brand-new Jeep Cherokee for their cross-country drive. And just last week, three seconds before Martin was going to confess, she revealed that she had arranged for "an incredible surprise" that was going to make their journey West "even more epic." Martin fell into a daydream about stops at luxury spas and iconic National Park lodges, and Julie hung up before he could say more than "can't wait."

Obviously, he'd let it go on too long. But he had been lost, so lost, since he received the selection committee's letter in March. Endlessly freefalling from a rocky precipice, too bewildered to right himself, too terrified to look down. The worst of it was he had so enjoyed being her hero—the man whose bravery inspired her, whose confidence fueled her, whose poetry saved her life—that he couldn't let it go, even after the ground beneath her adulation turned to mud. But that ended today. They were scheduled to leave the next morning to start their trip to Elko, and of course, he couldn't let it begin. Lies of omission were one thing from a thousand miles away, quite another from three feet across a Jeep's console

And yet, he couldn't tell her until he had his tickets to the *Cowboy Poetry Hour* in hand. He had to go to the show. Back in March, he had thought that he could walk away from cowboy poetry, since cowboy

poetry had so blithely walked—no galloped—away from him. And he
did stop practicing his orations. The last poem he proclaimed out loud
was on the morning before he received the rejection letter, a rousing
recitation of S. Omar Barker's "Purt Near!" into his shaving mirror.
But he still listened each Friday to the *Cowboy Poetry Hour*, out of habit,
out of longing. Since January, the performances were all part of the
Farewell Tour. Martin could hear finality in every syllable Vess Guffry
spoke, demise in every fiddle lick a guest artist bowed. The shows were
funerals, and Martin was a man who believed in paying one's respects.
Tonight, Martin would say his final goodbyes to cowboy poetry.

Juan Palimino, the maître d' at Emilio's, greeted Martin from the
reception podium. "Mr. Martin, welcome. Are you going to the cowboy show? We have a special pre-theater menu." Juan had worked at
the restaurant for fifty years, starting as a teenaged dishwasher and
rising through the ranks to part owner and maître d'.

"Julie's joining me. We're going together," said Martin. Juan knew
Julie. He knew every Pierrite or ex-Pierrite who had ever dined out—
which was by no means all of them, sit-down restaurant food still
seen as the equivalent of a private jet or an in-house masseur in some
blue-collar circles. Martin dined here at least once a week. His favorite
table was next to the wood-fired steak ovens, and Juan sat him there
now. "What's the pre-theater special?" asked Martin.

"The same as always, but we cook it faster and earlier," said Juan.
"I'll bring Miss Julie straight away when she comes. A cocktail, perhaps?"

"Just a ginger ale for now," said Martin. His stomach ached, though
he doubted the soda would cure the malaise. A blast of heat hit Martin's left cheek, he heard the sizzle of fat on flame, and he smelled
lighter fluid and seared flesh.

"A well-done T-bone is a waste of meat and fire," said Orville, the
steak guy, and poked what looked to be a chunk of charcoal into the
three-foot blaze.

Martin nodded back. Orville regularly complained to Martin about
philistine steak orders, and Martin always agreed. Orville was about
six foot seven inches and jabbed at his fires like the devil at his brim-
stone. Martin usually ordered vegetable malfatti so as not to further
enrage the cook.

He took the selection committee's letter out of his back pocket and set it, still folded, on the table in front of him. He wouldn't be able to enjoy the Cowboy Poet, knowing that Julie's considerable rage would be unleashed on him after. So he would get the tickets from her, then hand the letter over. He hoped that, having toadied to Orville on all matters meat, he might come to Martin's defense should her fury turn physical.

"Howdy, cowboy."

For a minute, backlit by the fire from Orville's ovens, Martin saw not Julie but a mirage of Ginger. She wore a brown lambskin jacket trimmed with hair-on cowhide and turquoise metallic fringe, with a turquoise camisole to match. Her jeans were tight, and her boots looked vintage, a hand-painted peacock feather design running the length of their outer edges.

"Juan, you still got that Veuve Clicquot?" said Julie. "Bring us a bottle."

"You look great," said Martin.

"And you look like a podiatrist on his way to his first craft beer tasting. What happened to the clothes I bought you?" said Julie.

Martin wore a forest-green cotton T-shirt under a black linen jacket, jeans, and Frye Venetian slip-on loafers. He had packed his cowboy gear in U-Haul boxes and stored them in the basement of Final Paws.

"Let's see those tickets," said Martin once Julie had settled, and Juan shuffled off after the wine. "I know the theater pretty well. I'll show you where we'll be."

"Third row, center left, aisle," said Julie. "They're excellent seats."

"I guess I've wanted to go to a *Cowboy Poetry Hour* taping for so long, it's like I can't believe it's really happening until the evidence is in front of me."

Julie laughed and opened a red leather handbag with *Cowgirl* spelled out in rhinestones on one side. She pulled out two printed pages and passed them over.

"You ought to take a look at this too," said Martin, and pushed the selection committee's letter across the table. He tried not to mouth breathe. She unfolded it. A hush fell on the dining room, the only noise the sizzle of a steak.

"What is it?" she said, and the meat crackled along with her falling voice. "Martin, it says they didn't pick you." She shoved her chair back. "This is from March." She stood up. "You let me take time off work, borrow from Lee, get rooms, get tickets, pay for your fucking Howdy Doodie get-ups and your aborted riding career."

"That was not my fault," said Martin. "The vet said Zach was a coronary waiting to happen."

Julie took a couple of steps back from the table. "This is like cancer all over again. You're like cancer. You betrayed me." She pointed at Martin. "You tumor. You carcinoma."

Martin stood too. "This is not like cancer. You don't have cancer. Cancer kills people. Cancer killed my mom, a horrible, painful, unfair death. Cowboy poetry couldn't save her, and it can't save you. The only person it might have saved is me, if I'd been able to pursue it, if all you—" he almost said *womenfolk*, thought better of it, switched to *easterners* "—if all you easterners hadn't needed tending to first. Cattle move only as fast as the weakest calf, and from day one, I've been stuck with nothing but downers in my herd."

Juan approached the table, a silver ice bucket stand in one hand, the champagne in the other.

"Shall I open it?" he said, waggling the thick green bottle. "What are we celebrating? Maybe an engagement?"

"Gimme that," said Julie and grabbed the bottle. She unwired the top, gave one hard shake, aimed it at Martin, and fired the cork into his belly. He bent, gasping for breath, holding his sides, checking his fingers for blood. Julie slammed the foaming bottle on the table, wheeled around, and stomped from the room. The only sounds were of the steak overcooking, the champagne foam dripping onto the floor, and the subtle clicks of the other diners turning on their cell phone cameras. Martin kept his eyes down, trying to decide how much of this he deserved and to remember whether appendixes could be burst by outside force.

"Surprise! Am I late? I see the bubbly's already opened."

Martin looked up. Before him stood an older, seedier, but definitely recognizable Bob Lattner, dressed in jeans, a straw hat, and a Jerry Jeff Walker T-shirt, Clicquot bottleneck in his fist, wine streaming over his bony wrist.

"Where's Julie?" he said, then raised the bottle and swigged.

Where the Ponies Come to Drink
by Henry Herbert Knibbs

Up in Northern Arizona
There's a Ranger-trail that passes
Through a mesa, like a faëry lake
With pines upon its brink.
And across the trail a stream runs
All but hidden in the grasses,
Till it finds an emerald hollow
where the ponies come to drink...

Down they swing as if pretending,
In their orderly disorder,
That they stopped to hold a pow-wow,
Just to rally for the charge
That will take them, close to sunset,
Twenty miles across the border;
Then the leader sniffs and drinks
With fore feet planted on the marge...

My old cow-horse he runs with 'em:
Turned him loose for good last season;
Eighteen years; hard work, his record,
And he's earned his little rest;
And he's taking it by playing,
Acting proud, and with good reason;
Though he's starched a little forward,
He can fan it with the best.

Once I called him—almost caught him,
When he heard my spur-chains jingle;
Then he eyed me some reproachful,
As if making up his mind:
Seemed to say, "Well, if I have to—
But you know I'm living single..."
So I laughed.
In just a minute he was pretty hard to find.

Some folks wouldn't understand it—
Writing lines about a pony—
For a cow-horse is a cow-horse—
Nothing else, most people think—
But for eighteen years your partner,
Wise and faithful, such a crony
Seems worth watching for, a spell,
Down where the ponies come to drink.

13

Martin and Lattner rode to Theater-on-the-Lake in Lattner's fire engine red '71 Mustang coupe. Lattner steered with his knees and used his hands to fiddle with a Bee Gees cassette tape. Martin clutched his bucket seat on both sides and stared at the road racing towards his nose. Five inches lower, and his ass would be dragging along Myrtle Avenue. Lattner spent the first half of the trip explaining how Julie had brought him back to Pierre, and Martin spent the second half of the trip explaining how he had driven Julie away from Pierre.

Telling her the truth hadn't gone as he'd planned. And it wasn't that he had expected her to be gracious or understanding. He knew she'd be furious. But to compare him to cancer? He was no hero, cowboy or otherwise, but he wasn't a malignancy. He was just a crappy friend. And so was she. It had never been about him getting to Elko, it had been about her learning to live again. Even with his mom, it had never been about helping her die, it had been about Julie replacing Bitsy. Martin may have violated the spirit of the West with his lies and his failures, but at least he tried to live up to something bigger than himself. Julie lived for Julie.

They skidded to a stop at a light, and the car shook and babbled like a stuttering sheep broadcast through a subwoofer. The smell of gasoline was so strong, Martin wondered if there was a spare can in the back seat. He peeked over at Lattner, who looked about to fall asleep. His eyelids fluttered, and a few stray wisps of white hair danced in time. A triangle of fuzz, a refugee from his morning shave, sat mid-cheek, pointing North. A greasy ring orbited a small tomato chunk on his collar.

Here was a man who knew how to live. He was aggressively unmoored. He went where the most favorable wind blew him, not hero, not villain, not knowing or caring where he rode next. Martin could learn from this man.

"She'll get over it," said Lattner. "You know how she is."

"Angry," said Martin. "And this time it's justifiable."

"The worse kind," said Lattner. "She was lamentably overinvested in having you wow 'em at the confluence. Ergo, me." Julie had begged Lattner to join them in Elko, arguing that he'd always been a mentor to Martin. Plus, Lattner could do PR for what she believed was going to be Martin's full-time gig as a breakout cowboy poet. Accompanying them from Pierre to Nevada was Lattner's idea.

"So what are you going to do now?" Martin said.

"Not stay around here," said Lattner. "But I can't go back to rehab in Tampa until I've been clean for a month." He accelerated through the green.

"Julie didn't mention she was in touch with you," Martin said as Lattner turned into the Theater-on-the-Lake West parking lot. "Did you know about Mrs. Trinkle?"

"Irene. Never been another like her." Lattner jerked the car into a spot.

"Why didn't you go to the funeral?" said Martin

"Because I'm not obsessed with death, like you," said Lattner. He chewed on the right side of his mustache and edged the Mustang up until it was bumper-to-bumper with the car opposite. "If they're gonna to hit my baby, I don't want them to get up any speed."

"It's not really a rave sort of crowd," said Martin, trying not to sound as morose as Lattner apparently thought he was.

"But they do serve beer inside," said Lattner. "I called ahead to check."

Up in Northern Arizona
there's a Ranger-trail that passes
Through a mesa, like a faëry lake
with pines upon its brink,
And across the trail a stream runs
all but hidden in the grasses,
Till it finds an emerald hollow
where the ponies come to drink.

Martin blew a hoppy gust and wedged further into the Theater-on-the-Lake's ungenerous but, thank God, padded seat. He winced as the ache in his knees travelled to his hips, and he silently ticked through the warning signs of a pulmonary embolism. He settled his Sam

Adams on the crest of his belly and tried not to begrudge Lattner the aisle seat.

The Cowboy Poet was starting the show with "Where the Ponies Come to Drink." His pitch-perfect timbre rang through the theater, piped through the speakers, but the curtain remained shut.

"Is this how it always starts?" Lattner whispered over his bottle, which owl-hooted harmony.

"With a poem, yeah," said Martin. "I don't know when he shows up. I've only heard it on the radio before."

Was it a recording or live? Martin wondered and worried. Worried that perhaps the Cowboy Poet did not appear in front of audiences anymore, that he was reading from behind the curtain, or worse, that this was a track off one of his CDs. Martin worried because there were rumors—of physical decline, of mental frailty, even of death followed by a vast NPR conspiracy involving low stage lighting and dubbed-over archival material. But surely they would not go on this much-ballyhooed last tour if they only had a cowboy corpse.

A cough and a pause and the voice of the Cowboy Poet continued to wrangle those ponies through *the bunch-grass and the gramma* and *cross the little stream.* A sign of life there, right? Wouldn't someone have edited that out if this were anything but live, if the Cowboy Poet were anything but alive? Martin shifted in his seat and forced himself to thrill to the easy jog of the poem's Western gait.

"Where the Ponies Come to Drink" was one of Henry Herbert Knibbs's poems. Martin was a Knibbs devotee; most lovers of cowboy poetry were. He was a pioneer, one of the most consistent and memorable voices yodeling at the turn of the twentieth century, the Golden Age of Cowboy Poetry. And yet, and perhaps this was why he had homesteaded such prime real estate on Martin's epicardium, Knibbs had never worked as a cowboy, never ranched, never roped the hell-bent bull from the back of a cayuse.

Martin had recited "Where the Ponies Come to Drink" at his mother's funeral, some thirty years before, primarily because guilt drove him to choose something horse associated. He could not bring himself to read "Chopo." That night, as he had wandered the first floor of their house, collecting wadded napkins, crumb-infested paper plates, and fringe-topped toothpicks from the after-service reception,

Frank's Sony Walkman hooked onto the waistband of Martin's black wool trousers, he had listened to the first *Cowboy Poetry Hour* broadcast live from Elko and the Second Annual Elko Cowboy Poetry Confluence. Mid-show, the Cowboy Poet, back then identified only by his given name, Vess Guffry, recited the same poem.

But for eighteen years your partner,
wise and faithful, such a crony
Seems worth watching for, a spell,
down where the ponies come to drink.

Applause echoed around Martin and even Lattner pushed his bottle between his knees and wolf whistled. As the stomps and calls died down, the curtain rose, not on the great man, but on Caitlyn Jordan and her violin. She was a slip of an ingenue whose piping recitation, deft fiddling, and homeschooled sterility had won over gritty and whiskey-soaked veteran poets at Elko the year before. She had been on the show several times since, and Martin had not been impressed. Now, in person, he liked young Caitlyn even less. She stood so straight, spoke so cleanly, pointed her white, unblemished chin so bravely toward the upper stage lights. She had too much of the feel of someone, or something, who had spent too much time in the valley of the uncanny.

Caitlyn raked out one more note of longing for the Montana mountains and homage to a dewy morning and praise for griddle hot biscuits, flashed a toothsome grin, and tripped off the stage. Lattner pointed at his empty beer bottle, then at Martin's half-full one, and made to get up. The stage lights dimmed, and Martin heard the distinct clomp of a horse hoof, caught the scent of hay. He lay a thick hand on Lattner's arm. Again, but this time without amplification, the voice rang clear:

But for eighteen years your partner,
wise and faithful, such a crony,
Seems worth watching for, a spell,
down where the ponies come to drink.

The Cowboy Poet took the stage, his sorrel mustang, Hero, falling in at his side.

Later, Martin would say that he should have known what was

coming. Much later, he would believe that he had. But at first, on that night, he only wondered whether it was the fire code that kept the Cowboy Poet from riding Hero onto the stage, as Martin had assumed he would.

The Cowboy Poet patted Hero's dark nose, cleared his throat, and chanted:

Sunny summer day it was when loping in to Laramie,
I overtook the Walking Man, reined up and nodded "How!!"

Of course. The riderless stallion made perfect sense. The Cowboy Poet was paying homage to the classic "The Walking Man," Knibbs's ballad of a wrangler's ambulatory penance for the horse that saved his life. Perhaps this show would be a Henry Herbert Knibbs's tribute. Wonderful, thought Martin. Wonderful and appropriate.

"Pity the intern that has to clean that up." Lattner elbowed Martin and nodded toward a pool of loose dung collecting in spurts behind Hero. Martin saw and sniffed at an odor akin to sewage. Something was wrong.

The poet must have known it too. He froze one line into the third verse, his thumbs shoved in the waistband of his jeans, his shining belt buckle kicking the stage lights back in a spray of stars. A minute ticked by. Hero stretched his muscled neck and hung his great head low. Someone off stage squeaked out the missing stanza: "If good people go to heaven, do good horses go to hell?" Hero went down on his front knees.

"Is he going to roll over?" Lattner sat up and placed his beer bottle on the ground.

Martin leaned forward too but didn't answer. Something was wrong. And he knew what it was. In fact, after cowboy poetry, what was wrong was something he knew more about than almost anything.

"Is Hero falling?" A child's voice floated from somewhere behind Martin.

"No," Martin whispered, to the child, to Lattner, to himself. "Hero is dying."

"No," Martin whispered to himself. "Hero is dead."

He grasped the railing of the Theater-on-the-Lake mezzanine balcony and looked down past the multi-tiered glass chandelier into the lobby. The fire alarm continued to clang. He was alone on this level, having climbed the foyer staircase over the objections of the zit-splattered usher moving the crowd to the parking lot.

"I'm with the show," Martin had growled at the boy, who blinked back but did not insist.

The theater had cleared quickly. The swath of earth on which Pierre sits is also the stomping ground of a particularly ferocious breed of tornado, and residents are hardwired from birth to move to the nearest ditch whenever an alarm sounds. Even Lattner bolted from his seat at the first flash of the red emergency lights, though Martin suspected that was the old newspaperman's urge to get to the story rather than any instinct for self-preservation.

"My phone's in the car," Lattner yelled over his shoulder as he headed for the side exit, straight-arming a retired elementary school teacher and leapfrogging a sobbing toddler in a straw bowler.

Martin, gassy and faint with horror, leaned on the mezzanine railing. He belched, smelled stale sweat, probably his own, and stared at the terrible tableau below. In the center of the royal blue carpet, atop a ten-foot woven replica of the Pierre lighthouse, complete with swooping seagulls and tacking sailboats, lay Hero. From this angle Martin could see both that she was dead, and that she was a she. Had the shock of the horse's demise not sucked the blood from his brain, this would have surprised him. The manly Hero a mare. But he was too caught up in the scene below to ruminate on the horse's gender fluidity. She appeared as if she were in full flight. Her ink-dipped tail spread from her haunches, well away from her back legs kicked forward and her front legs kicked back. Her bleached blonde mane feathered rear from her sinewy chestnut neck, blown, it seemed, by the same stiff breeze keeping the shag-rendered seagulls aloft.

The angular frame of the Cowboy Poet appeared from under the balcony. He brushed past Dr. Wiseman, the local vet, who stood several feet from Hero's body, consulting with a middle-aged brunette in embroidery-splattered jeans and a red-checkered shirt. The poet went straight to Hero, dropped on one knee, and cupped the horse's sooty muzzle in both hands. Martin couldn't see beyond the brim of his black Stetson to make out whether the man was talking or crying or both. Martin sensed both.

The clang of the alarm cut off with a click, and the buzzing silence that followed hurt Martin's ears. Through it, he heard the woman's raised voice and then the vet.

"Dead," he said. "Graveyard dead."

Martin was not sure if it were he or the woman who keened at the vet's epitaph, but he suspected it was he. She and Dr. Wiseman turned to look up at Martin. The vet said something to the woman, and she continued to stare at Martin, working her jaw as if she were chewing gum in a flavor she hated. Then she nodded and pivoted back to the horse and grieving master. Dr. Wiseman locked eyes with Martin and, with one finger, beckoned him down to his destiny.

The vet introduced the brunette to Martin as Lina Sharpe, the Cowboy Poet's administrative assistant, then excused himself with a "more your department than mine, I'm afraid." Martin and Lina clasped hands for too long. She said nothing, her eyes on the still kneeling Cowboy Poet. Martin heard himself blathering on about "nonhuman mortality solutions" and "organic tonnage hygienic disposal." When the poet stood, Lina dropped Martin's hand.

"Vess," she said, but he walked without a word toward the exit. She followed and after her, Martin, still jabbering about the tarps they had used to move Zach, "probably double the poundage in equine meat."

The Cowboy Poet stopped under a parking lot light and addressed Lina.

"How can I?" he said.

"I'm sure there's something else," she answered.

He shook his head and turned toward the tour bus emblazoned with an eight-foot high rendition of Hero, alive and galloping across a starry sky.

Martin continued to thrash in the throes of Tourette's: "fluid to flesh ratio...local sanitation regulations...bloat and drainage options." Lina edged back. He could feel this moment—his moment with the Cowboy Poet, the moment Martin returned to cowboy poetry, his moment to be of use to the art he still loved—on the verge of drowning in his infernal words, not poetry but a treatise on the practicalities of modern equine mortuary science.

But then, like the cavalry over the butte, Lattner and his red sports car thundered into the parking lot. The roar of the Mustang's engine

stunned Martin into silence and halted the Cowboy Poet's retreat.
Lattner jumped out of the car, pink Canon Powershot around his
neck, and reached for the hand Vess Guffry had extended—the now-
smiling Vess Guffry had extended. Had extended right past Martin.
As if Martin were a lamppost or a speed bump. A speed bump who
could not stop talking about large animal corpse recycling.

"'71, right?" The Cowboy Poet circled the back of car. "A coupe."

"That it is," said Lattner.

"I had one of these. New. Christ, what a great car. Are you with
him?" The poet jerked his long chin at Martin but kept his eyes on
the Mustang.

"It's his car," Lattner said. Martin swung his head around but kept
his mouth shut, unsure what gruesomeness might pop out if he tried
to object.

"Part of your business? Part of that pet cemetery stuff?" asked
the Cowboy Poet, finally looking at Martin, and Martin nodded, lips
pressed tight. Lattner, operating, he admitted later, on a selfless instinct
that he had never experienced before and would never experience
again, said, "Oh yes, this is the star of Final Paw's memorialization
motor fleet."

"Well, maybe we can work with them," the Cowboy Poet said to
Lina. "You figure it out."

"Obviously NPR will do whatever Vess wants, but we're not HBO,
and canceling the rest of the tour is a financial nightmare. Maybe if
Vess could do a couple of the shows, plus Elko. Really, he's got to do
Elko."

The man talking had been introduced to Martin as Mac some-
thing-or-other, an executive out of the NPR Chicago office. He
looked to be in his late thirties and stood shining in a tailored dark
gray suit, pinstriped shirt, and corn-yellow tie, pressing both hands
so firmly into the laminated wood top of the conference table in the
Final Paws' Family and Friends Comfort Room that the tips of his
fingers had turned white. He faced a framed poster of neon pink and
orange cartoon dogs and cats tripping over a rainbow bridge toward
a heaven of winged rawhide chewies and haloed squeaky toys. Martin
should have told Annie to bring them into his private office, where

the decor ran more to Remington prints and Annual Elko Cowboy Poetry Confluence posters.

"I told you, he'll do Elko," said Lina. She wore the same rumpled checkered shirt tucked into the same stretched and creased jeans she had had on when they had been introduced twelve hours earlier, over Hero's corpse. She stood at the window, staring out to the parking lot, her back to Mac but her profile in Martin's view. She turned beclouded eyes to the thud of the door opening, the smell of Bunn-burned French Roast, and Annie, with the machine's glass pot in one hand and a stack of Styrofoam cups in the other. "Hope no one wants cream. I don't like storing, you know, live human stuff in the fridge over the weekend."

Lattner was on her heels, arms full of papers. "I brought some of the price lists and ceremony options. And this." He tossed a newspaper clipping on the table. "From *USA Today*. From when Martin did the service for Zach."

Martin felt a bubble of pleasure gurgle in his gut. His old boss and friend had seen, cut out, saved, and chose to produce the article, a short account of the town's over-the-top funeral for the beloved Zach. The piece included a rather striking photo of Martin at a lectern in the Bandstand-on-the-Lake and did not include a mention of his role in Zach's last moments, so Martin considered it a public relations coup.

Lattner spread the Final Paws brochures—titles like "Best Buddies and Bereavement" and "Dispatching Your Large Animal over the Rainbow Bridge"—in front of Mac and started fussing with the coffee cups, inserting himself into the business as he had been doing throughout the all-night process of moving Hero out of the lobby of the Theater-on-the-Lake and into the Final Paws Large Animal Funereal Facility. And now Lattner was prattling on about urns and faux marble memorial plaques to an increasingly grim Mac. Martin stayed silent. He was exhausted from navigating the crooked and continuing course of last night's catastrophe: experiencing yet another live action horse death; hearing in person, seeing in person, meeting in person the Cowboy Poet; possessing a skill of use to the Cowboy Poet. And now, talk of a funeral for Hero in Elko, at the Thirty-Second Annual Elko Cowboy Poetry Confluence, broadcast live in lieu of the final

Cowboy Poetry Hour, with Martin as the director of it all, the chief memorialist and mourner.

Through the murk of his fatigue and sorrow, one lantern beam shone through, and he moved toward it steadily and gratefully: He would perform at Elko. Not as an outsider, not as a Midwestern pet funeral director with delusions of a Western alter-ego, but as one with a role, the most solemn role, the master of the dispatch of that most famous of horses of that most famous of cowboy poets. He was on the course he had sought forever but had glimpsed only on the far horizon and only a few times. He had glimpsed it but never before had he felt its hard grit under his boots, its gentle incline towards the high desert. He had glimpsed it, but never before last night had he stepped on the road to Elko.

He had tried to call Julie several times over the last twelve hours, but she hadn't picked up. At five a.m., he finally texted *Going to Elko, for real. U still in?* She replied in less than a beat: *F-U.*

Lina crossed to the conference table and accepted a cup of coffee from Lattner. She passed her free hand over the spray of glossy paper on the table in front of Mac.

"I like this, a memorial book," Mac said, picking up one lemon-hued pamphlet from the pile. "We could take it to the shows, let people pay their last respects to Hero."

"Like Princess Di," said Annie. "I heard they had a book for Princess Di. It went all over Michigan."

"Nice. Princess Di," said Mac, buffing his tie with his fist and bobbing his head. "We could wheel the body out at the beginning, and Vess could, you know, say a few words and, like, for a ten dollar pledge, people could sign the book."

"Like Stalin," encouraged Lattner.

"Whoa, whoa, whoa," said Annie. "They did not bring Princess Di's body over here. I think it was all burned up anyway. They just had a book, you know, of condolences and some pictures."

"There's no sanitary way to keep a corpse of this tonnage on, as it were, ice for that period," said Martin. "And under the stage lights, I am afraid that the situation with fluid dispersal—"

Lina interrupted. "It doesn't matter. There are no more shows. Mac, it's settled. He'll do Elko and the funeral, and then he's done.

He's an old man, and he just lost his best friend and partner. The end."

Mac sucked his lips in, looked at the ceiling, and exhaled. "Shit."

"He'll do the funeral," said Lina and sat heavily on one of the conference table chairs, flicked at an information sheet on the Final Paws' new high capacity crematorium. "He's going back to the ranch until Elko, and he'll meet up there with Hero—I mean, Hero's remains, however it is they get there."

"I think Mr. Guffry has already seen and approved of the Final Paws' hearse option," said Lattner.

"The '71 Mustang?" said Lina. "Oh, Vess will love that."

"The stallion goes home on a stallion," said Mac and fanned his hands as if seeing it in lights. "I like it."

"You do know Hero's a mare, right? Was a mare," said Martin.

"Technically," said Mac. "But for press purposes, she's always been a stallion. And we're going to have to do press on the funeral, text PETS and give ten dollars in memory of Hero or some other dead animal. Or a live one. We've got to recoup some of the loss. Part of the spring fundraisers maybe."

"I don't care what you do," said Lina. "Just leave Vess out of it."

"I'll coordinate any media through you," said Mac. "And"—he swiveled around to Martin—"your press folks?"

"We don't—" said Martin.

"That's me, Bob Lattner," said Lattner, handing Lina and Mac a card. "That's my direct line."

"You okay with social media?" said Mac, running a finger over the card's edge, which curved as if hand cut.

"Oh yeah, pretty much all I do these days," said Lattner.

"Settled then." Lina stood up, drained the last of her coffee, and carried the cup to the trashcan by the door. Mac followed her.

"Wait," said Martin, bustling to the conference table and grabbing a fist of brochures. "We haven't talked about funeral arrangements. There are a surprising number of choices."

"Yeah," said Annie. "We had these one clients who had us bury the head and hooves of the horse and render the rest, because they said that's how they do it in Kentucky."

"Well, don't do that," said Mac. "Whatever's cheapest. Without being tacky. Or gross."

"Whatever gets you on the road to Elko the fastest," said Lina, leaving the room. "Let's get this over with."

The next morning, Martin paused in the doorway of the Final Paws' crematorium and contemplated the suspended mustang corpse.

"Wait," he said.

Mike Hueypipe, an auto mechanic, Annie's ex-boyfriend, and the Final Paws IEB Series 100 Cremation System batch load operator, backed away from the button controlling the stainless steel leviathan's electric-hydraulic loading door. Martin stepped forward. He placed his hand on Hero's stiff snout. Cold. Also cold: the cement floor radiating up through Martin's loafers, the mulch-laced May breeze blowing through the open sliding door of the tin building, the still air encasing the carcass dangling over the SmokeBuster burners.

Martin thought he should say something, some last word before the IEB-100 went to work reducing Hero's mortal remains to a trunk-worth of greasy sand and bone bits. Mike seemed to expect it, too, and stepped back from the machine's control panel, bowed his head.

Martin shut his eyes but nothing came. He couldn't recall any cow-boy poems that featured a mare, though he was sure they existed and that he had heard them. It disturbed him only a little that the Cowboy Poet had lied about Hero. After all, the stories the cowboy poets told were allegories, not census records, meant to shape lives, not count heads. Hero died, and because of that, Martin was going to Elko. Gender had nothing to do with it.

Mike cleared his throat. Martin opened his eyes, removed his hand, and spun out the first Knibbs that came to mind, the ultimate verses of "Do You Remember."

> *Beyond each step there spread the deep Unknown;*
> *Below a hidden stream sang ceaselessly;*
> *We rode together—yet each rode alone,*
> *Do you remember, friend, who rode with me?*

As he intoned the last words, he opened his eyes, looked at the dead horse, and realized he was talking to Julie as much as Hero. She should be here. More than that, he needed her here. As excited as he was to ride the trail ahead, he wasn't sure he was ready "to flirt with death" with only Lattner flanking him. Mike joined Martin in front of the open IEB-100 loading door.

"Thanks, man," Mike said. "Really, I mean it. Thanks. A tribute, that's what that was. A fucking tribute." He patted Martin's back. "You know how to send a soul into the fire, man. Makes my job easier."

Martin sighed and turned to exit the tin building. Behind him, the IEB-100 doors clanged shut and the SmokeBuster burners whooshed on.

Martin headed from the crematorium to his office but stopped off at the doorway to the Family and Friends Comfort and Conference Room, where Lattner and Annie were planning for the cross-country trip. Lattner shouted orders into a Bluetooth headphone set, setting up some sort of press event on the following Thursday, when they planned to start the drive. The funeral was scheduled for the Saturday of the Thirty-Second Annual Elko Cowboy Poetry Confluence. That gave them two weeks to get to Elko, more than enough time to navigate any unforeseen—but in Martin's case, always expected—detours. It also gave them time to meet Mac in Denver at the office of NPR's KRCC, so the final details of the ceremony could be worked through. Or any details, Martin thought with a touch of contempt, though on the whole, he was pleased Mac and Lina seemed to be leaving it up to him. He mentally congratulated them for recognizing his rare amalgamation of cowboy poetry and large companion aftercare experience.

Annie looked up at Martin. "If you drove straight through, you'd be there in twenty-five hours." A bowlegged, squirrel-brown shih tzu with black-tipped ears and glaucoma-shaded fruit bat eyes stumbled out from under the table, bumped into Martin's right ankle, and started licking the top of his shoe.

"We are men of a certain age," said Lattner, flipping through the state maps. "There will be stopping."

"Down, Fancy Pants," Annie said to the dog, who squinted at her, then bent to probe Martin's sole with its tongue. She turned to Martin: "Bob needs an iPad. Can I use the card?"

Martin nodded yes. "Start an NPR account." No one had spoken of paying for all this, and he had not felt he could ask. He was deft at working financing matters into discussions with grieving pet owners, but this was different. Hero wasn't just a pet. He was Martin's entry ticket to Elko on terms he had long thought unattainable. Anyway, this was public broadcasting, not Bernie Madoff. They'd pay the bills.

"Try to find a refurbished one," he said to Annie.

Martin shook his foot. Fancy Pants flipped onto his back with a howl, and Martin continued to his office. The cost—and there would be cost—of Hero's funeral didn't concern Martin per se, but he wanted to leave Final Paws on sound financial footing. Because he was leaving, right? When he and Julie had talked about this year's confluence, they had never said this would be the beginning of a new life out West for Martin, but it had been assumed. He had assumed it, then and now.

His preparations over the next week reflected that certainty. He arranged his files of proven eulogies and creative burial options so Annie could continue to minister to the lofty standard he had set. He emptied his refrigerator and freezer and donated the two cases of Diet Coke he had bought on sale to the YMCA. He labeled a box "Ship to Martin Oliphant or bequest to the Pierre Public Library" and filled it with cowboy poetry: tomes like: *Steering With My Knees* by Paul Zarzyski, *New Cowboy Poetry: A Contemporary Gathering, One Hundred Poems* by Waddie Mitchell, *National Cowboy Poetry Gathering: The Anthology, Towards Horses: Poems* by Shadd Piehl, *Bitter Creek Junction* by Linda Hasselstrom; recordings of Wally McRae and Glenn Ohrlin and Georgie Sicking and Red Shuttleworth and Sandy Seaton Sallee; back issues of the *Dry Crik Review of Contemporary Cowboy Poetry* and *American Cowboy;* the works of the masters of the golden age: Henry Herbert Knibbs, Arthur Chapman, E.A. Brininstool, Bruce Kiskaddon, Curley Fletcher; and the books of the early collectors, John Lomax and, of course, Jack Thorp.

Early morning on the day of their departure, Martin placed *Songs of the Cowboys* on the top of the pile and covered it with a few old photos: his mom and dad, pre-cancer and pre-stroke, in tennis whites, waving matching Wilson T2000s at the bubble's gloom; Lattner and Mrs. Trinkle posing behind her typewriter, stiff bearings, open smiles; Martin and an infant Frank at a forgotten beach, Martin staring into the camera, Frank squalling on a striped blanket; young Julie, long hair gilded in a beam of winter sunlight, holding his mom's hand. Martin closed the cardboard flaps, secured the top with a double measure of packing tape, and left the box in the middle of his mostly empty living room.

The walk from his apartment to Final Paws was a short one, and he pushed into the front doors an hour before the mortuary opened, planning on going over his files and his final instructions to Annie one last time before anyone showed up. At his desk, he found Lattner, head in his hands, staring into a tumbler. A half-empty bottle of Jack Daniels sat atop the files Martin had come to review.

"Mac called me last night," Lattner said. "Some contract snafu with the Cowboy Poet. He said we had to cancel the press event. I got through to the churro booth guy and told the PPHS band director to deploy the phone chain. So we'll have a nice, quiet exit."

"What about the funeral?" said Martin, his heart bungee jumping to groin-level, twanging back to his throat.

"Still on as far as I know," said Lattner, pouring himself half a glass of whiskey. "Mac didn't say not to come."

"Right," said Martin, though it didn't feel right. This had always been his greatest fear. He would arrive at Elko without portfolio. He wouldn't find Beaufort or Ginger or any of their like, just strangers, who would look at him with laughing eyes and ask: "Who are you again?"

"So what do we do if the funeral's off?" Martin said.

"Have a few beers with the cowboys and listen to some poetry, I guess," said Lattner. "Isn't that what this whole thing's about?"

The girl in the blue uniform with the maize braid leaned over the hood of the Mustang and puffed at her piccolo like a glue sniffer huffing at a paper bag. Martin shut the car window against the atonal cheeping and the accompanying and lackadaisical tapping from the snare drummer next to her. The PPHS Marching Band phone chain had not stretched to these two, and they had shown up determined to peep and pound through their musical tribute to Hero, undaunted by the absence of the rest of their corps.

Martin had twice slammed the car door and thrice opened it, the third time just now. The choice was to endure the musical piece to its ear-scraping end or suffocate. The space in which air could circulate through the car's black leather-clad interior was limited, and what

oxygen molecules there were had to squeeze between the strawberry-fig mist emitting from the Febreze car vent inserts and the fog of
blue cheese seeping from Lattner's oversized hard-shell Samsonite.

The latter was wedged behind the passenger seat and pushed at its
back. Martin doubted he could bear the vertical posture this arrange-
ment imposed for another ten minutes, forget the twenty-five road
hours it would take to get to Denver then Elko. Next to the Samsonite
was a plastic tub holding the earthly remains of Hero, and on top of
both, was Martin's bag, a red LL Bean duffle with "Julie Oliphant"
embroidered in script on its side.

The piccolo piped unabated, and Martin wished he had volunteered to drive the first shift. He would have started up the car, just
to let them know it was time to trill off into the sunset. He wouldn't
have hit them, maybe just nudged the bumper up to the creases in
their band uniform pants.

The piper and drummer paused. Martin feared they were looking
for more sheet music.

"Start the car, goddamn it," he barked at Lattner.

Lattner scrabbled with the keys and switched on the ignition. The
Mustang rumbled then roared, black smoke puffed from the tail pipe,
and the PPHS band members scurried. Lattner shifted into first gear
and let the beast inch forward on the gravel drive. Annie and Mike
waved from the steps of Final Paws.

As they pulled out onto Niles Avenue, Martin heard a final drum
roll from the snare and Mike's fading salute: "Easy on the clutch,
man."

Lattner weaved into the turn lane on Niles Avenue, and a grey
dump truck honked, swerved, and sprayed gravel onto the road behind.

"Watch it," said Martin. "Can you handle this thing?"

"I got it here, didn't I?" said Lattner. "It's just this." He pointed to
a long wisp of white hair that had deserted his comb-over and was
buzzing in front of his eyes as if pulled by a tethered bee.

"Shut the window then," said Martin.

"The car smells of horse remains," said Lattner.

"If there is an odor to the cremains, it is the odor of the earth and
pastures from which our beloved friends have come and will return,"

said Martin, quoting an International Association of Pet Cemeteries and Crematories educational brochure entitled *Grief Doesn't Have to Stink*.

"Bullshit," said Lattner but rolled up his window anyway.

Several minutes of silent and straight driving ensued, and Martin closed his eyes and let the essences of Febreze, Roquefort, and—Lattner was right—wet cremains battle for dominance of his nostrils. Maybe they should move the computer equipment to the back and put Lattner's case in the trunk. Hero presented more of a problem. The tub was temporary storage for the twenty-plus pounds of ash and bone until Annie could FedEx Martin the western-styled box that would be Hero's final resting stall. The tub wouldn't fit in the trunk; they had tried.

Lattner began to hack, a guttural clanging, like the frying pans on a runaway chuckwagon. When he took his hands off the wheel to pound on his rattling chest, Martin said, "Why don't we pull off and repack? Your bag can go in the trunk and Hero on the rack. The Febreze is with us for the duration, I'm afraid."

"The lesser evil," said Lattner and turned left into The Apple Place, a fresh fruit and vegetable stand which, in mid-May in Pierre, had at least another month before there were any frost-blacked greens or stunted strawberries to offer. The plank shelves in the open wooden shed stood empty and a hand-printed sign announcing PUMPKINS lay on the dirt drive.

Lattner continued around the abandoned sales area on a rugged dirt path to the back of the shed. The Mustang pitched, the lid of the tub popped free on one end, and Martin whacked his knee on the gear shift.

"What are you doing?" he said.

"Just in case we were followed by press," said Lattner, jerking to a stop in front of a canting wooden apple hold. "I don't want it getting out that we've run into technical difficulties this soon."

Martin got out of the car, avoided a gopher hole and a small pile of dog shit, and unloaded the trunk: two laptops, Lattner's scribble-infested legal pads, Martin's Luccheses, jumper cables, and a plastic crate containing a roll of paper towels, a water-damaged copy of *A Confederacy of Dunces*, several torn pages from the tic disorder section of the DSM-IV schedule, a bag of organic mangos, a child's wooden hammer, and a set of bungee cords.

Martin held up the cords. "Excellent, these will work for the tub."

"'Be prepared,' that's my motto," said Lattner, picking up a DSM-IV page, smoothing it, and placing it back in the crate.

The two men sorted and secured their baggage and re-situated themselves in the front of the Mustang. Martin had offered to drive, but Lattner insisted he would do it.

"I enjoy actively taking leave of Pierre," he said. He turned the key but no rumble, no roar, just a whirr and a single click.

"Problem?" said Martin.

"Needs to warm up," said Lattner.

Martin settled back and stared out the window at the apple trees tentatively offering up tight blossoms to the frost gods. He was learning to live with the stench of strawberry-fig.

"Why did you go?" said Martin. "Besides the lawsuits."

"That was a part of it," said Lattner, eyes fixed front, "but mostly it was for you. And Irene."

"She was a wreck," said Martin, remembering Mrs. Trinkle cleaning out her desk, tears blotching her pale cheeks, hair askew, white cardigan buttoned wrong and stained with coffee. "She threw out her typewriter. And yours."

"Yeah, and she moved to Cabo with Paul, like she'd wanted to do for twenty years," said Lattner.

"But she died," said Martin.

"She died happy," said Lattner.

"What about me?" said Martin.

"You?" said Lattner. "I thought you'd go west."

Martin had suspected that. "I'm going now. It had to be right."

Lattner reached over and patted Martin's thigh. "You patch it up with Julie?"

"She won't take my calls," said Martin.

"Give it a few more days," said Lattner. He tried the ignition again. This time it took, and the Mustang sprang forward. "Then tell her you're sorry."

As they bumped back out The Apple Place's driveway, Martin considered whether he should listen to the old man on the subject of

Julie, or women in general, or anything to do with the human race at all. Still, Martin knew he would have to apologize. He'd been selfish and cowardly. Julie got hurt because she believed in him, the him he wanted to be, the him that he could be if he could just get Hero to Elko.

They turned onto Niles Avenue, and Lattner stepped hard on the Mustang's accelerator. "Good, good," he mumbled, his eyes on the steadily climbing speed gauge.

"Slow down," said Martin. "You're going to miss the turn."

Lattner passed the sign for I-94 West. "Do you smell smoke?" he asked. "Because I see smoke." He adjusted the rearview mirror and slowed.

Martin looked back. A plume of gray fanned out behind them.

"Is the Mustang on fire?" said Lattner.

"I don't think it's the Mustang," said Martin, watching the blue plastic lid of the cremains tub cartwheel down the shoulder. "I think it's Hero."

NPR Cancels Cowboy Poetry Hour Final Tour after Horse Death

Jayden M. Jones, USA TODAY 7:21 a.m. EDT May 13, 2016

NPR has cancelled the last two weeks of cowboy poet radio personality Vess Guffry's *Cowboy Poetry Hour Farewell Tour* after Guffry's horse Hero died on stage during a performance in Pierre, Michigan. According to NPR special projects spokesman, Mac Cooper, Guffry and his program will broadcast the final *Cowboy Poetry Hour* on Saturday, May 28 from the 32nd Annual Elko Cowboy Poetry Confluence in Elko, Nevada, as previously scheduled, and the show will be expanded to carry live the funeral for the mustang Hero.

Cooper refused to comment further on rumors that the tour cancellation and refocus on Hero's funeral was the result of contract disputes between Guffry and NPR on the terms of the Cowboy Poet's departure from the long-running program. For the last several years, the once popular *Cowboy Poetry Hour* has suffered from declining ratings and stories of dissention among what one source has called a "bloated" staff. Another anonymous source from the NPR fundraising department told *USA TODAY* that the program brought in far less in pledge dollars than it spent on Guffry's salary, the expenses of the travelling show, out-of-court settlements with several past employees, and compensation for guest performers "who have less to do with the West or poetry and more to do with who Guffry's screwing or owes money to."

Bob Lattner, press spokesman for Final Paws Pet Mortuary 'n Cemetery of Pierre, Michigan, the business handling the funeral arrangements for Hero, denied strongly the suggestion that the horse's funeral was a ploy to distract attention from the *Cowboy Poetry Hour*'s financial and personnel problems. "Vess Guffry is one of the most decent, talented, and honorable cowboys I have had the honor to meet. That he would want, and that NPR would grant, a public and fitting send-off for his longtime trail companion, Hero, speaks volumes about the character of both the man and the institution. A stallion of a funeral for a stallion of a horse is in the finest tradition of the American West and the patriotic spirit of our beautiful America."

14

Martin fell asleep that night to the sounds of rain and visions of Hero's cremains, a muddy swirl flowing into the storm drains off Niles Avenue. All night, the specters clung to him like Pomeranian hair on black gabardine—Hero charging across a dusty plain then bursting into flames; Annie and Lattner dancing with sputtering torches around his mother's cancer-clawed corpse; Ginger turned succubus, raven hair on fire, plunging her head into his lap while Julie applauded.

The clock radio alarm he had not set snapped on to wavering static at six a.m., and he batted at it for ten full minutes before he could get it to shut off. Through the thin walls of the Lime City, Iowa Super 8, he could hear Lattner snoring and considered waking him and making an early start of it, though of what he wasn't sure. A funeral procession sans remains. Hero's final ride, sans Hero. Hard to justify rushing.

He pulled his laptop from the nightside table, opened it, and loaded Skype. Julie had blocked his cell number several days before, but he hoped she hadn't gotten around to purging him from all her contact lists. He'd send a message. Something along the lines of: *Help, what am I supposed to do now?* And an apology. Maybe the apology first.

The program blooped on, and Martin saw that, not only had Julie kept his account open, but also that she was online right then. Forgetting the elegant missive of regret he had planned to compose, he hit the video call icon and tapped on the desk edge to the beat of the sing-song ring. After two choruses, a click, and a dark silhouette filled most of the frame. Whatever light she had on in the room was directly behind her head. He was relieved not to have to look in her eyes.

"Hey," he said. "What's going on?" This was not the tone he had meant to set, but it was the best he could do in his current state of unbalance.

A pause, during which Martin was certain the screen would blink off, then: "I'm buying sheep. Jacobs. I like their horns. You know, you can buy sheep online, pay-now button and everything. I think I'll make an awesome shepherd."

Martin didn't know what to say to that, so he said the wrong thing: "Are you drunk?"

Another long pause, a deep sigh, the clink of ice against glass. "Drinking, not drunk. What do you want?"

Now or never, thought Martin. "To say I'm sorry. About Elko, about everything."

"Worked out for you, though, didn't it?" she said.

"But not for you," he said.

She snorted a laugh. "Don't worry about me. In fact, I should thank you. You gave me the bitch-slap I needed to get back on track. You made me see how stupid I was to latch onto such a stupid dream, and it wasn't even my stupid dream."

"That's a lot of stupid," he said.

"Yes, it was," she said. "I had a long drive back to think about it."

"I wish you were still here," he said. "It's not going that great. Lattner's crazy and we lost Hero's ashes."

Julie laughed again, this time in a tone thawed a degree or two from subzero. "Use dirt instead. It's not like anyone's going to be running DNA tests."

"I thought of that, but the deception really bothers me." It wasn't that he couldn't live a lie. He could. He had. He was a master lie-liver, honed the talent over the last thirty-odd years, a sizable chip off his father's shape-shifting block. But Martin couldn't live this lie, a lie to Elko.

"Lying to me was okay, but not to your cowboy poet friends—excuse me, imaginary cowboy poet friends? You do know, don't you, that everything about your beloved cowboy poetry is a lie. Have you ever looked up your hero, Vess Guffry? He grew up Morry Cohen, the son of a shoe salesman in Queens, got his start in radio reading Christian inspirational poetry for the local station's Saturday shut-in programming. From the time he was about twenty until he was almost forty, no record of Morry, though there are rumors of jail time for statutory rape and bookmaking. He shows up again in the late seventies in Dallas as Vess Guffry, a rodeo announcer. He gets his first public radio gig from the station manager down there, a gambling addict with a taste for the sort of high-stakes games Morry-slash-Vess liked to run. The rest is history, maybe not poetry, but history. There's your sanctified Cowboy Poet. So I wouldn't sweat a little subterfuge in the funeral prep."

Martin knew about the Cowboy Poet's East Coast origins, but not the rest of it. And he didn't believe it. "Really?" he said. "What tabloid did you read that in?"

"Wikipedia," said Julie. "Vess Guffry isn't famous enough or interesting enough to get covered by the tabloids or any of the online gossip sites that people from this century read. You could have looked it up yourself. But you're lazy. All those years, I thought you were so noble, living by this strict code of honor that demanded you silently suffer and help others along the trail and keep your eyes on that far mountain horizon. But that's pure bullshit. You just set your sights on something so unattainable and unreal that you never have to make the effort to take the shot. You're not idealistic. You're lazy."

Martin gulped back a sob. "What do I do?" he said.

"Prove me wrong," said Julie. "Take your box of dirt and get your ass to Elko."

After Julie hung up, Martin lay back on the bed and, stunned by her call to action, passed out. Two hours later, he awoke to a pounding on the connecting door between his and Lattner's rooms.

"I got donut holes," Lattner yelled.

Martin unlocked the door to a showered and shaved Lattner. "You've got to read this *USA Today* piece," he said, waving the paper in the hand not clutching the Dunkin' Donuts bag. "Our funeral's gone national."

Martin took the paper and scanned the article, dated that morning. "Nice job," he said, trying to shake off the funk of Julie's words. "You sound very professional. Vess and Lina have got to love it."

Lattner popped the donut hole in his mouth, choked, recovered. "I am professional. And Lina did love it. She called this morning, looking for you."

"Does she know about Hero?" said Martin.

"Know what about Hero?" said Lattner. "She wants you to call back."

Martin decided to shower first. He also decided not to mention the premature scattering of Hero's cremains. Not because of what Julie said, but because it didn't matter, he realized. Nor did Vess Guffry's sanitized history. Or whatever the Cowboy Poet had done to get himself in trouble with the NPR legal department. A yarn, embellished with cowbells and whorehouse piano tinklings and talking broncos, was in the fine tradition of cowboy poetry. So why should Martin have a problem lying about, or simply not explaining every little detail of, the funeral to Lina? He climbed into the plastic tube that passed for a shower at Super 8 and ran the water until it steamed. He rubbed his fingernails with a washcloth until his cuticles bled and his hair with a sliver of Wyndham branded soap until his scalp burned. He rehearsed what he would say to Lina and what he should have said to Julie and washed his body like every inch of it was made of Lady Macbeth's bloody hands.

Martin returned to the office, took out his cell, and punched the number Lattner had given him.

"Martin." Lina picked up before it could ring. "I only got a minute. Vess has me picking up some new spurs for Elko, but I just wanted to say thank you. That article could have been a disaster for him, for us both, but your PR guy saved the day. We're getting calls now from NPR top brass about making even a bigger deal out of the funeral, and they've stopped all that trash talk about contract violations. And PBS wants to record it for later broadcast, you know, like Aretha Franklin at the White House. Or that guy from *Full House* on the Capitol lawn on Fourth of July. Vess is so happy. He's accepting it all, retirement, Hero's death, the last show at Elko, with the kind of good grace I haven't seen out of him since—I don't know—since the first Hero."

"First Hero?" said Martin. "There was another Hero?"

"Oh my God, there've been at least fifteen, maybe close to twenty," said Lina. "Some sucked on stage and we sold 'em off for pets or to dude ranches. Others were just mean or couldn't be properly broke. Let me tell you, if we had to do it again, which thank God we do not, we wouldn't start with a mustang, that's for sure."

"What happened to those?" said Martin. "The mean ones."

"The kill pen, usually," said Lina. "The West has unrideable mustangs like that latest Hero had flies, God rest her itchy soul."

"Of course," said Martin, trying to take in her cavalier roll call of the dead and murdered Heroes of the past. Lie upon lie. Taint upon taint. Riding to Elko on the back of a bunch of slaughtered frauds.

"One sec," said Lina and then something else in a muffled tone. The familiar Cowboy Poet's bass bore into Martin's right ear, and he instinctively reached to turn the radio down:

> *The pony drinks, but with gasp and sob,*
> *And wan is the man at its side;*
> *The way has been long, past butte and knob,*
> *And still he must ride and ride.*

"Arthur Chapman," said Martin. "'Pony Express.'"

"Will you recite it, Martin?" said the Cowboy Poet. "Will you recite it for Hero, for me? Will you read at Elko?"

Yes. Of course. He would read over the fake ashes of a fake Hero, one of a line of fake Heroes. Yes, he would answer the call of his hero, flawed mortal though he may be. Yes, he would rise to Julie's taunts, be a man of action and find his place in a Western world of Beaufort and Ginger and cowboy poets living and dead, a world he believed—he knew—was real.

"I will read at Elko," said Martin. "Count on it." And he hung up.

Forgotten
by Bruce Kiskaddon (1878-1950)

Yes, he used to be a cow hoss
that was young and strong and fleet.
Now he stands alone, forgotten,
in the winter snow and sleet.
Fer his eyes is dim and holler
and his head is turnin' gray,
He has got too old to foller—
"Jest a hoss that's had his day."

They've forgotten how once he packed 'em
at a easy swingin' lope.
How he braced his sturdy shoulders
when he set back on a rope.
Didn't bar no weight nor distance;
answered every move and word,
Though his sides were white with lather
while he held the millin' herd.

Now he's stiff and old and stumbles,
and he's lost the strength and speed
That once took him through the darkness,
'round the point of a stampede
And his legs is scarred and battered;
both the muscle and the bone.
He is jest a wore out cow hoss
so they've turned him out alone.

They have turned him out to winter
best he can amongst the snow.
There without a friend and lonesome,
do you think he doesn't know?
Through the hours of storm and darkness
he had time to think a lot.
That hoss may have been forgotten,
but you bet he ain't forgot.

He stands still. He ain't none worried,
fer he knows he's played the game.
He's got nothin' to back up from.
he's been square and ain't ashamed.
Fer no matter where they put him,
he was game to do his share.
Well, I think more of the pony
than the folks that left him there.

15

Martin sank into a modern—if by modern one meant awkwardly shaped and ugly—tall-backed office chair in the windowless conference room in the *Cowboy Poetry Hour's* suite at the Denver Creek Office Complex and Condominiums. The room smelled of carpet cleaner, and a thigh-high wall vent blew cold air through the mesh on Martin's chair. He worried the sweat that had collected in the small of his back might ice over.

He was the first to arrive and so considered moving to another seat to avoid the draft. But he already had his folder of possible funeral poems, a virgin yellow legal pad, and two pens set in front of him and his briefcase leaned against his chair leg. He was phlegmatic at the moment, and the flurry of resituating would make him less so. Martin checked his phone for messages from Lattner, who had opted out of the meeting to go find a place to get the Mustang detailed, preferably a car wash with saloon attached. "We're in the West, my boy," he'd said. "Who knows what wonders await!"

"Martin, thanks so much for coming. Don't get up." Lina circled the table and laid a concealer-caked cheek on Martin's freshly shaved counterpart. She reeked the waxy reek of too much make-up. He put a hand to his face and examined the greasy residue transferred to his fingers.

"Oh my God, I must look like an Oompa Loompa," said Lina, taking a seat and touching her own cheek. "I was doing an interview for the PBS guys. They're treating this show like the bleeding Olympics, you know, with short features on the athletes, about how they grew up in some hut with no feet?"

"Show and funeral," said Martin.

"Right. It's getting really complicated. Wyatt Wendt is involved. We should have known he'd horn in, and there's all sorts of questions about timing. Mac will be in in a minute. He's photocopying."

Martin sniffed and wrote *photocopying* on his legal pad. Looked at it. Underlined it twice. Thought about what it meant that Wyatt Wendt, the second most famous cowboy poet after the Cowboy Poet, would be part of Martin's funeral. Hero's funeral. On one hand, there's no denying the upside of having star power illuminate his Elko debut. He would perform with two of the greats. Except for having a neoclassical arch erected at the front door to the Elko Convention Center, entrances don't get much more triumphal than that. But on the other hand, the left hand, sinister, the one that hides with the pistol while the right one shakes "howdy…"

"Sorry, guys, toner was low."

Mac pushed into the room with an armful of stapled documents and dumped them on the table. "One each," he said, slid a packet to Martin and another to Lina, took his own, and sat. Martin looked at the top sheet, gasped, then fake-sneezed to cover. First in the numbered index was the item: Order of Service/draft program. Martin flipped to find the page. He had not sent them anything on the service, though he had his ideas. What if it were all set? With Wyatt Wendt and Vess Guffry (and maybe even Nina Totenberg) and Martin relegated to the overflow room to watch it on a rented TV. He found the page.

IN THANKSGIVING FOR AND
IN CELEBRATION OF THE LIFE OF
BENJAMIN CROWNINSHIELD BRADLEE
AUGUST 26, 1921-OCTOBER 21, 2014

"I had no idea he died," said Lina.

"Copeland processional, Sousa recessional," said Martin, flipping through the program, deep breaths of relief. "Nice choices, though I think it's unlikely we can get David Ignatius for the eulogy. Not on such short notice."

"Top notch logistics work here, Mac," said Lina.

"It's just an example, of what we could do," Mac said and fiddled with his bolo tie, the one concession to the West in his otherwise pure Brooks Brothers, Michigan Avenue corporate uniform. "I found it online."

"Could do, if Hero had been a revered editor of a major paper credited with bringing down President Nixon," said Lina.

"The TV people needed something." Mac's face flushed, and Martin feared the young man had garroted himself with his neckwear.

Lina sighed, looked at Martin, bit her bottom lip, and smiled.

Lipstick remnant smeared like blood from eyetooth to eyetooth, a raccoon after a chicken kill.

"There are a couple things we know for sure," she said. "One, the red Mustang will deliver Vess to the funeral but won't be in the processional. We finally got him to agree on that. There'll be a mounted honor guard up first, then the celebrants, or mourners, or whatever they're called. That's you, Martin, and Wyatt and whoever else pushes in once they find out it'll be on TV. And Vess. We're still talking about this, but Vess wants you all to be on horseback, and he would walk, the walking man, that poem, you know it right?"

Martin cleared his throat:

Sunny summer day it was when loping in to Laramie,
I overtook the Walking Man, reined up and nodded "How!!"
He'd been a rider once, I knew. He smiled, but scarce aware of me,
He said, "If you would like me to, I'll tell my story now."

"Oh, no need, Martin," said Mac. "I've got a lunch, and we have more to get through."

"It's a poem," said Lina.

"Knibbs," said Martin.

"Great," said Mac.

"So riding is okay?" said Lina to Martin.

No, of course it was not okay. It would, in the best possible of circumstances, add a Jerry Lewis-like slapstick quality to the proceedings, and, in the worst, kill Martin and probably at least one of the horses.

"When I ride, I prefer my own mount, Vesuvius," said Martin. He pressed his lips together and tried not to say anything else. He feared more regrettable words were about to flow, like the toxic lava from the volcano after which he had just named his imaginary horse.

"Because the other option is for you to ride on the caisson, with Hero's remains, which might actually be more appropriate."

"Oh, absolutely," said Martin, so pleased he had opted for the classiest of cremains chests to hold the handful of surviving Hero ashes and several shovels of dirt from an I-80 traveler's plaza. The container was a handsome thing, with its engraved hasps and russet leather straps and distressed wood slats and discreet Plexiglas holders for two portraits of the deceased. It would photograph well on the back of a horse-drawn hearse. And he would cut a poignant figure in his black Circle S suit with the double peak backed Western yokes and the center vent for ease of movement. It would be cowboy poetry in motion. Performance cowboy poetry. Might even make the poster for the confluence one year.

"And," said Lina, "show Martin that picture, the one Vess found on Pinterest. This is something we've got to do."

"At the end of the handout," said Mac, not meeting her eye and in a tone that suggested he had not forgiven their reaction to the Bradlee funeral template.

Martin flipped pages. The last was a color print of Princess Anne, a fur hat straddling her chestnut bouffant like a poisonous fungus atop a forest stump. She held one gloved hand to the gleaming amber muzzle of a horse, his head drooping from the back of a sleek trailer marked with the royal seal in flourishes of gold. If Martin had not known the steed was dead, had not been able to make out the silken sling, colored the same deep brown as the animal, that kept its head up, he would have assumed it was just bowing in deference to its royal owner.

"You know it?" said Mac.

Martin counted to ten, tried not to pant. Of course he knew it. What pet memorialist worthy of his title didn't know about Starwood's funeral? 2009. Carried live on CNN and CSPAN. Seven thousand people in attendance at Gatcombe Park, including Prince William and newly minted Secretary of State Hilary Clinton. A tribute medley performed by Elton John and Lady Gaga. Twenty-three bottles of embalming fluid and two cranes to lower and secure the body in the custom-designed combination horse trailer, casket, and tomb. Martin had spent many hours convincing grieving equine owners of the impracticality and prohibitive expense of the "Starwood Service."

Lina looked at Martin and Martin looked at Mac. "What is it you like about this picture?" Martin said, trying hard not to screech. Maybe, just maybe, what they liked were the clothes. That instead of Western, the clearly dementing Cowboy Poet had decided he wanted the funeral to look like a day at the Royal Ascot.

"It's her." Lina pointed to Princess Anne.

"If we can't get David Ignatius, I am fairly certain Princess Anne won't be available," said Martin.

Lina ignored him. "Vess wants to do that. That final pat good-bye. We showed it to the PBS folks, and they went nuts. It might even be the reason they decided to tape it for TV. So read "Walking Man" or "Where the Ponies Come to Drink" or "Yankee Doodle Dandy" for all I care, but we've got to get that shot." She tapped the picture three times.

"You can do it, right?" said Mac. "Because if not, well, I mean I know some people in London. We could talk to the undertakers there."

"Pet memorialists," said Martin and blacked out.

Later that day, still in Denver, or at least in its foothills, in another windowless conference room, at another faux wood veneered table, Martin contemplated another framed poster of the Maroon Bells and yearned to get out of enclosed office spaces and take a look at the Rockies for himself. He had a hard time believing there were really that many lupines.

This conference room smelled of iodine and cat piss. And the McDonald's french fries Lattner was eating one at a time, dangling each in front of his mouth, as if it were a worm on a hook, nibbling delicately, leaving the very tip intact.

Martin's stomach tilted, and he held the ice pack Julie had given him to his forehead. No bruise yet, but definitely a knot where he had cracked his head on the edge of the conference table in the *Cowboy Poetry Hour's* offices. He remembered discussing the Bradlee and Starwood funerals, a flash of that room's Maroon Bells poster, and black. He had heard Lina's nasal diagnosis—"altitude"—and a door slam. Next thing, the young receptionist in the Radio Lab dancing cat sweatshirt was guiding him to the elevator, one manicured hand at his elbow, pressing a plastic bottle of water on him.

"Hydration, it's the key to everything," she had said as the elevator doors shut. The key to everything! That's just what he needed. A key to everything. Or, at minimum, a key to turning Hero's paltry remains and rest stop dirt into an embalmed horse corpse in a funereal trailer.

"Why are we here again?" Martin asked Lattner.

"Because you need a dead horse, and Julie works for a vet," said Lattner, not moving his eyes from his work arranging french fry tips into letters.

Julie walked into the room, paused, as if considering what sort of greeting this called for, tilted her head, and sighed. "Bob says you need a dead horse. Again."

"Chopo was alive when we took him," Lattner said.

"Has it ever occurred to you, Martin," said Julie, "that the cost of your literary hobby, in terms of equine lives, is oddly high?"

"You were right," said Martin. "If I want to go to Elko, I've got to do what it takes to go to Elko. And what it takes right now is a dead horse. Again."

"Also, has it occurred to you that I work for a vet?" Julie continued. "And that the job of vets is to keep animals healthy and alive, not to serve as a Shoppers' Food Warehouse for every wacko in need of a horse corpse? And how's your head?" She walked around the table to where Martin sat, placed a hand on his ice-bedewed bump. Her touch was warm and dry. Martin leaned into her.

"Okay," he said.

"Oh, Martin," she said. "You idiot."

Martin shut his eyes and was mortified to feel tears escape onto his cheeks.

"We can pay," said Lattner.

"Actually, we can't," said Martin, turning away from Julie. "We've maxed out my credit cards and blown through any cash Final Paws had on hand."

"Ask Lina for an advance," said Lattner.

"To buy the body for her funeral?" said Martin.

"Listen to me," said Julie, who had taken the seat next to Martin. "I don't have a corpse to sell." She hung her head for a moment, as if exhausted. "But there's an auction tomorrow. I can take you. You can pick up something from the kill pen and for not that much. But you will need cash."

At sunrise the next day, Martin pulled the Mustang onto a parking pad at 414 Mumford Drive, Evergreen, Colorado.

"You have reached your destination!" Martin's GPS chirped as she had been chirping since he made the turn into the driveway. Normally, he appreciated her enthusiasm at the end of a successful journey. But today he thought he heard a buzz of condescension just below the surface of her usual panegyrics. Maybe he had just had enough of her this morning, and she of him. It had been a long ride, with multiple turns and switchbacks, through the foothills to Frank's mansion.

Martin rocked himself out of the bucket seat, looped back around the car, and tested with one booted toe the inlaid river stone path to the front door. It shone slick as if recently hosed down, and perhaps it was. This looked like the sort of place where a uniformed lackey might creep out at dawn to sprinkle the walkways and dew wash the staged natural outcroppings of rock and native wildflower.

Martin stopped several yards from the front door to admire the mountain view.

Did you ever stand on the ledges,
On the brink of the great plateau
And look from their jagged edges
On the country that lay below?

Martin had not heard this particular paracusia before, though he knew who it was: Bruce Kiskaddon, the poet. Most knew him for "When They've Finished Shipping Cattle in the Fall"—perhaps the saddest, truest portrait there is of a wrangler without a steer to wrangle. But "The Time to Decide" was one you didn't hear that often. Martin had videotaped himself reading it for this year's Elko entry, hoping to impress the known Kiskaddon devotees on the panel.

Beyond the stone facade of the house, the Continental Divide floated in a cushion of backlit cirriform clouds. Martin placed his hand on a boulder and took a deep breath. The air bit at his nose with the scent of flowers and ice. He looked for, but couldn't see any, lupines.

How long had it been since cowboy poetry had come to him like this, unbidden? It seemed it had always been there when he was younger, much younger. Always whispering in his ear, waking him at night, reminding him of who he was, or at least who he was meant to be. When had it stopped chasing him, when had he started chasing it? That must have been when he went wrong.

"You're not going to faint, are you?" Frank stood silhouetted in the golden light streaming from his open front door. "Lots of you flatlanders can't deal with the altitude. Come in and have some water. FIJI Water, the expensive kind."

Martin followed his brother into an open kitchen; glowing amber cabinets of polished wood encased stainless steel and black gloss appliances. It was the most beautiful wood Martin had ever seen, and not just the cabinets. The floor, the chairs at the obsidian granite kitchen island, the built-in window seat with beige leather top, the round table there, the living room beyond. A river of wood, the felled and planed bodies of virginal wood nymphs, wood flowing around sleek couches and armoires, wood floating rugs of muted and intricate design, wood rising up beyond the stone fireplace in graceful shelving. Wood in the browns of single malts, fawns' coats, and coffee con leches; in the oranges of hearth fires, winter sunsets, and Velveeta; in the reds of summer's roses, Irish Setters, and their mother's favorite lipstick shade, Divine Wine.

Frank stood on tiptoe on a patch of this glorious wood and poked in the higher regions of a massive kitchen cabinet.

"Is it too much to ask that we keep chia seeds in stock? How am I supposed to have this without chia seeds?" Frank pointed at the green drink he had pulled from the refrigerator. Martin did not answer because he could imagine no condiment, chia seed or otherwise, that would induce him to ingest what Frank had introduced as a "power gut smoothie." He had offered Martin one too, but Martin chose to stick with the FIJI Water, the expensive kind.

"Halle knows that this is a problem," said Frank, pouring the sludge into a pint glass and abandoning it on the kitchen counter. "We have food intensities that have to be respected." He walked around the island, at which Martin had taken a seat, onto the expanse of, of course, burnished wood between the kitchen and the living room, and squatted.

"Chair pose," he said.

"I thought her name was CeeCi," said Martin.

"CeeCi's the wife. Halle's the chef and supposedly a certified nutritionists and herbalist," said Frank. He straightened up, stood on his right foot, wrapped his left leg over the right, twined his arms in front of his head. "Eagle pose," he said.

Martin watched his brother contort and tried, and failed, to see any familial resemblance. Frank was lean, and his muscles bulged and stretched into easily identifiable individual units, as if he were an exhibit at a science museum, one of those crystalline castratos, rotating on a pedestal above clumps of snickering middle schoolers, its organs lighting up one at a time as a sonorous voice drones *the liver, the testes, the heart.* Martin's muscles—and they were there, he was not a weak man—were smothered in cellulite, his stomach a perfect moon he carried just in front of his own orbit.

"Is she home, CeeCi?" Martin asked.

Frank untwined, spread his arms, and opened his fingers. "Mountain."

Martin looked out the curving picture window, as if a tiny CeeCi might appear on the side of the range just now emerging from the morning fog.

"Mountain pose," clarified Frank. "CeeCi's at Rancho La Puerta running a seminar. She does a lot of them. Good money. But the pantry goes to shit every time." Frank spun away from Martin, dropped to the floor, stretched on his back and propped his head up. "Fish."

Martin looked into his brother's upside-down eyes and flashed to a long-ago summer. Frank hung like a sloth from a low branch of a maple in their backyard. Martin stood at his head, spotting him. Frank stretched back, smiled, shut his eyes, and let go. Martin reached out, caught Frank, tumbled with him, giggling, into a pile of leaves. Was that the last time they had laughed together? Was that the last time Martin had cared whether Frank cracked his head open or not?

Frank hopped back on two feet and faced Martin. "You want money, right? That's why you're here."

"No," said Martin, though he did. But he didn't just want money. He needed it.

"Look, you already owe me for the meat grinder," said Frank.

"Large capacity companion crematorium," said Martin. "And this is for a business expense, for a trip. To Elko." Martin had said too much. But for a second, maybe it was Frank's upended head, maybe it was remembering hanging onto to him, cushioning his fall, but for a second Martin thought Frank might get it.

"Oh shit, your cowboy stuff," said Frank. "Then the answer is definitely no. Grow up, bro. You're redefining pathetic." He hopped to his feet, padded back to the kitchen, picked up the glass of green gunk, and tilted it in the sink. "I'm going running, then I'm going to the Highland Frank's for a demo of some Mamba 8.1 Creekers. Whitewater kayaks. You ought to come. We've got rapids, inside. It's awesome."

"I'm sure it is," said Martin, who suddenly felt sick. "Can I use your bathroom?"

"Yeah," said Frank. "Use the one in the master—it's that way. Let me show you; you got to see the view. We had this house built so we could lay in bed and look at that view."

Martin followed Frank around a large stairway, with a slate-framed babbling brook as its bannister, and into a bedroom suite as large as the large living room and with the same curved floor-to-ceiling windows facing the Continental Divide. The vision of the range, now purple and dappled in flickering morning light, stunned Martin. He forgot about the bathroom.

From behind him, Frank said, "I'm just grabbing my shoes and going. Take as long as you need." He sniggered. Martin thought, but did not note aloud, that perhaps Frank's lifelong preoccupation with toilet humor was at least as pathetic as Martin's own lifelong preoccupation with cowboy poets.

"Finish the water if you want. Have another," Frank continued. That Martin was so obviously impressed with Frank's view seemed to have made him generous. "The front door locks automatically." Martin turned from the mountains and watched Frank emerge from a walk-in closet. He waved one hand at Frank's back and swiveled again to the windows.

It was as if Martin were looking at an inverted triptych in the vibrant hues of the cleaned-up Sistine Chapel. First the quivering rows of aspens, their spring leaves more yellow than green. Then the pointed and stretching pines, emerald and beryl and tall. And finally, the mountains themselves, filmy, dreamy, removed, as if separated from all that vert by a sheet of fine-spun gauze.

Martin had to look away. That Frank had this frontier majesty at his feet every night. That Frank lived here in this house of Western timber for walls and mountain streams for handrails. That Frank lived in the West at all and that Martin did not. Martin choked on the waves of privilege and pine scent, gasped for even the smallest breath of justice. All of it had been easy for Frank; all of it had been hard

for Martin. He had nursed their mom and their dad, then stayed by
their graves to mourn them. And for that, he had received almost no
thanks and a pet cemetery. And Frank got this, Martin's West.

Martin moved to leave and caught the glint of something—fire,
one could only hope, or water or something on one of the bedside
tables. He looked closer. The blink was of diamonds, a money clip,
topped with winking white stones shaped into a *C*. The top bill, Martin
could see, was a hundred. He walked to the bed and picked up the clip,
rifled through the edges of the notes compressed there. Hundreds, all
of them. Martin slammed the money back on the table. He pushed his
hand into the diamonds and felt them bite into his palm.

Martin needed one thing, cash for a Hero corpse. And Frank had
everything. CeeCi wasn't even here. It was probably just her spare
money, probably one of ten or twenty money clips she left lying
around, littering the landscape, clogging up the disposal, tempting
poor sods like Martin. He couldn't unglue his hand from the tabletop.
He appealed to the mountains, for perspective, for truth. And Kiskaddon, again, whispered the answer in Martin's ear:

> *While you're gazing on such a vision*
> *And your outlook is clear and wide,*
> *If you have to make a decision,*
> *That's the time and place to decide.*

Martin closed his hand on the clip and left the room.

"Hero's a chestnut, right?" said Julie.

She and Martin leaned on the chipped blue metal gate that led into
the corral of loose horses. Maybe twenty of them, many lame, with
overgrown hooves or open sores, the few healthy ones scared and
skittering. They shifted and pawed the dust and bit at their neighbors'
flanks and shivered away flies in a space suited for ten animals, no
more. Martin couldn't tell where Julie was looking. He saw a lot of
grays, a white, or more likely a cremello, a palomino.

"More sorrel than liver," said Martin. Both were shades of chestnut, though liver was, to Martin's eye, straight-up brown. Sorrel was
reddish gold, the color of the sun, or a new penny, or Hero when he
lived.

Several years ago, Martin had taken pains to learn the specialized lexicon of horse coats and their tones and marks, sensing that there was poetry therein: dark bay, blood bay, chestnut, brown. Dapple gray, rose gray, brindle, dun. Appaloosa, varnish roan, palomino, pearl. Piebald, skewbald, silver dapple, white. Several years after that, Martin had heard a young Montanan on the *Cowboy Poetry Hour* read a poem cataloging the colors Martin knew and some he did not. He was gratified his instinct was correct. He was crushed his contrivance had been co-opted.

Julie stepped up on the lower rung of the corral fence, leaned over the rail, and nickered. A golden head shagged with a blonde mane pushed between two darker horses and headed for Julie's outstretched hand. Martin had to agree. It looked like Hero.

The horse edged close to the fence and settled its muzzle into Julie's chest. "She's been handled. Somebody loved her," said Julie. "And she's a mustang." Julie ran her hand over the just visible BLM brand on the horse's neck. "And a mare." The horse cocked her head and one chocolate eye flicked between Martin and Julie.

"God, I hate this," Julie said as the horse bobbed her neck against Julie's open palm.

"What do you think she'll go for?" said Lattner, joining them and blowing on a steaming Styrofoam cup, carrying with him the smell of slightly burnt coffee mixed with a waft of horse manure, a potpourri Martin was coming to understand as definitively Western.

"I don't know. Virgil Ermine is over there. He's a meat buyer, and he's not going to want to pay more than seventy-five dollars a head, but then again, I don't know how big his order is and there aren't that many here." Julie pushed the horse's snout away and, after a baleful look at Martin, the mare bumped her way back into the thick of the herd.

Now she's stiff and old and stumbles,
and she's lost the strength and speed
That once took her through the darkness,
'round the point of a stampede
And her legs is scarred and battered;
both the muscle and the bone.
She is jest a wore out cow hoss
so they've turned her out alone.

Bruce Kiskaddon again. Maybe it was his birthday or something. What other reason, except of course, their utter applicability to Martin's current situation, would the poet's words keep ping ponging through Martin's psyche. This time, though, it was no auditory hallucination. This time, it was Julie.

"'The Forgotten,'" she said. "Bruce Kiskaddon."

"How do you know that?" said Martin.

"We were friends for a long time," said Julie. "You and me, I mean. Not me and Bruce Kiskaddon."

"He died before you were born," said Martin.

"Anyway, I don't hate cowboy poetry," said Julie. "Sometimes it gets things just right." The Hero doppelgänger pushed her head out of a scrum of bickering animals and whinnied.

"Exactly," said Martin, rocking back on his heels, thrilled to the point of gulping. He looked at Lattner and grinned a "you too?"

Lattner cleared his throat. "There once was a cowboy named Puckett…"

"But cowboy poetry doesn't always get everything right." Julie dusted off the front of her jeans. "I like it sometimes, but it's not my North Star, Koran, Lonely Planet Guide to the Galaxy, and Magic 8 Ball all wrapped into one." Martin must have let his crest fall too obviously, because she patted him on the arm and added, "Sometimes I look at my horoscope too."

The chestnut mustang was almost the last up for auction, and Virgil Ermine pushed its price up over $400.

"Goddamn it," said Julie, flicking her number the last time. "He thinks I'm with Colorado Mustang Rescue. He's trying to bankrupt us."

"Why would he think that?" said Martin.

"Because I volunteer with Colorado Mustang Rescue. How do you think I got a bidding number?" said Julie.

"What does he care?" said Martin. "Mustangs can't go for meat. It's the law. I signed a letter to my Congressman." Martin remembered how empowered he had been when he put his name on the online petition to save that great symbol of the West, the American mustang, from the slaughterhouse. He was sure the legislation had passed. He'd shared a Facebook status about it.

"I once called in about the minimum wage," said Lattner. "Fat lot of good that's done."

"There's a law," said Julie. "But there are plenty of slaughterhouses in Mexico. And there's lots of bad men who are happy to haul off unwanted horses, mustangs, thoroughbreds, you name it." She put her hands on her hips and squinted toward where Virgil Ermine was using a bull whip to move frightened horses toward his truck. The mustang, their mustang, stood alone in the center of the pen, shifting its feet, crouching away from the rest of the caterwauling, head-tossing, balking mass of horseflesh. Julie whispered more than said the poem's final lines.

She stands still. She ain't none worried,
fer she knows she's played the game
She's got nothin' to back up from.
she's been square and ain't ashamed.
Fer no matter where they put her
she was game to do her share
Well, I think more of the pony
than the folks that left her there.

Lattner took a few steps back, cracked the empty cup in half. Martin watched the slaughterhouse-bound horses, then looked at the one he had bought. Or that CeeCi had bought. He fingered the money clip buried deep in the pocket of his tan duster coat. The mare took two small steps in their direction.

"C'mon, let's go load your corpse," Julie said and turned from the corral.

Martin was sulking. He ignored Julie's fiddling with the radio. She switched it off, hummed, and blasted the air conditioner. He studied the strange rock formations and scrubby brush whipping past along the side of the highway. In the side mirror, he watched Lattner, also fiddling with the radio, follow the horse trailer attached to the bumper of Julie's F-10.

"Be reasonable," Julie said after turning the radio on and off one more time. "It's called the 'kill pen,' not the 'kill-ED pen.'"

"You told me that the horses that aren't bought from there are

kill-ED," said Martin, still concentrating on the mirror. Lattner looked
to be texting.

"Well, Helen was sold. To us," said Julie. She had dubbed the mare
Helen. "And if we hadn't bought her, she would have been kill-ed,
horribly killed at the slaughterhouse, if she didn't die in transport,"
said Julie.

For many years, Martin had agreed to purchase the 4-H blue-
ribbon-winning hog at the Pierre County Fair. As the first freckle-
faced lad who had talked Martin into the deal had explained, he had
to do nothing but write a check. The prized pig would come to him
cut into recognizable hams and roasts or ground to sausage and sealed
in airtight packaging. He had thought the kill pen would be a similar
experience, sans, perhaps, the dismemberment and vacuum-sealing.

He had been wrong. And now they were pulling a very much living
Helen. She had tripped up the ramp into the trailer Julie had borrowed
from her boss. He had used it for house calls until last year, when an
epidemic of goat giardiasis swelled the practice's coffers and allowed
him to buy a three-bay number. Julie suggested that the vet might be
willing to sell for nine or ten bills off CeeCi's roll of hundreds, still
thick and warm in Martin's left front pocket. There were bloodstains
on the trailer's wooden floor, equine dentistry gone wrong, which
made the vehicle too morbid for most weekend equestrians. But it had
the slings Martin needed to prop up the dead Hero—soon-to-be-dead
Helen—and it was, if not exactly black, then dirty gray. It would do.
It would have to do. But for a dead horse, not the live one they were
transporting.

As they continued into the Denver foothills, Martin couldn't shake
Kiskaddon's censure. *Well, I think more of the pony than the folks that left her
there.* But Martin hadn't left her, someone else had. Someone else had
condemned her. Martin was just a pawn, or maybe the pawn was Hel-
en, or Julie. In any case, it was all just pawns now, no kings, no power,
just pawns in an increasingly costly and complex journey to Elko.

"So what's the plan?" said Martin, though he knew the plan. He
just wanted to hear Julie explain it again. Frankly, she had muttered,
"She's a good horse" one too many times today. He was afraid she
might be having second thoughts.

"Back to the office, we, or I, euthanize this girl. We'll leave her in the trailer. It's got these strappy things Lee uses when he sedates horses to work on their teeth."

Lee, not Dr. Strachen, Martin noted. Dr. Lee Strachen was Julie's boss and, Martin was beginning to think, her lover. Julie lived rent-free at his five-bedroom log lodge, complete with wrap-around plank porches and wide rockers, hummingbird feeders, hanging geraniums, and mountain views straight out of *The Sound of Music*. Housesitting, she said, while he did his frequent charity work; he had left that morning to spend a week at a street-dog rescue shelter in Rio. The lodge was on the same grounds as Dr. Strachen's office, Conifer Veterinary Associates. Martin wasn't jealous, exactly, but Julie seemed to have a good thing going on out here. Out West. A good thing without Martin. Out West. He had spent his whole life striving to get here, so why was it he was the last to arrive?

"What did you tell your—Lee about me?" said Martin.

"You mean after you lied to me and ruined our cross-country trip?" said Julie.

Martin said nothing. He had no desire to go through this particular lecture again.

"Truth is," she continued, "I told him from the start you were a woman, a high school girl friend with severe depression who needed a Thelma and Louise type adventure to buck her up. I didn't say anything about Elko because I knew Lee would think it was stupid. Because it is."

Martin chose to ignore the dig. "What was my name?"

"Louise," said Julie.

"Very creative," said Martin. "And what happened to the trip?"

"You, Louise, died in a crane accident the day I got to Pierre."

"I was a crane operator?"

"Bystander."

Martin supposed he deserved the ignoble fictional death. He watched the rock walls of the foothills rise to either side of the truck.

"Why are you doing this?" said Martin. "Helping me."

Julie answered as if she had rehearsed. "Helen was going to die either way. Colorado Mustang Rescue doesn't have enough money to go to every auction. No one was scheduled for that one. Too small. And I didn't really think we would find a match."

That last part, to Martin, at least sounded honest.

"But we did," she said. "And this way, Helen can go out with some dignity. Even a little pomp, right? Besides, I still do want you to succeed, I really do. I know it's dumb to still care. But you've taught me something Martin, you and Frank and cancer and your mom. It's not how you play the game, it's whether you win or lose. I want to be with the winners. I want my friends to be with the winners. And you're still my friend." She flipped her eyes to her rearview mirror and honked. "What the hell is Bob doing back there? He's all over the road."

Martin swiveled his head around in time to see Lattner drift onto the shoulder, overcorrect, kick gravel every which way behind him.

"You know what she does?" said Julie.

"Who?" said Martin.

"CeeCi," said Julie. "Her seminars. They're about cancer, like treating cancer, preventing it, 'Don't Say Ta Ta to the Ta Tas,' as she says on her website."

CeeCi preached the power of positive thinking as the ultimate balm for the breast cancer sufferer. Her "Banish the Thought!" weeks, offered at top-dollar destination spas throughout the West and West Coast, schooled mostly young, mostly healthy women on how vitamin D and daily affirmations could keep cancer away and, should some negativity accidentally slip in with the sunlight, could cure cancer without resort to chemo or other therapy.

"Blame the victim," said Julie. "That always works. It's a medical fact." She banged her palms twice at ten and two on the steering wheel. "It's how they met, you know, she and Frank. She was counseling him on how to help me not be so sick." Julie banged again, and Martin readied himself to grab across and steady the car, if need be.

"Frank's an ass," said Martin, and meant it, as he always did, but felt it mightily right then.

"I know," said Julie. "I'm better clear of him. But goddamn it, I built those stores with him. Now they run themselves and the profits fund her 'don't metastasize, be happy' bullshit. I'm glad you took her money. I'm glad we're buying a dead horse with it. Only thing better would be if we could leave its head in her bed."

Julie jerked the wheel to the right and skidded onto an exit ramp. Lattner followed smoothly, his faulty wiring apparently better able to handle erratic driving then the alternative. They kept on past a strip mall with a boarded-over video store and a Kick It Out Little Dancers studio, then turned left into a long valley with foothills and mountains on all sides. Another left through a tall lodge pine gate, the sort that only worked when the sky was this big, and they were bumping down the dirt road to Conifer Veterinary Associates.

Julie bypassed a concrete block clinic building and continued to a parking area next to a large log barn that matched the main house a hundred feet beyond. Martin turned around to make sure Lattner was still with them, but Julie kept her head fixed forward, staring across the yard of shin-high sagebrush, where a middle-aged man strode toward the truck.

"Shit," she whispered. "Change of plan. Tell Lattner."

Martin turned back. Julie snapped off her seat belt and opened the door.

"Lee, I thought you'd gone," she said.

Dr. Lee Strachen was short, Martin was pleased to note, and almost completely bald. He walked with bowed legs, not like a rodeo rider, more like a former wrestler with a touch of arthritis. He had a big grin that spread out the entire bottom of his tanned face. When he reached Julie, he kissed her cheek. "Never left. The flight was cancelled, damn LIAT. I'll try again Monday."

Martin unwound himself from the seatbelt and hopped out of the truck. He heard Julie introduce Lattner to the vet and heard the vet address Helen's rear end.

"Who do we have here?"

Martin came around the back in time to help lower the trailer ramp. He received his own introduction to Lee, who, with Julie, then set about moving Helen out of her confinement. As they fussed over the mare, Martin tried to mime to Lattner to let Julie do the talking and believed Lattner mimed back that he was not a complete idiot.

"She's sound," said Lee, patting the mare's neck. "And well trained."

"Kill pen, if you can believe it," said Julie distinctly, enunciating each syllable as if she were miscast in a poorly rehearsed community theater production of *Black Beauty*. Martin waggled his eyebrows at her. She opened her eyes wide and hunched her shoulders up.

"We need to be able to use our words," Lattner hissed in Martin's ear, and Martin nodded with vigor. But it wasn't until much later that evening that they got that chance. Lee turned out to be an enthusiastic and ever-present host. Insisting they stay for dinner, stay the night, take a hike in the nearby mountains, take a nap in the porch hammock, no friends like old friends, right, Jules?

Jules?

Over the course of pre-dinner G and Ts, Julie brayed out their cover story with such persistence and at such volume that Lee leaned over to Martin and asked, "Is your friend Bob hard of hearing?"

They were going to deliver Helen to Mustang Manor in Elko, a nonprofit run by a dot.com magnate's ex-wife with whom Lee, Julie, and Colorado Mustang Rescue had worked before. And wasn't it marvelous that Julie's childhood friend and her first real boss were, at the very same time, traveling to Elko for the Thirty-Second Annual Elko Cowboy Poetry Confluence. Oh, how wonderful to have some company for the long drive! Oh, how forced the whole thing sounded, and Martin couldn't believe that Lee was buying it, but he was. Such is love.

"You two must have known Louise," said Lee at one point. "I'm so sorry for your loss."

Martin blanked for a moment on the tragic life of his doppelgänger, but Lattner picked up the slack. He took Lee's hand, looked in his eyes, and said, "Thank you. It's been difficult, but she would have wanted us to continue." Go with it. Lattner should have the motto tattooed across his forehead.

The evening passed from Bombay gin to an Oregon Bordeaux to a local whiskey artisanally aged in first-use American oak casks, the composition and making of which Lee knew more about than Martin thought seemly in a man without a financial stake in the distillery or a serious drinking problem. They talked of cowboy poetry. Lee hadn't heard of the confluence, thank God, and showed polite interest, but not so much they had to fear he might look it up. Lee loved NPR, but only the morning shows, *Morning Edition* and *BBC News Hour*, thank God, and gave no sign that he had listened to the *Cowboy Poetry Hour*. Lee knew Martin was Frank's brother—the less said about him the better they all agreed, thank God—and did not seem to view Martin as any sort of ally to Julie's tormentor or rival to her affections. Thank God.

After the second tumbler of Whiskey River's blended malt scotch, Lee excused himself. He had to get up the next morning for church.

"Church?" said Lattner, once Lee had left the room, and grabbed the bottle, poured them each another slug.

"Unitarian," said Julie. "So not really."

"Is that Mustang Manor stuff real?" said Martin, pulling his glass toward him.

"Of course, it's real," said Julie. "They have over nine hundred square miles and at least a thousand rescued mustangs."

She would bring what she needed to euthanize Helen with them and do it on the road someplace, she had decided, since offing the animal at the clinic wasn't a possibility with Lee in the house. Martin could drop the body at the rodeo ring at the fair ground, which was where the PBS crew was staging the funeral, according to Mac.

"Done and done," said Julie. "Our only problem will be if Lee gets too attached to Helen. She's a nice horse." There it was again. "And it's happened before. He's got two in his barn right now that started out rescues and ended up pets. But he's off again Monday. When do we need to leave?"

"It's eleven hours to Elko," said Lattner, looking at his phone. "Up through Salt Lake City then straight across."

"We're not due in Elko until Wednesday night," said Martin. "NPR got us rooms at the Red Lion Casino. I'd like to do it in two days, but I maxed out my last card at the Quality Inn."

"I'm not camping with a dead horse," said Julie.

"How much of CeeCi's money is left? After we pay for the trailer," said Lattner.

Martin pulled out the clip and tossed it on the table. Julie picked it up, counted out eight bills, then unfurled two more. "Oh my God," she said.

"I don't know how long it has been since you've stayed in a Motel 6," said Martin, "but we need two rooms and two hundred is not going to do it. And don't even think about a Hilton Garden Inn. Plus we've got to eat."

But Julie wasn't looking at the bills, which lay crumpled and glowing ochre in the candlelight filtered through her scotch glass. She held a black card. "The Centurion," said Julie.

Martin turned to her and she showed it to him. He had never seen one before. The most exclusive credit card in the world. American Express, invitation only. Membership fees of upwards of $7,500 per year. Million-dollar annual spending floor. No spending ceiling. And the promise of exclusive, gilded, magical money doors open to exclusive, gilded, magical places all around the world.

"It's not yours," said Martin.

"Oh, but it is," Julie said, squinting at the card's face. "Or was. Look." She held up the card. "Julie Oliphant. These things don't expire. Looks like the bitch was too lazy to get a new one."

"You didn't change your name back?" said Martin.

"Not on my license. I renew by mail," said Julie. "Good thing, right? Another point for inertia as a lifestyle choice."

Lattner was still looking at his phone. "Given this surprising but welcome change in our fortunes, I propose a couple of days at a Canyon Ranch. There's one due west of here, outside of Moab."

"That place books up a year in advance," said Julie, then looked at the card. "But I suppose…"

"…they could find a room for the fabulously wealthy Mrs. Oliphant," finished Lattner.

Martin pushed his chair back. He understood that by taking the money and the jeweled clip from his brother's bedroom, he had committed grand larceny. But this would be larceny on the grandest of scales. And to no noble end, just a couple of days spa vacation for a trio of embezzlers. He reached across the table for the credit card, but Julie snatched it and held it above her head.

"This is not a game." He could taste tears in the back of his throat.

"Maybe not," she said. "But if it was, I'd be winning for once. For fucking once."

Martin banged his glass on the table and headed out of the room. He had no more words for this, a situation even cowboy poetry could not find fertile. He was losing a focus he had had since he was twenty years old. He was a day's drive from Elko, four days from the confluence, a week from reciting at the biggest event ever held at the confluence. He was where he had always known he would someday be, about to do what he had always known he would someday do. His path was clear, and it was clear he had strayed from it.

As he turned onto the stairs up to the bedrooms, he heard the clink of fresh ice on glass, and Lattner's lowest and most sinister chuckle.

Mac.Cooper@WBEZ.NPR.org
To: Lina Sharpe, Martin Oliphant, Bob Lattner
Reply-To: Mac.Cooper@WBEZ.NPR.org
RE: RE: Site for funeral—FINAL WORD

So, after all that, the Elko Fair Grounds folks say we can't do the burial/service ANYWHERE on their property. They say they've got too much toxic shit leeching into their well water to feel copacetic with adding embalmed dead horse to the mix. I tried the local cemetery, only one for miles, run by the Perkins family for genera-tions. There's a story there, but who's got the time, right? Anyway, they said no animals in the graveyard, not even allegedly famous horses. But good news is, as long as the old lady's granddaughter can twirl her batons for the cameras at some point, they'll let us do the service there. So the body will trailer back to the Red Lion after and the renderer will meet the Final Paws crew there. Would have liked the grave, first clump of dirt, etc. for the cameras, but at least we get Vess at the trailer. Thanks everyone for hanging in through all this.

THREE. MORE. DAYS.

Mac Cooper
Special Projects, Communications and Branding, NPR National

16

They reached the Red Lion Casino right before the sun dropped into a miasma of pink and orange. Julie had had the Centurion concierge request a temporary corral for Helen, complete with hay feeder and watering trough, adjacent to the parking lot. Martin had questioned whether they would really go that far to accommodate even one as fake rich as Julie.

"This card will buy you anything," she had said. "Just ask Lattner. You know he proposed to the spa technician who drained his lymphs at that resort in Salt Lake City." Martin had not pressed.

Julie checked in, settled Helen, and begged to be excused from dinner that evening. Lattner left his bags in the car, explaining to Martin that he could have their room to himself.

"I'm staying with a sister of a friend," he said, handing Martin a card from the "Rose Briar B&B, Elko's oldest and cleanest bordello, since 1973."

Martin walked to the front desk alone, picked up a schedule for the confluence, then navigated the smoky casino's spinning wheels and clanging bells and planted himself at the bar between two cowboys in leather vests, black Stetsons, and waxed mustaches. He tried to read the order of events for the next few days but found his eyes swimming in tears he desperately hoped would not spill. He breathed in the air of Elko and found it more nourishment than the two Coors and an overcooked hamburger with bacon and Swiss he'd ordered from the bartender. He was home.

The next morning, Martin perched on the wide marble edge of an indoor planter and balanced a tiny Styrofoam cup of black coffee on his knee. He watched through a glass wall into the Elko Convention Center's entry hall as men in cowboy hats, crisp blue jeans, and belts with massive gold buckles greeted women in tight leather vests, perfect ponytails, and hand-stitched boots. An hour before the official opening of the Thirty-Second Annual Elko Cowboy Poetry

Confluence, and Martin had already been there an hour. Every once in a while, others seeking a place to sit and drink their dollar-coffee, proceeds to the Elko Mining Museum, would join Martin in the small atrium. They looked toward him politely, as if they knew him, because they must have thought they did. Everyone seemed to know everyone. Hugs all around. Back pats and cell phone snaps of the grandkids. Everyone had been here every year that Martin had not. Everyone knew everyone, but no one knew Martin.

He waited until the wall clock indicated a polite five minutes after nine a.m., the official opening time of the registration desk. He rose and squeezed around a group of Native American women in beads and rugs and out into the main hall. He collected his commemorative pin, which doubled as his pass to all the confluence's events, at a set of folding tables manned by high school rodeo princesses. He also asked about his speaker's badge; he and a bright-eyed brunette searched for it unsuccessfully among rows of plastic-encased nametags arranged alphabetically on a red-and-white tablecloth. The display was a roll call of living cowboy poet laureates: Wyatt Wendt, Jerry Brooks, John Dofflemeyer, Linda Hasselstrom, Chuck Hawthorne, Yvonne Hollenbeck, Ross Knox, Wally McRae, Doc Mehl, Waddie Mitchell, Joel Nelson, Glenn Ohrlin, Shadd Piehl, Vess Quinlan, Henry Real Bird, Pat Richardson, Randy Rieman, Kent Rollins, Sandy Seaton Sallee, Georgie Sicking, Paul Zarzyski. And Giles, right there between Dick Gibford and D.W. Groethe. Beaufort Giles.

When Martin saw the name, his joy that the old man was alive, his thrill that they would meet again, maybe today, swamped his rising shame at not being able to locate his credentials. The brunette princess called over her supervisor, an older woman, who was dressed in the sort of blue jumpsuit favored by French sanitation workers.

"When are you on again?" she said.

"Hero's funeral, Saturday." The supervisor peered at him through green paisley-framed reading glasses, and he added: "Cowboy Poet? PBS is filming?"

"Oh, Wyatt Wendt's thing," she said. "That's separate. We don't have tags for that." She turned away from the table and hugged a small man in a beaded leather shirt and an eye patch.

"Sorry," the rodeo princess said. "Want some Doublemint? It's free."

Martin refused the gum and set himself back up with another coffee in the atrium to monitor the entrants for Lina, for Beaufort, maybe for Ginger. Definitely for Ginger.

But it was Caitlyn Jordan whom Martin recognized first. He had not thought of the juvenile fiddler since the night she had performed in Pierre, right before Hero died. She flittered at the edge of a group surging in behind a wheelchair holding a bent and grizzled cowboy. A bent and grizzled Beaufort Giles.

Though changed, so changed over the last thirty years, it was Beaufort, Martin was certain. He glimpsed the old man's profile between the wasp waist of the child protégé and the legs of a cowboy closing ranks behind her. The old man's head was slumped forward, but Martin could see that Beaufort was smiling a tight half-smile. Martin remembered it from all those years before, saw it again as if it were filmed in Blu-ray and streamed through his optical nerves. Beaufort's chin jutted out and the sides of his mouth nudged up his tanned and lined cheeks. He looked as if he were about to drop a punch line, rag on an old friend, or laugh.

Martin tucked his coffee cup into the ivy and stones behind him and stood. He inched by three robust matrons in elaborate woven shawls. The fringe from one caught in a wooden button on his corduroy vest, and he lost several minutes in polite apologies as the shawl owner fiddled to get free in an overly intimate manner, and her companions whispered and giggled over scatological weaving double entendres.

"Are you a poet too?" asked one, and Martin answered "no" without thinking.

Once in the main hall, it took Martin several minutes to locate Beaufort and his posse. Or what was left of his posse, which was a pile of bulky coats and Caitlyn leaning against the wall next to his wheelchair. Both she and the old man stared straight ahead, not speaking. She rested a small hand on his thin white shirtsleeve.

Martin made for the pair, struggling through the crush of confluence attendees, as if he were thigh-deep in Class IV rapids and heading for shore. Something told him this was his last chance. Not Hero's funeral, but this. He had paused his life at Beaufort thirty years before and had never figured out how to hit play again.

Determination and fear must have been etched on his face because, as he barreled toward her, Caitlyn started and moved closer to the wheelchair. Beaufort's gaze and nascent smile remained fixed at some point right in front of the men's room across the way.

"Can I help you?" asked Caitlyn, all but her eyes composing into the demeanor of a polished performer. The eyes stayed wide and darting, an appropriate reaction, Martin supposed, to the approach of the sweaty, panting, needy beast he could feel he'd become.

"Beaufort," whispered Martin, and the old man looked up. His pupils black moons in the flat blue of his irises. Martin remembered that gaze, clear and steady and, unlike the rest of Beaufort's face, unmarred by decades of sun and wind, ice and dirt. His hair, still reddish brown, escaped from his straw hat and floated past his ears in uncombed wisps. More wisps, this time of white, flecked his chin and ropy neck. A black scab the shape of South America sat above his left eye and another, Antarctica, on his right temple.

"Do you know Mr. Giles?" Caitlyn said. Beaufort, eyes still set on Martin, raised a shaking arm and offered a cupped and gnarled hand.

"Yes," said Martin. "Yes, from a long time ago." He took Beaufort's hand and held it. Beaufort quaked some more and said nothing. "It's Martin, Martin Oliphant. From Jimmy Sneedle's," Martin said.

Beaufort continued to hold Martin's hand but turned to Caitlyn. She looked back as if she were reading his thoughts.

"Jimmy Sneedle's. That was a long time ago," she said.

Martin moved closer to the wheelchair, pressed Beaufort's hand, and the old man winced.

"You sent me *Songs of the Cowboys*. I should have brought it. I meant to return it."

Martin was speaking loudly, maybe yelling, he realized. A couple of men who had been chatting in the middle of the hall started toward him.

"I'm here because of you. Cowboy poetry. I read at Jimso's Jamboree and Talent Show."

Caitlyn's slender fingers dug into Martin's damp sleeve. With both hands, she tugged him back from the chair. "Look, Mr. Giles, it's J.T. …Mr. McJunkin." J.T. McJunkin, the corpulent poet with the waxed and silver handlebar mustache, edged Martin away from Beaufort and squatted in front of his chair, taking a metal armrest in each hand and tilting his black Stetson until it met the rim of Beaufort's straw hat. Martin stepped away. Blocked, again. But by J.T. McJunkin, the great poet J.T. McJunkin. Martin had all his books.

"Do you want some coffee?" Caitlyn asked, still clinging to Martin's sleeve. "It's free for performers."

Martin went with her. He heard a burst of laughter that had to be J.T. McJunkin, and then Beaufort, his voice thinner than Martin remembered, but clear:

Oh, here they come to Heaven,
Their campfire has gone out.

Martin followed Caitlyn through a cafeteria into an annex where powdered donuts and a coffee machine were set out on a folding table. Standard-issue round eight-tops ringed with beige plastic chairs dotted the room, only a few occupied. The poet and mule packer, Ross Knox, sat at one, holding a mug of coffee under his chin and leaning in toward a taut older cowgirl. Martin was fairly sure it was Deena Dickinson McCall, author of *Mustang Spring: Stories and Poems.* He had considered using one of her pieces for Hero's funeral.

"Why don't you sit here, sir, and I'll get you some coffee," Caitlyn said, guiding Martin to an empty chair at a table toward the back of the room. Her eyes jumped to the door where her father, a famous poet and singer in his own right, had materialized, hands in his pockets, shoulders hunched, head cocked. Caitlyn blinked something at him. *I'm fine.* Martin assumed because the man slipped back out of view.

He watched Caitlyn flit to the food table, smiling and offering a word to the volunteer manning it, a light tap to the old woman in the bright green fedora sitting alone, a wave to the boy with buck teeth tuning a fiddle in the corner. She returned with a steaming Styrofoam cup. The scent of Ivory soap battled with the aroma of the brew as she leaned over Martin.

"There," she said. "You have to forgive Mr. Giles for not recognizing you. He isn't well. And he is very, very old. I'm Caitlyn, by the way. And you're?"

"Martin," he said, "Martin Oliphant. I know who you are."

Caitlyn nodded, as if she was not surprised.

"How do you know Beaufort?" he said.

"Everyone knows Mr. Giles. He was one of the first. When the confluence just started." She folded her hands in front of her and bent over them. "This is probably the last time he'll be here." She looked to either side and whispered, "Cancer."

"Oh," said Martin and took a sip of the coffee to keep her from noticing the flush he felt crawling up his face. The drink burned his throat and he coughed. He stared at the far wall, trying to sort his feelings. Loss? No, he had lost Beaufort years ago. Grief, maybe, but for whom? Anger, maybe, but at whom? Caitlyn's eyes darted around the room, as if she was planning an escape. He should let her go, but he needed to know.

"Do you know Ginger? Beaufort's—Mr. Giles's—daughter?"

Caitlyn's head snapped back toward Martin, an early bird setting its beak at the worm. "Oh yeah," she said. "Everyone knows about Ginger Giles."

"Is she here?" Martin said, jamming his belly into the table's edge, almost tipping his coffee.

"Not here here, like in this room," Caitlyn said, "but I heard she's coming. With her husband, whom we don't know, most of us. She hasn't been for years and years."

"Husband," said Martin. He knew. He had always known. Why should she have waited for him for thirty years when he hadn't waited for her for ten minutes?

"Where's she been?" he said, and Caitlyn sat up straight, opened her eyes wide, flared her nostrils.

"Columbus," she said. "Ohio." She shook her head. "It's such a sad, sad story."

As Martin listened, he had to agree. Ginger's story was sad, sad: marriage at twenty-two to Thatch Bourne, a broken bull jockey twice her age; two weeks later, an errant hoof off Ginger's mare to Thatch's already dodgy left knee; crutches to walkers to wheelchair; an unsuccessful transition from bronc busting to mortgage banking; bankruptcy; one too many painkillers after one too many shots of Jack.

"A widow at twenty-three," Caitlyn exhaled. Her eyes bore into Martin's eyes for one beat more, then flicked away.

"What happened then?" he said. "How'd she get to Ohio?"

"I don't know," said Caitlyn, placing her hands on her thighs and craning her head to the left. "She just did. Married a rich guy. Like a banker or something." Caitlyn stood. "I really should go. The opening ceremony is soon." She patted Martin on the shoulder and walked away.

"Sad," he said to the seat she had abandoned. "Sad."

Martin found himself wondering if horses—bad ones, dead ones, fictional ones—had littered the landscape of Ginger's essence in the way they had his. Perhaps they had that in common. He wondered what would have happened had he made it to Elko as a young man. Caitlyn had been unclear on the timeline of Ginger's second marriage. Martin worked on quashing the thought that he was the Midwesterner who had been meant to pick up her pieces after Thatch's death. He, not some Buckeye banker. Martin would have come to her. He never would have taken her away from cowboy poetry, her father, her Western skies and purple plains.

Martin sat, palms flat on the table, half-filled cup of coffee in between them, until the bottom of his thighs lost feeling, and he couldn't distinguish them from the top of the seat. He sat as the room drained, refilled, drained, refilled again, drained again, never more than one or two others joining him at the table, not speaking but examining torn notebook pages or worn books or the fold-out confluence schedule. He sat until a third wave filled the room to capacity, and a young man with a white-blond crew cut and red bandana bent over to ask to use the empty chair next to Martin. He nodded his assent, sniffed at the fellow's plate of spareribs, coleslaw, and cornbread, and stood up. It was lunchtime. He had been at the confluence for four hours, his first four hours at any Annual Elko Cowboy Poetry Confluence, and he had heard but one sad story and no poetry at all.

Back in the main hall, Martin pulled his copy of the schedule out of his satchel and considered his options for the rest of the afternoon. He recognized two of the poets listed for "And We Shall Ride" starting in fifteen minutes in the Cedar Room. He found a seat up front, settled, decided he was too conspicuous. Moved to the back, took a center seat, became claustrophobic when three Stetson-wearing women in matching bowling shirts sat between him and the door. Shifted to a seat on the center aisle, placed his bag next to him, moved it to make room for the videographer setting up there. Debated removing his leather jacket in case it got stuffy, did remove his leather jacket and arranged it on his seat back, apologized to the videographer for knocking into one of her tripod legs, and glared at the white-haired, sloped-shouldered woman who had turned to shush him as the program started.

First up was a fireplug of a Jillaroo in a sky-blue cordovan and matching cape. She recited "The Horse Drawn Hearse" by Bush poet Jack Drake. Martin had not made much of a study of the Australian cowboy bards, but he knew this piece and appreciated it as the omen it was, though whether good or bad, he remained undecided. Second came a cheerful guitarist from Alberta, who chirped and plinked about love and loss to a bouncy beat more suited for the coffeehouse than the saloon. And finally, the young poet Shadd Piehl. His blank verse was angry, lyrical, literary, smart. Martin heard his younger self in every stanza.

He stayed in the Cedar Room for the next show, an open mic session. He had had no idea such events went on at Elko; they had never been broadcast during the *Cowboy Poetry Hour's* coverage, and yet they were scheduled every day, sometimes twice a day, thrice on Saturday. Had he just attended one year, he would have discovered he could have performed, with no more qualifications than the ability to write his name on the sign-up sheet.

Once the recital began though, Martin decided he was glad he had waited for a higher profile, if less conventional, onramp to Elko. A dentist from San Francisco read an ode to home brewing from a spiral bound notebook. A hunchbacked matron in a pink polyester tracksuit used most of her time to bemoan her long-dead father's decision to leave the family ranch to her younger brother. In her last few minutes, she read an original work titled "When Daddy Carved the Turkey." After, she took the seat in front of Martin, and he smelled malt liquor, IcyHot, and nerves in the sweat soaking her jacket's back. The last act was a half-hearted Caitlyn imitator—waist a little thicker, braid a little looser—who belted out S. Omar Barker's "Purt Near" as her mother offered up lines in a stage whisper from the front row.

The session made Martin sad. This was real life at its thinnest, and that was something he never thought he would find at the confluence. That such people were here and reciting and, more than he, fitting in, hit him in the chest like a round of buckshot. He rose to go, but the smelly and bitter hunchback in front of him tugged at his sleeve.

"Don't leave," she said. "People have been waiting in line to get in for the next show. Glenn Mayfield, Austin Miller, Beaufort Giles. Keep your seat, young man."

Martin sat and nodded a thanks, for the tip and for the "young man." Of course, he would stick for Beaufort. And Mayfield and Miller were legends. Martin checked his schedule. The program was called "Western Characters."

Miller led off. He stroked with two thumbs his wooly white mustache, glanced at the two other poets, frail in their folding chairs, and said, "If you look around this year, there's a bunch of us turned old."

That led to cackling and a few stray claps and set the tone for the show, which Martin soon realized was more storytelling than poetry. The warm bite of Miller's voice, his open stance, the way the other two old men put their hands on their knees and leaned forward to laugh. Martin felt he was back in Jimmy Sneedle's barn, Beaufort and the hands teasing him about his pronunciation of "Cayuse" or the crease ironed in his Levi's. When Miller ended a long story with the punchline, "There ain't no figuring women or sold-off cattle," Martin laughed until he cried, though he had no idea what that meant.

This was what he had imagined all those nights, days, months, years he had imagined Elko. These men talking to Martin in their wise and lilting way. These cowboys who knew where they were going and didn't mind at all if Martin tagged along. The road to Elko had been so crooked, he had almost come to believe it was a dead end. But he was wrong. He had arrived.

Glenn Mayfield stayed seated, recited "Dangerous Dan McGrew," sang something about sage, and told a joke Martin had heard before but struck him as new and hilarious when rendered in the ancient cowboy's slushy drawl. Miller did another round and recounted a man he once knew. "He never had religion," said Miller, "but he never raised no hell." The poet managed to make it sound like the worst sort of insult.

And then it was Beaufort's turn. He rose from his seat at the pace of the morning sun rising in winter and walked with creaking knees and a fortitude that radiated like a force field from his bent frame. His two friends eyed him with set frowns but did not raise their hands to spot his progress. They let him walk. He smiled and nodded at each then turned and smiled, at Martin? It seemed so.

Beaufort raised a shaking, spotted hand to his forehead and shut his eyes. He coughed once. Martin leaned forward. He closed his eyes too, waiting for the words to spin out and catch hold. He sensed in his tightening chest what came next, a rush of hot dry wind and thirty years gone. He sniffed for the smells of the barn, listened for the boot scuffs of the hands, and ached for Ginger's cool touch. He would feel that hard ground under his feet one more time.

Beaufort began:

Through rocky arroyas so dark and so deep
Down the sides of the mountains so slippery and steep
You've good judgment, sure footed, wherever you go
You're a safety conveyance, my little Chopo.

Martin reared back, clipped the knees of the woman behind him with his metal chair, and yelped in unison with her.

"No," he said and felt as if he were spiraling down. The barn and the hands and Ginger whooshed to a pinpoint and blinked out.

"Sit down," hissed someone to his left. He sat heavily and the woman behind him moaned.

"I know this isn't everybody's favorite." Beaufort's voice wasn't as Martin remembered. It was an old man's voice, raspy and tired, ready to be done with it all. "But my mother used to read it aloud, and it's been on my mind lately, so I'll ask you to struggle through it with me."

And struggle Martin did. He didn't hear every line, though he hardly needed to. The poem was etched in acid on his swiftly disintegrating psyche. The words he did grasp, he heard in his mother's quavering keen. He shifted left and right in his seat, tried looking at Beaufort and looking away, but it didn't matter. Martin was back in their living room, urine and bleach fumes mingling with the steam off Julie's Campbell's Chicken and Stars. A blast of blood, a burst of iron, the smell of rotting grass as the pony crumpled and fell. Vomit and wet dirt and the whiskey on Dr. Broad's breath, the gardenias at the funeral home and the Jiffy Pop his dad left burning on the stove after the reception. It swallowed Martin, and he would have run if he could have stood, and he would have screamed if he could have spoken.

Chopo my pony, Chopo my pride
Chopo my amigo, Chopo I will ride
From Mexico's borders 'cross Texas Llanos
To the Salt Pecos River, I ride you Chopo.

Then it was over. Martin looked up at Beaufort and saw nothing but an old man. An old man Martin didn't know at all.

Mayfield did one more song, but Martin wouldn't have been able to tell you what it was. He was sobbing so hard, the hunchback turned around and asked if she should go for the defibrillator. Martin buried his face in his hands and tried to gasp delicately until the final applause for the trio died and the murmurs of the departing crowded faded. He sat there still as a young woman unhooked the mike from the podium. He sat there still as the lights thunked off and the air-conditioning wooshed on. He sat until his mother and Beaufort and the cowhorse Chopo faded and were replaced, not with an image but with a vow. This had gone far enough. Helen would not die.

Julie slugged a frozen margarita out of an enormous clear bowl on a cactus-shaped stem. A clump of crushed ice dribbled from the right side of her mouth and plopped onto the burgundy tablecloth. Martin guessed she had started drinking some hours before they met that evening at the Red Lion's Aspen Bar and Grill.

He stared down at the overdone ribeye on his plate. The cooks at Aspen's broiled beef to just north of burned, no matter how rare he asked for it. He picked up his oversized steak knife and held it aloft, considering how it would be easier to plunge it into his own heart than attempt to saw off a hunk of the beef. He cleared his throat.

"The first poem he reads, and it's 'Chopo.'"

Lattner picked up his glass and made to toast with the woman to his left, whom he had introduced as "Baby." She was a squat bleached blonde with enormous and most certainly fake breasts distorting a glittery tube top with BABY spelled out across the front in metal rivets. She rolled her wide and tired eyes toward him and then to the four shrimp cocktails and three tequila shots arranged before her. She picked up one of the shots, touched it to the rim of his glass, downed it in one, and banged the jigger upside down on the table. She then went back to sucking, with mechanical precision, pink tiger shrimp from their tail shells.

Julie licked at the salt on the rim of her glass. "Sometimes your mom just pops into my head. Just being like she was at the end."

"She was so sick," said Martin.

"I was thinking she was so nice. But yeah, she was pretty sick too."

Lattner looked up. "They ought to get you another steak. You said rare, bloody, *bleu* in the language of a culture that knows how to handle *du boeuf.* That piece of charcoal is an abomination, an insult to the culinary traditions of an allegedly cattle-centric culture."

"I can't go through with it," said Martin. He stabbed the meat with the knife and left it standing there, a temporary grave marker.

"They even gave you the little pink toothpick." Lattner pulled the plastic marker out of steak, shook it at the back of a passing waitress, and stuck it in his teeth. "You need to stand up for yourself. This was a deliberate misrepresentation."

"I mean the funeral. I can't go through with the funeral. Killing Helen or asking you to." Martin nodded at Julie.

Baby glanced at him and buried another shot. Julie wiped her nose with a damp cocktail napkin and waved for another round of drinks.

"I'm serious. I'm done with it all. I'm leaving Elko. Tonight. It's not what I thought it was, the confluence, any of it. And I'm taking Helen with me. Or letting her go. Or something."

Julie bleated once, without mirth. Lattner reached for a shrimp. Baby batted his hand away without looking at him.

"Noble sentiments, my old friend, but unnecessary. Julie has come to the same general conclusion, but as is her phlegmatic Midwestern wont, she's done so in a more practical and, may I say, less selfish way," Lattner said.

"I can't kill her," Julie said. "I think I knew it before we left Conifer. But I got sort of wrapped up in it all, you know? It was fun, in an outlaw sort of way. Like with Dewitty."

Lattner chuckled.

"My mother died that night." Martin inhaled once, twice, found he could not exhale. His ears popped. The acid of partially digested mozzarella sticks burned at this throat. "My mother died that night." He thought he might black out.

"God rest her soul," said Lattner, and Baby crossed herself.

Martin could almost feel the bat in his hand again. His fingers ached with gripping. His arms shook and the wooden shaft crashed on Lattner's skull, sliced through the top of Julie's head, exploded into Baby's breasts. A wave of paranoia pressed Martin back in his chair and smothered him in a blanket of red, the red of the blood he envisioned covering the table, washing around the broken glasses, splattering the piles of shrimp shells.

"Jesus," he said. He drained half a margarita, and Baby clapped softly. "Why didn't you say something? Jesus. When were you planning to tell me? Before or after my reading? Before or after PBS started filming?"

Martin cupped his hands over his nose and mouth and tried to calm his breathing. Anger felt better than fear, so he focused on that orange heat. He realized that he had rarely revisited the night his mother and Chopo died. He had let it go as one of the many and sudden and unexpected ways that cowboy poetry shaped his destiny. He forgot it and waited for the next stampede, the next freak thunderstorm rolling over the mountain. And yet in Elko he met his mother and Chopo around every turn, pinching at him like a misshapen saddle, puncturing his skin with their fangs like a startled rattler. Julie looked into her lap, and Lattner put an arm around Baby.

"Well?" Martin's voice rang out. He realized he had achieved some moral elevation, and this settled somewhat his muddied innards.

"We weren't going to tell you," mumbled Julie. "We were going to drug Helen and let her sleep in the straps for the service, like Lee does when he floats horses' teeth."

A waitress delivered two more shrimp cocktails to Baby.

Martin took a long breath. The blood was receding, dripping off the table, flowing over the worn and diamond-patterned blue carpet, swirling its way back into the kitchen.

"And then, when, to the strains of my recitation of 'The Walking Man,' they backed the trailer into the grave and dumped two tons of dirt on the sleeping Helen...what?"

"There's no grave." Lattner looked up and grimaced. "Didn't you see Mac's memo?"

Martin shook his head. He'd been leaving the logistics to Lattner, who seemed to enjoy answering Mac's ten or twenty thousand emails a day.

Lattner pulled a reusable Kroger's bag from under the table and dug in it, retrieving and rejecting torn and stained scraps of paper. He stared at one, moving his lips silently, then presented it to Martin.

"Is this it? I don't understand. No burial?" said Martin, after reading the note through twice. "What renderer? I didn't arrange a renderer."

Lattner dipped a shrimp in cocktail sauce and popped it in his mouth. "There is no renderer," he said through his wet chewing. "Julie will take Helen to Mustang Manor."

"So we didn't even lie to Lee," said Julie. She grinned, as if she had not thought of this side serving of rectitude before.

"Ah," said Martin and thought: *No.*

All that time following cowboy poetry in search of firm ground. Following blindly over whatever mountain cliff, into whatever desert chasm, onto whatever bed of campfire-heated coals it chose to drag him. For a moment this afternoon, right before Beaufort started to recite "Chopo," Martin believed he had finally found his footing. But the sands shifted yet again, and yet again the way was no more clear than it had been the night he killed Chopo, carried his mother's battered body into the house, and lay it on the floor beside her bed. He knew he needed to blaze his own trail, to part from Beaufort and the *Songs of the Cowboys* and the hope of Ginger. Out of habit, he waited for the words of the West to help him explain this to Lattner and Julie, now both beaming at him with blurry moon faces. Kiskaddon, Barker, Charles Badger Clark. Always hissing in his ears. Nipping at his shoulders and back. Shoving him this way and that. Silent now. Thorp, Chapman, Henry Herbert Knibbs. He hadn't asked before, hadn't even questioned. He moved his lips and prayed that syllables would follow.

Grave cold silence.

"The funeral is off," he said finally, then paused to listen to the echo in his head. It wasn't poetry. The words were his. "I'm telling Lina and Vess the truth."

Baby snorted and spit a blob of cocktail sauce on Martin's cheek. "You don't know nothing about truth," she said.

Lattner smiled at her, patted her hand. "We're engaged," he said. Baby drained her last shot.

"She's right," said Julie, listing toward Martin's shoulder. "What's true about your cowboy poetry? How's that going for you, living your life by the code of the trail-worn troubadour? Read at Elko, make a splash, fuck that Ginger-bitch, get it out of your system. Please."

Martin leaned back and away from the anger in her voice. What right did she have? Was he not allowed his own tragedy? They had conspired against him, against his dream or whatever distorted image they had of it. They had, again, aided and abetted his most foolish instincts. They were not his pardners, never had been.

"Really," said Lattner. "You aren't the only one invested in this. All you have to do is what you have said you've wanted to do ever since I first met you waving your dick at a bunch of drunk welders at The Silver Dollar."

Martin nodded. They didn't understand. This wasn't about him. It never had been about him. He stood up and headed for the parking lot and Helen's corral.

July 27, 2016 at 8:07 PM

Mac.Cooper@WBEZ.NPR.org

To: Lina Sharpe

Reply-To: Mac.Cooper@WBEZ.NPR.org

PANIC

Ran into Bob Lattner. He says Oliphant wants out, something about the Hero corpse not Hero, not dead? HE WAS NOT DRUNK. You need to talk to Bob or Martin.

Should I tell them the grave's back on? Will that help?

Mac Cooper

Special Projects, Communications and Branding, NPR National

July 27, 2016 at 8:24 PM

LSharpe@CPH.NPR.org

To: Mac Cooper

Reply-To: L.Sharpe@CPH.NPR.org

Re: PANIC

leaving stockmans for red lion now to find bob and martin doo not do anything else do not tellthem anything else ill take care of it

Sent from my iPhone

July 28, 2016 at 1:04 AM

LSharpe@CPH.NPR.org

To: Mac Cooper

Reply-To: L.Sharpe@CPH.NPR.org

Re: PANIC

Found Bob then Martin. Crazy story, but I worked it to a happy ending. Everybody's back on board. DO NOT mention the switch back to the grave to ANYONE from that crowd, not even that Julie chick. Will make for unnecessary complications. I'll keep them away from the rehearsal.

Lina Sharpe

Chief of Staff

Cowboy Poetry Hour

17

The second time the heel on Martin's Lucchese boot slipped on an oil patch on the concrete, he slowed down. The third time, he gave up his march to Helen and reentered the casino through the doors to the hotel reception area. He waved at the raisin-faced lady behind the desk with his key card. He needed to go back to his room and think.

As he waited for the elevator, he imagined himself sitting on the puffed polyester king bedspread, listening to the electric buzz of the radio alarm, and sniffing the decades of exhaled tobacco leeching from the crushed red and orange shag carpet, so like the one in his family's Pierre living room. It was the kind of hotel that didn't stock the minibars. The elevator bell rang, and the metal doors opened onto an overlit interior and a framed ad for the Red Lion Casino Sports Bar. He let the doors close and looped back toward the bar.

The border between the bar and the casino was a porous one. Waitresses dressed in black pants and button-down white shirts rushed plastic cups of complimentary booze from the bar to the blackjack tables, and big winners wandered in to buy the better stuff with puce chips. Martin took a seat on a red leather swivel chair, swung around to the bar, cracked his knees into its faux mahogany base, and yelped a curse at the designer who had bolted the seat to the floor. Around him, the slot machines bleeped and trilled and screeched and clanged. He had to repeat his order, Jack Daniels on the rocks, twice to the dusky-eyed waiter behind the bar.

"Any luck?' the bartender asked.

"None whatsoever," Martin answered and pulled his tumbler toward him.

He couldn't simply set Helen free, as he had visualized doing when he stormed out of Aspen's. He had wanted to witness her charging off under an honest Western sky, the image of Hero memorialized on the Cowboy Poet's bus. But the Red Lion sat, as did most of Elko, on a main street that paralleled Highway 80. The stars weren't visible in the lemon glare of the streetlights and oncoming semi high beams.

Set loose, she would probably get run over, killed, taking out a few innocent cars and trucks as she fell. That was hardly the point he was hoping to make. Not that he really knew what that point was. Something about reining in cowboy poetry before it rode him into yet another tree.

As his rage began to dissolve in the smoky acid of his whiskey, he had to admit that Lattner and Julie's plan for Helen wasn't bad. In two days' time, the mare would be repatriated to a cushy rescue ranch, perhaps a little groggy, but alive, safe, and having committed no greater crime than providing a little solace to the masses of Cowboy Poet fans. It was not a lie that hurt anyone. But it was a lie Martin could no longer sit easily. After so many lies, this was the lie that had finally thrown him, trotted off without him, and left him gasping on the dirt of the rodeo arena, dust in his ears, mentally inventorying his body for broken bones. He needed to stand up, tip his hat to the indifferent crowd, and exit Elko. He ordered another whiskey and took out his phone to search for flights out of Salt Lake City.

"You a cowboy poet?" The bartender put Martin's drink on a coaster advertising Red Man chewing tobacco.

"No," said Martin.

"A cowboy?" The bartender's nametag said his name was Andy, but Martin didn't think so. The man held his sharp chin tight to his chest and his narrow head sandwiched between shoulders frozen in a half-executed shrug.

"Not a cowboy either."

"Then you can run a tab." He crumpled a piece of white receipt tape and tossed it on the floor. "You here for the mine?"

Martin briefly considered answering in the affirmative. Yes, indeed, a traveling mine equipment salesman, here to hawk shafts and picks, an honest laborer who wants nothing more than that the riches of the Western sacred grounds be unearthed and pressed into commemorative medallions. But that would be a weak start to his new life of rigorous honesty.

"I came for the confluence, but I'm leaving tonight."

The bartender retrieved Martin's bill from the floor and smoothed it out on the bar. "We don't take checks," he said. Martin pulled his last fifty from his rear pocket.

"Put mine on that too. I'll have what he's having."

Lina swung into the chair next to Martin. She smelled of cigar smoke and beer. She bared her teeth, which might have been an attempt at a smile, but it was hard to tell as the sides of her mouth did not turn up one whit. Martin stared at a brown flake centered on her incisor.

"Were you at the show?" Martin gestured at the clumps of what had to be cowboy poets streaming into the bar. Some still clutched the playbill from that night's main stage performance at the convention center. Martin had had a ticket but had forgotten about it in the swirl of anger and betrayal and memory that had overtaken his evening.

"Shit no," said Lina. "I was at Stockman's having a drink or ten with a guy who used to be a sound engineer for the *Cowboy Poetry Hour*. You know, at the beginning, before it got big, we had fun. I loved my job."

"You don't now." Martin didn't phrase it as a question, and Lina didn't answer.

"I ran into Lattner. He told me you were getting cold feet about the funeral." She hiccupped. "That's kinda funny. Cold feet for a funeral. Don't you think so, Andy?"

The bartender put down Lina's whiskey. "My name is Elbek. I'm a Chechen. It means 'lord.'"

"Anyway, I just want you to know, it's okay if you want to quit." She waved Elbek away. "There's only about two thousand Cowboy Poet wannabes wandering around here who would give their left nut to recite on the same stage as Wyatt Wendt. So, whatever." She put her nose in her drink and slurped.

Martin blinked. He was certain he wanted nothing to do with the funeral or performing in Elko. But it hadn't occurred to him that the show would go on without him. He, too, hid his nose in his drink.

"Like Jess over there," Lina said. She took off her ivory Stetson and waved it at a man in a buff Carhartt duck coat on the far end of the bar. "Jess, want to perform Saturday with Wyatt and Vess? It'll be televised." The man gave her a thumbs-up and a wide smile.

"What am I reading?" he yelled back.

"Vess and Jess," said Martin. "That could make a mockery of the funeral commentary. I think it's an unfortunate choice. And aren't the programs printed already?"

Lina turned to Martin. "What were you going to read?"

"Recite," said Martin. "I was going to recite 'The Campfire Has Gone Out.'"

"The campfire one," shouted Lina across the bar.

"I know it," Jess replied and stood up on the rungs of his barstool like he was standing in the stirrups of his saddle. He began:

The railroads are coming in,
And all the work is gone.

His voice was high and reedy. Lina nodded at Martin, who leapt to his feet and bellowed, "No! That's not how it goes."

"Oh yeah?" Jess pushed back from his end of the bar and moved toward Martin and Lina. He staggered a bit as he pushed through other similarly dressed drinkers, most sporting the confluence commemorative pin. He shook a beer bottle at Martin. "Oh, yeah?"

Lina hopped off her chair and put a hand on Jess's arm. "You're drunk. Just leave it."

"I know the fucking words," he said and put down the beer bottle, opened his coat, and pulled out a Glock 21.

Martin stood up too. "It's about a lot more than just knowing the words," he said in a bass so deep he felt it had its roots in the ground beneath his feet. He pushed Lina gently back with one hand and with the other took the pistol from the cowboy and set it on the bar. Elbek scooped it up and slid it under the counter.

"Next round's on me," Elbek said in a whisper.

Martin took another step toward Jess, looked past the top of his head, and roared:

Through progress of the railroads,
Our occupation's gone;
We'll get our ideas into words,
Our words into a song.

"Okay, dude," squeaked Jess and backed up as if gut punched. He turned to Elbek, who had poured himself a whiskey and was gulping it as if it were lifesaving antibiotics. "Can I get my gun back?"

"Nyet," he said and drained the glass.

Martin continued in a softer tone, now addressing Lina, who steadied herself on her chair.

First comes the cowboy—
he's the spirit of the West;
of all the pioneers I claim
the cowboys are the best.

Martin took a breath, raised his hand, and cupped Lina's chin. She looked into his eyes, placed a hot hand on the fly of his jeans, and said, "Keep going."

They consummated the first stanza in the elevator, Lina's mousy ponytail slapping the plastic over the framed ad for the sports bar. The second and third were completed on Martin's king-sized bed amidst sweat-scented sheets and crumpled denim. He even managed a brief reprise of the last chorus, though by that time Lina seemed exhausted, and Martin was just showing off. The lovemaking was more mature and sustained than his time with Julie at Jimmy Sneedle's and all the times with women who were not Ginger, or even Julie, after that. But it was no less intense or lyrical.

Martin watched a shirtless Lina fumble in her jeans pockets, pull out a crushed cigarette, and attempt to light it. He did not feel compelled to point out that it was a no smoking room, and that recklessness began to rekindle his lust. He propped himself next to Lina on the bed and reached for one of her creased breasts. She batted his hand away.

"You really do love this cowboy poetry stuff, don't you?" she said.

He inhaled her exhaled smoke and thought he could taste the bright pink lipstick, traces smeared on her thin lips.

"And you don't?"

She sighed, stubbed the cigarette fragment out on the bedside table, and reached for her shirt. "I knew you did when Lattner told me about that crazy plan with the drugged horse."

Martin sat up and choked. He had forgotten about that and about his revulsion at the deception. The reciting, the sex, the power had all taken him back to the first days of his lust for cowboy poetry.

"I was going to tell you," he said.

"I think it's fantastic." Lina snapped the small pearl buttons on her red and white checkered blouse. "Genius, really. The lengths you're willing to go to make the last *Cowboy Poetry Hour* really mean something. God, you care more than Vess. You should have been the

Cowboy Poet." She retrieved her boots from under the bed and pulled them on. "You would have been great."

He would have been great, thought Martin. He could still be great.

"So what are you going to do?" he asked.

Lina stood up. "That depends on what you're going to do. Will you go through with it? Will you read?" She walked to the door of the room.

"Of course," he whispered, then repeated louder: "Of course, I will read at Elko."

"Great," said Lina, opening the door. "I'll email you the schedule." She walked out, leaving Martin alone with the salty smell of sex, trembling inner thighs, and an overwhelming joy that his campfire had not yet gone out.

Martin arrived at the convention center early Friday morning, hoping to see Beaufort again or catch the symposium on leather braiding before he had to meet Lina for lunch at the whiskey-tasting table. They were to drive together over to the dress rehearsal. Martin was ready to play his part and play it well. Less than an hour after she had left his room the night before, she had emailed him a draft of the final program for Hero's funeral. During the processional, which kicked off right at noon, Martin would ride shotgun in the caisson pulling drugged Helen's trailer, Vess walking behind. After the two of them had their Princess Anne moment for the cameras, Martin would open the proceedings with "Of Horses and Men," then turn it over to Wyatt Wendt, who would recite "Make Me No Grave." Some group called the YeeHaw Yellars would sing a few jazzed-up hymns, Marilou Perkins would twirl her baton for no more than three minutes, leaving Vess twenty minutes to eulogize. Martin would finish with "The Campfires Have Gone Out," and the YeeHaw Yellars would pluck them off with "Amazing Grace." Forty-two minutes, give or take a couple, and since it was PBS, that was fine. They could always cut Marilou after the fact.

He was punching up a text when he caught sight of her across the main hall.

Ginger.

He froze, took her in. He would have known her anywhere. She was still slender though seemed to have grown taller. Perhaps it was the square heels on her black boots, lace-up not cowboy, well-polished and probably pricey. Her jeans were black too, as was her simple turtleneck. She didn't wear a hat, and her hair still shone, though it had darkened to the ochre of a tarnished penny and gone white in streaks, like the potash crystals in the Elko Mining Museum display over by the coffee sales table.

She turned to a paper she was tacking up next to the conference room, and Martin took one step forward. She seemed to be alone, but he wondered whether the man in the blue blazer talking on a cell phone and leaning on the wall nearby was the Ohio banker. Martin hoped so. The guy had the sort of Kewpie-doll male patterned baldness that left a tiny tombolo of hair right above the forehead.

Ginger turned her back on her notice and swept the hall with eyes in which Martin thought he could detect youthful spark and earned melancholy and eternal kindness. But he wasn't sure, because he avoided those eyes, dropped his head, feigned interest in Lina's message. All those years of dreaming of this moment, and he wasn't ready.

Fucking Fuck-Up, Lina's text read. Martin forced himself to read every word before he looked up again. If he did that, then Ginger would be gone, and he would be able to breathe. *BB busy Vess drunk. No time for lunch, putting out fires. Rehearsal off.*

K, he typed back and still could not lift his head.

"Martin?"

Oh God.

"Martin? Right? You haven't changed a bit." Ginger laughed, the same laugh. She touched his sleeve. He inhaled three times, held his breath, looked up.

"Ginger, isn't it? Ginger Giles?"

"Yes, yes." Her face was lined now but soft and creased like an old blanket. "Jimmy Sneedle's. You read at the talent show. You were good. I think about that all the time. Do you remember?"

Ginger had thought about him. She had thought about him all the time. *Cogitat ergo sum.*

"Yup, I believe I do." Martin worked at screwing up his face to feign great effort at recalling the event. Ginger kept her hand on Martin's arm, but her smile began to fade.

"I don't want to bother you," she said. "I remember it so well, maybe because it was our last Christmas there, before we went to Wyoming. But you were good, I do remember that. I'm not at all surprised you're part of the confluence."

"I'm not," he said, too quickly. "I'm not. I mean, I am. Part of the confluence. Or at it. I mean, it's my first time."

"Really?" She smiled again. "Well, then, have you seen Dad? You have to. You should sign up." She gestured back toward the paper she had pinned up. "You should read. He's MC-ing the open mic tomorrow at 12:30. He would love that. I would love that. You did 'Campfires,' right? You could do that."

"Actually, I'm reciting tomorrow at noon," said Martin. "At Hero's funeral." Ginger tilted her head. "You know, Wyatt Wendt?" he pressed on. "Vess Guffry, the *Cowboy Poetry Hour*?"

Ginger removed her hand from his arm. "Oh, that. I heard about that. Vess Guffry. I've never met him. I've listened to the show once or twice. It's okay, for what it is."

For what it is? She had eviscerated him without a blink or a pause. "I kinda like it," he said, hesitated. "For what it is."

"I guess I shouldn't talk," Ginger said. She was looking over Martin's head now toward an industrial chandelier above the hall. "I moved away from it a while ago. But it just seems to me, cowboy poetry is for cowboys, by and for cowboys. There isn't much left that's as simple as that anymore. And when you put it out over the radio and say it's for everybody? Well, it isn't."

She scratched at her cheek, then looked at Martin and nodded. "I tell you what. I'm going to put you down to read on the sheet. If you make it, fine. I'd be pleased to hear you. And if not, well then, you take care of yourself, Martin."

Martin nodded back, could not speak, watched her walk away. Willed himself to say something. Had no idea what that might be. Turned and headed toward the center's front doors.

HELEN

Saturday, 11:16 a.m.

Martin stared into the grave, and it yawned back at him like the tooth-less nightmare it was. A small house could fit in that craw. An unsus-pecting small house full of small children and their small puppies, singing "Jesus Loves Me" and rolling around belly laughing like that Coke commercial from an eon ago. A small house with small children and small puppies—or a regular-sized trailer with a regular-sized, drugged mustang.

He looked around for Lina, Vess, Mac, anyone. Didn't see them. He thought everyone was supposed to be here by eleven, but he only spotted a few cemetery workers and the PBS camera and light crews. Martin trotted to the other side of the hole and looked around again, looked into it again. A misunderstanding, that's what this was. Lina would have said something, in her memos, or after sex, when they had talked about Helen. She had to have known about such a substantial change in the obsequies. That was one big hole. They had probably been digging it for days.

Make me no grave within that quiet place
Where friends shall sadly view the . . .

Reverb sliced through Knibbs's words. *Test, test, no grave, ma ma ma make me,* more reverb. Martin turned to the stage dwarfing the other end of the cemetery. He couldn't make out the speaker, dressed all in black, erect among three slouching sound engineers, but Martin guessed it was Wyatt Wendt. A professional, that's what he was. Doing his own pre-show check. Had anyone told him that "Make Me No Grave" may no longer be the best selection?

Martin tramped back around the hollow plot, avoiding bouquets of Asiatic lilies, blue delphinium, and Western sunflowers, many tied with sashes bearing Hero's name or likeness. He headed to the parking lot and staging area for the processional. Maybe he had time to catch Julie, whom he had left with the caisson driver, a man who moonlighted as an Abraham Lincoln impersonator and looked it. They were hooking Helen's trailer to the horse-drawn hearse. If Martin could find Julie, they could just take the sleeping horse straight to Mustang Manor. Fuck the funeral. Fuck Elko and NPR and PBS and especially Lina. Because even if she hadn't remembered about the grave on Thursday night, she must have remembered after, and yet no mention in the texts and emails she had bombarded him with since. She knew, of course she knew, and she was going to let him go through with it anyway. What was another dead Hero to her? Well, he wouldn't. Not today, not tomorrow, not ever. He wouldn't go back to Pierre either. He would just keep heading west, hitch a ride with Lattner and Baby as far as they'd take him. Go to California. Go to Hollywood. Open a winery, learn yoga, eat sprouts. Forget cowboy poetry, forget Beaufort, forget Ginger. Reinvent the dream.

Martin caught sight of a Bobcat puttering toward a shed. He waved at the driver, diverted toward him.

"You dig that grave?" Martin yelled, gesturing widely.

The driver shut off the engine. "I dig all the graves."

"The big one, with the ramp into it. Did you dig that one? Who told you to?" said Martin.

"Crazy people," the man spat. "A bunch of crazy people with cameras."

Martin continued at a fast walk to the parking lot. The red Mustang coupe was parked off to one side. Lattner stood next to it, a hand on Vess's shoulder. Baby leaned on the driver side door, her head thrown back, a cigarette pointing toward the peaking sun.

Martin looked at his Seiko. 11:38. Kickoff was at noon. In the distance, Wyatt Wendt finished the poem.

And I shall find brave comrades on the way:
None shall be lonely in adventuring,
For each a chosen task to round the day,
New glories to amaze, new songs to sing.

Loud swells the wind along the mountain-side,
High burns the sun, unfettered swings the sea,
Clear gleam the trails whereon the vanished ride,
Life calls to life: then make no grave for me!

Martin jogged toward the caisson, passing Marilou Perkins juggling flaming batons at the front of the slowly forming processional, a program change that probably explained the grave. *New glories to amaze, new songs to sing.* For most of his life, until this year—in truth until the last couple of days—he had held onto to that. That promise, of cowboy poetry. And damn it, damn it. He would not let it go now.

Life calls to life. Life calls to life.

"Hang on, Helen, I'm coming," Martin bleated.

He ratcheted up to a run. The caisson was twenty feet ahead. The Percheron stood stolid in its harness. The cart, which would normally hold a casket, was empty but for a wilting bunch of roses. Lee's trailer was hitched behind it. Julie's truck was gone.

Also missing, Honest Abe. Martin wheeled around the back of the trailer, assuming the driver was on the other side. He slowed only a second to check Helen, who was snug in the slings, dead asleep. Dead asleep but breathing audibly. What a shitty plan this all had been.

Martin caught sight of the driver's stovepipe hat bobbing along a tree line on a lot across the access road from Elko's main drag. He blessed PBS and NPR for being too cheap to provide porta potties for the performers.

He climbed up onto the bench and picked up the reins. One snap, then two. The leather thwacked on the horse's gleaming haunches. It turned its head, blinked its cyclopean eye, and farted. Again, Martin thwacked and again the horse did not move. He felt tears well up. The Percheron shuddered from shoulder to tail, clanking its halter and rigging.

11:52. Lina was running toward Vess, who had returned to the Mustang and was sharing the cigarette with Baby. A woman with a handheld video camera ambled by, swooping the lens up to the sky, then back toward the processional. A balding man in Bermuda shorts and a down-filled vest barked unintelligible instructions into a bullhorn. Marilou Perkins and her soaring sticks of fire high-stepped forward a few paces.

Martin leaned over his knees, hands on his thighs, and gasped for air. The Red Lion was just a half-mile up Main Street. He could see its blinking sign from the caisson perch. If he could just get Helen back there, before the death march began.

"Move, move, please move," he sobbed. He thrashed the reins every which way until they flew from his grip and fell onto the Percheron's immobile ass.

Martin should have figured that, in the end, it would all come down to horses. Two live ones, as it happens, and he might be forgiven for not foreseeing that twist. But those stinking, twitching beasts. Those most idiotic of large mammals. They transform him now to the cowboy poet he was born to be. He doesn't rescue the schoolmarm from the flaming ranch house. He doesn't repel the ravenous coyote. Or defeat the rustlers or outrun the dust storm or count in the herd at the end of the trail. He saves a drugged kill-pen mustang from being buried alive by driving her in a Percheron-led hearse to a casino parking lot. You get what you get, a young Dottie Oliphant used to say, long before she devoted her life to getting what she did not have. You get what you go for, Julie will say later, when she tells the story at her and Lee's wedding breakfast. You get what you need, Mick Jagger promises on classic rock stations pretty much every day of the year. And, as Martin realizes as he stares down at the unmoving back of the draft horse, sometimes you get it all at once: who you are, what you have to do, and where to go from here.

Martin sucked his lungs full of dusty air. He dragged from his hippocampus the twenty or thirty minutes of non-crisis-laced instruction he had received at *Anyone Can Ride!* and on the back of Zach. And, without another thought, he coiled, sprang, landed on the draft horse's broad back, and hit the animal's sides with a kick that, he took only a second to note, could not have been executed by a less substantial man. By a less substantial cowboy poet.

The horse, the cart, and the trailer jerked once, then rolled steadily toward the road.

12:37 p.m.

Julie dropped Martin at the front door of the convention center and waved. He watched the back of the trailer pull out of the roundabout, Helen's heavy head visible, swaying in its straps. Julie would stay with the mare until she woke up, then turn her over to Mustang Manor.

Martin pushed through the doors, paused in front of the Elko High School bake sale table, and checked his reflection in the side of the stainless steel coffee urn. He straightened his bolo tie. There was nothing to be done about his black shirt, which had lost three buttons in the front, or his jeans, which had split along his inseam to his right knee. He entered the mostly empty hall and headed for the Cedar Room.

He brushed by the volunteer manning the door. Beaufort stood at the podium, gnarled hands grasping it at both sides. He looked up at Martin and smiled.

"Well, our first performer has made it after all. Martin Oliphant is a talented young man I had the opportunity to work with thirty years ago on the Giles family ranch in Wickenberg, Arizona. I don't know where he's been since, and I don't suppose it matters all that much. We're just happy to have him back."

Martin walked down the center aisle and climbed onto the stage. He stopped at the podium to hug Beaufort and help him to his seat. Then he stood dead center on the platform.

Lattner and Baby were on their feet in the back. Lattner flashed a thumbs-up and Baby waved a small Canadian flag. About halfway through the full house, J.T. McJunkin sat next Glenn Mayfield, J.T. with his arms loose at his side, Glenn clutching his fiddle, both with open faces turned to the stage. In the front row, Caitlyn perched ramrod straight next to her father. "Go, Martin," she hooted, then clapped her tiny hand over her mouth and popped her eyes wide. On the other side of the aisle, Ginger grinned and held hands with the balding man to her right.

Martin bowed his head for a moment and said a wordless prayer. Wordless because he did not have the words for this moment. Wordless because he did not need them. He began:

Through progress of the railroads,
our occupation's gone;
we'll get our ideas into words,
our words into a song.
First comes the cowboy—
he's the spirit of the West;
of all the pioneers I claim
the cowboys are the best.
We'll miss him in the round-up,
it's gone, his merry shout,

the cowboy has left the country,
his campfire has gone out.

Martin took a breath, unzipped his fly, dropped his jeans, and moved on to the second stanza.

ACKNOWLEDGEMENTS

My heartfelt thanks go out to the following people and institutions:

Regal House Publishing editor-in-chief Jaynie Royal and managing editor Pam Van Dyk, who took a chance on a weird story, then worked tirelessly to get it to readers in its best form.

Kathy Daneman, a master publicist, who has tackled this project with heart, drive, and so many brilliant ideas.

The Western Folk Life Center, who labor so diligently to preserve and promote the work of the real cowboy poets and put on the annual National Cowboy Poetry Gathering each January in Elko, Nevada.

The Center for Western and Cowboy Poetry, whose site, cowboypoetry.com, makes public an encyclopedic record of cowboy poetry and poets, both classic and modern.

Fred Veil, executive director of the Sharlot Hall Historical Society, who figured out how to get me permission to use a stanza of Hall's poem "Beyond the Range," and cowboy poet Shadd Piehl, who let me open the novel with my favorite cowboy poem, his "Sweetheart of the Rodeo."

Rainbow Trout Ranch, a dude ranch as magical as Jimmy Sneedle's is cynical, and especially co-owner (along with the rest of the Van Berkum family) Jane Van Berkum, whose spirit, love of horses, and endless enthusiasm were the inspiration for Ginger's appealing personality. My family has vacationed at RTR for twenty years, and without exception, we are all in love with Jane.

The James River Writers, and especially Katharine Herndon and Phillip Hilliker, who awarded *Four Dead Horses* first prize in its Best Unpublished Novel Contest, which led to an excerpt published in the *Richmond Magazine*, a generous sponsor of the contest and Virginia arts in general, and an introduction to contest judge and master thriller author Brad Parks, an early and consistent supporter of the book.

The magazines and journals that accepted my short work and gave me hope and the motivation to keep writing something longer—in particular *WhiskeyPaper* and its editor, the effervescent author Leesa

Cross-Smith, who published the first thing I ever had published; Jersey Devil Press, which ran the short story that introduced the character of Martin; and *Jellyfish Review*, *Pank*, and the *Kenyon Review*, whose editors I hope realize how much their kind and generous attention meant to a novice writer like me.

The Tinker Mountain Writers' Workshop and legendary author Pinckney Benedict, who convinced me both that Martin was a character worthy of a novel and that I needed to go to the MFA Creative Writing Program at Queens University in Charlotte to learn how to write it.

The Queens MFA program instructors who read chapters, sections, and entireties of early drafts, constantly pushing me to make them better: Pinckney Benedict (again), David Payne, Dana Spiotta, Myla Goldberg, and Fred Leebron. Myla, my thesis advisor, in particular provided characteristically honest, detailed, and insightful direction.

My workshop mates Shawn Miklaucic, Walker Smart, and Milo Silver along with workshop leader Fred Leebron, who helped me start the novel.

Fellow Queenies Hannah Cohen, Robert McCready, Pam Van Dyk, Alan Bell, Jay Hefron, and Eddie Ackerman, who were always there with advice and encouragement.

Author and teacher BK Loren, who led the Taos Writers' Conference seminar that workshopped the first draft of the novel. BK led me through a complete and vital restructuring of the book then and has remained since then a steadfast supporter, vigilant editor, and dear friend. I will always be in awe of her immense talent and her fierce advocacy for (and insistence on) the well-written word.

Author and professor CJ Hauser, who has been with me and Martin, cheering and collaborating, from the first word of the first story, through every draft, and on into the launch. CJ believed in this book long before I did, and without her energy, friendship, and advice, it would not have happened. Not to mention, she gave the book its title.

My beloved family, who have offered unflagging support and reassurance, no matter what they thought (and kindly kept to themselves) about my career-shift from paid work to novelist: Jeff Telgarsky, Jack and Ann Sparks, Brenton Auclair, Austin and Liz Auclair, Vanessa and Max Grenader, Fredda Sparks, Will Root and Vivian Telgarsky, and Nick Auclair. Jeff, Jack (who is not Frank), Max, Fredda (a.k.a. Mom), Viv, and Nick all read and commented on drafts. Viv and Will designed and maintain my website, which, as a result, is much more stylish than I. Mom brought her clear editor's eye to several versions of the book, as she has for most of my writing for most of my life.

And in the end, Viv and Nick, I am forever grateful to and for the both of you. You are my home and heart, and all of it, always, is for you.